TRIAL
BY
FIRE

Also by Frank Simon
in Large Print:

Veiled Threats
Walls of Terror

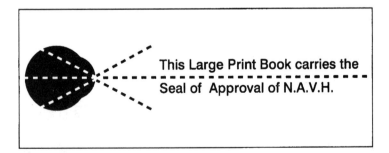

TRIAL
BY
FIRE

FRANK SIMON

Thorndike Press • Thorndike, Maine

Published in 1999 by arrangement with Crossway Books, a division of Good News Publishing.

Thorndike Large Print ® Christian Mystery Series.

The tree indicium is a trademark of Thorndike Press.

The text of this Large Print edition is unabridged. Other aspects of the book may vary from the original edition.

Set in 16 pt. Plantin.

Printed in the United States on permanent paper.

Library of Congress Cataloging-in-Publication Data

Simon, Frank, 1943–
    Trial by fire / Frank Simon.
        p.   cm.
    ISBN 0-7862-2143-7 (lg. print : hc : alk. paper)
    1. Germany — History — 1918–1933 Fiction.
    2. Architects — Germany Fiction.   3. Large type books.
    I. Title.
    [PS3569.I4816T75   1999b]
    813′.54—dc21   99-38783

In memory of
Juliet Ridley Simon

Acknowledgments

I want to thank the people who helped make this book possible:

My wife LaVerne, who said to me one day, "Would you like to hear an idea I have for a story?" She also served as my first editor and research assistant.

My friend and agent Les Stobbe, who advised and encouraged me and suggested the title.

Mark Werth of Stuttgart, Germany, for his help in researching the facts. If there are any mistakes, they are mine, not his!

The fine people at Crossway Books who made it all possible: Jill Carter, Marvin Padgett, and Lane Dennis. My special thanks to Ted Griffin for his help "above and beyond" in editing. And to Cindy Kiple for her cover art.

Prologue

On this beautiful day in June 1929, brilliant shafts of sunlight slanted through the summer home's front window. Johanna Kammler, about to become a teenager, stood back a little, shading her deep blue eyes as she watched the butler and maid scurrying around the wooden table in the front yard, distributing napkins, paper hats, and party favors. The heavy mantel clock ticking over the fireplace seemed to keep time with the servants' activity. Johanna smiled at the thought. She ran a hand absently through her shining blonde hair but found no imperfections. The long, silky strands were all in place. She looked down and smoothed her blue linen dress, still immaculate from the maid's iron. The fresh scent of starch lingered on her white lace collar.

June marked the first week of the Kammlers' vacation in Bavarian Berchtesgaden, a small town in a deep valley surrounded on three sides by Austria. A medieval abbey and a castle reminded visitors that the town had once boasted princes of the Holy Roman Empire and later had been the summer residence of Bavarian kings. Hovering over the town stood a mountain, Obersalzberg.

The Kammlers were leasing the same two-story brick house they had for years. Berchtesgaden was a welcome relief from the bustle of Frankfurt am Main, but it also took Johanna away from her friends. She turned her head and looked down the brick walk to where it went through the thick front hedge. Soon her guest, invited by her father, not by her, would be coming up that path. Her jaw set in irritation.

Her younger brother, eight-year-old Bernhard, dashed past and slid to a stop at the front door. "Waiting for your boyfriend?" he asked.

Johanna made a lunge for him. He yelped with glee as he raced away from her. She caught one of the straps of his *lederhosen,* but he twisted out of her grasp and ran up the stairs.

"He is not my boyfriend!" she shouted after him.

Heavy footsteps sounded in the hall leading to the back of the house. Walther Kammler frowned as he neared the entrance. "What is this disturbance?"

8

"Papa," Johanna said, her eyes flashing, "Bernhard is mocking me."

"Nonsense. He is just a little boy having fun with his older sister. Since when can't you take a little teasing?"

She pouted as she struggled with how helpless she felt. "Why did we have to come down early? If we were in Frankfurt, all my friends could have come to my party. Here I am stuck with Bernhard and Sophie — and Erich!"

She saw her father's expression turn sour. Why did he *never* take her seriously? she wondered as she struggled to maintain her composure. Why could she never get him to change his mind?

"Yes, I know," he said. "Such a cruel blow for someone turning thirteen. I am sorry we are taking our vacation early, but it could not be helped. The new linen factory will be finished in July, and I must be back for that. It is my business. Be thankful for what we have, Johanna. Many in Germany must do without."

Johanna clenched her teeth as she listened once again to her father's tired lecture on how hard things were for most Germans. But of course her father was *not* an ordinary German, to hear him tell it.

"I know, Papa," she replied, trying to use

the proper tone of sincerity.

"Do you? I wonder. Besides, what is wrong with young Erich, hmm? His father happens to be the architect of my new factory. The von Arendts are a fine Berlin family."

"But I have never *met* him," Johanna said in exasperation. She longed to tell her father to stop controlling every part of her life, but knew it would do no good.

Walther laughed. "That has been taken care of. It was at my suggestion that my friend Karl rented a cottage here for the summer, which made it possible for me to invite his son to your birthday party. Your mother and I are trying to do our best for you. I thought you would be pleased."

"Papa, you told me he's two years older than me."

"And that is to be preferred. You are a mature young lady. I'm sure you two will get along just fine."

"Papa!"

"That is enough. This is only a birthday party. Herr Erich is *not* coming to ask for your hand. I will hear no more of your whining. I have provided you with a fine party, and you will enjoy it."

"Yes, Papa."

He turned and left.

Hearing a faint sound, Johanna looked up and saw seven-year-old Sophie tiptoeing down the stairs.

"Were you spying?" Johanna asked. She tried to maintain her stern expression but couldn't keep it from turning into a smile. Sophie was the only person Johanna got along with. She was sweetly innocent and adored her older sister, which Johanna didn't object to at all.

Sophie shook her head slowly as she joined Johanna. "I wouldn't spy on you." Her smile showed deep dimples. "Who is Erich?"

"For someone who wasn't spying, you seem to know a lot."

"Is he your boyfriend?"

"You saw what happened to Bernhard, didn't you?"

Sophie nodded gravely. "Yes. But I was just wondering."

Johanna sighed. "Yes, I know. I have never met this boy, yet Papa asks him to my birthday party. This is *my* party. Why can't Papa ask *me* about it?"

"He might be nice," Sophie said with a smile. "He might even be handsome. And he will bring you a present."

Johanna gave a short laugh. "You have this all figured out, don't you?"

"No. But I am sure the party will be nice."

"I *hope* it will be nice," Johanna grumbled, though she thought that most unlikely. She looked outside again. Her thoughts ranged far from Bavaria. She longed for Frankfurt and the certainty of her own circle of friends. But her yearning didn't change anything.

Johanna stood on the front walk and looked past the hedge that separated their property from the narrow country road. Skillfully arranged flower beds provided just the right accent for the manicured lawn. Fluffy white clouds sailed along beneath the blue summer sky. Birds flew in and out of the tall trees, their calls a constant background to the activities below. The traffic on the road was light — mostly hikers, a few bicycles, and an occasional car. Curiosity struggled with dread as Johanna wondered what Erich would look like. If this had to happen, she decided, she was glad her Frankfurt friends were *not* here.

Elsa stood by her daughter. "You look lovely, dear," she said.

Johanna glanced at her brother and sister sitting on the same side of the table facing the walk. She saw the keen look in her brother's eyes. "Did you tell Bernhard to be good?" she whispered.

"I did. Don't worry. It will be a lovely party."

"When it's over. Where is Papa?"

"He and Herr Maser had to go into town to see Herr von Arendt."

"Who is Herr Maser?"

"Your papa's plant superintendent. There's some problem with the factory plans, I think."

Johanna pouted. "And that is more important than . . ."

"Hush, now. I believe your guest is arriving."

Johanna saw the top half of a tall young man appear above the hedge. He looked toward the house. Johanna watched his eyes meander over the house, drifting down until they finally settled on her. And there they stopped. And he stopped. The rapid crunching of his footsteps was replaced by abrupt silence.

Johanna caught her breath. The young man's blue eyes regarded her as if she were the last thing on earth he had expected to see. Then he smiled. It was a shy, boyish smile devoid of all guile. He wore a light green shirt and had a brightly wrapped present tucked under his left arm. He came through the break in the hedge and started up the brick walk.

Johanna could now see that the rest of his attire suited the warm day — brown shorts, white calf-length socks, and hiking boots. He was an attractive boy, she had to admit. She had assumed the worst when her father had sprung his surprise on her. The vision of a misshapen gnome vanished on the warm breeze. Those eyes and that engaging smile went well together.

Johanna was aware of her blossoming beauty, and she was pleased with how this affected boys, and by the increasing amount of attention she drew. That Erich would find her attractive did not surprise her; however, she preferred to do the choosing. But now that Erich was here, she found that his attention did amuse her, so she smiled.

Erich's eyes locked on Johanna until he stood before her, and his gaze quickly shifted to her mother. A sudden breeze ruffled his well-groomed brown hair.

"Frau Kammler?" he asked.

She nodded. "And you must be young Erich. I am so glad you could come to Johanna's party."

"Thank you for inviting me." He turned

to Johanna and extended his gift. "Happy birthday, Johanna. You look . . ." And there he froze.

She looked up into his eyes, grateful he wasn't a lot taller than she was. "Thank you," she said as she accepted the package. Why had he stopped? she wondered, secretly pleased with how she affected him.

A quiet snicker sounded behind them.

"Bernhard!" Elsa snapped. Suddenly it was quiet again.

"That is my son, Bernhard," she told Erich. "And next to him is my other daughter, Sophie."

Johanna blushed. "Erich, please excuse my brother. He doesn't know how to behave before guests." She glanced toward Bernhard and was glad to see that her mother's threat was apparently holding him in check.

Erich cleared his throat. "There is no problem. It is a lovely day, and . . ."

She waited for him to continue, but he didn't. She smiled as she watched him squirm. "And what?"

Erich gulped. He felt the sudden chill of panic as his mind churned frantically for the right thing to say. His face grew hot. He knew he was blushing, but there was nothing he could do about it. This was not at all what he had expected when his mother had informed him of the party. He had complained, only to have his father cut him off abruptly. Erich's thoughts swirled around one central impression that would not go away, and nothing else would come to mind. He knew he had to say it.

"And I think you are the prettiest girl I have ever seen."

Silence settled over the yard. Johanna blushed. She saw from his eyes that he meant it, but why did he have to *say* it in front of everyone? She glanced at her mother, who appeared stunned as well. Johanna noted the wicked gleam in Bernhard's eyes. Sophie alone seemed to think it was all wonderful.

Elsa recovered first. She waved her hands vaguely toward the table.

"Johanna, take your place at the head of the table. And, Erich, please sit here beside her." She turned to the butler. "Herr Exner, bring the cake and ice cream."

The servant nodded and went inside, returning with a large white layer cake with fluted white and pink icing. After serving each guest, he brought out a wooden tub of hand-cranked vanilla ice cream. Seeing that everything was in order, Elsa and the butler went back inside.

Bernhard and Sophie grabbed their forks, lowered their heads, and made short work of their cake. Johanna and Erich ate theirs slowly, stealing glances at each other between bites. Johanna's mind raced as she sought a way to fill the awkward silence.

"Is this your first summer in Bavaria?" she asked.

"Yes. We usually vacation in northern Germany."

"Do you think you will like it here?"

"Oh, yes. It is very beautiful. I have always wanted to visit Bavaria."

Johanna and Erich finished their cake and started on the ice cream. Bernhard and Sophie had already finished and were looking about the table impatiently.

Bernhard's paper hat slid forward over his eyes. He pushed it back and grabbed his favor. He yelped with glee when he saw it was a noisemaker. He grasped it with his left hand and pulled the string with his right, producing a sharp bang. Smoke poured out, and the stench of gunpowder drifted over the table. Johanna wrinkled her nose at the smell but tried her best to look adult.

Sophie overcame her initial fear and picked up her favor. She held it as if it might get away and pulled on the string. But her grip wasn't strong enough, and the string slipped through her fingers. Bernhard laughed at her, which made her try all the harder, but with no greater success.

Erich got up and walked around behind her. "Here, Sophie, let me help you."

She looked up at him. "It won't work!"

"I'll hold it, and you pull the string. Use both hands."

He took the noisemaker and held it firmly. Sophie grimaced as she gripped the string with her small hands. On the second jerk, the string came out, bringing forth a satisfying bang and the heavy smell of sulfur.

"I did it!" she said, beaming.

"Maybe Johanna needs help with hers," Bernhard suggested.

Erich's eyes narrowed as he looked at him. "Maybe *you* could help her, Bernhard."

Bernhard kicked at the table leg. "I think she would rather you do it."

Johanna's eyes flashed in anger. "Bernhard!"

"Well, wouldn't you?" he persisted.

Erich stood there looking at her. "Would you?" he asked with an open smile.

She grabbed the noisemaker suddenly as if she would yank it, then stopped. Boys were all alike, she thought. Well, if Erich wished to play, she would let him. She smiled helplessly.

Erich hesitated a moment, then came around behind her. She caught the fresh scent of soap as he reached around and took the favor. She grasped the string and pulled briskly. The string broke. She turned her head and saw him looking down at her. At first she thought his smile mocked her, but she quickly realized that was not so.

"They didn't make it right," Erich said.

He grabbed his and held it out to her. This time the noisemaker went off. He stood over her for several moments. Johanna's heart beat faster as he lingered.

"That's all it's going to do," Bernhard informed everyone.

Erich looked at him in bewilderment, then looked down at Johanna. He put the noisemaker down and took his seat.

"What did you bring her?" Bernhard asked, pointing.

"Did someone leave you in charge?" Erich asked with a good-natured smile.

The little boy eyed the package. "I was just wondering."

"Why don't we see what *you* got your sister."

Bernbard pointed to a flat package. "That's it."

Johanna picked it up and opened it. Inside were four small, finely embroidered handkerchiefs.

"Thank you, Bernhard. They are very pretty."

"Yes, they are," Erich agreed. "You have very good taste. Where did you get them?"

Bernhard tapped his fork on his plate. "Mama picked them out for me." He looked quickly at his little sister. "She bought Sophie's gift also."

Johanna unwrapped that one and held up a small book. "A diary. Thank you, Sophie."

"Mama and I picked it out together."

"That was very thoughtful, Sophie," Erich said.

One package remained unopened. It was rectangular in shape and several inches high. Johanna tested its weight while regarding Erich, trying to decide whether to tease him or not.

"What is it?" she asked.

Erich gulped. "I don't actually know. My mother bought it in town after Papa told us about the party. She wrapped it before I could see what it was. I didn't ask." He paused. "But I am sure it is nice," he added. "Whatever it is."

Johanna laughed. "I am sure it is, whatever it is. Shall we see?"

"Please."

She removed the bow and ribbon and peeled off the bright paper. Inside was a delicately carved wooden music box. She held it up, turning it so she could examine the sides and top.

"It's beautiful, Erich. Thank you."

"You're welcome. I guess actually you should thank my mother."

"I wonder what it plays." She wound it and raised the lid. The gentle strains of *Für Elise* drifted out. "She has good taste in music."

"We hear that all the time," Bernhard volunteered.

"Do you play?" Erich asked Johanna.

"Yes. The piano."

"But she isn't any good," Bernhard added. "It's the same thing over and over. It hurts my ears."

Johanna pointed at her brother. "Enough of this, Bernhard. One more word, and I will tell Mama."

Elsa opened the door and stepped out. "Bernhard! Sophie! Time to come in."

Sophie stood up and started toward the house. Bernhard made a face, then turned to see if his mother meant it.

Elsa stood still as a statue. "If you do not come, I will inform your father."

Bernhard jumped up and hurried after his sister. Halfway to the house he turned and began walking backwards. "Johanna has a boyfriend," he sang.

Johanna's glare promised him he would pay for his audacity later. Bernhard whirled about and dashed onto the porch, past his mother, and into the house.

Johanna waited for the door to close. "That boy drives me crazy," she said as she turned and sat down.

"I think you have a nice family," Erich said.

She looked at him in disbelief. "Even Bernhard?"

"Even Bernhard. I don't have any brothers or sisters."

"It must be nice, having your house to yourself."

"It's lonely."

"Maybe you would change your mind if you had brothers or sisters, especially if they were like mine."

"I don't think so."

"Well, at least Mama has rescued us."

"So it would seem. You said you played the piano. I would like to hear you play sometime."

She smiled. "Perhaps I will. Do you play?"

He sighed. "I took lessons on the violin for several years, but I don't have the talent for it. Or the interest, I guess."

"Maybe we could play together."

"I think a piano solo would be better. I do know enough about music to appreciate it." He paused and gazed at her. "I appreciate beautiful things."

Johanna felt her face grow warm. She knew she was blushing but could do nothing about it.

"Shall we go in?" she said finally. "I could play for you now."

"Yes, I would like that very much."

He got up and helped her with her chair. "Johanna?"

"Yes?"

He hesitated, then took her hand as they walked toward the house. "I would like to see more of you this summer. This is my family's first summer here. Is there much to do in town?"

"It is quite different from Frankfurt, but yes, there are things to do."

He opened the door for her. Johanna led

the way through the hall to a small conservatory at the back of the house. A grand piano graced the center of the room. Johanna sat on the bench while Erich stood facing her.

"What's this?" he asked, picking up a book lying near the music rest.

Johanna finished adjusting her music sheets, then peered at what he was holding. "Oh, that's a gift from one of Papa's British customers. It's a first edition — quite rare."

Erich examined the English title and scanned a few pages. "Can you read this?"

She laughed at his serious expression. "Yes, at least a little. My tutor has been teaching me English. I'm most of the way through book 1."

"What is it?"

"In German the title would be something like *A Two Cities Tale* or something like that. It's by Charles Dickens."

"And you understand it?"

"For the most part. Sometimes I have to ask my tutor for help. Shall I read to you, or shall I play?"

Erich put the book down and smiled. "Please play for me. But before you do, can I ask you something?"

"I guess so. What is it?"

"Papa said he invited your family to dinner this Saturday. Can we talk about doing things together this summer then?"

Johanna thought of the long summer ahead, far from her friends in Frankfurt. The specter of boredom took shape in her mind. Erich had his good points, she decided. He was handsome and pleasantly attentive. And it would be a long time until she returned to her friends in Frankfurt. He could be a welcome diversion from the tedium.

She smiled at the thought and nodded. "Yes, I think that would be nice."

One

In 1936 the world was still struggling with economic depression. Germany had bitter memories of unemployment and unbelievable inflation, but things were looking up. Since Adolf Hitler had become chancellor in 1933, more Germans were working, and he was dealing with political anarchy. This new leader lifted their heads and told them it was grand to be German, as long as one had the proper genealogy.

Johanna was only vaguely aware that these developments benefited her. It grated on her that others, her father mostly, were continuing to determine her life for her. The only facet beyond her father's reach, so far, was her music, which offered her a marvelous gateway into the world of art and intellectual pursuits.

The slanting rays of the late spring sun beamed through the conservatory's tall windows, providing cheery lighting. It was comfortably warm inside, unlike the brisk coolness outside. Johanna sat at the piano as the final chords of *Für Elise* died away. She smiled to herself, pleased that she had not made any mistakes. Ulrich Remer, her instructor, nodded critically and for once found nothing Johanna needed to correct.

"Excellent," he said. "You are making wonderful progress."

She turned toward him. "I would hope so. I've been taking lessons for a long time now."

He came and sat beside her on the piano bench. Her pulse raced as she caught the scent of his cologne.

"So you have," he agreed. "But it takes talent as well. I think you may have what it takes to pursue the piano professionally." He paused. "That is, if you are willing to make the commitment."

She tried to hide her sudden irritation. She had seen other musicians practicing for hours, practicing far longer than she did. Being a professional musician appealed to her, but she didn't like the idea of slaving away at the keyboard for long hours. "What are you saying, Ulrich?" she asked.

He shrugged. "Simply that you have talent. But to take your career further requires work — lots of work. You have taken lessons long enough to know that. Your father is wealthy, Johanna. Work is something you do not have to do unless you want to. The choice is yours."

She nodded. "Yes, I know." She looked at him, her eyes painfully serious. "I would like to be a professional musician. But I also realize it would take years of hard work. I just don't know."

"No need to make a decision today. Think about it."

She nodded. "I will. But right now I feel the outside calling me."

Ulrich glanced toward the doorway. "Do not look now," he said in a stage whisper, "but we are being invaded by the string section."

Johanna looked around and saw her friend Christabel lugging a cello secure inside its case.

"I heard that, Herr Remer." Christabel parked the well-worn case beside the window and pulled up a chair. "The orchestra has all kinds of instruments. The string section is quite important to the overall effect."

Johanna giggled. "So is the wind section. You apparently excel at both."

Christabel's eyes narrowed. "I didn't expect that from a friend."

"Then don't leave such an opening."

"I'll be on my guard," she said with a smile. She looked through the sparkling windows at the side garden. "Isn't that gorgeous? I love the spring flowers — they make me think of the French impressionists."

"Anyone in particular?" Ulrich asked.

"Oh, I don't know — Claude Monet, I guess. How about 'Impression: Sunrise'?"

"That doesn't have any flowers in it," Johanna pointed out.

"I know, but it is such a beautiful painting. And it does give Impressionism its name."

"Of course, Monet *did* paint flowers. A lily pond and a Japanese bridge, for example."

Christabel held up her hand. "I surrender. I am done talking about painters. What started all this anyway?"

Ulrich nodded toward the window. "The garden. And it *is* a perfectly gorgeous spring day. Shall we go outside and inspect the garden — be our own impressionists?"

Christabel shook her head. "I must be off." She stood and struggled out with the cello case.

Ulrich waved his hand toward the door. "Shall we?"

They maintained a proper distance as they left the conservatory. Passing the side flower beds, soon they were deep inside the sprawling formal gardens in back. Ulrich took Johanna's hand as they followed the gravel path to the secluded stone bench they considered their own. They sat down and gazed at the skillfully arranged flowers whose bright colors seemed to shout that it was spring. Johanna thought again of what Ulrich had said, trying to imagine herself as a concert pianist, wondering if the effort would be worth it.

"Do you really think I could be a professional musician?" she asked as she snuggled close to him.

He looked askance at her and put his arm around her shoulder. "I was thinking of other things, but yes, if you really work at it. I think you have some understanding of what would be required, but believe me, it's harder than you can imagine."

She nodded. "I'll take your word for it and think about it. But right now I'm just enjoying being with you. You're good for me, Ulrich. No one else understands me."

He kissed her gently on the cheek. "Yes, I understand you, Johanna. And I love you."

She put her hand in his. "I love you too, Ulrich."

She leaned eagerly toward him, and he softly touched her lips with his, then again, just as lightly. She closed her eyes. He pulled her toward him and kissed her again, firmly this time. Johanna felt her heart race as she returned his kiss with a passion that both thrilled and scared her. She gasped for breath when they finally broke apart.

"I wish we had more than these secret meetings," she said.

"So do I."

"If only Papa would let you court me."

He shrugged. "You know what we are up against. Your papa will want the son of a prominent businessman for you. No one else will do. Our only hope is if you can convince him otherwise."

She felt the familiar frustration within her again. She resented how her father controlled every aspect of her life. She knew what he thought of Ulrich, to the extent that he thought of him at all — as a servant, nothing more.

"I know," Johanna replied. "I have tried everything I can think of, without being too obvious. But he doesn't hear a thing I say. He continues to invite various young men over — the sons of his friends." She smiled. "So far I have not had too much trouble discouraging them."

He hugged her. "That's my Johanna, resourceful as ever. All I can say is, keep trying. If you keep running them off, he may relent yet."

She looked at him hopefully. "Do you think so?"

"Only time will tell."

She sighed and laid her head on his shoulder. He put his arm around her and hugged her gently. Johanna gazed into the distance as her mind reran the tight track of all the schemes she'd tried on her father. It appeared as if the trap she was in had no exit. *But there has to be a way,* she thought angrily.

Ulrich sat at the small desk the conservatory grudgingly allowed him. He had just finished with his last student for the day, the son of a Frankfurt glassware manufacturer. Despite Ulrich's praise, the young man would never excel. He lacked talent and the discipline to work hard — a deadly combination for a pianist. Ulrich snorted. The father probably knew Herr Kammler. The young man was probably one of those who had been spurned by Johanna.

A sudden movement roused him from his reverie. He looked up with a start and saw a slim figure standing in the slanting rays of the afternoon sun. Even with her face hidden in the glare, he knew who it was.

"What are you doing here, Dorothee?" he demanded.

"Aren't you going to ask me to sit?" she asked in a hurt voice.

"No, I am not! I told you *never* to come here. My work at the conservatory has *nothing* to do with the White Cat Club."

"I saw you with that girl." Her tone was subdued, but Ulrich knew that could change quickly to accusing.

"I will *not* have you spying on me. There is nothing between me and her." He paused. "What made you think there was?"

"I saw you walk out of here with her. I saw her eyes — and yours."

"That's it?"

"Yes."

"Really, Dorothee, you must do something about your jealousy. I'm *supposed* to take an interest in my students. I walk with them, go over their progress, encourage them. It's expected. My job at the club doesn't pay all the bills."

"So you still love me?"

"Of course I do." He exhaled as softly as he could. "Now, what brought you down here?"

"I was lonely. On the days we don't rehearse I don't have anything to do until the club opens. I missed you."

He ran his fingers through his hair as his mind raced. Had anyone seen her come in? Had Johanna? He frowned as he struggled for the right words. "Well, you must leave at once. Now listen to me — do not *ever* come here again. The directors of the conservatory would not understand. If you get me fired, that would be very serious business. Do you understand?"

"Yes, Ulrich."

"Good. I will see you this evening."

Karl von Arendt paused to catch his breath after climbing the steps. He unlocked the door to the spacious two-story home in the stylish Schlachtensee section of Berlin. He pulled the door open and waited as his wife Julia and their son Erich walked into the entrance hall. They shed their coats and hats, grateful to be out of the brisk March weather. Karl's pear-shaped figure seemed to relax now that he was home. He smoothed the thin brown hair over his bald spot.

Erich took his time hanging up his overcoat and hat. The Sunday morning service echoed in his mind like the reverberations of a heavy gong. "What did you think about the service?" he asked his father.

Karl frowned as he looked up at his son. "What about it? The pastor went on too long, but that's nothing new."

Erich considered dropping the subject but decided to press on. "I know how you feel, Papa. But I think church is important — at least to me it is." He knew he was expressing himself badly but did not know how to put it more skillfully. But there was one fact he was sure of — Jesus was the Son of God.

Karl's frown grew deeper. "It seems we have produced a devout Christian, Julia."

"Perhaps Erich is right," she replied. She, like her husband, was short and stout.

"I have had my sermon for today, Julia. I don't need to hear one in my own home."

"Yes, dear."

Karl and Erich went into the front sitting room as Julia retreated upstairs. Karl sat heavily in a large overstuffed chair, while Erich stood by the window looking out at the street.

Erich glanced at his father. He didn't want an argument, especially on Sunday, but one point in the sermon simply would not go away. "What did you think about the pastor's comments on Herr Hitler sending the army into the Rhineland?"

"Violating the Treaty of Versailles? How absurd! The Rhineland belongs to Germany. Of course our leader is right! And that meddling pastor of yours better watch his step." He looked at his son suspiciously. "And what did *you* think?"

Erich turned toward his father. "It concerns me that Germany is violating the treaty. Even if it is unfair to us, we *did* sign it." He could see his father was about to erupt. "I know the Rhineland is ours, Papa. And we do need someone to lead us back to greatness — and maybe Herr Hitler *is* the one to do it."

"Is that what you really think?"

"Yes."

"Good. Then we are agreed. That sanctimonious charlatan needs to keep his mouth shut."

"I didn't say that, Father. Pastors are supposed to prick our consciences."

"Well, I will thank him to stay away from mine. I have enough trouble without someone trying to make me feel guilty all the time."

Erich sat down. It concerned him that his father did not understand the importance of faith, but he had little hope that would ever change. Nevertheless, he felt he could not give up. "The sermon was not about Herr Hitler and the Rhineland. The pastor only mentioned that in passing."

Karl arched his eyebrows. "Is that correct? Then what *was* the sermon about?"

Erich had to think quickly. The text eluded him for a few moments before he managed to snare it. "He preached on 'God is love.' The pastor said that in order to please God, we must love our fellow-man."

"And keep the army out of the Rhineland," Karl finished for him.

"That was not the point, Papa."

Erich knew his father was goading him, but it still hurt. These discussions always forced him to reconsider what he really believed about his faith. Even though many years had passed since his confirmation, he still remembered being taught about how Jesus had died for his sins, how he had announced to the congregation that he had trusted Jesus Christ as his Savior. He smiled. He had not changed his mind.

"And what is so amusing?" Karl grumbled.

"It is not amusing. I was just remembering when I became a Christian. It's a comforting thought."

"For some perhaps."

"I wish it was for you, Papa. Mama and I

are concerned for you."

"I'll thank you both to leave that up to me."

"We have no choice. No one can decide for you."

"Thank goodness for that."

Erich sensed his father's discomfort and hoped it would prod him to think about eternal matters.

Karl's eyes wandered about the room, as if trying desperately to locate some other topic of conversation. His eyes finally stopped on the desk.

"Oh," Karl said. He levered his bulk up from the chair, walked to the desk, and sat down behind it. "All this foolishness made me forget. I have something I need to discuss with you."

"What is it?"

Karl smiled as he tapped a letter with a letter opener. "What do you think of the Kammlers?"

Erich felt a pang in the pit of his stomach. His pulse quickened as he remembered the previous summer's vacation in Bavaria, one of several. He had tried to monopolize Johanna's time, to the extent he had been allowed. They had attended concerts and plays, and there had been the usual round of parties — and the long walks. *But why is Father bringing this up now?* he wondered.

"I'm not sure what you mean."

Karl laughed. "I'm surprised at you, Erich. You have no thoughts concerning this fine family?"

Erich grinned self-consciously. "Well, now that you mention it, I seem to remember that their eldest daughter is quite remarkable."

"Remarkable? Only remarkable?"

"Actually, she is the most beautiful woman I have ever met."

"Do not be rash. There are many women you have *not* met."

"Father, I think you know how I feel about Johanna. I love her. I can't think about anything *but* her. And Frankfurt is so far away . . . I wish we lived closer."

"Looking forward to this summer?"

"You have no idea."

Karl arched his eyebrows. "I understand and remember, son. I was not always the old burned-out shell you see before you. Your mother, I assure you, could stoke the youthful fires."

A shocked expression came to Erich's face. "I didn't mean . . ."

Karl grinned suddenly. "Oh yes, you did. I was young once myself, and I was sure my papa did not understand how it was with me." He paused. "Son, Walther and I have been having some serious talks lately."

"What about?"

"About you . . . And about Johanna."

Erich felt his mouth go dry. The distant hope he had held for years suddenly came to life. He watched his father's smiling eyes, waiting for what he longed to hear.

"What about us?" he croaked.

"I know how you feel about Johanna — I would be blind not to. Walther and I have discussed the two of you from time to time over the last few years. We believe your marriage would unite two fine German families. He gives his wholehearted approval, as I do myself."

Erich closed his eyes in happiness just before a sobering thought crept in to give him pause. No one had said anything about courtship in the years he had known Johanna. It had never been far from *his* mind, but he had never discussed it with Johanna. They had simply enjoyed being in each other's company. Erich just assumed . . .

"Have you nothing to say?" Karl asked.

"I don't know what *to* say. I'm thrilled — it is everything I have dreamed of for years.

But Johanna and I have not discussed this. Did Herr Kammler say how Johanna feels about this?"

"Well, no, but I assume Walther has discussed it with her. I'm sure she is as delighted as you are." He paused. "Am I to understand that you two have never talked about marriage?"

Erich suddenly felt hot and knew he was blushing. "Not in so many words, Father." He paused. "I haunt their house when we go to Frankfurt or vacation in Bavaria. She knows how I feel — I've told her I love her. I was planning to ask you to help me approach Herr Kammler this summer."

Karl's serious expression eased a little. "Well, it seems I've beat you to it. And I assure you, Walther could not have been more enthusiastic. He has promised a magnificent wedding. I think perhaps we should visit Frankfurt in a few weeks and firm up the plans — give you and Johanna time to discuss this. How does that sound?"

Erich put his head back and closed his eyes. "Like heaven."

"I have already had my sermon, thank you. Let us come down to earth, hmm?"

"Oh, heaven will come someday, Papa. But this will definitely do for now."

★ ★ ★

Walther Kammler looked up from the newspaper propped up on his ample middle. The peaceful strains of Beethoven drifted from the conservatory as Johanna practiced on the piano. Walther smoothed his moustache and struggled to his feet. He smiled as he strolled to the conservatory door and waited.

Johanna saw a flash of movement and looked up, leaving Beethoven hanging in mid-note. "What is it, Papa?"

He entered the room, pulled up a chair beside the piano, and sat down. "You play beautifully, Johanna," he said.

She smiled. "I agree with you. But I suspect that is not why you came in here." She smoothed her long blonde hair and struggled to maintain her composure as her mind hurriedly considered the possibilities.

"I can hide nothing from you, daughter. I have news — good news. Something we have dreamed of for a long time."

Johanna felt both anticipation and dread. "What is it?" she asked breathlessly.

He nodded, smiling broadly. "I knew that would get your attention. Your mother and I are not unaware of the affairs of your heart."

Johanna's vague dread solidified into real

fear as her mind raced ahead. She struggled to maintain an outward appearance of calmness, hoping she was misreading her father's intentions.

"What do you mean by that?" she asked, unable to suppress her obvious concern.

Walther's broad smile disappeared. Johanna longed for a way to prevent what she feared was coming, but she knew there was nothing she could do. Her wishes had little effect on him.

Walther cleared his throat and began again. "I . . . rather, your mother and I have noticed . . . well, every summer young Erich von Arendt and you have been constant companions. Parties, family picnics." He laughed nervously. "Every time I turn around he is underfoot — not that I mind, of course. He is a *fine* young man from one of the great German houses."

Johanna closed her eyes for a moment. Her stomach felt like it was tied in a knot, and she struggled to contain a twinge of nausea. "What does his social standing have to do with me?" she asked slowly, stressing each word.

Walther drew himself up. "Germany is entering a new era under our Führer. And that new future includes us. You are twenty now, Johanna. It is time to be thinking of marriage and a family."

Johanna wanted to scream but instead protested, "Stop! Do not say another word!"

Even though it was cool, sweat suddenly appeared on Walther's forehead. His expression hardened. "Johanna, I will thank you to remember that I am your father! You will listen respectfully to what I have to say."

All she could do was stare at him with her mouth open, as if she were in the path of a speeding train she could not avoid. She waited for the inevitable.

He shifted uneasily in his chair. "Karl von Arendt and I have come to an understanding. You and young Erich are to be wed early this summer."

Johanna shook her head. Tears welled up in her eyes.

Walther hurried on, "You and he have been constant companions on our vacations. It is obvious Erich loves you dearly — he *worships* you, Johanna."

She could hold in her sadness no longer. She turned her head away from him and felt in her pocket for a handkerchief. Bitter tears fell as she sobbed. All her dreams were crumbling before the whim of her uncaring father.

"What is the meaning of this?" Walther demanded in a bewildered voice.

"Please leave me alone," Johanna begged.

Walther sat for a few moments before struggling to his feet. Then he left the room as quickly as his ruffled dignity would allow.

Johanna's parents did not object to her frequent afternoon walks. However, she never went out at night unless suitably chaperoned. This her father insisted on, which she hated, but these rules also insured her privacy and what little freedom she had during the day.

As she walked past her father on her way out, she sensed he wanted to say something, but she hurried past so he wouldn't have the chance. She knew he could have stopped her, but he apparently decided not to.

She hunched her shoulders and pulled her coat tighter around her as the biting wind tried to find an opening. She reached the street as the tram ground to a stop. She rushed up the steps, tossed her fare into the meter, and sat down. The small car lurched into motion. The electric motor whined away under the floorboards as the power pole sparked along the wire overhead.

Several blocks later the car rounded a curve. The elegant homes of Sachsenhausen gradually gave way to smaller dwellings in need of repair. The tram crossed the Main River and entered the business district. Johanna watched the plate-glass windows as they drifted past, their painted signs beckoning to the passing shoppers. She remembered Ulrich telling her the White Cat Club was no place for a well-bred young lady. He had said it in a joking way, but she knew he was quite serious. She felt a little guilty about going there, but she *had* to talk to him.

Johanna shifted so she could see past a tall passenger, hoping she would recognize the club from Ulrich's description. A block away she saw a sign shaped like a cat. She reached up and pulled the cord to ring for her stop. She stood up, bracing herself as the tram squealed to a halt. She stepped down and hurried to the sidewalk.

Half a block ahead a small sign hung over a dingy doorway advertising the entrance to the White Cat nightclub. She struggled with apprehension as she walked steadily toward her destination. Pausing before the door for a moment, she knocked timidly. She waited almost a minute before banging more sharply on the glass panel. A hand pulled aside the shade, and a young man peered out. The shade fell back.

"We're closed," came the muffled voice from inside. "Come back this evening."

Icy pangs of panic welled up. "Wait!" Johanna shouted, more loudly than she intended. "I have to see Ulrich Remer."

After a few moments the lock clicked, and the door opened a few inches. The man's eyes ran up and down her as if he didn't understand what he was seeing. "You are a friend of Ulrich's?"

"Yes. Is he here?"

In answer, the man opened the door wide.

Johanna walked past him and paused inside, allowing her eyes to adjust to the gloom. The thin young man who let her in retreated to the back without another word.

Johanna wended her way through the deserted room and took a seat at a small, round table well back from the stage. She wrinkled her nose at the musty, close smell of the place. She tried to imagine what it was like at night, with all the tables filled and the spotlights on the performers. Dim overhead bulbs bathed the stage in an

47

even, unflattering light. She looked up at Ulrich as he pounded out a loud accompaniment on a battered piano. A pretty young girl clad in a tight black gown struggled with her impression of a Marlene Dietrich song. Johanna winced as the performer missed a high note by a considerable margin. If this bothered the singer, she gave no sign. The pianist glanced toward the tables and saw Johanna. He muffed a few notes but quickly recovered. Johanna watched the singer rehearse her lyrics and sultry moves, wondering what it would be like to be a nightclub performer.

Ulrich finished the song and closed the piano's keyboard cover. "That is enough for now, Dorothee. We'll go over the routine one more time half an hour before opening."

Johanna flinched as the young woman hurried over to Ulrich. She couldn't hear what Dorothee was whispering, but it was clear she was angry. Ulrich gave a terse reply that the singer cut off. She pointed toward Johanna as she continued her whispered tirade.

Ulrich stood up, obviously provoked. "I've heard *entirely* enough! Go calm down, and we will discuss this later."

Dorothee glared at him, turned briefly

toward Johanna, and finally flounced off the stage. A few moments later a door banged shut.

Ulrich descended from the stage and walked between the tables toward Johanna. A smile quickly replaced his frown.

"My darling, what an unexpected pleasure," he said as he kissed her. He pulled a chair up beside her and sat down. "I hope that unpleasantness did not upset you." He waved toward the empty stage.

Johanna leaned closer. "I couldn't hear what you were saying — until you told her to leave. What's the matter with *her?*"

He waved a hand in disgust. "She's inexperienced and insecure as a performer. She felt you were interrupting her rehearsal. Don't worry about it." He paused and looked into her eyes. "Now tell me, what brings you here?"

Johanna lowered her head. "Something horrible has happened." She brought up her handkerchief as the tears began to flow.

"What's wrong?"

She leaned toward him. He put his arm around her and hugged her.

"You have to help me," she pleaded.

He waited for a moment, then sighed. "I am not a mind reader, Johanna. Why are you here?"

She sniffed and looked down. "I don't know where to begin."

"Pick a place," he suggested. "If I get lost I will ask for directions."

A sob escaped. "You're making fun of me."

"Not at all. Tell me what's wrong. You have my undivided attention." He took her hand and patted it reassuringly.

"There is this man I know . . . not well . . . Our family and his vacation together . . . His name is Erich." She blinked away her tears as she struggled to control the anger rising inside. "Today Papa told me I am to marry Erich." She looked at Ulrich, depending on him to provide a way out.

Ulrich drummed his fingers on the table. "Do you love him?"

"How can you say that, Ulrich? I love *you*. I long for you every moment I am away from you." More than anything she wanted him to get up and take her in his arms, to tell her he was hers forever. "I love everything about you. We share the same interests . . ."

"I love you too, Johanna. You have no idea what you mean to me. We are both fine musicians, we enjoy the same art, we have fine discussions on the future of Germany. That is all well and good. But you did not answer my question. Do you love him?"

"No. I told you — I love you."

He caressed her hands. "Good. And I love you. You know that."

"Yes, of course. But what am I to do?"

He stroked her soft hands before answering. "I really don't know. I don't see what you or anyone else *can* do. You certainly can't go against your father's wishes — not if you wish to keep your inheritance."

"I don't care about that. I can't marry a man I don't love."

Ulrich sighed. "Yes, you can, my dear. And I happen to know you *do* care about your inheritance and all that goes with it. You are used to the good life, Johanna."

"Do you want me for my money?" she asked with a pout.

He shook his head. "Not at all. I love you dearly, you know that. But only a fool would give up her inheritance. And you, Johanna, are no fool."

"Perhaps Papa will change his mind."

"I think that very unlikely," Ulrich said. "We can hope, but unfortunately I think your fate is sealed."

She pounded the table. "But this is so unfair!"

"Life is unfair, Johanna. A few have

power, and the rest of us do not. Those with power have their way."

"But *I* have power. I can leave home. Take me with you, Ulrich. We can be married and pursue our music together."

He sighed. "No, Johanna. That would never work. Your father would be furious, and he could ruin my career at the conservatory. And even if he did nothing, we would have to leave Frankfurt because we would not be able to live on what I make here." He paused, a sad look coming to his eyes. "I suppose I always wished for a way to make myself acceptable to your father. I knew it was unlikely but kept convincing myself it was possible. Now there is no hope."

In a flash of insight she knew Ulrich was right. She burst into tears and lowered her head to the table. *It's unfair,* she thought. *Papa can do as he pleases with me, and I can do nothing about it.*

"I'm sorry, Johanna," Ulrich said.

She gave no indication she heard.

It was nearly 8 P.M. on Monday. Erich von Arendt looked out through the large windows of Berlin's Romanische Café, across the street from the Kaiser Wilhelm Memorial Church. Located on Kurfürsten-

Damm, known locally as Ku-damm, the restaurant was one of the most popular in the city. Erich glanced at his watch, wondering how late his friend Franz Brant would be this time. He took a sip from his beer stein and set it back down.

A tall man pushed through the front door and looked around the crowded room. He had blond hair and blue eyes, looking very much the young Aryan that Adolf Hitler so praised. He spotted Erich and headed for his table. He sat down and signaled for a beer at the same time.

"So you have good news," he said as he pulled his chair up to the table.

Erich's smile grew even wider. "Indeed I have. The best."

"Well, tell me."

"Johanna and I are to be married. Papa told me yesterday. It's all arranged."

"That's wonderful. But I guess this is not too much of a surprise. After all, she is all I ever hear you talk about."

Erich grinned. "What are you saying? We talk about other things as well."

The beer maid placed a large stein on the table. Franz took it without looking at her and gulped down several swallows, wiping the foam away with the back of his hand.

"Erich, this is your friend talking. I am the one who has to listen to your lovesick chattering."

Erich shrugged. "Anyway, the date is set. We will be going to Frankfurt in two weeks to meet with the Kammlers, make the announcements, and all that."

Franz raised his stein and looked over it as he took another drink. "You *have* talked to Johanna about this, I assume?" he asked as he put the beer down.

"Well, no, not in so many words. But we have known each other since I was fifteen." He laughed self-consciously. "We vacation every summer with the Kammlers. Johanna and I go everywhere together. I certainly have never been interested in anyone else." Erich paused. "Franz, I really couldn't talk to Johanna about marriage unless I was officially courting her. I intended asking Herr Kammler about that, but he and Papa beat me to it."

Franz looked down at the tabletop. "Then I'm sure everything will be fine." He looked up, his eyes bright. "This calls for a better celebration than sitting around here. Berlin has *much* more to offer, you know."

"Hitler has closed all those places down."

Franz winked at him. "Not all of them. There are a few left, and *I* know where they are. What do you say? One last fling while you are still free?"

Erich flushed in embarrassment. "No, Franz, I could never do that. It wouldn't be right."

"As you wish. So, where will you and Johanna be setting up house?"

"I have bought a house in Schlachtensee. It will be convenient to Papa's architectural firm."

Franz swirled the beer in his nearly empty stein, then drained it. His eyes hardened and locked with Erich's.

"So you still plan to work for your father when you finish school?"

"Of course. It's what I studied for all these years. Why shouldn't I?"

"You should do what is best for you," Franz said as he signaled for another beer.

"I intend to. But what about you?"

Franz looked surprised. "Me? Getting kicked out of the university limits my options a little, yes?"

Much as he liked Franz, his friend's wild life disturbed him. He could not understand why school was so unimportant to him.

"You could go back."

"Yes, I know. And maybe I will. But I have been thinking of joining the SS. It would be a lot more interesting than drawing up building plans the rest of my life."

Erich laughed uneasily. He had heard disturbing things about Herr Himmler and the SS. Then he remembered what his pastor had said about the remilitarization of the Rhineland.

"I guess lots of things are more interesting than architecture." He paused. "Franz, what do you think of our Führer?"

Franz sat back in his chair. "I think he is the best thing that has ever happened to Germany. You know what we have been through since the Great War — the humiliation, the poverty, the riots, the Communists. Look what Hitler has done so far. Germans can hold their heads up again, for the first time since the end of the war."

"Yes," Erich replied with hesitation.

"You don't sound so sure."

"You're right — some things are much better."

"Then what are you concerned about?"

"I've heard some things about Hitler's tactics that worry me."

"Are you listening to the tales of old women? It takes force to correct the problems Germany has. Thank God our Führer has the strength to see it through."

"I know Germany needs a strong leader. I only hope he is the right one."

"Oh, he is the right one all right. Just wait and see."

Two

Johanna sat in the chair beside the dresser and stared out into the night. She had spent all of Monday inside, her mood alternating between bitter sorrow and icy rebellion. A thousand scenes had played themselves out as she sought a way out of her dilemma. But they all foundered on the same rock — her father. Elsa had been up several times, urging her to come down, at least for meals. But she had refused each time.

She heard the grandfather clock strike 9 downstairs. Moments later she heard soft footsteps coming up the stairs. She chose not to answer the muted rap at her door. It sounded again, louder this time.

"Johanna?"

"Leave me alone, Mother," Johanna replied more loudly than she intended.

The door opened slowly, and Elsa came in.

"Please come downstairs. Your father and I want to talk to you."

Johanna continued to stare out the window. "No. Now go away."

She waited for her mother to leave, but

all she heard was silence. With mounting irritation, Johanna turned around.

"Your father says you are to come down at once," Elsa said in the voice of a reluctant messenger.

Johanna knew there was no appeal. She stood and followed her mother downstairs. They entered the front receiving room, where Walther stood by the fireplace mantel, a coal fire at his back. His eyes followed her all the way into the room.

"Sit down, Johanna," he said, motioning toward a chair by the window. Elsa took her place beside her husband.

Johanna sat down and lowered her head.

"Look at me." He waited until her eyes met his. "Enough of this foolishness. Your mother and I are not going to put up with any more of your bad manners and ingratitude. This will cease at once."

"But, Papa . . ." Johanna began, tears welling in her eyes.

"Silence. You will listen to me. I have worked hard to provide for my family, and it's time you realize that with privilege comes responsibility. The Kammlers are prominent in Frankfurt society, and I intend to see you married into a suitable family."

He paused and shook his head. "I do not

understand you, Johanna. The only young man who has been introduced to *me* as your suitor is Erich von Arendt. You and Erich have known each other for seven years now. Erich comes from a fine Berlin family, and he's going to be a partner in his father's firm. Good family, outstanding financial and social prospects — it will be an *ideal* marriage."

"But . . ."

"Do you think I'm a fool? I know all about Herr Remer, if you're wondering about him. The investigator I hired was *most* thorough and discreet. This music teacher, who betrayed my trust, got better than he deserved. Herr Remer took the money my attorney offered him and has agreed that he is never to see you again."

"Papa!"

"Enough! I'm not playing games with you, Johanna! Erich is the only acceptable suitor you've ever had. I have talked with Karl von Arendt at length. He assures me Erich loves you *dearly* — something I was well aware of. I would not have agreed to the arrangements otherwise. I have not met a finer young man."

She looked up, her eyes pleading, but knowing protest was futile. It felt like her whole world had caved in. With Ulrich removed, she had no one to turn to except her friend Christabel. But with Ulrich gone, what did anything matter anyway? Bitterness welled up inside her, knowing she had to accept the control her father had over her. There was no other way.

Walther's stern gaze never wavered. "In a few weeks the von Arendts will come here for the official announcement and the receptions. And in June you *will* become Frau Erich von Arendt."

Erich looked out at the spring countryside as the Frankfurt express train neared its destination. So much had happened in the preceding two weeks that he couldn't express it all, except to say that the time had not passed quickly. The train slowed as it came into the city and finally drew into the station.

"There they are," Erich said, pointing to the family on the platform. "Even Bernhard is there. I bet they had to tie and drag him."

Julia laughed. "Of course they are all here. This is *not* a summer holiday in Bavaria, Erich. They are welcoming you into their family."

"Yes, son," Karl agreed. "This is a marriage of families."

Erich waved to Johanna. After a moment she waved back. The train came to a stop, and Karl and Julia stood back to allow Erich to step down first. He walked slowly over the platform, oblivious of the multitude swirling around him. All he could see was the strained smile on the face of his bride-to-be. She turned her head delicately, and he gently kissed her cheek. He had to swallow before he could speak.

"You look lovely, Johanna. I can't tell you how I have longed for this."

"Thank you, Erich," she replied, casting her eyes down.

He took her hand in his and squeezed it.

"Welcome to Frankfurt, my boy," Walther said. "Let me congratulate you."

He shook hands with Erich, then greeted Karl and Julia.

"Let me be the second to congratulate you," Bernhard, now fifteen, said, extending his hand. "And I suppose Sophie will be third."

Sophie giggled.

Erich took Bernhard's strong grip. "Well, you were right."

"About what?"

"The first time I came to visit, you said I was Johanna's boyfriend."

Bernhard glanced at his older sister.

"True. That is something Johanna has never let me forget. I thought it was a rather astute observation."

"Johanna said you were being a pest," Sophie observed.

Bernhard shrugged. "Well, she never has appreciated my true gifts."

Walther gave instructions for the baggage and ushered his family and guests outside where two chauffeured Mercedes touring cars waited.

He pointed out the second one to Erich. "Perhaps you and Johanna would like to take that car?"

"Well, yes, thank you," Erich said. "I appreciate that."

"My pleasure. I'm sure both of you have much to talk about." Walther's gaze lingered on his daughter until he caught her eye. She nodded.

The young couple settled into the comfortable leather backseat while the chauffeur took the wheel. The driver followed the first car out into the traffic.

"Do you remember what I said the first time I saw you?" Erich asked as he took her hand.

Johanna gazed out the window. "No." It seemed to Erich that she stiffened as she spoke.

Erich looked a little surprised. "I said you were the most beautiful girl I had ever seen."

She laughed. "Oh yes, I remember now. I don't know who was more shocked — you or me."

"I know. But I meant it. And I mean it now. Johanna, you are the most beautiful woman I have ever known."

"How many have you known?"

He blushed. "A few, as acquaintances. You know, parties, dances — the social scene. But you are the only girl I have loved. And I love you so much."

He put his arm around her and tried to pull her close.

She reached for her handkerchief. "Thank you, Erich." She dabbed at a tear and sniffed.

"What's wrong, Johanna?"

She smiled at him. "Nothing. Women get emotional at times like this. It is something you will have to get used to."

"But you are happy, aren't you?"

"Very." She squeezed his hand and looked away.

His momentary concern faded as he caught the scent of her perfume. "I promise you a good life, Johanna. I'm joining my father's architecture firm. And I've found us a house in Schlachtensee. It definitely needs a woman's touch, but I think you will like it."

"I'm sure it will be quite nice," she said evenly.

"I think it's more than nice," Erich said in surprise. "I assure you, Schlachtensee houses are not cheap."

She smiled. "I'm sure you're right, Erich. Berlin is your home, so you would know."

The car turned south onto Schweizerstrasse and crossed the Main River.

He grinned. "I guess we shall see about that." He squeezed her hand. "I think you'll like our honeymoon."

She turned to him, her eyes wide. "What?"

He blushed. "I meant where we're going. Franz told me . . . I did tell you about Franz, didn't I?"

Johanna sighed. "Yes, Erich, you've told me about Franz — many times."

"Well, anyway, Franz told me about this intimate inn in the Bavarian Alps, not far from Berchtesgaden. Nothing around for miles — beautiful and remote."

"It sounds primitive."

"Oh, no. It's quite exclusive and has the very best accommodations. I know you'll like it."

"I'm sure I will. Now, let's enjoy the drive to our house."

Erich settled back in the seat as the Mercedes purred its way through Frankfurt. He watched Johanna out of the corner of his eyes. He knew he was very nervous and wondered if that explained his concern about her reactions. Finally he decided she was probably just as nervous as he was.

All too soon the weekend was over. To Erich it was a kaleidoscope of memories, of things he had to do, people he had to meet, getting the wedding announcement in all the Frankfurt and Berlin papers. And all too little time spent alone with Johanna, which was all he really wanted.

They stood on the platform in the Frankfurt station. Erich's parents boarded the train, and Johanna's said their good-byes and retreated. The Berlin express huffed in the background, a shrill whistle announcing its imminent departure, as the young couple hesitated, each unsure what to say.

"Are you sure you can't come up to Berlin before the wedding?" he asked.

"Yes, I'm sure. I have much to do before June. Mama and I have to pick out my dress and have it made. Then there are all the parties my friends will insist on."

"But . . ."

"Don't *you* have things you have to do? Like finishing school, getting the house, going into business with your father?"

"Yes, I do. It's just that I will miss you so."

The whistle sounded again.

"And I'll miss you. Take care. The time will pass."

He pulled her close and kissed her. His pulse hammered in his ears, and his knees began to tremble. A series of thuds sounded as the locomotive edged forward, taking the slack out of the car couplings.

She pulled out of his arms. "You'll miss your train, Erich."

"Good-bye," he said.

He kissed her again and ran for the train. He jumped up into the doorway and turned to look back, then waved to Johanna until the train was clear of the station.

The time went by faster than Erich had thought it would. Much faster. By early June he had his degree in architecture, and his wedding date was fast approaching.

Karl von Arendt looked up as Erich entered the cottage behind their house.

"Been checking on your house?" he asked.

Erich sat down with a weary sigh. "Yes. The workers have finished with the structural work. But I think I'll wait until Johanna and I move in to begin the redecorating."

"A wise decision."

"I think so. One of the things I appreciate about Johanna is her artistic sense. I can't wait to see what she does with the house." He paused. "I'm glad I have a job lined up. Fixing up that house is going to be expensive."

Karl stroked his moustache. "I'm afraid you won't be working for me, son."

"What do you mean? I was depending on that." He ran a hand through his heavy brown hair. "Papa, I *must* have that job. I have many bills for the house, and my wedding is next week. I can't make ends meet without that job."

Karl held up his hand. "Let me explain — it's not as bad as it sounds. Another architect has been trying for some time to get me to go to work for him, but I turned him down until recently. Then I got an opportunity to sell the firm at a substantial profit. It was too good to pass up. Part of the proceeds will go to you. Furthermore, the man I will be working for needs another architect. He'll employ you for the same pay I was offering."

Erich's furrowed brow eased a little. "This is a shock, Papa. I trust your judgment, but I wish I had known about this beforehand. Who are you going to work for?"

"Have you heard of Albert Speer?"

Erich's eyebrows shot up. "The one who's doing all that work for the Führer?"

"That's him. Herr Speer needs architects *now*, and he's looking for the best. When I finally agreed to talk about employment, I showed him some of my work. I hope you don't mind, but I also showed him one of your school projects."

"I guess I don't mind, though this is all a bit unnerving."

"I know, son. I wish I could have warned you, but it all happened so fast. Herr Speer was quite impressed with your work. I think this will be a better opportunity for you than I could've provided; otherwise I wouldn't have done it."

"I trust your judgment, Papa. I just need time to make the adjustment. Who did you sell the firm to?"

"Another architect — no one you know — who has been after me to sell for a long time. He's ambitious, has money, and knows a good practice when he sees it. I'm getting a good price. When the offer from Herr Speer came, I had to sell. I hope you understand."

Erich took a deep breath. He had enough to think about with the wedding and the repairs on his new house. To have his work plans changed added to his jittery nerves. But the more he thought about it, the more intrigued he became. Working for Herr Speer would certainly be exciting — if he could measure up. The man *did* have a reputation as a taskmaster.

"Well, yes, I guess so. Papa, I've dreamed of being your partner ever since I started school. But this does sound like a wonderful opportunity."

"I really believe it is — for both of us. Wait until you meet Herr Speer. Germany is destined for great things. And with all the work Herr Speer is doing for our Führer, I think we'll be right in the middle of it all."

"When do I get to meet our new boss?"

"Tomorrow."

Albert Speer rose from his desk as Karl and Erich were ushered into his office. Albert had a trim figure and was quite tall.

Erich was immediately struck by the man's piercing eyes, his bushy eyebrows so black they looked painted, and his charming smile. But at the same time there seemed to be a strange reserve that put a slight chill on the man's outward charm.

"Herr von Arendt," Speer said, shaking his hand warmly. "And this must be your son Erich." Erich took the man's hand, noting the firmness of his grip. "Please sit down." Albert returned to his seat behind the large desk.

"Thank you for seeing us," Karl responded. "I know you're busy, but I wanted my son to meet you. After all, I did change his career plans without warning."

"I understand completely. I also wanted to see you before we get down to our task. I can promise you interesting work, and I want you to know what I expect." He turned to Erich. "I looked over your school project, Erich. You show exceptional talent for one so young." He laughed suddenly. "And you're a better draftsman than me. I always had trouble with that."

"Thank you," Erich said self-consciously.

"What will we be working on?" Karl asked.

"The Nuremberg Stadium initially — architectural drawings and a wooden model. Have you heard about the project?"

"Yes, but not any details."

"The Führer has given me this huge project for the Nazi Party Rally Site. At the end of the new processional avenue will be a raised colonnade for the regimental flags. Behind this will tower the 400,000-seat Great Stadium." His eyes grew wide. "This will be the largest stadium ever built — by far. So, I think you can see this will be a project with immense importance."

"I should say so," Karl agreed.

"I never dreamed I would be working on something so magnificent," Erich said.

Speer waved a hand and laughed. "This is only the beginning, I'm sure. Herr Hitler has great plans for Germany. Several times he has hinted to me that he's planning a major reconstruction project for Berlin."

Subtle troubling thoughts tugged at the back of Erich's mind. Some of the things he'd heard about the Nazis bothered him, such as the Nuremberg laws that severely limited the social rights of Jews. But he could not deny Adolf Hitler's powerful effect on him and on most Germans he knew. And the Führer *was* dealing with problems like no other German leader since the Kaiser. Erich knew this was not the time to bring up his doubts.

"Sounds wonderful," Erich said. He looked toward his father. "When do we start?"

Albert smiled. "Your papa tells me you have some personal business to take care of. Is that so?"

Erich blushed. "Yes. I'm getting married in a week."

"Wonderful. My congratulations to you both. Then we'll see you here after you return from your honeymoon."

He stood and led them into the hallway. "We've already begun the stadium model. Let me show you the progress before you leave — something to whet the appetite, yes? Straight ahead is my model shop."

At the end of the hall Albert opened the double doors and led his guests into the large brightly-lit room. A rough horseshoe-shaped wooden skeleton dominated the center of the room, standing over seven feet tall. Two easels flanked the embryonic model, each supporting blueprints providing the stadium's details. One part had been completed — the massive colonnade flanked by heroic statues sitting upon the front-stepped platform. High walls flanked the monumental building, guarding the open end of the stadium.

"What do you think?" Speer asked, obviously proud.

The visitors stooped to view the colonnade from eye level. "The detail work is the best I've ever seen. And it looks exactly like pink granite," Karl said.

"You have a good eye," Albert replied. "The exterior will be pink granite and the stands white."

"Four hundred thousand seats? Will those at the top be able to see anything?"

Albert laughed. "I wondered the same thing. We did a study and found it was better than I expected, although the lower seats are better, of course."

The door behind them banged open, and a frantic young man ran in. "The Führer is here!" he gasped.

Karl and Erich looked toward the door in surprise, but Albert appeared calm. "Is he in my office?"

"No! He's coming back to the model shop. I ran back here as fast as I could."

Albert smiled. "No need for concern. The world is not coming to an end."

The doors opened, and Adolf Hitler strode in. Erich's eyes grew wide as he saw the familiar face that had captivated almost all of Germany. Seeing him up close had a powerful effect on the young architect.

Erich found himself fascinated — that unforgettable, magnetic expression, the immaculate Nazi uniform, complete with iron cross and red armband with the stark black swastika on a white circle. It surprised him that Hitler was alone.

Erich waited for Albert to deliver the Nazi salute and the familiar "Heil Hitler" and was prepared to join in. But his new boss did neither, and Hitler did not seem to expect it. Erich could sense a powerful bond of mutual interest that apparently transcended political customs.

Hitler's blue-gray eyes locked with Albert's. "I must see the model," he said in a rush. "After seeing the drawings the other day, I could think of nothing else."

"But it's not finished, my Führer. As you can see, we have only begun."

Hitler turned toward the model and walked slowly toward it as if he had suddenly found a pearl of great price. Karl and Erich silently stepped aside to allow Germany's dictator to pass. Hitler seemed not to notice them.

"It is magnificent, Herr Speer," he said reverently.

His eyes glinted with joy as he stooped down to see the colonnade's details. "Imagine all the regimental flags in there.

Row after row of colors, the emblems of the future glory of Germany." He shifted his view a little. "Perhaps a large perpetual flame in the center, hmm? Would that not make a nice touch?"

"I am sure it would, my Führer. I will have drawings made for a bronze torch at once."

"Good," Hitler said with a curt nod.

He turned suddenly and started toward Erich, who was standing in front of the left-hand easel. Erich tried to get out of the way but stumbled. His hand brushed against the easel, causing it to tip and clatter to the floor, scattering drawings everywhere. Hitler stared in shock at the blueprints for a moment, then frowned as he turned to Erich. The young man felt the blood drain from his face as an icy chill settled in his stomach.

"Who are you?" Hitler demanded.

"Erich von Arendt, my Führer."

Albert stepped up quickly. "These are my two new architects, my Führer. In fact, they will be working on the stadium model."

Hitler's smile returned. "Architects, you say." He locked eyes with Erich. "Wonderful profession. To build on a grand scale — there is nothing better." He paused.

"There was a time I wanted to be an architect. I still sketch occasionally."

"And quite well, my Führer," Albert
said.

Hitler waved a deprecating hand. "And
what projects have you worked on?" he
asked Erich.

"I have just graduated from university,
my Führer. The only thing I have worked
on was the final project for my professor."

Hitler nodded. "And what was that?"

Erich cleared his throat nervously.
"Plans for a new central train station for
Berlin, one built on a scale to rival the
Americans' Grand Central Station in New
York."

Hitler's eyebrows shot up. "What an interesting idea. I wish I could see your
drawings."

"Herr Speer has them in his office."

Hitler turned to Albert. "Do you? May I
see them?"

"Surely you are too busy, my Führer,"
Albert said.

"I will be the judge of that, Herr Speer.
Fetch the drawings."

Albert nodded and hurried out. A
minute later he returned with a large port-
folio. He opened it, took the drawings out,
and handed them to Hitler, who placed

them on the right-hand easel. The blue-gray eyes flitted over the top drawing, drinking in the station's exterior ground-level view. He turned to the interior renderings, his head nodding slowly as he checked detail after detail.

"Good. Very good." He appraised the young man standing nervously before him. "And where would you place this new station?"

"This was only a school project, my Führer." Erich smiled. "I was concentrating on doing the drawings rather than getting carried away thinking about sites."

Hitler glanced at Albert before returning to Erich. "But you *did* think about it, didn't you?" Hitler's eyes glinted. "I know how you architects operate. Now, where would you place the station?"

Erich looked at the drawings. "South and east of Tempelhof Airport, I think."

"What of the existing rail lines going into the city center?"

"Why not reroute them? Anhalter and Potsdam stations and their rail lines clutter the heart of Berlin. Removing them would revitalize our capital."

Hitler flipped back to the first drawing. "Yes, I think you are right. And this would certainly be a magnificent replacement.

Bigger than New York's Grand Central Station, you say?"

"I believe so, my Führer." Erich grinned. "If not, it could be made so."

Hitler's smile matched Erich's. "Yes, I am sure it could. I will keep that in mind. So, when will you be starting on the stadium project?"

"In a few weeks. I am to be married next week."

"Is that so? How wonderful. Do you have a photograph of your intended?"

Erich pulled out his wallet and showed him Johanna's picture.

"What a *lovely* fräulein. My congratulations to you both." He glanced at Albert. "Now the beautiful Frau Speer will have competition."

Hitler spotted Karl standing by Albert. "And you are the other new architect?"

"Karl von Arendt, my Führer. I am Erich's father."

"Ah, yes. I see the resemblance. You have a talented son."

"Thank you, my Führer."

Hitler turned back to Erich. "Are you and your father Nazi party members?"

"No, my Führer."

"Easily taken care of. I will leave word at party headquarters in Berlin that I will sponsor both of you."

Karl saw Erich stiffen. "How kind of you, my Führer," he answered for both of them.

"Not at all," Hitler replied. "I'm vitally interested in these projects. I expect to see more of both of you." He turned to Albert. "I'm pleased with the progress. I can't wait to see the finished stadium model. I expect your best."

"You will have it, my Führer."

Hitler nodded and hurried out.

Erich sighed as the excitement began to drain away. Seeing Hitler in person reinforced the sheer magnetic effect the man had on Erich, the effect he had seen so often on others. But despite the charm, Erich also felt uneasy. Some things the Nazis did bothered him. But of course what government was perfect — or what leader for that matter? So much of what Hitler did was right, Erich decided. He would just have to wait and see.

Three

Johanna sat by her bedroom window and looked out at the bright summer day. She reached for her handkerchief and dabbed at her tears. She had held on desperately to the hope that Ulrich would show up and take her away from her fate, but she now realized this would not happen. She had tried to reach him by phone only to find that he had moved and left no forwarding address. She scowled. Papa had been his usual thorough self.

A knock sounded at the door. Johanna ignored it. It came again.

"Johanna," her mother said.

"Leave me alone."

The latch clicked, and Elsa pushed the door open. She came in and closed the door, then sat on the edge of the bed.

"How are you, dear?" she asked.

Johanna blew her nose. "What do you care?"

"Perhaps more than you know."

"How can you know how I feel?"

Elsa sighed. "Married life is not like a romantic fairy tale, Johanna. For many, there is not even love to speak of, at least not at first. It was like that with your father and me."

Johanna looked surprised. "Then why did you marry him?"

"Because it was my duty. We were suitable for each other, and our families agreed it would be a good marriage."

"But to marry someone you don't love . . ."

Elsa smiled. "It was the right thing to do. Walther has been a good husband, and I think I have made him a reasonably good wife. We face life's problems together and have produced three wonderful children. Maybe we do not love each other as you think of love, but Walther and I do care for each other. We've had a good life together."

"But that isn't what I want, Mother!"

"Quiet, dear, and listen to me. I *know* it isn't what you want, but it's what you have. I'm sorry if Erich isn't your choice. But if you would indulge your mother a moment — I think Erich will make you a good husband, Johanna. He's dependable, he has fine character, and I believe he really loves you. These things are very important. I know Ulrich has told you he loves you, but I think he's unreliable. And from what I've heard, he's been cheating on you."

"You believe Father's spies?"

Elsa's gaze hardened. "Yes, I do. Character counts. Erich is a fine young man. Why not give him a chance?"

Johanna looked down without saying anything.

Elsa got up. "Please think about it. Your happiness depends on how you face up to this. Listen to me — you wouldn't be happy with Ulrich, not in the long run. I believe you and Erich can be happy together. But it depends on you."

Elsa left and closed the door softly. Johanna's mind felt numb. She didn't — wouldn't — believe what her father had told her about Ulrich; it had to be a ploy to keep them apart. Her tears flowed as she realized once again that her father had won. He had decided she would marry Erich and that was that. She collapsed on her bed and wept bitterly.

Erich tried to get comfortable as the cab made its leisurely trip from the hotel to the church. His starched shirt chafed, and his collar was too tight. He ran a finger around the snug fabric to try and get some relief, but it didn't help. His black cutaway was immaculate, and his shoes shone like mirrors. A fresh carnation adorned his buttonhole.

Karl gazed at buildings they passed, noting the ones with interesting architectural details. Julia alternated between beaming at her son and dabbing her eyes with a soggy handkerchief.

"I hope I'm doing the right thing," Erich said, almost in a whisper.

Karl's head snapped around. "What? After all these years of seeing no one but Johanna, you're having doubts? What do you mean by this?"

Julia took her husband's hand in hers. "Now, Karl, I'm sure this is normal. This is a big step for our Erich. And as I recall, you had cold feet before our wedding."

"Who told you that?"

Julia smiled. "Your mother."

He looked disconcerted. "Well, I . . . Never mind." He removed his hand and resumed his survey of Frankfurt architecture.

"Do you want to go through with it?" Julia asked her son.

"Mother, I love Johanna with all my heart. I've dreamed of this day for years."

"You didn't answer my question, son."

Erich's stomach went ice-cold as he saw

the church approaching on their left. He gulped and nodded. "Yes. Yes, I do."

"Are you sure?"

"Yes, I'm sure. But it's a big responsibility. I will be living with Johanna the rest of my life. I have to be a good husband and . . ." He gulped. ". . . and a good father."

She smiled and patted his hand. "You're right. It *is* a big responsibility. But it'll be all right, Erich. Trust God — He will see you through."

The cab pulled up behind a floral truck. The von Arendts got out as the deliveryman struggled up the front steps of the church with a huge floral spray.

"Wonder who that's from?" Julia asked.

"A friend of the Kammlers, no doubt," Karl muttered as he took a look at his watch. "Come now, we must be going inside."

They entered the heavy stone structure together. An usher escorted Julia to her seat as Karl walked behind. Erich took a side aisle to a small room off the chancel. He opened the heavy wooden door and entered.

"So you decided to go through with it," Franz said with a grin.

"Absolutely," Erich said, shaking his

hand. "Now don't make me sorry for asking you to be my best man."

Franz laughed. "I thank you. You must do the same for me, if I can find a woman who will put up with me."

"It will be an honor. Is Johanna here?"

"Relax — your beautiful bride-to-be is here. The Kammlers arrived at the same time I did. The ladies disappeared into a room to fuss over Johanna's dress. Take it easy, Erich."

"I'm trying to, but it's hard. You do have the ring?"

"No, I threw it in the Main River."

"This is nothing to joke about!"

Franz pulled the ring from his pocket and held it up. "Yes, I have the ring. I'm taking care of you, my friend."

"Yes, I know. It's just that my nerves —"

The door opened, and Bernhard burst in. His cutaway was splendid, and he would have looked elegant had his grooming matched his clothes. Tufts of blond hair stuck out, defying his mother's earlier attempts to control it.

"Guess what happened?" he asked.

Erich's heart began to race. "What?"

"The Führer sent flowers! The delivery-man gave Mama the card. It says, 'To Erich and Johanna on your wedding day.

With my very best regards, Adolf Hitler.' What's going on? Why would the Führer be sending you and Johanna flowers?"

"This isn't easy to explain," Erich said slowly. "Papa and I met him last week. We were meeting with our new boss, Albert Speer, when Herr Hitler simply showed up. We talked . . ."

"You talked to the Führer?" Bernhard interrupted.

Franz's mouth dropped open. "You *know* our Führer?"

"If you two will let me finish — Papa and I met him *one time*. He came by to see the architectural model we'll be working on. We talked a little — that's all. Somehow we got around to my marriage plans."

"You must have made *some* impression if he sent you flowers," Franz commented.

That Hitler remembered him pleased Erich greatly. He looked forward to working on the great architectural projects of Germany's leader. But at the same time, Erich still could not shake his feeling of uneasiness. Most of what was happening in Germany Erich agreed with. But there were also certain new regulations and laws, along with rumors concerning some of the Nazi organizations.

In the sanctuary the organ music stopped. The pastor stuck his head in. "Erich, Franz, it's time."

The three men walked to the chancel and turned to the front of the church. The interior was dark except for the brilliant kaleidoscope of colors blazing through the stained-glass windows. The organ swelled with the processional march, and Johanna started down the aisle on the arm of her father. Erich's heart skipped a beat as he watched his bride-to-be glide toward him. Her white gown seemed to light up the church. Her veil moved slightly as she took each measured step. Finally she was there. Walther, beaming at Erich, released Johanna's arm. Erich offered her his, and together they faced the pastor. Franz took his position beside the couple.

A momentary wave of panic swept over Erich as he realized he could not remember what he was supposed to say or the order of the service. The pastor's lips were moving, but Erich's mind was not making any sense of the words. He gulped as he felt sweat trickle down his cheeks.

Then the pastor stopped speaking. After a few moments of awkward silence, he waited until he caught Erich's eye. "Erich, will you have Johanna to be your lawfully wedded wife?"

"Yes."

To Erich, his response sounded like a squeak, but the pastor seemed satisfied and promptly asked Johanna her vows. After a brief pause, Erich heard her soft voice respond with timid affirmation.

The rest of the service seemed surrealistic to Erich as he stumbled through his lines. The pastor received the rings and gave Johanna's to Erich, who almost dropped it. The young groom's heart pounded as he slid the ring onto Johanna's slim finger, realizing he was becoming one with her before man and God.

At last the ordeal was over. At the pastor's invitation, Erich turned and lifted Johanna's veil. He was momentarily shocked at her damp, red eyes, but he had been warned she would probably be emotional. He leaned over and nervously kissed her. Then the pastor presented Herr and Frau Erich von Arendt to the congregation. Erich took Johanna's arm and walked back up the aisle and out the large open doors. They squinted as they descended the stone steps under the bright sunlight. The brilliance dimmed suddenly, and the previous warmth disappeared as a large cloud passed in front of the sun.

Franz held the passenger door of Erich's Mercedes sedan, and the couple gratefully ducked inside. Franz closed the door and got in front, then wheeled the large touring car out into the traffic.

Erich took Johanna's hand and was surprised at how cold and damp it was.

"Are you all right?" he asked, looking at her in concern.

She nodded. "I'll be fine. You must forgive me. This is a very emotional time for me."

He put his arm around her. "Is there anything I can do to help?"

She shook her head. "No. Just give me time."

"Do you feel up to the reception?"

"Yes, Erich. We *have* to attend the reception. It's expected."

"I know, but . . ."

"This is how things are," Johanna interrupted. Her expression softened a little when she saw how serious he was. "Relax, Erich. I am all right."

Franz guided the car through the light traffic and out into the countryside. After traveling several miles, he turned off the road and through the gates of a large villa belonging to one of Walther Kammler's friends. The reception dinner was held in a large guesthouse in back of the main residence. Erich's mind was in a whirl as he met the cream of Frankfurt society. He was quite relieved when it was all over and he and Johanna could change clothes. As they said their final good-byes, Franz stood beside the car waiting for them.

"You two can relax now," he said as they left the villa far behind. "Just forget I'm here and enjoy the ride."

"Thank you," Erich answered for them.

Franz shook his head. "It's the least I can do for my best friend. Oh, I almost forgot . . . back there on the floor."

Erich reached down and picked up a wrapped package. He removed the ribbon and paper and opened the box. The rich smell of Moroccan leather escaped into the car. Erich lifted a large purse and handed it to Johanna.

"This is beautiful, Franz," he said.

"Yes, thank you, Franz," Johanna said, almost in a whisper.

"There's more," Franz answered. "Look under the paper."

Erich lifted the paper and saw a large leather briefcase. "Thank you, Franz," he said, fingering the meticulous stitching. He opened it and looked into all the dividers and pockets. "I don't think I've ever seen one so exquisite. I can really use this."

Franz glanced into the rearview mirror. "I got both of them in a fancy leather shop in Berlin. I'm glad you like them."

Erich sniffed the rich aroma again and put the briefcase back in the box. Johanna put her new purse on top of it, and Erich closed the box. He leaned toward his new wife and put his arm around her. The large touring car raced effortlessly over the narrow roads.

The sun sat on the western horizon, deep red and very large. Slowly it merged with the wooded mountaintop and finally disappeared. The road up ahead curved around to the left. The Mercedes swept past some outlying Bavarian houses, still clearly visible in the warm afterglow of the sunset. Franz took his foot off the gas and let the car coast as they approached the tiny alpine village.

"We're here," he said.

Erich leaned forward to look through the windshield. "What hotel did you say it was?"

Franz laughed. "The Bayerhof. It's the only one in the village, so I don't think we'll miss it. And if we do, it won't take long to turn around and try again."

Franz turned onto a side street that was more like a path. He slowed the car almost to a stop, shifted into first, and started cautiously up the hill. The dirt path was rutted and grew progressively more steep and narrow.

"Looks like I'll have to back down when I leave," Franz remarked. "I don't think there's room to turn around up there."

The dirt track ended at a two-story Bavarian inn whose steep pitched roof spoke of heavy snowfalls. Franz stopped the car, set the parking brake firmly, and left the transmission in gear. He jumped out and opened the rear door.

"And here we are."

He helped them in with their luggage, said his good-byes quickly, and was gone. Johanna hung back as Erich approached the heavyset innkeeper who stood behind his tiny desk with the registration book open before him.

"May I help you, sir?" he asked.

Erich attempted an easy smile. "Yes, I have a reservation."

"Excellent," the proprietor said. "Would you please sign the register."

Erich took the pen from its holder as if it were an unfamiliar instrument. With nervous strokes, he wrote his name on the next available entry and put the pen down. The innkeeper's smile never wavered, but he pointed to the signature. Erich felt his head grow very warm, and he knew he was blushing. He wrote in "Herr and Frau" above his signature. The man turned quickly, removed a large brass key from a hook, and gave it to Erich.

"Welcome, Herr and Frau von Arendt. I hope you will enjoy your honeymoon with us. Will you be having dinner in our dining room, or should I have a tray prepared for your room?"

Erich glanced back at Johanna. She appeared embarrassed and merely gave a shrug.

"We will come down for dinner," he said, turning back.

"Very good. We will be waiting for you — no hurry. Shall I take your bags up to the room for you?"

"No, I can get them."

Erich turned to Johanna. He grabbed their bags and led the way up the narrow stairs to the second floor. Eight rooms lined the center hall, and theirs was at the end at the back of the inn. Erich opened the door and held it open. Johanna entered and looked around. As Erich set their bags by the large window, he felt a strange mixture of elation and apprehension wash over him. His pulse quickened as he realized that what he had longed for all these years had now begun.

He had to clear his throat before he could speak. "Are you ready to go down to dinner, my darling?"

"In a little bit," Johanna replied. "I need to freshen up."

She turned toward the bathroom.

"Being 'Herr and Frau von Arendt' is going to take getting used to," he remarked. "And calling you 'darling.' "

"You could have called me 'darling' when you were courting me."

"Well, yes, but somehow I felt it wouldn't be proper." He smiled suddenly. "But I will get used to it. Johanna, the vows I made to you today . . ."

"Yes?"

"I meant every word. I will be a good husband to you, dear."

"I know that, Erich. And I will be the proper wife to you." An impish grin came to her face. "Now perhaps I should get cleaned up before the innkeeper wonders what is delaying us."

She entered their private bath and closed the door. Erich blushed again, but there was no one to see.

Most of the tables in the small dining room were taken when Erich and Johanna entered. A stout woman came out of the kitchen and seated them at a table beside a window, took their order, and left.

Erich smiled. "This is the first time we have been alone, except for the short time we were in the room. Are you feeling better?"

"Yes, I am," she replied. A flicker of a smile crossed her face. "I'm just tired. It's been a very emotional day for me, and the trip was long."

"Yes, it was. Maybe we should have stayed in Frankfurt the first night, but I was anxious for you to see this place."

"It *is* a lovely place."

He paused a few moments, then added, "I can't tell you how I've longed for this. My heart is yours, Johanna. Thank you for becoming my wife. You have made me happier than you can ever know, dear."

Johanna looked down. "It's the marriage of two great families, as Papa keeps reminding me."

Erich's smile waned. "Yes, I guess it is. But far more important than that, it's the joining together of two people who love each other. When we said our vows this morning, I meant every word, Johanna. As God is my witness, I'll be the best husband to you that I can."

"Thank you, Erich. I'm sure you will."

Johanna struggled to quell the dread welling up inside her. Ulrich was lost to her, and now she was the wife of Erich von Arendt. Her mother's advice came back to her. Could she make a marriage work despite the lack of romantic love? she wondered. She gazed at Erich, so serious and obviously concerned. That was nice, she had to admit. And he was quite handsome. But somehow she could not forget that she was here because men controlled her life. Her father. Erich's father. And Erich. Could she never make her own choices?

The combination cook and server made her appearance and set their dinner before them. Erich's heart was full as he enjoyed the company of his wife. Johanna ate slowly and was unusually quiet. Erich ordered the apple strudel for dessert, but Johanna declined.

"Then I won't have any either," Erich said.

"Nonsense. Enjoy your strudel. I'll have some coffee."

"Are you sure?"

"Yes. I'll have some tomorrow. I'm too full tonight."

Erich savored the rich dessert, and the dark aromatic coffee too. Johanna sipped delicately as she waited for him to finish. They both realized dinner was over at the same time. Erich felt his pulse quicken, and his hands grew moist. He cleared his throat.

"I guess we'd better go upstairs," he said at last.

Johanna nodded.

Erich smiled at their hostess as they left the dining room. She nodded and returned his smile.

They climbed the stairs, and Erich opened the door. Once inside, he stood by the window as his bride gathered her toiletries. His eyes grew round as she dug through her suitcase and drew out her blue silk robe and a sheer black negligee. Johanna disappeared into the bathroom. Erich sat in the chair by the window. In moments he heard the water running in the tub. He gazed at the heavy wooden bed, which seemed to anchor the room. He felt his pulse quicken as he thought about their wedding night.

After what seemed a long time, Johanna emerged from the steamy bathroom in her robe. Erich gathered his things and went in.

A while later Johanna removed the bedspread, folded it, and placed it on the wooden holder. She pulled back the smooth linen sheets and patted her pillow into shape. She slipped under the covers and pulled them up to her chin. She stared at the bathroom door, listening to the muted sounds of Erich bathing. Tears came to her eyes. She angrily wiped them away, taking care that they not spoil her looks. She was determined to be a proper wife to Erich — up to a point.

She thought of Ulrich Remer, of music, and of what would never be. *Papa has won,* she thought bitterly. *Business is more important to him than his own daughter's happiness. What does Erich know about art, stimulating conversation, passion for life — all the things that made Ulrich so exciting?* She felt her throat constrict as rage consumed her once again. She forced it back by sheer force of will. She would do what was expected of her, since she truly had no choice. She pounded the covers with her small fist and waited for her husband to make his appearance.

The bathroom door opened, and Erich

emerged wearing pale blue pajamas and a sheepish grin. He regarded Johanna for a few moments, then padded over the hardwood floor to his side of the bed and crawled under the covers. After a few moments he inched his way over until he felt the warmth of her body through the thin clothing between them. He extended his right arm, and she raised her head so he could hold her. She nestled back down, and he pulled her close.

"Johanna, I love you so much," he said, his voice low and husky.

"I love you too," she whispered. Even though it was a lie, it was what she felt she must say.

He turned toward her, looking into her eyes, feeling obviously eager but at the same time hesitant. He closed his eyes and gently kissed her. Then a wave of repressed emotion washed over him, engulfing both of them in their first honeymoon night.

Four

A week later, early in the morning, Franz again drove Erich's Mercedes up the narrow path to the inn. He parked the car and went inside. When he approached the desk, the innkeeper's wife inclined her head upward and told him the room number. Franz thanked her and took the stairs.

He paused by the door and knocked softly.

After a few moments of silence a sleepy male voice said, "What is it?"

Franz grinned. "It's your chauffeur. I'm here to drive you and Frau von Arendt to Berline — or had it slipped your mind?"

"Oh, no, Franz — I forgot we had to get up early."

"I quite understand," Franz said with a chuckle. "I can come back later."

"No, no . . . we'll get up. Give us a few minutes and we'll be down."

"No hurry. I'll be in the lobby drinking coffee. It's early for me also."

A half hour later, Erich and Johanna appeared in the lobby with their luggage. After saying good-bye to the innkeeper and his wife, they left. Franz helped Erich load the suitcases.

Johanna saw the Bavarian lakes, mountains, and forests, but she could not appreciate them as every mile carried her further from Frankfurt and what would now never be. Life in Berlin would be so different. She was not at all sure she would be able to fit in there. And lurking over it all was Johanna's uncertainty over her new marriage. She vacillated between her commitment to be a proper German wife and her desire to be free. How she would resolve the dilemma she had no idea.

Their route took them north out of the Bavarian Alps past the cities of Nuremberg and Leipzig, arriving at Berlin quite late. Franz drove directly to their two-story stone house in Schlachtensee, helped Erich with the luggage, then departed quickly.

Erich looked around the entranceway with its clutter of boxes.

"Your things got here from Frankfurt, I see, Johanna."

"Yes. Something to do tomorrow. But now I think I'd like to put my feet up."

She entered the large living room and sat down on the couch, and Erich joined her. He put his arm around her.

"Franz is a good friend," Erich said

with a sigh.

"That's what you keep saying," Johanna replied, unable to hide her irritation. She wondered at her husband's uncritical approval of Franz. Although she had not been around him a lot, there was something about him she didn't quite trust.

Erich looked at her in surprise. "Is something wrong, dear?"

She shook her head. "No. Nothing's wrong. I *know* Franz is your friend — you've told me many times. It's . . . it's just been a long day, and I'm tired." She looked into his eyes. "Aren't you?"

"Well, yes. But I hope you'll like Franz. He and I have known each other since we were boys."

"I'm sure I will," Johanna said, not wanting to discuss it any further.

Erich stood up. "What do you think of your new home?"

Johanna looked around. "The furniture is rather dreary."

Erich laughed. "Actually, it's dreadful. The previous owner sold it to me for a nominal price — something for us to start with. You can pick out whatever you like to replace it. And we'll also remodel the interior. You have a free hand."

"Thank you, Erich."

He pulled her close and kissed her gently. "I want you to have the best, Johanna. Shall we see the rest of the house?"

"Yes, I'd like that."

Erich led her into the dining room. "Another room that needs your touch, I'm afraid."

"Oh, yes," she agreed. "I see what you mean about dreadful. Nothing matches, and it too is in terrible shape."

"I can't wait to see what you do with it."

"Is the rest this bad?" Johanna made mental notes as she surveyed the clashing, outdated decor. Her plans for the house gave her a welcome outlet. She hoped it would help her make peace with her future.

"I'm afraid so," Erich replied. "Let's take a look at the kitchen." He opened the door and waited for her to enter. "This house may seem small compared to your father's home, but for Berlin it's quite nice. We have plenty of room for entertaining." He pointed to a door off the kitchen. "Through there is the servant's room and bath."

"Can we hire a housekeeper soon?"

"As soon as you like. The running of the household is up to you, after all. Do you like it so far?"

"I think it'll do nicely — *after* it's fixed up."

"I love your artistic sense. I can't wait to see what you do with all this mess."

The last stop was the bedroom on the second floor overlooking the street. Johanna's eyes grew wide when she saw the brass bed with its lumpy mattress.

"That most *definitely* has to go," she announced.

"It will be the first thing we replace," Erich agreed. "But for tonight, I am sure it will perform admirably."

The pantry being bare, Erich and Johanna ate breakfast at a corner café several blocks from their house. Johanna found herself intrigued by the fast, cosmopolitan atmosphere of Berlin, so different than the more provincial Frankfurt. She didn't know if this would make her new life with Erich more endurable, but for the moment she felt cautiously optimistic. But she also knew it would take a long time for her bitterness to dissipate, if it ever did. Erich glanced at his watch as he sipped his coffee.

"I have to leave soon," he said. "I don't want Herr Speer to get the wrong idea about me."

"What wrong idea would that be?"

"That I'm lazy or unpunctual."

Johanna grinned. "That would never do."

"Never. What do you have planned for today?"

"You said we could hire a housekeeper?"

"Yes, of course. The house is large, and a lot of work goes into keeping one up." He paused. "Johanna, have you ever cooked?"

She appeared surprised. "Well, no. Oh, I've cooked party foods from time to time, but we've always had a cook, as well as the normal house servants."

"That's what I suspected."

"What do you mean by that?" she demanded.

A twinkle came to his eye. "Only the obvious, dear. Growing up in a wealthy Frankfurt household, I would not *expect* you to know how to cook."

"You expect correctly." She shared his good-natured jest.

"Then I suggest you make sure the housekeeper can also cook."

She nodded. "I will. Where do I need to go?"

"Take the tram to Lindenstrasse. Turn right; in the middle of the block is a domestic agency. They should be able to provide what we need."

"What about food?"

"Why not wait until we hire the housekeeper? Let her do it. If it takes a few days, we'll eat out. Consider it an extension of our honeymoon."

"Berlin is *not* the Bavarian Alps."

Erich laughed. "No, it's not. Honestly, I'm looking forward to living, and dining, in our new home."

"Then I better get busy finding the housekeeper."

"It shouldn't take long." He folded up his newspaper. "Are you through with breakfast?"

Johanna looked down. "I think I'll have another cup of coffee before I go back to the house. I'll try the agency around 10."

"Very well. I'll see you this evening."

Erich leaned forward and kissed her. "I love you, dear."

Johanna felt a momentary twinge of guilt but decided that being a proper wife meant saying what was expected of her. "I love you too. See you this evening."

"See you then."

Johanna watched him go. He was so sincere, so full of energy. He really was a very nice person. She sighed. Would it get any better? she wondered. Was her mother right? Would she come to see her marriage to Erich as a good thing, even if it was devoid of true love?

True to his promise, the driver looked back and pointed as the tram approached Lindenstrasse. Johanna nodded and got up as the tram ground to a stop with squealing brakes. She stepped down near the center of the street and waited for a car to pass before walking to the curb. The sidewalks and buildings were surprisingly clean and well maintained. Johanna had observed the same result in Frankfurt when the Nazi party got serious about the rundown city centers.

Johanna found the agency right where Erich said it would be. She entered and in moments met the proprietor at the receptionist's desk. His slim build and neatly groomed moustache indicated he was all business. He ushered her back to his office and waved toward a large, comfortable chair while he retreated behind his desk.

"Tell me, Frau von Arendt," he said, wasting no time, "how may I help you?"

"My husband and I are looking for a housekeeper, Herr Schmidt."

"I see. Well, you have come to the right place. We place the finest domestics in all of Berlin."

"Oh, and she must also cook."

"Of course. I will call for some placement files. Can I offer you some tea while we wait?"

"Yes, please."

He nodded. He picked up the phone, issued curt orders, and replaced the receiver.

A few moments later the receptionist came in carrying a small tray with two cups of tea in china cups and a plate of small biscuits. After tending to the sugar and lemon, the receptionist left. No sooner had the door closed than it opened again, admitting a heavyset woman bearing a stack of thin files. She set them on the corner of the desk and left without a word.

Herr Schmidt handed the folders to Johanna. "Please review these. I assure you we have checked every reference."

Johanna took the files and opened the first one. "After I select one, how soon can she start?"

"How soon do you want?"

She looked up. "Today, if possible."

"That *is* a little quick, but we shall do our best. Do you wish to interview the applicants?"

"I suppose so. That is customary, isn't it?"

Herr Schmidt nodded. "Yes, it is. May I suggest looking over the files?"

Johanna felt unsure of herself, but she scanned the references on the first three servants anyway. Finally she realized she had no idea how to proceed and put the files back on the desk. "Do you have a recommendation, Herr Schmidt?"

He pursed his lips as he selected one folder and opened it. "Frau Bertha Liedig. Middle-aged, a widow. She has just concluded a long-term situation with a wealthy Berlin family and is looking for another position as soon as possible."

"Sounds like what we're looking for." Johanna paused. "Why is she leaving her present employment?"

Herr Schmidt cleared his throat. "The family in question is moving to America — New York, to be exact."

"Germans moving to America?"

"They are Jewish, I believe."

"Oh, I see." Johanna lowered her eyes and skimmed the neatly written letters of recommendation. "We require a housekeeper immediately, Herr Schmidt, and it seems Frau Liedig is in need of employment. When could I talk to her?"

"If you care to wait, she left a number where she can be reached. It should take less than a half hour I would think."

"Yes, please. I'd like to get this settled today."

"Very good."

Herr Schmidt had his receptionist place the call. After a short wait, Frau Liedig came to the phone and agreed to come at once to the employment agency. Twenty minutes later the receptionist let her into the office. Herr Schmidt stood in welcome.

"If you will follow me, I have a place where the two of you can talk in private."

He led them to a small room at the end of the corridor. He opened the door and held it while they entered.

"Frau von Arendt, I will be in my office after you have finished the interview. Ladies."

He bowed and gently closed the door.

Bertha Liedig stood waiting. Her blue eyes seemed to miss nothing. She was stocky, and her silver-streaked brown hair was done up in a neat bun. She impressed Johanna as a capable woman, even formidable.

"Frau Liedig, I am Frau von Arendt. Please sit down."

The middle-aged woman sat across the table from Johanna and waited.

"I have read your references. They are

excellent, and Herr Schmidt recommended you. My husband and I are looking for a housekeeper. We have a house in Schlachtensee."

"Yes, I know where that is."

Johanna paused, again feeling her lack of experience. "Frau Liedig, we need a housekeeper and cook. Can you do those things?"

Bertha's eyebrows raised slightly. "Have you read my recommendations, Frau von Arendt?"

Johanna felt her face flush in embarrassment. "Yes, I have. But what I really want to know is, can you do the job as well as your papers indicate?"

"Yes, I can. I guarantee you and your husband complete satisfaction. I have *never* displeased an employer."

Johanna nodded. "Very good. Herr Schmidt said you were looking for an immediate placement."

"Yes, that is so."

"Well, we are in immediate need. Could you start today?"

"Yes, I would like that. But what about the terms of my employment?"

"I'm sure my husband will be agreeable to matching your last salary and days off, that sort of thing. That's quite standard, I would imagine."

"Yes, it is."

"Good." Johanna paused. "Then I suppose we need to make the, ah, proper arrangements and . . . get started."

A flicker of a smile passed over Bertha Liedig's round face. "If I could suggest, perhaps you might ask Herr Schmidt about the customary procedures. I think you will find him quite informative and helpful."

"Why, yes. Thank you. I'll do that."

Bertha stood. "I will be sitting in the reception room while you and Herr Schmidt conclude your business."

The heavyset woman took her leave. Johanna found the agency's proprietor in his office. He stood and waited until she was seated.

"Do you think Frau Liedig will be acceptable, or shall we look at other applicants?" he asked as he sat down.

"Frau Liedig will do just fine."

"Very good. Now, do you wish to discuss the details of employment — pay, days off, that sort of thing?"

Johanna shook her head. "We will meet her previous pay. The rest is fairly standard, isn't it?"

"Yes, it is."

"Then I would like to conclude our business. Frau Liedig agreed to start today, and my husband and I need the position filled immediately."

"I understand." He opened a folder and placed a typewritten page before Johanna. "If you will sign here please."

She wrote her name in a tight, neat script, struggling a little with her new last name.

He kept the agreement and handed the folder to Johanna. "I suggest keeping this handy, Frau von Arendt. In it are the agreed upon wages, days off, things like that. My bill will be posted to you later." He stood. "It has been a pleasure serving you. If I may be of further assistance, please call on me."

Johanna got up. "Thank you, Herr Schmidt."

Johanna stopped by the reception room and gave Frau Liedig directions to the house. She left the office, grateful to have that task out of the way and hoping her inexperience hadn't been too obvious.

Two weeks later Johanna felt she was getting a grasp on managing the household. The accounts with suppliers had been set up, and a routine began to emerge. Today Johanna sat in the living room enjoying a mid-morning cup of tea while the efficient Frau Liedig worked away in the kitchen, tidying up the pantry after a grocer's delivery. *She's a Godsend,* Johanna mused, until she realized such thoughts were not relevant. *We make our own way through this life,* she reminded herself.

The sounds in the kitchen ceased, and moments later Bertha entered the living room. "I have put away the groceries, Frau von Arendt. They forgot the flour I ordered — they charged us for it though — and they made another mistake in the bill — in their favor. I will have them on the phone shortly and get it straightened out. Now, I think you said we were expecting some furniture this afternoon."

"Yes. A suite of furniture for the living room and a worktable, desk, and chair for Herr von Arendt's office. The lists I made are on the table by the door."

"Very good, madam. I will check everything off when it's delivered. If anything is damaged, I'll send it back."

"I'll leave it in your capable hands. Oh, and make sure they take away everything, including this wretched carpet."

"Yes, madam. Are they delivering a new carpet?"

"No. That will be tomorrow. We'll have to make do with bare floors until then."

Bertha nodded stolidly. "Shall I fix you lunch, madam?"

"No. I'll be going to Herr von Arendt's office shortly. I will be having lunch with him."

Bertha smiled. "Very good, madam. I will have dinner ready for you both when you get home."

"Thank you, Frau Liedig."

Traffic of all sorts competed with the tram for right of way. Cars passed on the right, while several times the tram driver had to slow to avoid pedestrian traffic, trucks, and horse-drawn wagons. Johanna took it all in as she noted the differences between Berlin and Frankfurt. She watched carefully for her stop, looking for the landmarks Erich had told her about. She rang the bell and stood up as the tram ground to a stop. She stepped down to the pavement and waited for a car to pass before hurrying to the curb. Erich's directions had proved accurate, Johanna noted as she spotted the appropriate building. She opened the front door and walked in.

The receptionist looked up from her work. "May I help you?" she asked.

"I am Frau von Arendt. I'm here to see my husband."

The young lady glanced at her watch as she got up. "It's nearly noon, and a lot of the men have left for lunch, but I didn't see your husband leave. I think he's in the back drafting room."

She led Johanna past the front office until they came to a door with a frosted window. The receptionist left and hurried back to the front.

Johanna opened the door and looked inside, but Erich was not there. One draftsman was in the room. He looked around, got off the tall stool, and stretched.

"Do you know where Herr von Arendt is?" Johanna asked.

The man nodded. "He told me he would be working on the stadium model. Do you know where the model shop is?"

"No. Could you show me?"

The man accompanied her into the corridor.

"See those double doors at the back?" he asked. "Go through there. The stadium model is against the far wall."

Johanna thanked him and walked to the end of the corridor. She pushed through the doors and into the large shop. Lights blazed down from high overhead, illuminating the various models in stark relief.

Johanna brought her hand to her mouth to suppress a giggle when she spotted Erich. Comically resembling Zeus, her husband sat in the midst of the horseshoe-shaped stadium model, atop a sturdy table. He had his back to her as he surveyed the tier of colonnades that wrapped around the top of the Nuremberg stadium. He had to look up since the model was over seven feet tall.

"Deciding where to throw your thunderbolts?" Johanna asked.

He stood and spun around, almost losing his balance. He smiled at her. Forgetting all about the architectural detail he was working on, he turned about in a stately pirouette.

"It does give one a sense of power," he admitted. "This stadium is going to seat 400,000 people, and I'm almost as tall as it is. Don't I look grand?"

"Of course you do," Johanna teased. "Did you escape from Valhalla?"

Erich's grin changed to a mock scowl. "Yes, my dear Valkyrie. And if you are not good . . ."

The rear door banged open. Johanna turned her head and froze as Adolf Hitler, in full uniform, strode into the shop and right up to the stadium model. There he stopped abruptly upon encountering the Brobdingnagian intruder in the new stadium. Erich stared down at Hitler, then belatedly raised his arm in salute. "Heil Hitler," he croaked.

Hitler brought his arm partway up but quickly dropped it. "What are you doing up there?" he demanded.

Rapid footsteps sounded behind Johanna. She turned to see Albert Speer hurrying in from the front offices.

"My Führer, what a pleasant surprise. Why didn't you let me know you were coming? I could have . . ."

Hitler waved him to silence as he kept his eyes riveted on Erich. "I am waiting for an answer!"

"Herr Speer has assigned me to work . . ."

Hitler's eyes brightened, and his scowl melted into a smile. "Oh, yes, now I remember. Herr von Arendt, I am afraid you surprised me. When I stopped by to see the stadium, I did not expect to see someone standing in the middle of it. What are you doing up there?"

"Examining the colonnades from eye level. It is the only way I can tell if the details and perspective are right."

"Absolutely," Hitler agreed, rapidly rubbing his hands together. "Give me a hand. We'll look at it together."

Erich's eyes grew wide as he reached down to help Germany's undisputed leader up onto the stadium model. They made a complete circuit of the colonnades, taking tiny, coordinated steps as if afraid of trampling Lilliputian players on the field below. Hitler peered into the columns, his keen eyes missing nothing.

Johanna watched in awe as the two men made their slow circuit. Her heart beat faster as she saw Hitler's obvious fascination with Erich's project. This private side of Hitler surprised her but in no way lessened the man's magnetism. She could see Erich was affected as well, in spite of his reservations about the Nazis.

"Well done," Hitler said to Erich. "Is this your work?"

"Yes, my Führer."

"I knew you would do well when I saw your plans for the Berlin train station."

"You remember that, my Führer?"

"Of course. And I've been thinking a lot about your design. That station *would* be a wonderful change for Berlin."

"Do you really think so?"

Hitler nodded. "I do." He looked deeply

into Erich's eyes. "It is fine men like you who are the future of Germany, Herr von Arendt."

"I don't know what to say, my Führer."

Hitler turned and looked down at Speer. "It progresses nicely, Herr Speer." Then he saw Johanna standing nearby. He turned his head slightly and smiled. "Who is this, please?"

"My wife, Johanna," Erich replied.

"Ah, the beautiful Frau von Arendt." He turned to Erich. "Help me down."

Erich jumped down and helped Hitler step to the floor. Together they approached Johanna.

"My Führer," Erich said, "allow me to introduce you to my wife, Johanna von Arendt."

Hitler smiled as he took her hand and kissed it. "If you will allow me to say so, your husband has excellent taste. I am so pleased to meet you, my dear."

Johanna felt her heart race as she looked into the mesmerizing eyes of Germany's ruler. Despite his heavy responsibilities, he appeared genuinely interested in her. How different this private Hitler seemed from the man who gave all those fiery speeches she had heard over the years.

"Thank you, my Führer," she stuttered

when she finally found her voice. "I am honored."

"The honor is entirely mine," Hitler replied. "I shall have to ask Herr Speer to bring you and your husband to a state dinner sometime. I am sure your presence will brighten an otherwise dull evening."

"Thank you."

Hitler bowed slightly and turned to Speer. "The model progresses well, Herr Speer. You have a good man working on it. I expect great things from you both." He turned again to Johanna. "Regretfully, I must leave now. Until we meet again."

He paused at the door and looked back. "Keep up the good work, Herr von Arendt." Then he was gone.

For a few moments no one moved. Albert recovered first. With a curt nod he left the model shop and returned to the front offices.

Johanna turned to Erich. Noting some wood chips beneath the stadium model, she became aware of the mundane once again as it swept away the grand feeling of only moments ago.

"Does he do that often?" she asked.

Erich exhaled slowly. "He meets with Herr Speer often, but this is only the second time I have met him."

Johanna couldn't keep the surprise out of her voice. "Only the second time? You make it sound so normal. Most people *never* see our leader up close like that."

Erich shrugged. "That's true. All I can tell you is that Herr Hitler watches what we do very closely. He's fascinated with architecture."

"There is something else I don't understand. Where were his guards?"

Erich laughed. "I asked Herr Speer about that. These are private visits. His driver and guards stay outside unless Herr Hitler brings guests along." Erich lowered his voice. "I think Herr Hitler considers Herr Speer his personal architect. The two of them work very closely together. It's quite informal."

Johanna looked into her husband's eyes. "I heard you say, 'yes, my Führer' several times while you were showing him the model. Have you changed your mind about the Nazis?"

Erich looked around the room quickly. "Don't say things like that in public, Johanna. Someone might hear."

"Are you avoiding my question?" Johanna watched him and wondered if he would put her off. She noted the pained look in his eyes as the seconds ticked by.

"It's hard to explain," he finally whispered. "I'm excited about what Hitler is doing for Germany. The anarchy is gone, the economy is under control, we're building for the future again. And I'm grateful for the part I get to play. But I hear other things as well — the rumors of persecutions, the new laws and regulations. I don't know . . . I just don't know."

Five

Johanna got up from her vanity when she heard the door open. "Where have you been?" she demanded, her hand gripping the hairbrush in anger. "Do you expect me to receive our guest by myself? That isn't fair, Erich!"

Erich dropped his briefcase onto a chair. "I'm sorry, Johanna, but it couldn't be avoided. Herr Speer is the boss, and sometimes he works us long hours. The stadium model is going to the Paris World's Fair next year, and I still have an unbelievable amount of work to do on it."

"Then perhaps you shouldn't have invited Franz over for dinner."

"Johanna, that's not fair. I didn't know I'd have to work extra hours when I invited him." He attempted to embrace her, but she turned away. "Besides, I *did* get home before he arrived. I had to promise Herr Speer I would be in early tomorrow to make up for lost time."

"But I didn't know if you were going to get here or not."

"I'm sorry. I should have called."

"Yes, you should have."

A muted bell sounded.

"He's here," Erich said. "I'll entertain him while you finish getting ready." He leaned down but hesitated when she stiffened. Finally he kissed her cheek. "I love you, Johanna. Please be patient with me. I'm still learning how to be a husband."

"Yes, well, Franz is waiting."

The boyish smile returned. "I'll see you in a little bit."

Erich hurried downstairs. Bertha Liedig turned when she heard him approach, obviously relieved to see him.

"Herr von Arendt," she said, "I was coming to get you. Herr Brant has arrived."

"Thank you, Frau Liedig."

She nodded and returned to the kitchen.

Erich led his friend into the living room.

"This certainly looks different than the last time I saw it," Franz remarked as he sat down in one of the new chairs. "Johanna is quite a decorator."

Erich smiled. "Yes, she is. She has exquisite taste. You know I did not pick this stuff out."

"And Frau Liedig . . . did Johanna pick her out also?"

"Yes. I gave her the name of the employment agency, but Johanna selected her. She's been wonderful. She's an industrious housekeeper and a marvelous cook — wait until you see."

"She obviously takes her duties seriously. But I don't think she likes me."

"How can you say that?"

"Oh, I can tell." He paused. "Sometimes I wonder about your powers of observation. But enough of that. I'm hearing wonderful things about Herr Speer and his talented company of architects. I rejoice on your behalf."

"It's interesting work, all right. But I have to work long hours — all of us do, including Herr Speer."

Franz nodded. "That's what it takes to succeed."

"The only time I see Johanna is in the morning and evenings — if she's still up. It's not fair to her, but I don't know what I can do about it."

"There is nothing you *can* do. Herr Speer is the boss."

Erich frowned as he tried to order his thoughts. He felt guilty about being away from home so much, but working for Speer was intoxicating. "That's what I keep telling Johanna," he said finally. "I like my work — I just wish it didn't take

127

quite so much time."

Franz glanced around the room. "It does pay the bills."

Erich nodded. "Yes, it does. Believe me, I'm very grateful for that."

"And it's good for Germany. Our Führer is leading us to greatness, don't you think?"

Erich frowned as a new thought added to his uneasiness. "For some of us perhaps. Do you remember Jakob Baum from school? We were both studying architecture. He was planning to practice here in Berlin."

Erich saw his friend stiffen. "Yes, I remember. What about him?"

"He called me a few days ago. He and his family are leaving for America."

"So? If they wish to live elsewhere, why should you care?"

"Because of the reason. They're Jewish. He said they were afraid of what might happen to them if they stayed."

Franz winked at his friend. "Why, I had no idea . . . our friend Jakob is a Jew?"

"This isn't funny, Franz. Jakob is a decent man from a fine family. I was going to ask my father if he could come to work for us — that is, until Papa sold the firm."

"I suspect your father would not have

thought that a good idea. But your friend is overreacting. You and I see Jews a little differently, I think, but there is no official plan to harm them. But let's not talk about that. I came to see how my newlywed friend is faring. What has Herr Speer got you doing?"

Erich frowned. "Do we dispose of this so easily?"

"Erich, as I have said, there is no conspiracy against the Jews. Now, I didn't come here to talk about that. I came to see how things are with you."

Erich sighed and forced a smile. "Very well. I'm working on the plans and model for the new Nuremberg Stadium. Papa is too."

Franz nodded. "I've heard of this."

"It's part of Herr Hitler's plans for revitalizing Nuremberg. The model is over seven feet tall, and the completed stadium will hold 400,000 people."

Franz waved his hand dismissively. "Yes, I'm sure that's quite exciting, if you're an architect."

"And I have met Herr Hitler twice."

Franz's eyebrows shot up. "Twice? I remember you telling me about the first time. And of course I saw the flowers. This Herr Speer must be going places."

Erich longed to share his friend's excitement. But the undefined dread he felt would not entirely go away.

"Yes, I think he is. He knows everything that we're doing — everything. I don't know how he does it. Papa is delighted, and on the whole I'm glad to be working there."

"But not entirely?"

"It's hard to explain. It's just something I have to work out for myself."

"I don't see what the problem is, but I'm sure you will figure it out. But tell me, what happened the second time you met our Führer?"

Erich shifted uneasily in his chair. "He came by to look at the stadium model, and I was working on it, so we examined it together. He was quite impressed with what I was doing."

"Really?"

"Yes. He met Johanna that day as well. She had come there to go to lunch with me. The Führer was most gallant. He even said he would like to invite us to a state dinner sometime."

"You're joking with me," Franz said.

"No. That's what he said."

"You *do* move in interesting circles, my friend."

"It would seem so. How are things with you?"

Franz thumped the armrest with his right hand. "As of last Monday my obvious talents have finally been noticed. I've joined the SS."

"You have?" Erich asked. "I'm surprised. I've heard . . . rumors about them."

"It is not wise to heed rumors."

Erich felt a sudden chill go down his spine. "I'll take your word for it. What will you be doing?"

"That's hard to explain. The SS has many divisions, but I assure you, I'm *not* in a police or military unit, although I do have a military rank. I'm not allowed to discuss my exact job, but I'm involved in economic and military production studies."

"I didn't know the SS was involved in things like that."

Franz smiled. "The SS is involved in *many* things, my friend. Herr Himmler is a very ambitious man. So, you see, you are serving Herr Hitler in one way and I in another." His eyes grew bright. "Our destiny is wrapped up with the Führer. He *is* the future of the Fatherland."

Erich's forebodings would not go away, although he couldn't deny the progress

Hitler had achieved. "Perhaps you're right," he said finally.

"There's no doubt about it."

Johanna entered the living room wearing a blue linen dress with a white lace collar and a narrow black belt. Erich and Franz got to their feet.

"Johanna, you look lovely this evening," Franz said.

She smiled, then looked toward her husband.

Erich felt his pulse quicken as her beauty made him temporarily forget what he and Franz had been talking about. "You do look lovely, Johanna. As always."

"Franz beat you to it."

It felt to Erich like she had dashed cold water on his expression of love. He looked into her eyes, hoping for a change of heart, but the hardness remained. He glanced at Franz. His friend seemed to be preoccupied with the painting over the sofa.

"Dinner is ready," Erich said finally. "Shall we see what Frau Liedig has prepared?"

Johanna nodded and led them into the dining room. Erich headed for Johanna's chair, but Franz got there first.

"Allow me, Frau von Arendt," he said. He held her chair while Erich retreated to the head of the table. Once Johanna was seated, Franz took his seat on the side.

Bertha entered from the kitchen and started serving the soup. Erich watched as she placed a bowl before Franz. She paused slightly, then glanced at her employer. Her frown disappeared when she realized Erich was watching her.

Erich and Johanna passed the first year of their marriage caught up in their own difficulties at home and Albert Speer's increasing demands on Erich's time. Adolf Hitler continued to solidify his hold on Germany while pushing forward his ambitious building programs. That summer he awarded Speer his greatest architectural commission, the rebuilding of Berlin on a grand scale. Then, in rapid succession, came the Olympic Games in Berlin, Hitler's Four-Year Plan, and his treaty with Italy and Japan. In 1937 Albert Speer's model for the Nuremberg Stadium earned a Gold Medal at the Paris World's Fair. Most Germans exulted in what Hitler had accomplished in such a short time — jobs and food and the promise that the humiliation of Versailles would be avenged.

Albert Speer's organization had never been busier. On the evening of Friday,

July 1, 1937, Erich arrived home at 9, which he considered early. Bertha Liedig greeted him at the door.

"Is Frau von Arendt in the living room?" he asked.

"No. Frau von Arendt went upstairs after dinner." She paused. "I think she was hoping you would not be late."

Erich sighed. "If Herr Speer were in town, I wouldn't be home until Sunday, if then."

Bertha nodded. "Shall I heat up your dinner?"

"No. I think I'll go upstairs."

The housekeeper stood her ground, and for a moment Erich wondered how he was going to get around her.

"Is there something else?"

"I'll fix you a sandwich and leave it in the kitchen," she said firmly.

In spite of his tiredness and worries, it touched him that she was concerned for his health. He couldn't help smiling. "That's very kind of you, Frau Liedig."

"And I expect it to be gone in the morning."

"I'll do my best."

She stalked back to the kitchen.

Erich tiptoed upstairs. He hesitated at the door, rapped on it once, and went in.

Johanna was propped up in bed. She scowled at him over the top of the novel she was reading.

"I'm home, dear," he said.

Johanna frowned as she glanced at the clock on the mantel. "You're early. It's *only* nine o'clock."

Erich sat in a chair at the foot of the bed. "You know I don't set the hours, Johanna. I wish I didn't have to work so late, but I have to do what Herr Speer says — if I want to keep my job." He saw a blowup approaching, but he didn't have the energy or desire to avoid it.

Johanna threw her book down. "Then maybe you would be better off with a different job." Despite her lack of love for Erich, she saw his job as a rival she detested. On strictly practical terms, his work schedule greatly limited her evening social life.

He shook his head. "We've been through this before. This is a very good job. No one else has projects like Herr Speer does, and I certainly couldn't earn as much money elsewhere."

"All you think about is your work. Besides, money isn't everything."

"The money pays for this house and everything in it. It pays for our car and our vacations — and your clothes and jewelry — don't forget that."

"My, we're in a grumpy mood tonight."

That stopped him. He knew she was right. "I know. I'm sorry, Johanna. I am not myself — something upsetting happened today. The Gestapo arrested Pastor Niemöller."

"What's wrong with that? He's been opposing everything our Führer has been trying to do."

Erich looked at her in disbelief. "But he's a man of God."

"So? You don't go to church. Why should you care?"

Erich's shoulders slumped as he felt all his energy drain from him. He walked to the chair by the window and sat heavily. "I'm a Christian," he said. "I may not be what I should be, but I do believe. And I know it's wrong to arrest a man of God."

"Even if he's interfering with what our Führer is doing?"

"Yes."

"I wouldn't let anyone else hear you say that."

He shrugged. A haunted look came into his eyes. "Johanna?"

"Yes?" The word indicated an openness to what he had to say, but the tense body language communicated the opposite.

"Are you happy?"

She sat up straight. "What has come over you, Erich? What kind of question is that?"

"It seems like we argue about *everything*. I don't want to do that — I love you. But no matter how hard I try to please you, it never seems that I can. Tell me . . . are you happy living with me?"

She hesitated. "Yes. I guess so."

Erich felt his throat constrict, and his eyes began to sting. "Johanna, I love you so much. You know that."

"I should. You tell me often enough."

"It's true, Johanna."

"Well, I'm glad."

He looked into her eyes, trying to read her thoughts. "We need to think about our future, dear. We need to start planning our family."

"I am not ready to discuss that."

Erich stood and started pacing. "That's what you say every time I bring it up. We've been married a year, Johanna." He stopped and looked her in the eye. "It's time we talked about it. It's time we came to a decision."

She looked away. "I'm tired. We'll discuss it some other time."

Erich's frown turned into a scowl. "No. I've been very patient. We'll discuss it *now*. When can we plan to start our family?"

Johanna's obvious anger startled Erich. "Since you really must know, I do *not* wish to have children."

He stopped pacing, then came and stood over her. "Why not?" he demanded.

She stared at him.

"Why not?" he repeated, his voice rising.

"Because I don't love you," she said slowly, her voice absolutely even.

Erich stood there unable to believe what he had heard. His world was dissolving, and he was powerless to prevent it. Whatever meaning there had been for his life was gone now, blown away by words he never thought he would hear. Feeling the tears come, he brought up a hand and tried to stop their flow but could not.

"I don't understand, Johanna."

"No, I suppose you don't," she snapped. "You don't understand any more than Papa does. My papa and your papa decided we were to marry, without even asking me how I felt about it."

"But I thought you loved me. You *married* me."

"Because our families arranged it. Erich, wake up! What choice did I have? None!"

"I didn't know you felt that way."

"Well, now you do!"

Erich paused. "Is there someone else?"

She visibly stiffened. "How dare you!"

He grabbed her by the shoulders with his strong hands. "Because I'm your husband! I have the right to ask . . . is there anyone else? Answer me!"

She pouted sullenly.

He shook her. "Johanna, answer my question!"

She looked at him, her eyes wide. "Will you beat me if I don't?"

"Don't be silly. But I won't leave you alone until I know."

She shrugged. "If you really must know, yes, I love someone else."

"Who is it?"

"No one you know — someone in Frankfurt."

He blinked away his tears. "Johanna, how can you do this to me? Doesn't my love mean *anything* to you?"

She turned away.

He stood there for a moment, not knowing what to do. Then he left their bedroom and trudged down the stairs. He paused in the entryway, then went into the kitchen. He turned on the light and saw the sausage sandwich Frau Liedig had prepared for him. He picked it up and took a bite. The bread tasted like sawdust in his dry mouth. He walked to the sink, spat, and left the kitchen.

He wandered into the darkened living room and over to the window. He pushed aside the drapes and looked out. A car drove past, and Erich watched as the red taillights dwindled in the distance. He shuddered as a feeling of loneliness and loss nearly overwhelmed him.

He sat in a chair by the window, tilted his head back, and closed his eyes. His world suddenly had no meaning, and there was nothing he could do about it. He looked about the room, his eyes brimming with tears. He wanted desperately to have some hope, but how?

A tiny thought crept into his mind, and he hungrily pounced on it. But what could prayer do in such a terrible strait? he wondered. Yet the thought would not go away. Since all he knew about his faith had come from pastors and Christian friends rather than from the Bible itself, he wasn't sure what to do next. And what little he knew about prayer had derived primarily from what his father called "feel-good speeches." Hot tears spilled down Erich's cheeks as he lowered his head in grief.

*Lord, please help me. I can't handle this —
I don't know what to do. You know I love
Johanna, and I would do anything to win her
love. I want this more than anything, but there
is nothing more I can do.* He paused and
wiped away his tears. *Lord, I ask You to do
whatever is necessary to win her love for me.
Please. You are the only hope I have.*

Six

It was early morning before Erich finally drifted off into a fitful sleep that offered no rest. The last thing he remembered was how cramped he felt. In what seemed moments later he heard heavy footsteps in the hall. He awoke with a start, at first not knowing where he was. He turned groggily and fell on the floor.

Bertha gasped. "Who's there?"

"It is only me, Frau Liedig."

"Herr von Arendt, what are you doing down here?"

Erich scratched his bristly face. "I'd rather not discuss that."

"No, of course not. Forgive me. You startled me."

He got up and joined her in the hall. "I'm sorry."

"Is there anything I can do?"

"No. I'll come back down for breakfast in a few minutes."

He watched as she hurried off to the kitchen. He turned and looked up the stairs toward the bedroom. Johanna's painful words engulfed him again as fresh grief threatened to overwhelm him. How could she do this to him? Why couldn't she see his love and respond to it? He wished for a way to avoid further conflict, but he knew he had to face her. He wearily ascended the stairs.

Johanna sat by the window, looking out at the gray dawn that echoed her mood. She heard the soft steps in the hall and turned toward the door. The lock clicked, and the door swung open. She had never seen Erich so unhappy, and for just a moment she felt a brief pang of remorse. Then she remembered why it had all happened. She saw him blink. Were there tears in his eyes? she wondered, not that it really mattered.

He cleared his throat. "We need to talk," he said softly.

She frowned. "What is there to talk about?"

"Us. What is to become of us, Johanna?"

"You could divorce me. You have grounds."

"That's out of the question."

"Why?"

"Because I love you. And I meant the vows I made to you before God."

"Suit yourself."

"Johanna, I don't understand."

"I told you, Erich. *My* father arranged this with *your* father without asking me how *I* felt about it. That I can never forgive."

"But what about my love for you? Does that mean nothing to you?"

Avoiding his eyes, she moved to the vanity bench. She sat down and began brushing her hair. The quaver in his voice bothered her conscience a little, but he had gone along with this whole unfair plan — he too had not consulted her about whether she wanted to marry him. Erich did not deserve an answer.

"What do you plan to do?" Erich asked finally.

She stopped brushing and glared at him in the mirror. "Since your *honor* will not allow you to divorce me, I will remain your wife — but in name only." She paused. "Oh, I will still be with you in bed, if you were worried about that. *But no children!* You, Erich, are the last of the von Arendts."

"You don't understand me, Johanna. How can you . . . ?"

She saw his tears but chose to ignore them as she fought to keep her exasperation in check. "No, I guess I don't."

"Isn't there something we can do — see a pastor maybe?"

"No, Erich. I don't wish to talk about it any further with anyone, including you. Now hurry up or you'll be late for your precious job. Herr Speer will whip you if you don't turn in a full day. Go away — I'll be down later."

Erich left and closed the door softly.

Johanna threw her hairbrush down, then looked at her reflection in the mirror and wondered what she should do.

A half hour later Johanna wandered into the kitchen. Bertha made a great show of straightening up the pantry while she assiduously ignored the woman she had served faithfully until now. Johanna tried to outwait her servant but finally decided it wasn't worth it.

"I would like some breakfast, Frau Liedig." The tone said, *How dare you ignore me!*

Bertha banged a quart jar down and turned. Her frown faded, but not before Johanna noticed it. "What would you like?"

Johanna noticed the lack of proper address and debated with herself on what to do, deciding she really couldn't let it pass.

"Is this your idea of respect? If you're unhappy, we can dispense with your services."

"Herr von Arendt is my employer."

"I hired you, Frau Liedig, and I assure you I can fire you just as easily."

"That may be so."

"But that's not what I want. What I want is an explanation."

Bertha looked down. "Herr von Arendt loves you. You are hurting him."

"How dare you! This is none of your business." Johanna waited a moment, but Bertha remained silent. "I expect an answer, Frau Liedig."

The housekeeper looked up, her eyes full of sadness and perhaps regret. "You are right, Frau von Arendt. It *is* none of my business. Please forgive me."

Johanna nodded.

"May I get you something to eat, Frau von Arendt?"

"Yes. I would like a poached egg, toast, and coffee."

"Very good. I'll make it right away. Shall I serve it in the dining room?"

Suddenly Johanna felt very weary. "No. I think I'd like a tray in the bedroom."

Bertha nodded and started preparing the breakfast.

What began as a thought of desperation solidified as Johanna ate her breakfast. By the time she had finished, it did not seem rash at all, but wholly reasonable and wise given the circumstances. It would be a notice to Erich and a welcome respite for herself. She quickly packed a small bag and made a call to the train station. She thought about calling her mother but decided to wait until she got to Frankfurt. She phoned for a taxi, waited a few minutes, then went downstairs.

Bertha stopped cleaning the living room as Johanna walked past and set her bag by the door.

"Are you going out, Frau von Arendt?" Bertha asked.

"Continue with your cleaning, Frau Liedig. This is none of your affair."

"But what am I to tell Herr von Arendt?"

"Tell him anything you please." Johanna struggled to contain her growing anger. "Tell him I'm going to visit my parents in Frankfurt."

"But . . ."

Johanna gritted her teeth. "Are my instructions unclear, Frau Liedig?"

"No, but . . ."

"But what?" Johanna snapped.

Bertha twisted her hands helplessly. "Herr von Arendt is a fine man. How can you leave him? Please . . ."

Johanna glared at her. "How dare you talk back to me!"

Bertha hung her head. "I am only speaking the truth out of concern for you and Herr von Arendt."

"Silence! Not another word! Go back to the kitchen and leave me alone!"

Bertha reluctantly nodded and left.

A few minutes later the cab came, and Johanna opened the door and walked out.

It was after 11 P.M. when Erich returned. He opened the door and was surprised to find Bertha waiting for him.

"Is anything the matter?" he asked. Fear gripped him as he saw her obvious distress.

"Frau von Arendt is gone."

The blood drained from Erich's face. "Gone? Gone where?"

"To see her parents in Frankfurt. She left this morning."

It was several moments before he could trust his voice. "Did she say why?"

"No, she did not."

"I see. I'm . . . I'm very tired. Good night."

He started up the stairs.

"I made your dinner, Herr von Arendt," she called after him.

Erich stopped but did not turn. "Thank you, but I'm not hungry."

"You have not been eating well. Come . . . Sit in the dining room . . . Let me bring you something to eat."

He felt his stomach tighten. "Good night."

"I'll leave a sandwich in the refrigerator."

He continued up the stairs in silence.

Johanna watched the countryside streak past as the train approached Frankfurt. The sense of unease that had haunted her for the last two hours was now erupting into near panic. What had seemed so reasonable and wise in Berlin now appeared ill-advised and rash. But Erich had forced the issue, she reminded herself. He had demanded to know how she felt about him, so she had told him. At least she had not lied.

She closed her eyes against the agony of her unhappy marriage. But added to this pain was one more, equally unfair — what would she tell her father? It was Saturday, so she knew he was likely at one of his factories. But she would have to face him sooner or later.

She dabbed at her tears with her handkerchief as she struggled to maintain control. She watched as the peaceful farms and tiny villages gradually gave way to larger towns. The train swept past gate crossings with lines of waiting cars and trucks. Factories and mills soon replaced the towns, and the brakes squealed and the sunshine lessened as the train entered the dimly lit station and pulled up to the platform.

Johanna retrieved her bag and stepped down beneath the cavernous ceiling of the terminal. Other passengers scurried around her as if they were sure of where they were going and why. Johanna stood there, wondering what to do.

"May I help you, fräulein?" a porter asked, touching the brim of his cap.

"No, no, I'm fine. Thank you."

He nodded and continued down the platform. Johanna shivered as she thought about placing a telephone call, but decided it would be best to take a cab to her parents' house. She walked slowly through the terminal and out the large doors. The dazzling sun outside did nothing to brighten her spirits. She continued toward the line of cabs. One driver opened the door for her, and she got in. She gave him the address and sat back. Her sense of dread increased the closer she got to home until it was almost unbearable. What would she tell her father, and what he would say? He was not known for his understanding. She briefly thought of returning to Berlin but knew that would solve nothing.

When the cab pulled up at the house, Johanna paid the driver and got out. She stood looking at the large, two-story home feeling very much like an intruder. She walked slowly up the walk and onto the porch, rang the bell, and waited. The butler opened the door. His eyes grew wide with recognition and shock.

"F-frau von Arendt," he stuttered, "w-what are you doing here?" He flushed in embarrassment. "Please forgive me, but you surprised me so. Come in. Let me take your bag."

He took her bag and held the door open.

Johanna tried to smile but could not. "You used to call me Johanna, Herr Exner."

He smiled. "Yes, but you are a married woman now. I did not think it proper. And how are you?"

Her eyes tightened as she struggled to

maintain her poise. "I'm fine. Is Mother home?"

"Yes, and your father as well."

"Father? Here? Who is tending his mills? Surely Herr Maser can't manage them all by himself." She watched for a reaction, but he ignored her sarcasm.

"Shall I announce you to your mother?"

"No . . ."

A door opened on the second floor, and heavy footsteps sounded ominously in the hall and down the stairs. Walther Kammler fastened his gaze on the person standing next to the butler. After a brief pause, he approached.

Icy pangs settled in Johanna's stomach as she struggled to maintain her tight smile.

"Hello, Papa." She saw him purse his lips as he always did when he was struggling with what to say.

"Hello, Johanna. How are you?"

"I'm fine, Papa. How are you?" The expected small talk felt to her like a nervous calm before a terrible storm.

He paused. "I am not sure. Why are you here, if I might ask? Is this merely a visit?"

She saw his expression begin to harden. "Father, I . . ."

"And where is Erich?" he added.

Johanna lowered her chin. "He is in Berlin."

"What is the meaning of this, Johanna?"

She cringed as she heard his rising tone. She knew what was coming.

"Papa . . ."

"You have left your husband?" he interrupted again.

She flushed and wished for some way to escape this scene she had chosen.

"Johanna . . ." Walther stopped as he remembered the butler. "Come. We will discuss this in my study."

He took her arm, but she refused to move.

"I wish to see Mother."

"You will come with me this instant, is that clear?"

Herr Exner turned and hurried toward the back of the house as quickly as decorum would allow. He passed Elsa who was coming from the kitchen. They passed without a word.

"Johanna . . ." she gasped. "What's the matter? Why are you here?"

Walther waved his hand. "I'll handle this, Elsa. Johanna and I are retiring to my study."

"I want Mother to come also," Johanna said with trembling confidence.

"No, we will discuss this alone."

"Unless Mother is there, I will stand right here."

The veins on Walther's neck began to bulge. "You dare . . ." He struggled to regain his composure. He glanced at Elsa, who was pleading with her eyes. "Very well. Shall we retire to my study, unless, of course, we wish everyone in Frankfurt to know all about this?"

He led the way and held the door while the others entered. Mother and daughter sat in chairs in front of his desk while he closed the door. He walked to the window and looked outside for a long time before turning to face them. Johanna shrank under his harsh gaze, as she had so often while growing up. What did he know about her needs and concerns? Why should he care?

"This has to start somewhere, Johanna," Walther said at last. "Why are you here in Frankfurt? Why have you left your husband?"

Johanna's eyes flashed in anger. "The only reason he *is* my husband is because you and Karl von Arendt decided he would be. No one ever asked me how *I* felt about it."

"You come from a privileged family —

you and Erich both. And with privilege comes responsibility. You made a commitment . . ."

"I've heard that all my life," Johanna interrupted. "Why is it that everyone else has rights, but I have none? Mother, don't you understand what I am talking about?"

Elsa's hands writhed in her lap. "I care about your happiness, dear. But you are a married woman now. You have certain responsibilities to your husband. You have your vows."

"You don't understand me either."

"I think I do — more than you realize."

Johanna's chin began to tremble. "No matter. I did have a love at one time, someone who cared for me, someone exciting to be with, someone I had something in common with. I have my memories."

Walther pointed a finger at her. "If you mean that piece of refuse Ulrich Reeder . . ."

She lifted her head. "Remer. His name is Ulrich *Remer*. Ulrich understood me. He cared about me. He loved me. Ulrich appreciates music, theater, the arts, unlike those in this house — and unlike Erich."

"Erich is your husband, and I will not have you speak ill of him. As for this Remer creature, he is long gone. I paid him well and made it very clear he was never to see you again."

"The family dictator has spoken."

"Enough! I am your father, Johanna. You will respect me."

She shrugged.

"I am waiting for an answer, Johanna."

"What do you want me to say?"

"That you are going back to your husband."

"I just got here. Are you going to drive me to the station right this instant?"

Walther glanced at his wife.

"Perhaps we could book her trip for tomorrow," she suggested.

Walther nodded. "Very well. I will take care of it."

"May I go up to my room?" Johanna asked.

"Yes," Walther replied, waving toward the door.

She got up and walked out. The hallway was deserted. She hurried up the stairs and at the top turned toward her bedroom. Reaching the door, she glimpsed a movement out of the corner of her eye. She glanced at the door across the hall. It was ajar, and a blue eye regarded her through the crack. Despite everything, Johanna couldn't help smiling.

"I see you," she said. "You might as well come out."

Sophie opened the door. "Can I come in and talk?"

Johanna shrugged and opened her door. "Yes, come in. I need to talk to someone."

Sophie entered, went to the chair by the window, and sat down. Johanna plumped up a pillow and placed it against the headboard. She plopped down wearily, rolled onto her back, and propped her head on the pillow.

"I suppose you want to know why I'm here," Johanna grumbled. "Everyone else does."

"Not if you don't want to tell."

Johanna looked at her curiously and shook her head. "Sophie, you're always a wonder. I think you're the only friend I have in this family."

Her teenaged sister shook her head. "No, you are mistaken. Mother cares. In our talks she keeps saying how she hopes you'll come to appreciate Erich's character." She paused. "And in his own way, I think Papa cares."

"Papa? That's absurd! All Papa cares about are his factories — that and dictating what everyone else does."

Sophie maintained her steady gaze.

"That's mostly true, Johanna. But I also believe he wants what's best for you."

Johanna's scowl deepened. "He only thinks about himself. He couldn't care less about what I want."

Sophie sighed. "I don't want to argue with you. I just wanted to ask how things were with you and Erich."

Johanna closed her eyes. Running off had seemed the right thing to do back in Berlin. However, once on the train she had begun to have doubts. And now with her father's reaction . . . She opened her eyes and saw Sophie's caring expression.

"Things are bad. Erich and I had a huge fight. He's at work all hours, he rarely takes me out to the theater or the philharmonic or art exhibits, and I don't have any real friends, not like I do in Frankfurt. Finally I just couldn't take it anymore."

"What was the fight about?"

Johanna exhaled audibly. "About what I just said. That and he asked me again about having children. He has before, but this time I couldn't put him off. I told him I didn't want any."

"What did he say about that?"

Johanna's eyes flashed. "He got mad, madder than I've ever seen him. I thought for a moment he would strike me."

"Just for that? That doesn't seem like Erich."

"Well, there was more. He asked if I was seeing anyone else. I said of course not but that I love another."

"Oh. So you told him about Ulrich."

"Yes. Erich made me so mad. But yes, I told him about Ulrich. Erich stomped off, and I guess that's when I decided to come home."

"I'm sorry, Johanna. I wish you could find happiness."

Her younger sister's words felt soothing to Johanna, and yet it seemed like all her emotion had drained out of her, that she was empty. "I wish I could too."

For the first time she allowed her thoughts to range beyond her own troubles, to the one member of the family she had not seen today. "Where is Bernhard?"

"He's at a Hitler Youth gathering in Nuremberg."

"How does he like it?"

"He really enjoys it. The local leadership have their eyes on him. Papa, of course, is delighted."

"Of course. Well, I guess I won't be seeing him."

"How long are you staying?"

Johanna scowled. "Papa's taking me to

the train tomorrow. He's probably calling my dear husband right now, apologizing for my dreadful behavior."

Sophie got up, put her arms around her sister, and hugged her. "I hope things get better for you."

Johanna exhaled slowly. "I do too."

The clock on the mantel struck 5. Johanna tiptoed downstairs, took the key from the cupboard, and unlocked the front door. The tight constriction in her throat made it hard to breathe as she hurried down the walk and didn't ease until she had gone several blocks. She looked over her shoulder several times as she made her way through the gray dawn. She did not have long to wait before the tram arrived at the stop.

She was both excited and scared, the closer she got to Christabel's apartment. She got off the tram and hurried through the nearly deserted streets. She found the apartment and walked up four flights. She knocked on the door, softly at first, then much harder. After several minutes she heard footsteps approaching.

"Who is it?" came the muffled voice inside.

"Johanna."

The door opened cautiously.

"Johanna, what are you doing here?" the sleepy voice asked.

"It's a long story. Please let me in."

Her friend opened the door the rest of the way, and Johanna hurried past and into the cramped living room. Christabel followed her, rubbing the sleep from her eyes. Johanna settled awkwardly in a chair.

"What's going on?" Christabel asked as she sat on the couch. "I thought you and Erich were living in Berlin."

Johanna burst into tears. "We are . . . were. Oh, I don't know what I mean."

"Slow down. What's happened?"

Johanna wiped her eyes with her handkerchief as she explained her return to Frankfurt and what her parents had said. Christabel listened patiently, nodding as her friend made each point.

"So, what do you want to do?" Christabel asked when Johanna was done.

"Do you know where Ulrich is?"

"You're really leaving Erich?"

"It's the only hope I have for happiness. I can't go back to Berlin, and my parents will force me if I don't get away. Ulrich will take me away, if I can find him. He loves me."

Christabel shook her head and looked

away. "If you say so."

"What do you mean?"

"Don't mind me. To answer your question, yes, I know where he lives. He's still in Frankfurt, though in a different apartment. He was forced to leave his old one."

"Yes, I know. Would you write down the address for me?"

"Sure." She laughed unexpectedly. "Since you roused me from my sleep, I feel like some breakfast. Care to join me?"

"Yes, I think I will. I didn't get anything when I left my house."

"Let's go into the kitchen and see what we can find."

Johanna felt hope spring up in her heart. She tried to imagine what Ulrich's apartment looked like and what part of the city it was in. She longed to be on her way to see the only one who would help her, the only one who had ever loved her.

Since Ulrich's apartment was only a few blocks away, Johanna decided to walk. It was mid-morning by the time she located the correct building and walked up to the second-floor apartment. She stood before the door for a long time until she could muster her courage. Finally she knocked. At first there was no answer, and she was about to turn away when the door opened.

"Johanna, what are *you* doing here?"

"Hello, Ulrich. Can I come in?"

"Why, yes, yes — of course."

He stood aside and closed the door after she was inside. Johanna looked around. The apartment was small but very tidy. Prints of masterpieces hung tastefully on the walls, and a bust of Beethoven glowered down at them from the mantel. The only piece of furniture that did not fit the decor was the upright piano wedged into one corner of the living room. Johanna sat on the sofa, and Ulrich sat beside her.

"Now," he said, "tell me how it is with you."

She laid her head on his shoulder as the tears came. "Oh, Ulrich, you have no idea how miserable I've been."

"It hasn't worked out with Erich?"

"No, not at all. He and I have nothing in common. The marriage was Papa's idea — and Erich's. They decided my life for me as if I have no feelings. It isn't fair."

"No, Johanna, it isn't. But not much in life is. I see you are finding this out."

She looked up at him and wiped away her tears. "You understand me, Ulrich. I can talk to you. You treat me with respect — and love."

He gave her arm a squeeze. "Yes, yes, we understand each other. The world is more than factories and drawing plans that other people build. What do they know of art, hmm? What do they know of Beethoven and Bach and Wagner, or Monet?" He laughed. "They are complete and utter philistines, but then again, they run the world. What can we do?"

"It isn't fair."

"Yes, I know. But let's not repeat ourselves. What do you plan to do about it?" He was abrupt, but in her pain she didn't notice.

"Take me away, Ulrich. Let's run away to the Mediterranean."

He raised his eyebrows. "You are heir to a fortune, Johanna. Are you willing to give up all that?"

"Yes. What good would it all be if I'm not happy?"

"Money can take care of a lot of problems. And the thing is, you've never done without. You have no idea what that is like."

"Whose side are you on?" Johanna demanded, suddenly perceiving Ulrich's possible lack of understanding or compassion.

"Yours, my dear, yours. I am just telling you something you need to know."

She closed her eyes. "Oh, Ulrich, I have

missed you so much. You have no idea how I've longed to be with you."

He put his arm around her and pulled her close. "You are sweet, Johanna."

"You do love me, don't you?"

"How can you even ask?"

He leaned over. His lips lightly brushed hers, and Johanna felt her pulse quicken. He kissed her again, and she returned it with a fierceness that frightened her. Ulrich gently reclined, taking Johanna with him.

The door suddenly rattled against its frame with a violent pounding.

"Police! Open up!"

Ulrich bolted upright in shock. "Does anyone know you're here?" he whispered.

Johanna shook her head.

"Open up or I'll break the door down!"

"Just a minute!" Ulrich shouted. "I'm coming!"

"Straighten up your dress," he whispered harshly.

Johanna stood, smoothed her dress, and tidied her hair. Ulrich hurried to the door. Pausing a moment, he opened it, only to see an officer of the law. Behind the policeman stood Walther Kammler.

"What have you done with my daughter?" he shouted, flecks of saliva hitting Ulrich in the face.

"I've done nothing with Johanna. She simply came by to visit me."

"You do remember the terms of our arrangement?"

"I do. But I did not seek her out."

The policeman looked decidedly uncomfortable. "Do you need me any further, sir?"

Walther looked at him as if he had forgotten he was there. "No, no. You may go. Thank you for your service."

"Not at all, sir." He put his hand to his cap and quickly left.

Walther turned back to Ulrich. "Allow me to put it in a way that cannot be misunderstood — if you ever see my daughter again, for any reason, you will regret it for the rest of your life. I will see to it that you never work again — not anywhere in Germany anyway. Do I make myself perfectly clear?"

"Perfectly."

"Very well. Come, Johanna."

She closed her eyes as she realized her nightmare was not going to go away.

"This instant, Johanna! Come with me! Your poor mother is waiting back at the house. How could you do this to us?"

She remained silent, but after a few moments she followed her father down to the car.

Seven

Erich watched the express from Frankfurt as it pulled into the station and ground to a halt. Weary travelers stepped down after their long journey, grateful to be at their destination. Families and friends gathered together in small groups and traded warm greetings. The stream of passengers continued for a long time, then slowed to a trickle.

Erich felt dead inside as he scanned each face. One part of him longed to see Johanna again, but he couldn't push aside her devastating words. He hoped with all his heart that she'd changed her mind about him, but his earlier phone conversation with his father-in-law had not been encouraging. Walther had tried to sound cheerful, but Erich sensed the man's tension.

Erich looked about the nearly deserted platform and began to wonder if he had misunderstood Walther. No, he thought, this was the correct train. Perhaps Johanna had gotten off before reaching Berlin.

Finally a thin figure stepped down from a car near the end of the train. It was

Johanna, standing alone on the platform. Erich's pulse raced. His eyes grew damp, and he wiped them with his sleeve. He started walking slowly toward her. As he drew closer, he could see the tension in her eyes. He stopped several feet away and waited for a passing porter to get out of earshot.

"How are you, Johanna?" he asked as he struggled to maintain his composure.

She met his eyes briefly, then looked down. "I'm well, thank you."

"Did you enjoy your visit?" he asked, deciding to play the game, unsure what else to say.

"Yes, but I am glad to be back home."

"Are you?" He regretted the impulsive sarcasm, yet also wanted to know where things stood.

She glanced up. Erich watched for some sign of remorse or love, but he saw neither. Instead she frowned.

"Please, Erich, I'm very tired. I've had a long, uncomfortable trip."

"Yes, of course. Forgive me, dear. You can relax on the way home."

He picked up her bag and escorted her out of the terminal, then helped her into his car. Neither said a word as he drove back to the house. Once inside, he set her bag beside the front door.

"Go on up and make yourself comfortable," he said in the entranceway. "I'll get Frau Liedig to make you something to eat. What would you like?"

She lowered her eyes. "Nothing. I'm not hungry."

"Are you sure? I'll be glad to get you anything."

Johanna tried to hide her exasperation. "Erich, I am *not* hungry. I just want to go upstairs and rest."

He felt a stinging sensation in his eyes. "Shall I stay down here then?"

"For heavens sake, Erich, do whatever you want." She hurried upstairs.

Erich caught a movement out of the corner of his eye. He turned and saw Bertha Liedig standing in the doorway to the kitchen, her shocked expression obvious. She hesitated a moment as if she didn't know what to do, then retreated into the kitchen and quietly closed the door.

A door slammed on the second floor. To Erich it sounded like the first peal of a death knell. His mind raced as he tried to decide what to do. His eyes drifted up the staircase to their bedroom door. He started up the stairs, his right hand sliding slowly over the banister, paused at the door, then opened it and went in. The sound of running water came through the closed bathroom door. He thought briefly about going in but decided to wait. He sat down in a chair by the bed.

His wandering eyes roamed the room until they fell on the music box he had given Johanna on her thirteenth birthday. *She may not love me, but she adores that music box,* he thought bitterly. He quelled the impulse to smash it. *I am forgetting — music is important, but I'm not.*

After a while he heard the water draining, and minutes later Johanna came out dressed in her blue robe, vigorously toweling her long hair. She hesitated a moment when she spotted Erich, then walked to her vanity and sat down. Erich waited to see if she would say anything. She picked up a brush and began brushing her hair.

"Johanna?" he began finally.

She turned her head until she could see his reflection in the mirror. She frowned and slammed the hairbrush down. "What is it?"

"I have to know. How is it going to be with us?"

"Nothing has changed, Erich! Since you refuse to divorce me, I will remain Frau Erich von Arendt. I have no say in this, as you very well know. As I said before, I will be the proper German wife to you, with the one exception that we will not discuss further. You *have* me, Erich! What more do you want?"

"Your love," he said simply.

She shook her head. "That is something you will *never* have."

He got slowly to his feet, struggling to maintain his composure. "I must be going, Johanna."

"Where?"

"Back to work. I didn't tell Herr Speer I was going to meet you at the station. I'm behind in my work. I'll probably be home late."

Johanna waved her hand vaguely. "Do whatever you have to. Don't you understand? I don't care anymore."

He hurried out to keep her from seeing his tears. The landing swam in his blurred vision, and he stumbled and almost fell down the stairs, catching himself at the last moment. He hurried out of the house as if he could outrun his troubles.

Johanna resigned herself to the dreary reality she saw her life to be. Erich's work consumed ever-increasing amounts of time. Their intimate moments became less frequent, and less satisfying. Johanna observed her husband's lack of interest and wondered if there could be another woman. This thought bothered Johanna a little, but she told herself it didn't matter. Why should she care *what* Erich did?

Their separate duties carried them through the rest of 1937 and into the next year like unwilling captives. In January Erich was assigned to the design team for Hitler's new Chancellery, an assignment at least as demanding as his former duties.

Erich took Johanna to operas and plays, but these diversions grew infrequent as his workload increased. Lonely and bored, Johanna began spending time with the wives of other Speer employees. Leisurely luncheons and teas at stylish Berlin restaurants occupied many afternoons, plus evenings at the Berlin Philharmonic or the opera. Johanna looked on these groups as uncultured and even insipid, but it was better than boredom in the home she now despised.

In March Hitler ordered Pastor Niemöller sent to a concentration camp. At first Johanna thought the action justified, but she could not shake the feeling that it was excessive despite Niemöller's meddling. She could see that the situation hung heavily on Erich's heart, which didn't surprise her. Johanna assumed that Erich's work on Hitler's new Chancellery would mean more normal hours, but Albert Speer's promise to deliver the building by January 9 made that impossible. By the time November came, Johanna and Erich hardly saw each other at all except for a few hours sometimes on Sundays. This irritated Johanna only because it meant she couldn't get out of the house as much as she wanted.

Johanna had a hard time understanding her emotions during this time. She had felt deep despair and self-pity on her return from Frankfurt, and this gradually eroded into apathy with brief outbursts of longing for something better though knowing it could never be. Most of the time Erich was wrapped up in his work, but he carried a sorrow so obvious that even Johanna saw it. She almost felt pity for him.

The morning of November 9 was cold, and Johanna shivered as she hurried down the stairs, down the hall, and into the chilly dining room. Erich looked up from his breakfast, obviously surprised at seeing her.

"Good morning," he said as she sat down. He glanced at his watch. "To what do I owe this honor?"

Bertha rolled her eyes and returned to the kitchen to prepare another plate.

"Good morning, Erich," Johanna replied. "You do remember we're going to the concert tonight?"

Erich closed his eyes and tilted his head back. "Oh no!" he moaned. "I'm sorry . . . I forgot. The work on the Chancellery is killing me."

"Erich, you promised," Johanna said, her voice rising.

"I know . . . I remember now. But I can't — not tonight. If I don't finish my plans, the workers will be idle tomorrow. And if that happens, Herr Speer will fire me."

"Your work *always* comes first, doesn't it?"

Erich sighed wearily. "I have no choice, Johanna. This is how I earn our living."

"Then go work for someone else."

He shook his head. "I could never earn as much elsewhere. Beside, no one else has projects like Herr Speer. I've always dreamed of working on commissions like this."

"I thought you disapproved of our Führer?"

Erich frowned. "Don't jest, Johanna."

"What about your precious Pastor

174

Niemöller? You said it was wrong for him to be sent to a concentration camp."

"Yes, I believe it *was* wrong."

"So you're being inconsistent, but never mind . . . *I* think Niemöller got what he deserved."

"How can you say that?" he demanded.

"Never mind that! What about me, Erich? I have looked forward to this concert for weeks. It's not proper for me to go unescorted, and none of the other wives are going this time. Erich, I don't ask much — you know I don't. And you promised to take me."

"Johanna, I can't. I'm serious — if I don't finish these drawings tonight, Herr Speer will fire me."

"Then I don't care about decorum. I'll go by myself!"

He stared at her in disbelief, his jaw set. "I forbid it!"

"You will *not* tell me what to do!"

"Johanna, I'm your husband! You will not do this!"

"And how will you stop me?" she asked, lowering her voice.

"I . . ."

Johanna watched him stand up and throw his napkin onto his plate. He turned away.

"Where are you going?" Johanna asked

as he reached the door.

"To work," he said over his shoulder just before he slammed the door.

"What are you working on?" Karl asked as he looked over his son's shoulder.

Erich sighed as he laid down his pen. He noted a slight nervous tremor and shook his hand to loosen it. "The lighting fixtures in the Chancellery's long gallery."

"Important work. How is it going?"

"Well, I think. I should be finished by 5 or 6 in the morning. Let me rephrase that — I *must* be finished by then. The workers are going to start installing the fixtures tomorrow." He glanced at his watch. "Hmm — just past midnight. Make that *today*."

His father smiled and patted him on the shoulder. "Keep at it, Erich. This is how a successful architect starts out." His eyes took in the details of the drawing. "You do good work, son."

"Right now I just wish . . . !" Erich exclaimed, more sharply than he intended.

Karl frowned. "Wish what?"

"Never mind." Erich saw his father's hurt look. "I'm sorry, Papa. I'm under a lot of pressure, and I really must get back to my drawing."

"I understand. I'll leave you to it."

★ ★ ★

Erich stole a glance at his watch. It was a little after 1 in the morning. He sighed as he put down his pen and leaned against the back support on his high drafting chair. He rubbed his eyes vigorously as he tried not to dwell on how much work he still had to do. The door latch clicked. Erich turned around expecting to see his father, but it was an unnaturally serious Franz who came in and quietly closed the door.

"What brings you here at this ungodly hour?" Erich asked, hoping his friend would not stay long.

Franz came close but did not sit. "Ungodly is what *you* would call it, I guess, and you may be right." He looked around the large drafting room as if to make sure they were alone. "You must not tell anyone I was here, Erich."

Erich frowned. "I am *not* in a mood for games, Franz. I'm tired, and I have a lot of work to do before morning."

"This is not a game, and I'm quite serious. Promise me you will not tell anyone I was here — anyone!"

"Oh, for heaven's sake, I promise I'll keep your blasted secret. Now, what is it?"

"I called your house earlier this evening. The formidable Frau Liedig reluctantly informed me that you were at work. I asked about Johanna, but . . ."

"Why would you be asking about Johanna?" Erich demanded harshly.

"I had a good reason, believe me. But Frau Liedig refused to discuss Johanna at all." He looked into his friend's eyes. "Where is she, Erich?"

"If you really must know, I think she went to some concert. I was supposed to take her, but this work — which you are preventing me from completing — didn't allow me to. I told her she couldn't go alone, but she defied me."

Franz looked away. "I wish she had listened to you."

"What do you mean?" Erich demanded.

"Do you know where the concert is?"

"Yes, I know where the concert is! Now tell me, what is going on?"

"She may be in danger . . . There will be riots tonight. They may have already started, I don't know. You'd better go get Johanna." He glanced nervously at his watch. "I must go. My boss doesn't know where I am. I must get back before he misses me and starts asking embarrassing questions."

"Franz . . ."

His friend hurried to the door. He opened it and started out. He looked back.

"I've told you all I can." Then he was gone.

With one glance at the unfinished drawings, Erich grabbed his coat and raced into the cold night air. His breath came in frosty puffs of white as he dashed across the deserted street. He wrenched the door to his car open, leapt in, and cranked the engine. It caught with a roar, and he put the car in gear and raced down the street. He reviewed the route to the concert in his mind, afraid for his wife — it went right by a Jewish business district.

Johanna gathered her cloak about her as she leaned back on the seat cushions, thankful to be out of the raw wind. The traffic was light as the taxi made its way through central Berlin.

Johanna had not enjoyed the concert even though it had been well done. The musicians had been brilliant, and the audience a choice sampling of Berlin society. But she had not been able to get over her fight with Erich, even though she had tried to convince herself it didn't matter. And somehow the fact that he had forbidden her to come weighed heavily on her, raising her irritation to a new level. She did *not* need Erich telling her what to do.

A movement up ahead caught Johanna's eye. She leaned forward and peered through the taxi's windshield. A dark undulating mass lined both sides of the street, and it appeared to be coming their way. Johanna gasped as the taxi's headlights picked out men in ragged coats running down the street. They broke off in twos and threes, bashing in store windows with crude clubs. Looters raced out with anything they could carry while others continued the mindless destruction.

"What's going on?" Johanna demanded.

"I don't know," the driver replied. "Hold on!"

He quickly braked and twisted the wheel. The taxi swerved to the left, barely making the turn onto the narrow cross street. But their way was completely blocked by an even larger mob coming toward them. The driver cursed, stood on the brakes, and fought for control as the car squealed to a stop. He threw the gearshift into reverse, gunned the engine, and let out the clutch. The rear wheels spun briefly as the car raced back toward the intersection.

Johanna twisted around in her seat and looked out the narrow rear window. She gasped as she saw the mob from the main street come through the intersection, blocking their escape route.

"Do something!" she screamed.

The driver searched frantically for a gap in the moving wall of flesh, but there was none. Scant feet from the intersection, he jammed on the brakes again. Johanna watched in horror as the back of the taxi slid toward the nearest rioters. She got a good look at their unshaven faces as they tried to get out of the way. She felt a sickening bump and heard a muffled scream as the car backed over one of the men.

Johanna recoiled in horror as a leering, bearded face with wild eyes appeared in her side window. The rioters flowed around the taxi like a human flood. A gaunt man swung his shovel and smashed the windshield. Johanna screamed and cowered in a corner of the backseat. The driver clung to the steering wheel as if it were his lifeline.

The taxi rocked on its springs as the men outside pushed on it. Johanna held onto the armrest as the car tilted further and further. Finally it stood balanced precariously on two wheels. With a wild cheer, the men gave it one final shove, and the car crashed down onto the passenger side.

Johanna lay sprawled against her door, looking up through the opposite side windows at the night sky and a nearby streetlight.

The windshield exploded inward, admitting a blast of frigid air. A heavy wooden club cleared the remaining glass from the frame. A huge man in a tattered coat several sizes too small for him knelt down and peered inside.

"Come with me!" he shouted at the driver.

He reached in with both hands, grabbed the terrified man by his shoulders, wrestled him away from the wheel, and dragged him out through the windshield opening. The driver disappeared into the milling crowd. The unshaven giant returned. Johanna shivered as he looked her over under the glare of the streetlight.

"Well, what have we here?" he said, an evil glint in his eye. "A little late for a pretty fräulein to be out, yes? Come here, darling." The heavy smell of schnapps drifted into the backseat.

Johanna shook her head and tried to back further into the corner. She was vaguely aware of the shouts outside and the continuous sound of breaking glass. The man pointed at her.

"Come here at once or I'll come in after you!"

"Stay away from me!" Johanna screamed.

"I warned you!"

The man crawled through the windshield frame, mindless of the glass shards that littered the inside of the car. Johanna scrambled to her feet and reached for the door above her.

"Oh, no you don't," the man growled.

He grabbed her ankles as she twisted the door handle and tried to push the door open. The man jerked her feet out from under her. Johanna screamed as she collapsed. The armrest dug into her side, and the broken glass cut through her coat and dress. She felt the warm trickle of blood. She lifted her head to get a better look. The man's face was in shadow, but she could see the glint of his teeth. She yelped as he tightened his hold on her ankles.

"Come out of there or I'll pull you out!" he demanded.

He released his grip and backed out of the car. Johanna, afraid to have the man corner her inside the car, cried out at the sharp pain as she rolled onto her side, then began crawling toward the man. Bits of glass slashed her knees and hands as she made her way over the seats and out the windshield. The man grabbed her by the wrist and jerked her upright. The alcohol on his breath was overpowering as he looked down at her.

"What a beautiful lady. Do you like me?"

Johanna squirmed in his grip, but he only clamped down harder.

"That hurts!" she cried out.

The man's voice was low, barely audible. "Come with me."

"No," Johanna whimpered.

The tinkling sound of breaking glass rolled over her like an angry sea against a desolate shore. The rioters swung their clubs against the windows of all the shops along the street. Others rushed through the breaches, returning moments later with armloads of plunder. A scream sounded from somewhere down the street, a scream that quit suddenly.

Johanna almost tripped as her captor pulled her through the throng and toward the sidewalk. His grip tightened, and she cried out in pain.

"We'll go in here," he said.

She looked at the remains of the shop window. *Goldstein's Delicatessen*, the sign proclaimed. Her captor dragged her past the smashed display cases and the empty cash register. A light from a storeroom provided dim illumination for the small restaurant at the back of the shop. The man pushed the tables and chairs to the side.

Johanna knew what was coming. "No," she whimpered.

He slapped her face hard. "Be quiet!"

She sank to her knees sobbing. Tears streamed down her face as she stretched out on the cold floor, then rolled over and started crawling toward the storeroom. The man grabbed the back of her coat and pulled, ripping the heavy fabric. He reached for her shoulder and flipped her over.

"Such a nice fräulein," he said. "Don't you like me?"

Johanna looked up into his eyes in terror. A sudden shadow flickered behind him as he reached for her. She saw a blurred motion as something arced down, striking the man on the head. She heard the sharp crunch and watched as her assailant fell flat on the floor. It took her a few moments to realize that the back of the man's skull was crushed. Only then did she look up and see the young boy holding a heavy fire poker, tears streaming down his face. The shouts of angry men and breaking glass sounded a little more distant now.

"You saved me," Johanna said in a whisper.

The boy said nothing. He stood there holding the poker and continuing to cry.

"Who are you?" Johanna asked.

The boy wiped at his tears with his left hand. "Michael Goldstein."

Johanna looked around. "Where did you come from?"

"I live here."

Johanna felt an iciness in her stomach. "Where are your parents?"

"They're upstairs." He broke down again. "They're dead," he gasped between sobs.

"Oh no," Johanna moaned.

A sound came from the front of the shop. Michael and Johanna looked past the rubble that had been one family's delicatessen. A dark shape was silhouetted in the gaping front window. Michael bolted for the back door.

"Wait!" Johanna shouted.

The boy wrenched open the door and dashed into the frigid night.

"Who's there?" the man up front asked as he started toward the back.

Johanna glanced at the open back door. She started toward it, but the man caught up and grabbed her by the arm, spinning her around. She expected him to be another of the unshaven thugs but was surprised to see that he was well-groomed and wearing a suit.

"So I've found a Jewess hiding in her hole."

"I am *not* Jewish!"

"No? Goldstein sounds Jewish to me. Do not lie to me!"

"I'm not lying! I am Frau Erich von Arendt. My husband works for Herr Speer — you may have heard of him."

"Herr Speer, you say. And what would Frau von Arendt be doing inside a Jewish shop in the middle of the night?"

"I was on my way home in a taxi when these . . . these thugs blocked our way."

"You can prove this, I suppose."

"Look in my purse — if it's still in the taxi."

"Very well."

They went outside. The man stopped one of the looters and had him retrieve the purse. Then he returned to where Johanna was standing under the streetlight. After examining her identification, the man returned her purse to her.

"I'm very sorry this happened to you, Frau van Arendt, and I apologize for my rudeness. It's not right for good Germans to be hurt by what these anti-Jew anarchists are doing. May I offer you a ride home?"

Johanna nodded. "Yes, I would appreciate that."

"Very well. My car is parked a few streets over. I would go and get it, but I must not leave you alone."

"No, no . . . I'll walk with you."

He took off his coat. "Here . . . Put this around you. It's quite cold."

Trembling from the night chill and from the dangers she'd faced, she accepted it. They walked to the corner and waited for a lone car to pass. The driver slowed as he approached the destruction.

"It's Erich!" Johanna gasped as she recognized the car.

"What?" the man asked.

"My husband . . . That's my husband." She waved at him.

The car slowed further and pulled over to the curb. Erich set the parking brake, jumped out, and ran around the car.

"Johanna! What happened?"

She felt the last dregs of energy drain from her. The horror of what she had been through came upon her in full strength, and she buried her face in Erich's chest. Great racking sobs burst forth.

He held her tightly. "It's all right. I'm here."

She began shaking.

"You'd better get her home," the man standing with her said.

"And who are you?" Erich demanded.

The man pulled out his wallet and showed him a card. "Herr von Arendt, you are a very lucky man. Now, I'm telling you to go home, and take your wife with you. You must not be here any longer."

"Yes," Erich mumbled. "Yes, we will go."

Johanna returned the man's coat and allowed Erich to help her into the car. As Erich drove away, Johanna leaned back in the seat, thankful for the security of the warm car. Feelings of guilt and anger tugged at her as she struggled to make sense of what had happened to her, knowing it could have been much worse. She knew it wouldn't have happened at all if she had obeyed Erich and not gone out alone.

At first she was grateful for Erich coming to find her. But then again, if he had kept his promise to her, none of this would have happened. *He could have found a way to take me to the concert if he had really tried.*

Though the night's events still frightened her, Johanna chose not to think of that but of her continuing anger against her husband. She saw once again how much Erich limited and stifled her. But the way things were, she could see no way out of having a miserable life.

Eight

Johanna could never drive from her mind the vivid memories of what the world later called *Kristallnacht,* the night when SS (*Schutz-Staffel*) and SA (*Sturmabteilung —* brown shirts) groups rioted, destroying Jewish shops and businesses. The horror of what had almost happened to her haunted her for a long time, and she blamed Erich for her trauma. She lost track of the number of times she awoke trembling from a nightmare that seemed all too real. And she could not forget Michael Goldstein's grief-stricken eyes. She told herself there was nothing she could have done, that she had not been responsible for what happened. The rioters were *not* the sort of people she would associate with. But the boy's dark, anguished eyes haunted her anyway.

The horror of that night and its aftermath mingled with Johanna's confused feelings of guilt. Her heart had reached out somewhat to her husband when Erich tenderly helped her into bed after a long bath that could not cleanse her thoughts or feelings. But she forgot all about that the next morning when Erich had to rush off to work. She soon learned that Erich nearly lost his job because the Chancellery drawings were not ready. But when Albert Speer heard what had happened to Johanna, he relented. She wished Erich had lost his position; then he could spend more time with her. She no longer loved her husband, and yet she wanted more of his time. She couldn't make sense of her own selfish musings.

Johanna's discontent grew steadily worse as Erich's workload intensified through November and December. The completion of the new Chancellery in January of 1939 brought only a brief respite, quickly swallowed up in the other projects that continued to pour into Speer's organization because of his position as General Inspector for the Construction of Berlin.

One day Johanna feigned interest as her husband told her about the monumental project of designing a new Berlin, which Hitler planned to rename Germania. Prachtstrasse (Street of Pomp), wider than the Champs-Élysées, would pass underneath the Arch of Triumph, which of course could nestle the Arc de Triomphe beneath it. The proposed Great Hall, the largest domed structure ever designed, anchored this grand boulevard on the north, while South Station guarded the other terminus.

Johanna responded with the appropriate compliments, and Erich told her that Hitler wanted the young architect's drawings to be used as a basis for the new South Station. Erich would be refining these drawings, while his father was assigned to working on the Great Hall.

As these events swept past Johanna, she felt as if she were an unwilling bystander. But the worst was yet to come. On September 1, 1939, Hitler forced Germany onto a political roller coaster by joining Russia in an invasion of Poland. Britain and France promptly declared war on Germany, but the western war did not start until the spring of 1940 with the invasion of Holland, Belgium, and Luxembourg. Then came the Anglo-French disaster of Dunkirk. Summer ushered Italy into the war, saw France completely occupied, and brought the beginning of the Battle of Britain. Though Germany's generals urged caution, Hitler strode boldly ahead, and almost everything he tried worked. Despite the rationing of food and clothing, national morale remained high.

By the time January 1941 rolled around, Hitler appeared invincible, making advances on all fronts against enemies ill-prepared for war.

Bertha Liedig pulled open the front door. "Welcome home, Herr von Arendt," she said. She took his heavy coat and hat and hung them in the hall closet.

"Is Frau von Arendt still up?" Erich asked.

Bertha's smile vanished. "Yes. She's in the living room."

Erich heard Johanna's quick footsteps approaching. His shoulders slumped as he awaited her appearance.

"Where have you been?" she demanded as she turned the corner into the hall.

Bertha clutched her hands together. "If you will excuse me," she muttered. She dodged past Johanna and rushed toward the kitchen as quickly as propriety would allow. The door closed with a solid thump.

"Please, dear, I've had a hard day," Erich said.

"You said you would be home early!"

He took a deep breath and let it out slowly. "It may surprise you to hear it, but there's a war on. You do remember the bombing raids on Berlin, don't you?"

"The Führer says these will stop. Our enemies are retreating on all fronts."

Erich shook his head. "Yes, yes . . . Never mind. To answer your question, I thought I *was* going to be home early. But Herr Speer had other plans for my time."

"So your work is more important than I am."

Erich stepped past her. "I'm exhausted, Johanna. If we really must discuss this, let's at least sit down."

She hurried after him as he led the way into the living room. He picked a chair by the window and collapsed into it. Johanna sat on the couch and tucked her feet under her.

"You said we would talk about vacation after work. You said you would be home early."

"I remember, and as I have already explained, I thought I *would* be home early. But after the Führer looked at the Berlin models this afternoon, he asked for changes in the South Station. Herr Speer said it must be done immediately."

"Herr Speer — Herr Speer . . . That's all I ever hear. Herr Speer has become your god."

"Don't say that, Johanna. Jesus is my Lord."

"Oh? So why don't you go to church?"

Erich hung his head. "I should, but I'm so exhausted all the time, and Sunday is the only day I have to rest."

"Rest? You work on most Sundays as well."

Erich sighed. "What do you want from me, Johanna?"

"What we were talking about this morning! I want a vacation. I want to get away. It's been more than a year since I've been away from Berlin. You know I hate Berlin!"

"We can't go away right now — not after what I was assigned today. Maybe this summer."

"That's what you always say. Later — always later! I don't even remember the last time I saw my friends."

Erich jerked his head up and scowled. "Is there anyone in particular you wish to see?"

Johanna paused. "What's that supposed to mean?"

"Your special friend in Frankfurt. The one who pleases you in ways I can't."

"I told you, that's over."

"So you say."

"You don't believe me?" Johanna asked, her voice becoming shrill.

Erich closed his eyes.

"I asked you a question," Johanna said.

"No, I *don't* believe you. Does that satisfy you?"

"How can you say that after the way I've sacrificed myself for you? I had no choice in marrying you, Erich. The *men* in my life arranged it for me without so much as an 'if you please.' But I went through with it anyway. And . . ."

"Enough!" Erich shouted.

Erich felt his world closing in on him. An ill-defined dread that had long lived in his mind was becoming horribly clear. He understood more clearly than ever before that continuing to live this way offered no happiness for him, or for Johanna for that matter. Their marriage was a sham destined for eventual failure. He felt a momentary flash of anger at Johanna's unwillingness to respond to his love.

"I will not listen to your whining story again. I gave you my love, Johanna. I did everything for you I could think of. If that is not good enough, then I think you should leave."

Johanna sat up straight. "What are you saying?"

"Go. If I can't make you happy, you may leave."

"Are you divorcing me?"

"No!" Erich paused when he saw her jump, then said more gently, "No. I will not divorce you, Johanna. I vowed before God that I would be your husband as long as we live. I will not break my vow to God."

"So what am I to do?"

"Just what I said — leave. Go back to Frankfurt, if you think that'll make you happy. Do whatever you want. There's nothing else I can do for you."

She shook her head. "You are so cruel, Erich. I have no money. How would I live?"

He slammed his fist on the armrest. "I'll provide for you! I'm *still* your husband! I'll give you an account in a Frankfurt bank with money to live on."

She sat there looking at him, her eyes wide.

His eyes flashed. "Well, isn't that what you want? To be free of me — the husband you hate?"

She brought her hand to her mouth. "This is so sudden. I've never had any say in my life, and now you're setting me free. I just don't know . . ."

He waited until he caught her eye. "Don't pull your 'poor me' routine. You keep telling me how miserable you are. Well, I'm releasing you. Go make your own happiness."

Erich felt a chill in his heart as he saw her making her choice. He knew this was finally the end.

"Very well," she said. "I'll leave in the morning."

Erich lowered his head. "Fine."

Johanna waited a few moments, then got up. She left the room and went upstairs.

Slowly the tears formed in Erich's eyes, then flowed down his cheeks as the dam of his emotions finally gave way. He broke down in racking sobs unlike any since childhood.

His agony over his marriage merged with his growing uneasiness over what he was learning about Adolf Hitler's plans for a new Germany. Despite his commitment to his work, gone was his earlier optimism as indefensible acts of the Nazi state weighed on his mind — the Nuremberg laws, Pastor Niemöller sent to a concentration camp, *Kristallnacht,* and the brutal occupation of countries declared to be enemies of the Reich. And Erich knew well the Nazi penchant for secrecy. *What other things are they doing of which I am not aware?* he wondered.

Erich looked around as a soft rap sounded. The office door opened, and Franz peered inside. Erich left his drafting table, grabbed his coat, and left the room.

"What's wrong?" Franz asked when he saw his friend's bloodshot eyes.

"Let's take a walk outside," Erich suggested.

It was still dark as the gray dawn struggled with the low overcast. The light sleet promised a raw winter day and a coming snowstorm. A few cars rushed past, having the road much to themselves. Erich rammed his hands into the pockets of his heavy overcoat and slouched forward against the wind.

"I need your help," he said.

"What's wrong?" Franz asked.

Erich brought up a hand and wiped away a tear. "Johanna and I are through. I told her to leave, so she's going back to Frankfurt."

"I'm sorry, Erich."

Erich nodded. "I'd like you to take her to the station. I can't bring myself to do it."

"I don't know what to say. But if it will help, of course I'll take her to the station.

What happened?"

"I don't wish to talk about it. It's too painful."

"Yes, I'm sure it is. What time do I need to pick her up?"

"Around 8." Erich handed him an envelope. "Here is her ticket and some money."

Franz stopped and caught Erich's eye. "Does Johanna know I'm taking her to the station?"

"No. But I instructed Frau Liedig to make sure Johanna is ready at 8." A bitter smile settled on his face. "You should have seen the look on Frau Liedig's face. I don't know who was more upset by this — me or her. Anyway, Johanna is supposed to be ready."

"Are you sure you don't want to . . ."

Erich shook his head. "I can't. It's over. I think it best if I never see her again."

Franz exhaled, his breath forming a large, white cloud. "Is there anything I can do to help you?"

"No. Just take Johanna to the station."

"Yes, of course."

"Thank you, Franz. You're a good friend."

Franz nodded and walked to his car. Erich watched as he got in and drove off into the frigid dawn.

Johanna was surprised when Franz showed up to take her to the station, but she tried to hide it. She sat in silence as Erich's friend drove her through Berlin's morning traffic. The car's tires whispered through the new snow, not yet dirty or packed. Franz parked and carried the bags in for her, turning them over to a porter. His farewell seemed cool to her but mercifully short. Then he was gone, leaving her alone in the chilly, cavernous terminal.

She looked around, wondering if Erich would show up before she left. A vague sense of guilt nibbled at the edge of her mind, but she refused to acknowledge it. In a way she wanted to see Erich before she left, to bring closure to this part of her life. But she didn't expect him to come.

A sudden thought struck her. She had no idea what to do when she got to Frankfurt. She would go to her father's house, but after that what? Where would Erich open her account, and when would he do it? And would he really do it, or might he change his mind? She felt a clammy chill that had nothing to do with the temperature inside the station.

The loudspeaker announced the express to Frankfurt. She boarded and took a seat by a window. Soon afterward the train pulled out of the terminal and into the gray day that so fit her mood. The day became even darker as the snow began falling hard.

A sudden noise jarred Johanna from her uneasy slumber. For a few moments she did not know where she was or what had awakened her. She heard the train's screaming brakes and the rumbling explosions at the same time. She put her head against the window and looked forward. Icy fear stabbed her as she saw black clouds spring up in the distance, a startling contrast to the blanket of white. The ground shook as the ominous dark puffs drew closer. She knew it was enemy bombers. Johanna could see the entire front of the train as it slid to a stop on a curve entering the outskirts of Frankfurt. A forest, its branchy canopies heavy with snow, stood on the right, while a road ran along the other side of the tracks.

Frantic passengers jumped to their feet. The conductor rushed forward from the back of the carriage.

"Everyone off the train!" he shouted as he passed. "Take shelter under the trees."

He was gone before Johanna could say anything.

She followed the others out of the carriage and jumped down. The snow covered the tops of her shoes as she ran for the trees. The marching explosions drew closer, each one shaking the ground like an approaching giant.

Johanna looked up as she reached the shelter of a large oak tree. She heard the droning rumble of the bombers. The high, thin overcast did nothing to obscure their targets, though heavy clouds on the horizon promised more snow before long. White streamers trailed behind the four-engine planes flying in formation. Black puffs of smoke sprouted overhead as the antiaircraft artillery tried to knock them down. Johanna gasped when one plane was hit. She watched as it slowly spiraled out of formation. Tiny white parachutes appeared as the crewmen bailed out. But most of the bombers rumbled on.

The bombs marched ever closer, much too close. Johanna's knees shook, and she placed her hands over her ears. A bomb erupted in an orange-red flash less than a hundred feet away, the sound deafening even through her hands. The explosion tossed snow, dirt, and trees upward.

Johanna fell down and tried to bury her face in the freezing snow. The stench of cordite rolled over her like the hot breath of death. The next bomb lifted her several inches off the ground. She cried out as she heard shrapnel scream past her.

The quaking explosions seemed to go on forever, and with each one Johanna feared her life was over. Her heart pounded as she waited for the end. She heard the sound of splintered wood and twisted metal behind her but was afraid to look. Gradually the terrifying sounds began to diminish, then stopped completely.

Johanna rolled onto her side, oblivious of the wetness of the snow. She gasped when she saw the extent of the destruction. The war had suddenly become very personal. Ugly brown craters pockmarked the new fallen snow like giant footprints. One bomb had hit the last carriage on the train, twisting it and the rails into grotesque scrap.

The conductor dashed through the snow. "Back on the train!" he shouted as he struggled to catch his breath. "Everyone back on the train!" A gust of icy wind flipped his hat off and sent it rolling over the snow, ending up in a bomb crater.

Johanna struggled to her feet, brushing

clods of frozen earth out of her hair. She ran awkwardly toward her carriage as the engineer and fireman struggled to uncouple the ruined last car. The conductor raced back to examine the rails under the car in front of it. Johanna boarded her carriage only to find a woman with two small children in her seat. The woman started to get up.

"We were in the last carriage," she explained.

A man several seats away got up quickly. "Please, take my seat," he said to Johanna.

She nodded and staggered past. The woman sat back down with her children in numb gratitude. In a few minutes the train lurched forward, resuming its interrupted trip. When they pulled into the Frankfurt station, everything seemed normal — except for the passengers' dirty clothes and haunted looks. Johanna wondered if she looked the same to them.

She stepped down from the train carriage and stretched her legs. It was cold inside the station. She sighed as she examined her ruined stockings and shoes and her wet, soiled coat. She signaled to a porter and told him where to find her bags. She took a change of stockings, gloves, and shoes into the rest room and repaired the damage as best she could. She stood before the mirror and brushed the clinging dirt off her coat. She paused to examine her work and was pleasantly surprised. Except for a damp overcoat, she looked quite presentable. She disposed of the ruined articles and returned to the terminal.

The porter stood patiently by Johanna's bags. She tossed her head as she tried to shake off the bone-weariness of the ordeal. She longed to get to her father's house where she could rest and try to recover from what had happened. She thought about calling Christabel but decided she would do that later.

She led the porter outside to the line of waiting taxis. The frigid wind took her breath away. She stepped carefully over the icy sidewalk.

The first driver jumped out and opened the trunk for the porter. Johanna opened her purse and pulled out the envelope Erich had given Franz. She saw a flicker of movement out of the corner of her eye. As she turned toward it, a blurred body raced past and plucked the envelope out of her hand.

"Stop!" she shouted.

Mindless of the snow and ice, the thief tore across the street, expertly dodging traffic. The young boy made it to the other side, raced to the corner, and disappeared around it.

Johanna saw a policeman emerging from the station.

"That boy stole my money!" she shouted. She pointed to the corner where he had disappeared.

The policeman nodded and ran in pursuit.

The porter shook his head. "He will not catch him."

"He took all my money. How am I to get home?"

"That I don't know," the porter said with a sigh. "If you will excuse me, I don't think there is anything further I can do for you." He left her and went back inside.

The cab driver scowled as he slammed his trunk and got back inside his car. Johanna ignored him and looked around, wondering how she would get home. She noticed a tram stopped in front of the terminal and briefly thought of asking the driver if he would let her ride for free but could not bring herself to ask.

Suddenly everything she had been through came crashing down on her. Tears welled in her eyes as she fought for the last vestiges of self-control. Through her blurred vision she saw an elderly man in work clothes approaching from the street. He was of medium height and had a solid build, but no indication of fat. He stopped before her and tipped his cap.

"I saw what happened," he said. "I'm so sorry. Is there anything I can do to help?"

The tone of his voice surprised her. She looked up into his kind, blue eyes and saw the evident concern. She wiped her tears away with her gloves.

"Thank you, but what can you do? That boy took all my money. I have no way to get home."

He pointed toward the street. "That's my tram. You're welcome to ride with me — there will be no charge."

Johanna glanced at the streetcar. It was the very line that went by her father's house. However, this was *not* how she would have chosen to return home. She knew she could get someone to call her father, but she was reluctant to do that.

"Thank you. I think I'll accept your kind offer."

He grabbed her bags and led the way back to the tram, then placed the luggage on an empty seat. Johanna took a seat near the driver. He released the brake and twisted the power lever. The electric motor whined to life, and the tram rumbled down the tracks.

"Is anything wrong?" he asked softly, making sure no one else could hear. He glanced back quickly, then resumed his vigilant watch for pedestrians and traffic.

Johanna looked around the nearly empty car in shock. "No," she said in a harsh whisper. "Why ever would you ask such a thing?"

He did not look back. "Forgive me . . . I meant no harm. You just seemed so upset — more upset than . . ."

"More upset than what?" she snapped, forgetting to keep her voice down.

"Than merely losing your money."

She glared at the back of his head. "I would say losing my money is *quite* important." Her mind dwelt briefly on the bombing raid. "But yes, there is more. The enemy bombed the train I was on, and I'm lucky to be alive."

"Yes, I see," the driver said. "I'm glad you were spared. But even so, some things are even more important than a narrow escape."

It surprised Johanna how calmly he said this, but then, it was not *his* money or *his* life. "Like what?" she demanded, her voice laced with sarcasm.

"Your soul," the motorman said simply.

For a long time she could say nothing. The tram stopped at an intersection, and a sour-faced old woman got off. Two middle-aged working men got on and walked to the back. The motorman rang the bell and started the tram moving forward.

"You sound just like my husband," Johanna muttered.

"He's a Christian then?"

"He says he is, but he doesn't take it seriously. He never goes to church."

"What about you?"

"I don't share his superstitions."

His glance was brief, but Johanna was surprised at the concern she saw there. "Oh, I'm sorry to hear you say that," he said, turning back. "It's not superstition. God *does* exist, and He loves you."

"I don't wish to discuss it."

"As you will," he said softly.

The tram left Frankfurt's central business district, turned south, and clattered up onto the bridge that crossed the Main River. Ahead lay Sachsenhausen, where apartment buildings soon gave way to stylish housing sections. Johanna watched the familiar neighborhoods drift past, each one more elegant than the last, each one decked out in white finery. Finally she saw her stop ahead.

"This is where I get off," she told the driver.

He glanced at her luggage. "Have you far to go?" he asked with concern.

"A few blocks only."

"I'll carry your bags to the corner, but I can't go any farther from my tram. I'm sorry."

A tall young man came forward to get off. "Permit me, fräulein. I'm getting off here." He tipped his hat and grabbed her bags.

Johanna stiffened. "I am *Frau* von Arendt." She considered the heavy bags, then lowered her voice. "But if you would help me with these, I'd appreciate it. My parents' home is only a few streets away."

"Of course, *Frau* von Arendt," he said with a nod.

The motorman stopped the tram and set the brake. Johanna started past him.

"A moment please," he said.

He pulled a scrap of paper out of his pocket and wrote quickly with a short stub of a pencil.

"If my wife or I can help in any way . . ." he said, handing her the note.

She looked up into his kind eyes, debating on whether to take it. Then she tucked it into her purse and followed the young man off the tram and back into the blustery January day. They looked an unlikely couple as he struggled with her heavy luggage. Two blocks later she led him up to the steps, fortunately cleared of snow. He put the bags down. He tipped his hat and turned to leave when the front door opened.

Walther Kammler walked slowly to the edge of the porch as if unsure who was invading his walk. His blue eyes peered down at the intruders through his glasses.

"Johanna? Is that you?" He frowned as he took a closer look at the other person standing there. "Who is that with you?"

The man looked like he wanted to run.

"Just someone who was on the tram with me. He was kind enough to carry my bags."

"Carry your bags? What are you doing here?"

"If you'll pardon me," the man said, "I really must go." He spun on his heels and hurried back to the street.

Elsa came through the door and joined her husband. "Johanna, what . . . ?"

"Mama, it's cold out here. May I come

213

in out of the wind?"

"Of course, dear."

Walther frowned as Johanna walked past. Elsa held the door open.

The butler stepped onto the porch. "I'll get the bags," Herr Exner said as he passed his employer.

"Leave them!" Walther said as he turned to go inside.

"I beg your pardon, sir?"

"I said leave them!" Walther thundered.

The butler scurried back inside.

Walther stepped through the door and slowly closed it. He glared at Johanna over the top of his glasses. "In my study, if you please," he said. Johanna and her mother entered the richly paneled room. "Sit," Walther said as he closed the door.

"Papa . . ." Johanna began.

"Why have you come?"

The events of the past few days whirled in her mind. The tears came, and she reached into her purse for a handkerchief. "Papa, I had no choice. My life was miserable in Berlin. Erich was working all the time, I never got to go out . . ."

He shook his finger at her. "Enough of this! Don't think you will fool me with your hysterical blather. Tell me what happened. Why are you here?"

Elsa glanced at Johanna. "Walther, perhaps you're being too hard on our daughter."

"You will leave this to me, Elsa. We've been through this before. As a married woman, Johanna has certain responsibilities, and we will *not* help her evade them." Those hard blue eyes turned on Johanna. His tone was low and menacing. "Now, tell me what happened, and stick to the facts."

"Erich and I had a fight. He said since he couldn't win my love I was to go."

"Am I to understand he's divorcing you?"

She shook her head. "No. He said his vows before God wouldn't allow him to."

"So you left him?"

She nodded, wiping a tear from her eye. "He said I should return to Frankfurt. He said he would provide me living money in a bank account."

Walther turned to the window. He watched as the snow started falling again, tiny flakes that swirled about in the wind, apparently having as little stability or foundation as his foolish daughter.

"Dear, what are we to do?" Elsa asked.

He turned and faced them. "We? Elsa,

we have nothing to do with this. Our daughter has made her decision. She has left her husband . . ."

"He *told* me to go," Johanna interrupted.

"Enough! Don't try any of your tricks on me. You gave Erich no choice. You *forced* him to let you go. Now you will have to live with the consequences. You will leave this house at once."

"Walther!" Elsa cried out. "You can't . . ."

"Silence! Get up, Johanna."

"Papa, it's snowing outside!"

"The tram is still running."

"I have no money."

He pulled out his wallet and handed her several bank notes. "Here. Now go."

Elsa got to her feet, her eyes pleading, but her husband ignored her. Johanna got up and walked slowly from the room. Her stomach churned as her mind clawed desperately for a way out. Where could she go? She was not ready for this. She had expected to make her plans from the comfort of her father's house.

Walther jerked the door open, allowing no further appeal. Johanna looked at him as she slipped past. The door closed with a solid thump. The snowfall was heavier now, and her bags were already covered with a thin white coating. The wind whipped around the eaves and tugged at her coat. She shivered as she stepped down from the porch and walked into the gathering storm.

Nine

Johanna examined the reichsmarks her father had given her. It was enough for tram fare and a few meals, but nothing more. She certainly could not afford to stay in a hotel. Her mind raced as she tried to decide what to do. It was snowing harder now. She pulled her coat tighter, but the wind seemed to cut right through it. She shivered. She had no idea when Erich would set up her account or how she would manage until he did. What if he decided *not* to provide the account? The wind felt even colder with that thought.

She thought of the odd tram driver but immediately dismissed the impulse that sprang into her mind. Lacking a plan, she picked up her two bags, gasping at their weight. She considered leaving them, but her pride would not allow her father that victory. Wheezing with the effort, she struggled out onto the sidewalk.

The tram stop seemed miles away as she trudged along. The bags rubbed against her legs, chafing them painfully. She found she could only walk a few paces until she had to drop her burden. But after each stop, she grabbed the handles again and continued on, her determination fueled by her anger at her father and at Erich. After what seemed like forever, she finally made it to the corner. She gratefully dropped the bags and struggled to catch her breath.

It was snowing much harder now. The frigid wind quickly stole away the body warmth from the exertion of her difficult walk. She shivered violently. She heard the tram before she saw it, the clanging bell and the whir of the electric motor piercing the curtain of snow. Then she saw the dim shape of the city-bound tram emerging from the gray. Its brakes squealed as the driver slowed down. Johanna grabbed her bags with determined energy and staggered into the street. Unfortunately, her right foot hit a slick spot, and her feet flew out from under her. She fell on her back, groaning as the impact knocked the wind out of her despite the heavy layer of snow.

She heard the rapid crunching of boots. She twisted her head up to see the motorman approaching. He slid to a stop, almost falling himself.

"Are you hurt?" he asked.

"No," she snapped in exasperation. "I'm fine. If you'll just help me up . . ."

"Yes, of course."

He took her hand and steadied her as she regained her feet. He took the bags and led her to the tram. She boarded and took a seat next to the driver, thankful to be out of the cutting wind. There were only a few other passengers. She paid her fare and settled back in the hard seat, then looked out through the frosty window.

Her stomach felt like a chunk of ice. Where could she go? What would happen to her? Having only a few reichsmarks certainly limited her options. She thought of the other tram driver. He had been very kind, but she resisted the idea of accepting help from someone she didn't really know, especially a common working man. As the tram crossed the Main River, Johanna looked down but could barely see the water through the snow.

The closer she came to the city center, the more desperate she became. Finally she pulled out the scrap of paper listing the driver's name, Wilhelm Hoffmann, and his address. She didn't recognize the name of the street but assumed it was one of the smaller streets in the heart of Frankfurt.

She stood up at the next stop. The driver looked at her in surprise, staring at her fine clothing. Johanna blushed as she showed him the scrap of paper.

"Do you know this address?" she asked.

"You're a friend of Wilhelm's?"

Johanna glanced around quickly to make sure no one else could hear. "Yes . . . I mean, no. I only met him today. He said . . . he said he would . . . help me."

The man nodded. "That sounds like Wilhelm." He released the brake and started the tram forward. "Get off at the next stop. Turn right at the corner, go down three streets, and turn left. He lives in an apartment about halfway to the next street. He's still working, but I'm sure his wife, Karoline, will be home."

She peered through the front windows of the tram. The heavy snow draped everything with a smooth, white blanket. The wind gusted, swirling the powdery curtain into evanescent shapes. The brakes squealed, and the tram slowed. Johanna turned when she heard heavy footsteps approaching from the back.

"A moment please," the driver said to the workman. "Would you be so kind as to help this lady with her bags? She has no one to help her."

The man's eyes grew round in surprise but quickly recovered. "Why, yes, of course. I'll be happy to."

221

Johanna showed him the address.

"Yes, I know where that is," he said. "Just follow me." He glanced at her expensive shoes. "Watch your step. It's very slick out there."

Johanna felt momentary irritation but simply nodded.

He grabbed her bags and stepped down from the tram. She followed, taking great care as she left the relative security of the tram's bottom step. The deep snow enveloped her feet, chilling her instantly. She felt the icy powder work its way into her shoes and start melting. She trudged after the workman, trying to stay within his large footprints. Her feet were soaked before she had gone one block. Her companion seemed indifferent to the weather as he plodded along effortlessly. Occasionally he glanced back to make sure she was keeping up.

Gusts buffeted Johanna, threatening to blow her down. The icy wind brought tears to her eyes, and she wiped them away as best she could with frozen gloves. Her face felt stiff and partially numb. She longed for shelter as she staggered along the deserted street. There was no traffic of any kind. The man crossed at an intersection, and she followed him as they entered a narrow side street with brick buildings on each side. Midway down the block he stopped before a worn door, then held it open for her.

"This is the address," he said. "The apartment you want is on the second floor. I'll carry your bags up for you."

"Thank you," she said, slurring her words.

She stepped into the hallway and stamped her feet to get rid of the clinging snow. She almost fell as her right foot came down on a piece of ice. The workman reached out and steadied her. His touch surprised her and, it seemed to her, embarrassed him.

She led the way upstairs and found the Hoffmanns' apartment. The workman put the bags down and waited as Johanna stared at the closed door. Finally she knocked. In a few moments she heard movement inside. The door opened, and a short, heavyset woman stood before them with searching eyes. Despite the dreary day, her eyes sparkled.

"May I help you?" she asked in a way that made Johanna believe she really meant it.

"I don't know where to start." She paused as she agonized over what to say. "Your husband . . ."

"Ah," the woman said, "you've met Wilhelm. Please come in." She looked past to the workman. "Forgive my lack of manners. I'm Karoline Hoffmann. Come in, both of you, and warm up. Let me prepare something to eat."

The man touched a hand to his cap. "Thank you for your kindness, but I must be going." He picked up the bags and set them inside.

"Thank you so much," Karoline said.

Johanna turned to him. "Oh, yes. Thank you for helping me." She reached into her purse. "I don't have much, but let me give you something for your trouble."

The man stiffened. "Nothing for me, thank you. I'm glad I could be of service." He turned to go.

"Well, thank you," Johanna repeated, her hand still inside her purse.

The man nodded and headed for the stairs. Karoline closed the door.

"I think I offended him," Johanna said.

"Helping others is a gift of God — to both."

"I don't understand."

"We'll discuss it later. May I ask your name, dear?"

"Oh, yes, of course. Forgive me. I'm Johanna . . ."

"Yes?" Karoline prompted after a few moments.

"I'm Johanna von Arendt."

Karoline's smile never wavered. "I'm so pleased to meet you, Johanna. Now, I suspect you'll want to change into dry clothing. Are you hungry?"

Johanna felt the last of her energy drain away. "Oh, yes! I'm starving."

"We'll attend to that. You can change your clothes in there." Karoline pointed to the bedroom. "I'll prepare some bread and tea."

Johanna opened one of her bags and took out fresh clothing. She changed quickly in the Hoffmanns' bedroom, grateful to be out of her wet things. A few minutes later she came into the compact dining area. Karoline entered from the kitchen carrying a tray with bread, plates, and tea. She placed the cups, saucers, and plates before setting the bread in the center.

"Please sit down," she said. "I'm afraid there's no sugar or lemon, but I'm sure we can make do."

They sat down, and Karoline bowed her head. "Lord, we thank You for this food and Your gracious providence. Please bless Johanna — You know her needs. I ask You to help her. In Jesus' name, Amen."

Johanna tried to smile. "Thank you for your kind thought."

"It's more than a thought, dear. It's a prayer."

Karoline took a thin slice of black bread and put it on her own plate. The other two slices were thicker, and each had a thin smear of butter.

"You've given me too much," Johanna said.

"Not at all. You're hungry after being out in this weather. I've been snug inside all day. Eat. It's good for you."

Johanna took a slice of bread and broke it. It was all she could do to refrain from gulping it down. She finished the entire slice before tasting the tea. Then she picked up her cup and sipped. The tea was hot and good, despite there being no sugar.

"This is wonderful," she said as she started on the second slice of bread.

"I'm glad you like it. Thank you for being my company on such a cold winter day."

Johanna struggled with her uneasiness. "Why are you helping me? You don't know me."

"I believe God brought you to my husband, and he sensed your need."

"I don't know about that. He wrote down your address when I left his tram to go visit . . ." She paused and looked down into the bottom of her cup . . . . "my parents." She was silent for a long time.

Karoline waited patiently. "Is there anything you want to tell me, dear?" she asked finally.

Johanna shook her head. Tears welled up in her eyes, and she wiped at them angrily with her napkin. She did not want to display weakness before this woman. She reflected on the unexpected reaction of her father but decided it really didn't matter. She would have her own bank account soon enough — unless Erich decided not to keep his promise. She shook that thought off. She knew him better than that. He always kept his word.

"Do you want to rest then?" Karoline asked gently.

"Yes."

Karoline got up. "I'll make you a bed on the couch. The toilet is at the end of the hall if you want to wash up. I can get you a towel if you want to bathe."

Johanna shook her head. "I'll just freshen up a little. I'm too tired to take a bath right now."

The toilet was cramped but clean. Johanna hurriedly washed her face and brushed out her hair. When she returned to the apartment, Karoline had her bed ready.

"Try to get some rest," Karoline said. "I'll be as quiet as a mouse. Do you want me to wake you when Wilhelm gets home? That's when we have dinner."

"Yes, please."

"I'll call you then."

Karoline disappeared into the bedroom and closed the door. Johanna prepared for bed quickly. Moments after crawling under the sheets she was fast asleep.

Johanna opened her eyes. At first she didn't know where she was. Then she saw Karoline standing by the couch, bundled up in a heavy sweater.

"Wilhelm is home," she announced. "He's in the bedroom, so you can get dressed now."

Karoline went into the kitchen. Johanna got up hurriedly and put on her dress. Since it was cold, she put on her coat as well. She shivered as she joined her hostess in the kitchen.

"I was going to suggest that," Karoline said. "Our coal ration doesn't allow us to heat the apartment all the time. Wilhelm will be out shortly. Then we'll eat."

He entered the kitchen still in his work clothes. He nodded at their guest. "Good evening, Johanna. Karoline told me your name when I got home. I'm sorry things didn't work out with your parents."

Karoline swatted at him with a hot pot holder. "Hush. She's upset enough without you making matters worse."

"It doesn't matter," Johanna said without feeling.

Karoline stirred a pot of potato soup on the burner. Sliced black bread was already on the table. The soup's aroma melded with the pungent odor of ersatz coffee.

"That smells good," Wilhelm said. He cast an eye at the coffeepot. "The soup anyway."

"And it's ready," his wife replied. "Sit down, both of you."

Wilhelm held Johanna's chair, then seated himself. Karoline ladled steaming soup into all their bowls. When she sat down, Wilhelm thanked the Lord for their food. Johanna watched him as he offered his simple prayer. She could not escape the disconcerting conviction that he believed in the One he prayed to. He finished and found her looking at him.

"Is something the matter?" he asked.

"Oh, no," she stammered. "It's just . . ."

"Just what?"

"Well, it seems you really think someone is hearing you."

"Someone *is* hearing me — God."

"Oh, I see."

He smiled. "I hope someday you will."

She looked up sharply, wondering if he was making fun of her. But she saw from the deep compassion in his eyes that he wasn't. She shivered.

They ate mostly in silence. Johanna felt self-conscious. The Hoffmanns seemed to welcome her, but she still felt out of place. There was, she realized, the social difference between them, but she knew it was more than that. Finally the meal was over, and they got up.

"Karoline and I usually read the Bible together after dinner," Wilhelm said. "You're welcome to join us."

"No, thank you," Johanna replied. "There's a book in one of my bags."

"Then we'll retire to the bedroom so we won't disturb you. If there's anything you need, please let us know."

Johanna felt ashamed as she saw the concern in his eyes. "I have everything I need. You've been so kind, though you don't even know me. Thank you."

"Don't thank us. Thank the Lord. He's the One who provides."

"Well, yes, of course," she said to be polite.

Wilhelm helped Karoline with the dishes, then they both retired to the bedroom. Johanna pulled out her novel and began to read. It was a story about a society rake and his adventures in the Berlin nightlife of the 1920s. She read a few pages, then put it down. The book had been interesting enough when she'd started it, but she just couldn't get into it this evening. She decided to get ready for bed.

Saturday dawned cold but clear. A bright blue sky dotted with fluffy white clouds greeted Johanna as she looked out the dining area window. Wilhelm came in from his trip to the toilet, toweling the soap from his face. Karoline clattered away in the kitchen, preparing their breakfast.

"I have the next two days off," Wilhelm said to Johanna. "Is there anything I can do to help?"

"No, thank you."

"Well, what will you be doing today?"

Karoline looked in from the kitchen.

"Wilhelm! Mind your own business!"

He glanced her way, then turned back to Johanna. "I think she means it."

"I do."

He laughed. "Shall we see what we have for breakfast?"

By midmorning Johanna made up her mind. Since the weather was clear, she decided to visit her friend Christabel. She longed to see Ulrich but knew he'd moved. Perhaps Christabel would know where. She examined her change. She had enough for tram fare both ways.

"I'm going to see a friend," Johanna called out.

Wilhelm and Karoline came out of their bedroom.

"Very good," Wilhelm replied. "One of us will be here all day if you need anything."

"Thank you."

Johanna hurried down the stairs with renewed energy. Outside, the crisp, cold air invigorated her as she walked along the sidewalks. Most of them had been shoveled. Only the streets made for difficult walking.

The tram ride to Christabel's was pleasant. Johanna hummed softly as she walked up the four flights to her friend's apartment. She knocked and waited and a minute later tried again. She knew Christabel still lived there because she had checked the registry downstairs. Johanna debated on whether to wait or come back later to try again. Finally she decided to return to the Hoffmanns'. Her friend, she knew, frequently stayed away for extended lengths of time.

She walked back down to the lobby and out into the cold. On the way back to the tram stop it occurred to her that the White Cat Club was nearby, and she had enough money to go there and return to the Hoffmanns'. She took the tram and got off at the familiar sign with a white cat on it. The doorway looked as bad as it had the last time she'd been there. She rapped on the door and waited. The shade slid to the side, and a familiar face peered out. It was the same young man she'd seen the last time.

"Let me in," Johanna demanded. "I have to see Ulrich. Is he in?"

The man opened the door for her.

"I don't know. I just got here myself. I suppose he's in his dressing room. You know the way?"

"Oh, yes," she assured him. Actually she

didn't, but she didn't want to admit it.

He nodded and disappeared into the back.

Johanna waited a few moments for her eyes to adjust to the dim interior. Then she made her way through the tiny tables and past the empty stage. She stopped and listened. She heard a phonograph playing somewhere. She followed the sound back into a dark corridor. It seemed to be coming from the last door. She tiptoed up to it and listened. All she could hear was the clear piano strains of Claude Debussy's *Clair de Lune*. She smiled. This was one of their favorite pieces. It was almost as if Fate had arranged it for their reunion. Johanna's pulse quickened, and she felt the delightful touch of desire for the first time in so long.

She opened the door and stepped in. Johanna gasped, her eyes round in shock as she gaped at the two heads turned toward her. She recognized the singer she had seen the last time she'd been to the White Cat. The young woman uncoiled herself from Ulrich and stood up. She hurried past Johanna as if afraid she might be struck. Ulrich's startled expression dissolved into angry disgust.

"Just what do you think you're doing

here?" he demanded as he got up off the couch.

The tears came so quickly, there was no way Johanna could stop them. Cutting herself off from Erich, the bombing of the train, her father's heartless rejection, and now this merged together into a whirlpool of despair. With each racking sob she felt her heart would stop beating forever. The idyllic strains of *Clair de Lune* continued in the background. Ulrich stomped over to the phonograph and angrily moved the needle across the record. Johanna winced at the savage scratching sound. She stared at Ulrich through a blur of tears.

"Ulrich, how could you? I thought somehow perhaps you still loved me . . ."

He approached her cautiously. "How could I what? You are a married woman, Johanna. You and I are no longer together. How dare you invade my privacy!"

"But I didn't love *him*. I always loved *you*."

"You're not making sense! If your father could have accepted me — a most unlikely situation — there might have been a chance for us. But not otherwise."

"Is that all I meant to you? Just a way to get at my father's money?"

He shook his head. "You never change,

do you? You seem to think the world was created just for you."

She glared at him. "Answer me!"

"Oh, now we're demanding, are we? If you really must know, yes, I was interested in your father's money. Johanna, you can be such an incredible nuisance! Do you not realize how incredibly selfish you are?"

"But we had such good times together. You have no idea how much I *wanted* you!"

He laughed. "So now we get to love, do we? You're so naïve. We never *did* anything, Johanna. You know absolutely nothing about loving a man, believe me."

"But . . ."

"If you expected to waltz in here and find me waiting for you, you're more of a fool than I thought."

"How can you say that?"

"Because it's true."

The last dregs of hope for love and happiness were draining away, and she could do nothing to stop it. Johanna threw herself on the couch and buried her head in her arms. She sobbed, the pain so intense she could hardly breathe. When she could stand it no longer, she gasped for air. She tried to speak, but at first no words would come. Ulrich stood there helplessly.

"I've lost everything," she managed finally. "Erich sent me away. The enemy bombed the train I was on. I finally got home, and my own father threw me out. And now this." She raised her head and stared at him. "What am I to do, Ulrich?"

He sighed. "That's your affair and not my concern. I will no longer play the game."

She lowered her head again. "Then I guess this is good-bye."

"Yes, I'm afraid it is. I feel sorry for you, Johanna, but yes, it's over. You must make your own way now."

It was still bright when she got outside, but a dark shadow had fallen over her heart. Her one last hope was gone, and she could see no way out of her despair.

Ten

Johanna stood on the street and tried to gather her thoughts. She dabbed angrily at her tears as the wind whipped around the corner and stung her cheeks. It felt much colder now. The earlier blue skies had given way to dingy gray. Heavy snow clouds marched along, dropping lower by the moment. The light sprinkling of snow soon became a suffocating curtain of white. She shivered and drew her coat closely about herself.

Her mind searched frantically for a safe haven, now that Ulrich had rejected her. She thought about returning to Christabel's but doubted her friend would be back yet. Her remaining money was enough to get her back to the Hoffmanns', but that was all. She thought about the only ones who had shown her any kindness. She did appreciate their help, but they definitely were not her kind of people. She knew she had to get away, make a life for herself somewhere, but that could not happen until Erich set up her account. And Monday was the earliest she could find out about that.

She pouted as she made her way to the tram stop. The wait was mercifully short as the wind drove a chill deep into her bones. She boarded the tram. All the seats were taken, but an elderly gentleman got up and gave her his seat. She nodded brusquely and sat down. The tram ground its way along through the deepening snow. By the time Johanna reached the Hoffmanns' stop, the car was almost stalled.

Johanna gasped as a fresh gust stole her breath away and threatened to knock her down. She lowered her head and trudged across the street and down the covered sidewalks. She tried not to think of how numb her cheeks were. Sharp pains stabbed her ears with the threat of frostbite. She cupped her hands over them, but that only made them hurt worse. She hit some hidden ice and fell heavily. She struggled to her feet and continued on.

She began to suspect she had missed the street, but finally it appeared. She quickened her pace, her breath coming in painful gasps. She ducked into the entrance and stamped the snow off her shoes. She walked slowly to the second floor and paused. She had not planned it this way. She had envisioned finding a new place to stay — if not with Ulrich, at least with Christabel — sending for her bags later. She knocked, and after a few moments Karoline opened the door.

The older woman smiled with obvious relief. "Come in. I was beginning to worry about you out in this horrible weather."

The apartment seemed almost as cold as the outside, but at least there was no wind. Johanna shivered.

Karoline shook her head. "You've caught a chill, dear. Come over here and sit down."

Johanna obeyed, her limbs still stiff from the cold. She grimaced as she sat by the dead fireplace. Karoline lifted the remaining chunk of coal from the pail and placed it on the grate. She prepared kindling and soon had a weak fire going. Gradually the coal began to burn. Karoline pulled some quilts from the hall closet and piled them on her guest.

"Is that better?" she asked.

Johanna nodded. "Yes. Thank you."

"That's good." The older woman prodded at the fire with the poker. "Did your plans go well this morning?"

Johanna considered ignoring the question but found she couldn't. She shook her head. "No, no, they didn't."

"Oh, I'm sorry, dear. I don't mean to pry, but is there anything I can do?"

"No. There's nothing *anyone* can do."

Karoline sighed. "Much of life is that way, Johanna. But God can help you through it, if you give Him the chance."

"I don't want to talk about it."

"Maybe later."

Johanna only shrugged.

Karoline glanced at the fire. "You should be feeling some warmth now. Stay there until you feel better. Can I get you anything?"

Johanna shook her head.

Wilhelm returned at dusk. He pulled off his gloves but left his coat on. Karoline came in from the kitchen. He kissed her and turned to Johanna, who was still bundled up in quilts.

"How was your day?" he asked.

"Not now," Karoline interrupted. "She needs her rest. Now, you go get ready for dinner."

He nodded, got a towel, and made a quick trip to the communal toilet in the hall. When he returned, Karoline ushered them to the table. Johanna savored her soup. She found it hard to look these simple people in the eye, especially since they were the only ones who had shown her kindness since her arrival in Frankfurt.

After Karoline cleared the dishes away, the three sat back and drank their coffee.

"I don't think I will ever get used to this ersatz stuff," Wilhelm said, making a face.

"Nor me," Johanna agreed.

"But I suppose it's better than nothing." His expression turned serious. "I don't know what you're going through, and I certainly don't wish to pry. But I want you to know that Karoline and I *do* care. God wants us to live our lives in joy, not in misery." He paused. "I think He's trying to reach you, Johanna. Why not give Him a chance?"

She closed her eyes and shook her head.

"Well, we'll pray for you. We go to church on Sunday mornings. Would you like to come with us? It doesn't hurt to listen."

"Thank you for your kindness, but no."

He nodded. "As you will." He glanced at his wife with a twinkle in his eye. "You'll find us not very exciting people on a Saturday evening. I normally read, and Karoline works on one of her projects. If you'd like your privacy we can retire to our bedroom."

"Oh, no," she said quickly. "I . . . I think

I'd like having company. I can read my novel."

"A quiet evening it is, then."

Karoline set up her quilting frame, found where she had stopped, and continued with her tiny, precise stitches. Johanna found it relaxing to watch the quilt's pattern slowly forming.

Johanna thought Sunday would never end. She got up with the Hoffmanns and ate breakfast with them. Then she sat by herself in the cold apartment while they went to church. She thought there might be something interesting to do that afternoon or evening, but it soon became apparent that her hosts savored their day of rest. She tried to read her novel several times, but each time it simply did not keep her attention. Finally Karoline could stand it no longer.

"Dear, it distresses me to see you so unhappy. Is there not something we can do?"

Johanna knew tears were close but was determined to hold them back. "No. You and Wilhelm have been so kind, and you don't even know me."

Karoline smiled. "It's our pleasure, dear. Jesus said we are to love God and each other. It's amazing how that changes life."

Johanna shrugged. "I'm glad that works for you."

"It works for anyone who gives it a try — who gives *Him* a try. I hope you find that out someday. But is there anything specific we can help you with?"

"Well, yes, but I'm embarrassed to ask."

"Please feel free. If we can help, we will."

"I tried to visit a friend on Saturday, but she was out. I'd like to try again tomorrow, but I don't have the tram fare."

"That's no problem," Wilhelm spoke up. "We'll give you the fare."

"I can repay you," Johanna said in a hurry. "My . . . a bank account is being set up for me. As soon as I find out where, I'll pay you back."

"I don't understand," Wilhelm began. "What . . ."

"And you don't need to, dear," Karoline interrupted. "Of course we'll help you, Johanna. We can talk about the other later, if you wish." She aimed an intense signal at her husband. He saw it and returned to his paper.

It was mid-morning by the time Johanna arrived at Christabel's door. A strong wind had blown the storm clouds away, but the beautiful blue skies did nothing to cheer her up. She knocked, half-expecting no answer. After a few moments the door opened a crack, then all the way.

"Johanna," her friend said in surprise. "Come in."

They went into the sitting room, where Johanna sat on the couch while Christabel took a chair by the window.

"I'm almost afraid to ask, but why have you come back to Frankfurt?"

Johanna closed her eyes briefly, emotionally drained for the moment. "It's a long story. Erich told me to leave."

"What!" Christabel gasped. She shook her head. "So he's divorcing you?"

Johanna shook her head. "No. He refuses to do that. But he said I was to return to Frankfurt. He's setting up a bank account for me."

"Does he have another . . ."

Johanna looked puzzled for a moment, then blushed. "No. There's no other woman."

"Are you sure?"

"Yes, I'm sure! Erich has many faults, but cheating on me is not one of them!"

"Take it easy. I'm just getting the facts straight."

"Christabel, what am I to do? I'm at my wit's end."

"I don't see the problem. You've never been happy with Erich, and now he's set you free and has even set up a bank account for you. Your father has that nice plush house with servants. Not bad — if you can forget about the war."

The tears came despite Johanna's determination not to cry. "You don't understand. My father threw me out of the house."

"Oh, my. Well, where are you staying?"

"A tram driver took me into his apartment."

"Johanna!"

"It's not like that! He and his wife are very nice. They're the only ones who have shown me kindness since this all happened." She paused. "There's more."

"This is like watching a circus."

"It's *not* funny!" Johanna snapped.

"I'm sorry. Please continue."

"I went to see Ulrich."

"Uh, oh. That wasn't a wise move."

"You knew he was involved with that . . . that tramp?"

Christabel sighed. "Johanna, you are so naïve."

"That's what *he* said."

"Johanna, did you really expect him to wait for you after you married Erich?"

"I don't want to talk about it."

"I could point out that *you* brought it up." She held up her hand when she saw her friend's reaction. "Forget it. So, what are you going to do?"

"Get in touch with Erich and find out where my account is, then find an apartment. Can you help me?"

"Johanna asking for help? This is certainly new."

"Please, Christabel. You're the only friend I have left."

"You're broke, right?"

Johanna nodded.

"OK, I'll advance you the money to call Erich, but you must pay me back. Times are hard."

"Oh, I will. Once I have my account, my troubles will be over."

"Oh, you think so," Christabel said with a short laugh. "Where are you planning to stay?"

"I'll rent an apartment."

"You won't find one in the city. There's a war on, Johanna. Housing is scarce, especially in Frankfurt. Too bad about your father. That would've been ideal."

"Yes, it would have," Johanna pouted. "But he rushed me out so quickly I didn't even have a chance to see Sophie." Suddenly she thought of her brother. "Or to hear about Bernhard. You knew he was in the army, didn't you?"

"You said they were calling him up in your last letter."

"Right. He's with the occupying forces in France, near Paris."

Christabel arched her eyebrows. "I guess there's worse duty."

"We're grateful, for now. But things could change. I know Mama's worried. I guess Papa is too, although he didn't write me much."

"I'm sorry for you, Johanna."

"Thank you. But right now I have to find a place to live. What am I to do?"

"Find someone to live with. That or go out into the countryside."

Johanna closed her eyes. She thought briefly about returning to Berlin but discarded the idea immediately. She could *never* do that, no matter what.

"Could I make a suggestion?" Christabel asked softly.

Johanna blinked. "Yes, I suppose so."

"Would you like to share expenses on my apartment? It might be a little snug for two, but it's a nice building with a great location."

"Oh, could I?" Johanna asked excitedly.

"Yes. But I'm serious about the expenses. We share everything, and no credit."

"Of course. I wouldn't have it any other way."

"Very well. Shall we go place your call to Berlin?"

Johanna remembered that phone call for a long time. Even with a bad connection, she could sense Erich's commitment to their separation. He gave her the name of the bank and said a curt good-bye. The two women went directly there, and Johanna drew out expenses for the first month. Then she and Christabel picked up the bags from the Hoffmanns'.

Much about this arrangement pleased Johanna, with a few exceptions. She and Christabel enjoyed the Frankfurt nightlife, attending the opera, plays, and musical presentations. Christabel had her own active social life, and she frequently went home with her male acquaintances. Johanna held back. She saw nothing wrong with the idea, but almost all the young men were in the army. There was nothing wrong with older men, she said to herself, but none of them seemed particularly interesting, despite the fact that many of them were obviously attracted to her. There had to be standards, she decided.

As winter gradually gave way to spring and early summer, Johanna tried to convince herself her life was looking up. True, she had not found a gentleman friend she cared for, but that would come in time. At least she was no longer chained to Erich. Although the enemy air raids were becoming more frequent, so far none had come close to where she and Christabel lived.

One June night Johanna looked up from her novel when she heard a distant rumble. At first she thought it was an approaching thunderstorm, but the shrill air raid siren dispelled that idea. She threw off the sheet on her cot in the living room, got up, and put her robe on. She looked back toward the bedroom. Christabel came out and padded over to the window in her bare feet. She pulled aside the curtains and peered out. Johanna joined her.

"Another false alarm," Christabel grumbled.

Johanna opened the window for a better view. "It looks closer this time. Look at the searchlights to the west. Maybe we should go to the shelter."

"You can if you want to. I'm staying here. It's late, and I don't feel like spending a sleepless night cooped up in a smelly shelter."

Searchlights continued to flash, ever closer to their building.

"The bombers are coming right at us," Johanna said in alarm.

"They'll miss us."

They could now hear the heavy rumble of the engines. The searchlight beams intersected on individual planes as the anti-aircraft artillery pounded away. Johanna gasped as she saw a bomber disappear in a brilliant orange flash. A few seconds later a second plane suffered the same fate. But the rest kept coming. A building a few blocks away erupted in a column of smoke. Flaming debris arced through the air, landing on nearby buildings. Red and orange flames licked up into the heavens, spreading rapidly. People poured out on the street, their screams drifting up from below. The raging fires made their way to the shelters. A woman carrying a little girl fell when a flaming timber tumbled onto her from above. She fell to the pavement and lay still. The child got up and looked down at her mother.

Johanna felt her blood run cold. "I'm leaving!" she shouted.

Christabel dashed for the bedroom.

"Wait while I grab my robe!"

Johanna hesitated. A bomb hit the building across the street. It disappeared in a cloud of smoke and dust. Sirens sounded in the distance.

Johanna ran for the door, threw it open, and dashed into the hall. All she could think about was the four long flights she had to descend to get to the street. She heard a faint whistling noise as she raced for the stairs. Wondering what it was even as she looked over her shoulder, she saw her friend start through the door at the same time that a blurred object crashed through the ceiling.

It all happened so quickly that only later did Johanna realize what it was. In an instant a dark shape smashed into Christabel before ripping through the floor. A moment later the deafening blast threw Johanna down, pounding the air from her lungs. She clamped her eyes shut. A split second later another blast lifted her off the trembling floor, throwing her about like a rag doll.

Terror gripped her as the building swayed beneath her. Her ears rang, and sounds seemed distorted and distant. She forced her eyes open. Fires in the next block provided an eerie glow, but she

couldn't see anything through the billow-
ing dust and smoke. Johanna gasped as a
hot wind blew the obscuring curtain away.
Both ends of the building had disappeared,
and ragged floorboards ended about
twenty feet away from her. She glanced
over her shoulder. She was roughly in the
middle of what was left of the tottering
structure. She tried not to think about how
high she was above the pavement.

A brick wall collapsed into the street,
sounding like a faint tinkling noise to her
impaired hearing. She heard something
else that puzzled her until she realized it
was the screams of those on the street. The
ruined building shifted, and for a moment
Johanna thought it too would come thundering down. She felt heat behind her. She
looked around and saw orange flames lick-
ing the exposed wood.

She struggled to stand. A floorboard
gave way under her left foot, and she
almost fell as she struggled to maintain her
balance. The intense heat at her back
urged her forward. She forced herself to
creep along the shattered floor toward the
drop-off. The closer she came, the harder
it was to make the next move.

Finally she stood less than two feet from
the abyss. Far below she could see a huge

mound of brick and splintered wood. People dashed among the wreckage as they tried desperately to get away. Johanna glanced back. The floor behind her was burning briskly, and she knew it would reach her in seconds. The floor lurched again. She looked up into the sky, where bright stars pierced the coal-black heavens. Searchlights slanted this way and that, but the bombers were gone. Johanna lowered her head, convinced she was most probably about to die.

"Help!" she screamed. Her voice sounded puny and lost in her ears.

She heard a strange groaning sound and looked around, but could not tell where it was coming from. Then she saw a drainpipe about a foot beyond where the building ended. The bent pipe sloped back toward what was still standing and scraped against the crumbling wall.

Johanna forced herself to inch forward again, steadying herself by gripping an exposed wooden post. She leaned out and looked down. The drainpipe was bent in several places, but it appeared to be attached to the wall. Whether it would bear her weight or not, she had no idea. The fire behind her popped, and Johanna screamed as a burning ember landed on her exposed leg. She flicked it away and looked again at the swaying pipe.

She slowly transferred her hold from the post to the pipe, gripped it with both hands, and swung her legs around. It swayed alarmingly, and for an instant Johanna, terrified, was sure it would collapse, throwing her to the street below. The bracket below her broke away, and the drainpipe leaned away from the wall and threatened to buckle. Johanna closed her eyes and waited. It held. She started inching her way down, trying to avoid making sudden moves.

It seemed to take forever. Johanna watched the flames engulf the structure above her. She could see the brick wall tottering. Increasing her pace, she passed the third floor and then the second. Finally she jumped down onto the rubble-strewn sidewalk. She dashed over the debris, not even noticing as the sharp edges cut her bare feet. People dashed past in every direction, screaming in terror. Johanna ran across the street. She looked toward where she had seen the little girl, but she was gone. Johanna kept going until she reached the next block, then looked back. Raging flames towered above the building. Then it crumbled and collapsed in a dust cloud capped with a torrent of flames and sparks.

Johanna fell down and wept. Chaos reigned all around her. The roaring flames and strident sirens provided a chilling background to the wailing misery she heard from every direction.

Eleven

Erich dropped the report to his desk as a quiet knock sounded at the door. The knob turned, and Bertha Liedig came in. "Herr Brant is here to see you," she said, making no attempt to hide her frown. Erich pretended not to notice,

"Thank you, Frau Liedig. Then I suppose he and I will be dining out."

"But I've prepared your dinner, Herr von Arendt."

"I'm sorry, but I didn't know if Franz would be able to come. His schedule is quite unpredictable."

"That's not the only thing," she mumbled.

Erich tapped a pencil on the report as he tried to hide his irritation. "Herr Brant is a guest in this house."

"Yes, sir. Please forgive an old woman's ill temper. If I've offended . . ."

Erich tossed the pencil down. "There's nothing to forgive. Your services here are greatly appreciated."

"Thank you, sir."

Erich knew he had to go downstairs to

greet Franz, but he wanted to know what lay behind Bertha's reaction. "Please close the door."

She looked at him in alarm but did as he asked. He got up and walked to the window. "You've never liked Franz, have you?"

Bertha wrung her hands. "Sir, please forget what I said and forgive me."

"I'm not mad, Frau Liedig. But please tell me . . . I know you don't like him, and I'd like to know why. I assure you, this is strictly between us."

She took a deep breath. "I know he's your friend, sir. Herr von Arendt, I have always sensed fine character in you. I don't sense the same values in Herr Brant. He has always seemed to me to be . . . well, cunning. I'm sorry, but I just don't trust him."

"Any specific reason?"

"No, sir." A bleak smile came to her face. "Perhaps it's simply how an old woman looks at everything."

He tried to return her smile. "I appreciate your concern — I know it's because of your loyalty to me, and I thank you. But I think you're wrong about Franz."

"I hope so, sir."

Erich nodded. "Now I must see to my guest."

"I'll be in my room." She left quickly.

Erich hurried down the stairs to where his friend stood in the hallway. "Franz, welcome. Glad you could make it after all." He caught a strong whiff of beer when they shook hands.

"I wasn't sure I would gain entrance," Franz said, slurring his words. "Your field marshal becomes more formidable every time I encounter her. It's a wonder Keitel doesn't appoint her to his General Staff."

"You exaggerate, as always. Come in and sit down."

Franz shook his head. "I've a better idea. I've managed an SS car for the evening. Let's be off at once."

He drove them to a small beer hall off Kurfürsten-Damm. They pushed through the front door and into the warm and humid atmosphere. Erich missed the relatively cool night air, but Franz seemed not to notice. They took a table in the corner.

"Two beers," Franz ordered as he sat down.

"And a sausage plate," Erich added before the beer maid got away.

The beers came immediately. Franz grabbed his stein and drained half of it.

Erich frowned. "So what did you want to talk about?"

His friend looked around and lowered his voice. "You must never repeat this."

"I'm not sure I want to know."

"That's probably wise, but I have to tell someone — someone I can trust not to betray me. When you first asked me what I was doing, I said I couldn't tell you."

"I remember." He took a sip from his beer. "You said you were in the SS — that's all."

"Yes, and that covers a lot of ground. Herr Himmler prefers to have all the potatoes in his pot, if you know what I mean."

Erich leaned forward. "Not so loud," he said in a harsh whisper.

"Don't worry — I'm being careful. Erich, you're the only one I can talk to."

Erich saw the pleading look in his eyes. "Go on."

"As you know, I'm not in a military branch — see, no uniform. My group administers transportation for slave labor."

"What did you say?" Erich asked, his voice rising.

"Now *you* must be quiet," Franz said with a wry grin. "Does my news surprise you?"

"Germany is involved in slave labor?"

"Erich, this is what I do — I've seen these people with my own eyes."

"But I've never heard of such a thing."

"Nor have the rest of our people. Only those directly involved know about it. Most of the slaves I don't care about — Jews, Communists, and gypsies mostly."

"But you *should* care. What is being done is wrong."

Franz frowned. "Yes, yes, I know," he snapped. "But that's not what I want to talk to you about, Erich. These SS people terrify me. You have no idea what monsters they are." He looked down at the tabletop. "It's bad, Erich — very bad. I'd get out if I could."

Erich took a long pull from his stein. "Then why *don't* you?"

"Even you know the answer to that. I can't. It would be prison or worse if I tried. No, I'm in this for the duration."

"I don't understand. What do we do with them?"

"The slave laborers? Have you heard of the Organization Todt?"

"Of course. Fritz Todt's organization, the Minister of Armaments. Herr Speer is acquainted with him, and we do some work for his organization from time to time."

"As I thought. Then you have observed that *most* German men our age are in the army?"

"Well, yes."

Franz laughed. "*We,* of course, are not because of how immensely valuable our services are to the Fatherland." His grin dissolved into a vacant scowl. "Wake up, Erich. Who do you think is taking up the slack in our factories, hmm? I'll give you a hint — it's not Herr Himmler or Herr Goebbels."

"Franz, will you watch what you are saying."

"This isn't such a great surprise to you, is it?" He paused. "Also, how does this affect your Christian sensibilities?"

Erich closed his eyes and leaned back in his chair. When he again looked at his friend, it seemed as if all his defenses had been stripped away. "When I stop to think about it, no, it doesn't surprise me. But slave labor is wrong, no matter what the reason."

"But your hands are clean, Erich, since you're not directly involved. Right?"

Erich shook his head. "No. This affects *all* Germans. What dishonors Germany dishonors us."

Franz drained his stein and signaled for another one. "Now you see what's bothering me."

"Yes. I wish I could help."

"You have. You've listened to me."

"That's not much help."

"It is. Do you know what I dream about?" He picked up his fresh stein. "I dream about the war being over. I dream of hiding away in some Bavarian castle, sitting on a whole boatload of reichsmarks, and *never* having anything to do with politics again."

"Sounds like a good dream to me."

"I hope I live to find out."

It was after one o'clock when Franz pulled up across the street from Erich's house.

"Looks like you have company," Franz said.

Erich leaned forward and looked out the driver's side window. "Oh, no. That's Herr Speer's car."

"Speer? What's he doing here?"

"How should I know? The man is all work. It's no social call, that's for sure."

Erich got out and stood on the sidewalk until Franz had driven off. Then he started across the street. It was a quiet night, and he could hear the gritty crunch of his footsteps on the pavement. As he neared the car, the driver's window rolled down. He couldn't see the man but knew who it was.

"Get in," the man ordered.

Erich walked around to the passenger side and did as he was told. The interior light revealed what he already knew. The light flicked off as he closed the door.

"Is anything wrong?" Erich asked.

"No, nothing's wrong. I just needed to see you." Albert drummed his fingers on the steering wheel.

"Is it about my work?"

The shadow moved. "No," Albert said quickly. "I mean, yes." He pounded the steering wheel. "Your work is excellent — it always has been. But I need you to start working on something else."

"Stop work on the station? Is the Führer displeased with what I'm doing? He always seems so excited when he looks at the model or my drawings."

"Erich, will you please shut up and listen! The Führer is *delighted* with your work. That's part of my problem. I have to convince him that someone else can do as well in finishing the drawings, and that will not be easy."

Erich waited in silence. In his mind's eye he could see those intense eyes underneath bushy black eyebrows. The stillness of the night seemed to close in around them.

"Erich, even though you're quite young, you're a gifted administrator. I watched you after I assigned you to coordinate the model shop. I know it wasn't easy getting all those architects and artists to work together, but you did it." He laughed. "You've experienced in a small way what I've been doing for years."

"Thank you."

"You may not thank me later. But we must all do what's expected of us, yes? In addition to my architectural work, the Führer has appointed me General Inspector for the Construction of Berlin. This organization, among other things, plans demolitions to prepare for the rebuilding."

"Yes, I was aware of that."

"It also means we're responsible for allocating all housing in Berlin. The people who are evicted when we demolish buildings must go elsewhere. This is a heavy responsibility, Erich."

"I can understand that."

"You will *come* to understand it, I assure you. Herr Dietrich Clahes is the head of the Main Division for Resettlement. I'm assigning you to help him in administration, at least until the bulk of their work is done."

Erich felt an uneasiness in the pit of his stomach. "What will I be doing?"

Albert cleared his throat. "For the good of the Reich, many people must be relocated — there is no other way. You will help in arranging transportation." He paused. "And carrying out the evictions."

"Where are the people going?"

"Wherever Herr Clahes decides!" Albert snapped.

Erich waited. He had observed this abruptness many times.

"This isn't an easy job, Erich. Some of these people will be relocated in other sections of Berlin. Many . . . *most* will go elsewhere. It can't be helped."

"I see." Erich didn't really, but it was all he could think of to say. "Will Papa continue to work in the model shop?"

"Yes, he will." Albert paused. "I'll miss you, Erich. I've come to depend on you. Rest assured, I'll get you back as soon as I can."

"When do I start?"

"Tomorrow." Albert gave Erich a folded piece of paper. "I've written the address for you. And one more thing . . ."

"What's that?"

"How Herr Clahes runs his organization is his business. I don't wish to be informed of what's going on over there."

Something inside Erich clamored for attention. He struggled to regain his composure.

"I will carry out my duties."

"I knew you would. That's why I picked you. Very well. I will not take any more of your time."

"Good night."

"Good night, Erich."

Erich got out of the car and slowly ascended the steps to his house. He stood there for a long time, wondering what he was becoming involved in. The more he learned about what the various Nazi organizations did, the more concerned he became. But why did his boss insist on remaining ignorant of what Dietrich Clahes did? He shivered under the burden of an unknown dread. Finally he unlocked the door and went in.

At seven o'clock in the morning, Erich entered the offices of the Main Division for Resettlement. He had not slept at all, adding to the exhaustion of working long hours on the Berlin construction plans. A secretary looked up at him as he approached.

"I am . . ." he started.

An office door flung open, and the frosted window glass rattled as the door hit its stop. A thin man of medium height looked out at him. "Are you Herr von Arendt?" he demanded abruptly.

"Yes."

"You're late! Come into my office." He looked at his secretary. "We're not to be disturbed."

"Yes, Herr Clahes."

Erich hurried in, trying to hide his growing apprehension. He took a chair by his boss's desk. Dietrich closed the door and sat down. His serious eyes probed Erich's.

"Herr Speer claims you are a wonderworker," he began without preamble.

"I don't know what to say to that."

"There is nothing *to* say. You either know what you're doing or you don't. I'll know soon enough. We must relocate in excess of 50,000 people in the next six months or so, which isn't going to be easy."

"That many?" Erich asked in astonishment.

"Probably more. Our quota for this month is 9,000, mostly Jews. You'll find complete orders on your desk, but I wanted to talk to you before you started. You must understand how important this is."

"Herr Speer said as much."

"And now *I'm* saying it. It will be very difficult, but I expect results. Do you have any questions?"

"No."

"Very good. You will find your orders quite complete. My staff will be most helpful if you require further information."

Twelve

Johanna awoke from her nightmare. It had all been very real. She had again seen that blurred object smash into Christabel before erupting into an inferno that pursued Johanna to the very edge of the tottering building. Only this time she was hundreds of feet in the air, not forty feet or so. But despite the height, she could see Erich watching her from the ground, waiting to see what she would do. Again the drainpipe provided the only escape. The fire licked at her feet and caught her robe on fire. Straining every muscle, she jumped and barely caught the pipe. It groaned and swayed, slowly at first, then more rapidly. With a horrible screech it tore away from the wall. Johanna screamed as she saw the ground rushing up at her. Then she awoke.

She struggled to catch her breath as she tried to figure out where she was. Reality came to her as the last cobwebs of sleep dissolved. The dim lighting and unpleasant smells reminded her she was still in the air raid shelter. It was Friday. She shuddered as she realized she was still wearing her nightgown and robe. She winced at the pain from the lacerations on her feet.

People were stirring now. A woman came past and stopped. Without a word she rummaged in a corner and found Johanna a work dress, but there were no spare shoes of any kind. Johanna swallowed her pride, accepted the dress from the lower-class woman, and dressed quickly. The woman took her to a soup kitchen a few blocks away. Johanna ate her soup hungrily and was indignant when she was refused a second bowl. Her benefactor tried to explain what she needed to do to get new papers and clothing. But Johanna had other ideas. Working-class Germans might have to do this, but not her. Her new friend shrugged and went about her business.

Johanna stood on the street for a long time as she pondered what to do. She thought of going back to the Hoffmanns' but dismissed that idea almost as quickly as it came. It had been hard enough to accept their help earlier, but now that she was much worse off . . . The fact that she had no money finally got her moving. She walked the long blocks to the bank, pretending not to notice the stares that followed her every step. She entered and got in line. But the teller and even the manager refused to believe who she was, since she had no papers.

She left and walked aimlessly to the corner. She watched a tram approach. Her heart lifted momentarily as she imagined it might be driven by Herr Hoffmann. But it wasn't. The bustle of Frankfurt swept past her on all sides, full of purpose while she had none.

Then the thought that had been lurking at the back of her mind came forward. Surely her father would not turn her away, not in these circumstances. She hated the idea of begging him for help after all he had done to her, but she could think of no other option. She considered asking a tram driver for a free ride but could not face the likelihood of refusal. She plodded along, each step sending jolts of pain upward from her feet. She looked down and saw a trail of red splotches behind her.

After a mile she felt panic welling up within her. Her feet felt numb, not really part of her at all. Halfway there, her energy drained away. In addition to the pain and her increasing fears, a dark foreboding festered menacingly. Bombed-out houses appeared before her in increasing numbers, tall piles of brick and splintered wood.

Many of the houses were burned, including most of those that had escaped the bombs. She gradually became aware that she had not seen a soul since entering this area of destruction.

Johanna hoped she would soon be past the blight, but it instead grew worse. Her neighborhood appeared to be at the center of a large bombing raid. She almost collapsed on the spot, but somehow she had to know for sure. She turned onto her street. Every house for blocks around stood in ruin, most blasted to rubble by bombs, the rest gutted by the firestorm that had followed in the wake of the raid. Every house but one. There in the middle of the block was her father's house, standing like a lonely sentinel amid the heaps of rubble and burned-out devastation. As she got closer, she saw there was some damage. A hole gaped in the roof, and the top of one of the chimneys was gone. Several of the front windows were shattered, and the exposed wood on the side was scorched.

Johanna hurried up the front walk despite her fatigue and the dull ache in her feet. Her hand froze as she reached for the doorbell — the heavy front door stood ajar. She slowly pushed it open and peered in. A vague anxiety formed in her heart and began to grow as she stepped inside.

A large trunk sat at the foot of the stairs. Her mother's favorite music box lay abandoned by the door. Johanna shuffled into her father's study and over to his desk. It was unlocked. She opened the drawers and found them empty. She went from room to room, opening every door and closet, ending up in Sophie's room. All the furniture was there, but clothing and personal items were missing. Panic threatened to overcome Johanna as she realized her family had left in a hurry. She flipped on a light switch, but nothing happened.

She hobbled downstairs and tried the water tap in the kitchen but only got a sucking sound and a few muddy drips. She opened the pantry expecting it to be bare. To her surprise she found half a loaf of moldy bread, a few tin cans of beans, a jar of peach preserves, and a large jug of apple cider.

She felt faint as she became aware of her hunger and thirst. She carried the bread and preserves over to the counter beside the sink, returning for the cider. She poured a glass, then tore off a chunk of bread and rubbed most of the mold off. She tried to remove the top from the preserves, but it was stuck. She rapped the top against the sink but to no avail. Finally she wolfed down the bread dry, washing it down with cider. The bread tasted surprisingly good. She decided to save the rest of the loaf even though she was still hungry.

Johanna went outside and made a slow circuit of the house. Huge mounds of rubble lay all about her like the graves of giants. She looked up as she heard a distant whining sound. Looking between the blackened heaps she saw a tram rumble down the cross street at the end of the block. It didn't stop — there was no reason to. The clattering noise of its passage dwindled and finally went away.

Johanna searched the house thoroughly, looking for something indicating where her parents had gone, but there was nothing. Late afternoon came. She thought about returning to the city but knew she wasn't up to it. She passed a restless night sprawled on her bed, drifting in and out of sleep. Finally, just before dawn, she fell into deep sleep induced by extreme exhaustion. She awoke Saturday in the early evening.

She stirred and groaned at the insistent throbbing of her feet. She looked down in horror at how swollen and bruised they were. She cried out in agony as she staggered into a standing position. She hobbled downstairs to the kitchen and looked out at the gathering dusk. She drank some cider and ate the rest of the bread, not bothering to remove the mold. Still hungry, she struggled with the preserves for a moment, then smashed the jar in the sink. She picked the peach chunks out of the glass and ate them. When she finished, her chin was wet and sticky from syrup.

Johanna felt her head with the back of her hand. It was definitely hot. A cold chill shivered down her spine as she realized how alone and helpless she was. She thought about the agonizing trip upstairs and decided it wasn't worth the effort. She shuffled into the sitting room and collapsed on the sofa.

She spent another night in feverish sleep. On Sunday she awoke near noon and returned to the kitchen. She picked at the remains of the preserves but stopped when her stomach turned sour. She knew she had to get help, but where? In her desperation she thought of the Hoffmanns but knew she couldn't walk to their apartment.

After a few minutes she struggled to her feet, crying out at the intense pain. She leaned against the wall until the throbbing subsided a little. She staggered through the house and out the front door. The heaps of rubble seemed unreal under the bright blue summer sky. Johanna shuffled down the walk, taking slow, deliberate steps, weaving in and out of the destruction as she made her way to the tram stop at the end of her street.

A tram heading toward the city approached as she made it to the corner. It ground to a halt, and the driver waited patiently as Johanna shuffled around to the front and up the steps.

"I don't have the fare," she said.

"Then you can't ride," the driver replied.

"I can't walk into town."

He paled when she showed him her swollen, discolored feet.

"Sit there," he said, pointing to a seat near the door.

She sank down on it gratefully as the tram rumbled forward. The desolation gradually gave way to sections with less damage, but every part of Frankfurt was affected to some degree. The bombing was like a cancer that had relentlessly eaten away at the city. The tram crossed the Main River and entered the central business district.

Johanna groaned when she saw her stop approaching. She struggled to her feet and tottered to the door. The driver glanced at her as she passed, obviously relieved to have her off his tram.

She stood in the street and shivered as the tram rumbled on its way. The few blocks to the Hoffmanns' seemed like miles. Only the thought of a safe haven drove her on. When she at last reached the appropriate corner, she stopped in horror. A tall pile of bricks and rubble marked where the Hoffmanns' apartment building had once stood. Johanna collapsed on the curb and wept. Then, with the last of her energy, she crawled into an alley and passed out.

Johanna didn't know what time it was when she awoke, only that it was very dark with the blackout in full effect. Her head burned, and sharp pains shot up from her feet. She pulled herself up on a box and slowly stood. The street beyond the alley stood out as slight gradations of intensely dark shadows. She hobbled out and looked both ways. Except for bright flashes caused by pain, she could see nothing. She thought she heard music somewhere to the right but dismissed it as a hallucination. She kept expecting it to go away, but it didn't.

She started toward the peaceful sounds. Gradually the music grew louder. A darkened building loomed suddenly as if through a fog. The music was nearby, but it seemed to be coming from somewhere below. The strong chords of a piano came upward, carrying joyous voices with it. Only then did Johanna recognize the song — "A Mighty Fortress."

She almost turned away, but the people sounded so happy. This made no sense to Johanna, not in this time and place. She saw a slightly darker shadow that she assumed marked the steps down into the building's basement. Curious, desperate, she felt for the first step with her foot, slipped, and tumbled downward. She hit hard and lost consciousness in a flash of stars.

Johanna heard a buzzing noise. She wished it would go away, but it was joined by a vague sensation of pain. The pain became more distinct, driving itself into the center of her brain. With a rush she was fully awake and in agony. She looked about the dimly lit room in panic, wondering where she was and what was happening.

"She's awake," someone whispered.

Johanna turned toward the speaker. She willed her eyes to focus and saw — Karoline Hoffmann! She blinked her eyes. Wilhelm stood beside his wife. Behind them hovered a man she didn't recognize.

"Where am I?" Johanna croaked, her mouth as dry as cotton. She struggled to rise.

"Don't try to get up," Karoline said, gently restraining Johanna. "You're in Ludwig Dorpmüller's apartment. He's a friend of ours from church. Now, stay where you are, and I'll bring you something to eat." She hurried out of the room.

Johanna slumped back onto the cot. She was in a crowded living room, partitioned by blankets hung from a taut cord. The two men stood in front of her, silently waiting.

Karoline returned with a steaming bowl of broth. She sat in a chair by the head of the cot and spooned the broth into Johanna's mouth.

"Oh, that's good."

"It's what you need," Karoline agreed. She took her time, making sure Johanna ate it all. Then she took the bowl back to the kitchen and returned with a cup of tea.

Johanna sipped it slowly. "What happened to me?" she asked.

Karoline smoothed Johanna's hair. "We don't know, dear. You sort of dropped in on us."

"What?"

"We were holding Sunday services in the basement where we meet, and you fell down the steps. Wilhelm was nearest the door, and he heard you. We brought you here."

Johanna shifted her legs, grimacing as jolts of pain shot to her brain. "My feet," she moaned, gritting her teeth as she waited for the agony to pass.

"They're infected, dear. The doctor's seen them. We've been applying salve for the last two days. They're better now. The doctor says you should recover completely."

"I've been out two days?"

"For the most part. The times you were awake, you were delirious. You've been running a high fever."

"What day is it?"

"Tuesday night."

"You've been taking care of me all this time?" Johanna saw that Karoline was clearly surprised.

"Why, yes. Of course we have."

Tears brimmed in Johanna's eyes. "But why? You barely know me — you wouldn't know me at all if I hadn't been on your husband's tram."

Karoline patted Johanna's hand. "You were brought to us by God. Wilhelm and I felt so the first time. We've prayed for you . . ."

"Even after I left?" Johanna interrupted.

"Especially after you left. We prayed that God would look after you. That and we also asked Him to bring you back if there was anything else we could do. See? He answered our prayers."

Johanna shook her head. "No, it's not like that. I was only trying to find your apartment. I fainted, and when I woke up it was dark. I stumbled around in the blackout and fell. That's all."

"Stumbling around in the dark you came to where we were having our evening service. We were in the middle of a hymn."

"Yes, I remember that."

"Do you know what we were doing right before that?"

"No." She stared at those loving eyes.

Karoline gently patted Johanna's arm. "We were praying. Wilhelm had just finished praying that God would bring you back to us."

Something seemed to touch Johanna's innermost being. She felt as if a dam had cracked within her, releasing emotions that had been pent-up her entire life. With sudden insight, she realized that her make-believe world no longer existed, in fact never had. Her dreams of becoming a concert pianist and enjoying a rich life among artists and intellectuals was gone. She squeezed her eyes tightly shut as if this would protect what was left of her dignity. She thought too of the greatest shame of all — Ulrich's betrayal. The tears came in a flood.

Karoline held her close, pulled a handkerchief out of her pocket, and gave it to Johanna. She turned to the two men. "Please leave us alone," she said softly.

Wilhelm and Ludwig left quietly.

"Do you want to talk, dear?" Karoline asked gently.

Johanna nodded, wiping her eyes with the handkerchief.

"Take your time. There is no hurry."

Johanna struggled to catch her breath. "So much has happened — I don't know where to start."

"Start anywhere you want."

"It's a long story."

"I'm not going anywhere. And we will not be disturbed. Why not tell me everything? It'll make you feel better."

Johanna nodded and took a deep, shuddering breath. "It's horrible. A bombing raid destroyed my apartment building. I was there when it happened and had to crawl down a drainpipe in order to escape. The building collapsed right after I reached the ground. My friend, Christabel, died right in front of my eyes — I saw the bomb hit her.

"I've never been so scared in my life. People were running in every direction, screaming. Once I got down, I looked for a little girl I'd seen earlier. I saw her mother die, but I don't know what happened to the girl.

"I managed to get into one of the shelters. It was awful down there. So many were terribly wounded. They were all bloody, some missing arms and legs. They were screaming and moaning and crying. Children were wailing. This went on most of the night. You can't imagine how bad it was."

"We've seen it too, dear," Karoline said. "We spent several nights in the shelters ourselves. The worst was when our building was bombed — the same night as yours, I imagine."

Johanna nodded in embarrassment. "Oh, yes, of course. I'm not thinking clearly."

"That's all right. Go on."

Johanna caught her breath in ragged gasps as she thought about her family. "The next morning I decided to go to my parents' house." She paused. "Papa sent me away when I came back to Frankfurt, but I thought under the circumstances . . ." She broke down suddenly.

"There, there," Karoline said, patting her arm. "We can stop if you like."

Johanna shook her head as she wiped her eyes. "No, I want to get it out. I thought surely Papa would take me in after what happened. But the whole neighborhood was destroyed, except for our house. And when I got home, no one was there — I have no idea where they went."

"What about your friends, dear?"

Johanna shook her head. "No one from the neighborhood is left — all their houses are bombed out. And my . . ." She paused. "My artistic friends weren't welcome at my house." She brightened suddenly. "But there is someone who might know where they are."

"Who is that?"

"Herr Maser. He's Papa's plant superintendent. I don't know where he lives except that it's close to the factories."

"Wilhelm will check for you tomorrow."

"I appreciate that." She stopped suddenly. Her head swam with emotion as her war experiences merged with what she'd been through with Erich. She considered keeping this to herself but decided she would feel better talking about it.

"There's more," she said.

"Go ahead, dear. I'm listening."

"I have an unhappy marriage. My husband's name is Erich. My father and his father decided I would marry him, without asking me about it. I've lived in misery for years, but I stuck it out until Erich finally told me to go home."

"He's divorcing you?" Karoline asked.

Johanna choked back her sudden irritation. "No," she said, struggling to maintain an even tone. "He said he would never do that." She sneered. "He says he can't break the commitment he made to God."

"He's a Christian then?"

"He *says* he is. But he doesn't go to church anymore. His job is more important to him."

"I see. So he's sent you away with no support."

"No. He set up a bank account for me. But it still isn't easy for me, being a woman, and with the war going on."

Karoline nodded. "Yes, dear, of course. Go on."

Johanna hesitated. "I've never had any freedom in my life. Early on, Papa decided I was going to marry the son of one of his friends — he said it would be the uniting of two great German families. Rubbish! But he had his way. I did marry Erich, against my will."

"What did your mother say about all this?"

Johanna looked down. "She sided with Papa. Said her marriage was successful and mine could be also. But what else *could* she say? She's married to him."

"Maybe she was trying to help you." Karoline paused. "How would you describe love, dear?"

Johanna looked at Karoline suspiciously but saw only care and concern. "Love is when two people think about each other all the time, when they can't stand being apart, when meeting each other's needs is as natural as breathing. Erich and I never had this."

"I see. Were there other things you longed for?"

"My talent. I could have been a concert pianist if all this hadn't happened. My teacher said I could make it." She looked down. "All it required was dedication."

"Perhaps you could pursue that later."

Johanna shook her head. "No, not anymore. Not after all that's happened. Not in the middle of this war."

"May I ask you a question, dear?"

Johanna hesitated. "Yes, I guess so."

"You've been through a lot. What bothers you the most right now?"

Johanna felt the tears coming again. "Realizing that my life means nothing. That I have nothing to live for."

Karoline patted her hand. "Oh, you're wrong there, dear. You have *everything* to live for. Don't even think such a thing."

Johanna glared at her. "How can you say that after everything I've been through?"

Karoline's smile seemed strangely confident and compassionate. "I think God is reaching out for you. He loves you and wants what's best for you."

"Well, He has a funny way of showing it."

"Sometimes what He does *is* painful. But what if this is the only way He can help you? You wouldn't want Him to give up, would you?"

"I don't want to talk about it. If God put me through what *I've* been through, I want nothing to do with Him."

Karoline looked down. "I hope you change your mind, dear. Please promise me you'll think about it."

She turned her head away. "No promises."

"As you wish. Is there anything else you want to talk about?"

Johanna sighed. She had never felt wearier in her life. "No, not now. I'm so tired."

"Then lie back and get some rest. Can I get you anything to eat or drink?"

"No. I just want to sleep."

"You go ahead. I'll make sure you're not disturbed."

Karoline pulled the bandages gently away and inspected the bottoms of Johanna's feet.

Johanna winced as she saw the blue-black tops of her feet. "How do they look?" she asked.

"Much better. They're healing nicely." Karoline washed them gently before applying the ointment and covering the wounds with fresh gauze and tape. "Would you like some tea and toast?"

"Yes, that sounds nice." Johanna smiled at the prospect.

A soft click sounded in the entryway. Both women looked toward the door in surprise. It opened slightly.

"It's me," came a familiar voice. "I have

Herr Maser with me. Can we come in?"

Karoline pulled the sheet and a light quilt up to Johanna's chin.

"Yes, dear. We're presentable."

Wilhelm pushed the door open and waited for his tall, thin companion to enter. Johanna looked from one to the other. Neither man smiled. Wilhelm closed the door.

"What's wrong?" she demanded.

"Perhaps you would like to talk to Herr Maser alone," Wilhelm suggested.

Johanna considered this but finally shook her head. "No, I'd like you both to be here. Herr Maser, won't you sit down?"

The man nodded and sat in a chair close to Johanna's cot. Wilhelm pulled two more chairs over. He and Karoline sat beside Johanna.

Johanna felt her mouth go dry. She felt an icy sensation grow in the pit of her stomach as she watched the superintendent's obvious distress. Johanna steeled herself to ask the questions she had to ask.

"Herr Maser, do you know where my family is?"

He nodded. "Yes, Frau von Arendt, I do. I am so sorry to have to tell you . . ."

Johanna closed her eyes. "Tell me what?" she interrupted.

"Your parents and fräulein Sophie are dead."

Johanna felt hot tears stream down her face. It took all her willpower to keep from breaking down completely. She felt Karoline's reassuring hand on her shoulder.

"How did it happen?" she asked in a shaky voice.

"These bombing raids are scaring everyone. Your parents' house was the only one left standing in the neighborhood."

Johanna nodded. "I know. I saw it."

"Then I suppose you can imagine how they felt. Your mother in particular was quite upset. Herr Kammler thought it best to go to the Bavarian house, for a while at least. He sent me into town to get you . . ."

"Papa knew where I was?"

"Yes, he did. But when I found your apartment building destroyed, I assumed the worst. And the civil authorities had no record of you. When I informed your papa, he was devastated, as were your mama and Sophie. This on top of what they had already been through. I saw them off." He paused. "Your father was driving. The car had a blowout just outside Munich, causing the car to swerve into an army transport. They were killed instantly."

"When did this happen?"

"Last Friday. The funeral was day before yesterday."

"They're dead and buried and I didn't know anything about it."

Herr Maser looked down. "I'm so sorry," he said, almost in a whisper.

A thought sprang to her mind. For the briefest instant it struck her as inappropriate, but she had to ask. "Herr Maser, I suppose Bernhard and I must attend to settling father's estate then."

The man remained silent.

"Don't we need to do that?" she probed.

Herr Maser sighed. "Yes, I suppose you must. But I'm afraid there is more bad news."

Johanna felt a sense of dread. "What is it?"

"Your father was facing bankruptcy when he died. All his mills were together in one block by the Main River. The same bombing raid that spared your house leveled the mills. And your father was heavily in debt because of our rapid expansion."

"Weren't the mills insured?"

"Yes, they were. But the policies exclude acts of war. The insurance companies won't pay a thing. Your father's creditors will claim all the assets in his estate, which won't be much since almost everything he had was invested in those mills."

Johanna looked at him in complete shock. "How do you know all this?"

"I witnessed the papers."

"You mean there's nothing — nothing at all?"

He nodded. "I'm sorry. I wish with all my heart it wasn't so. But, yes — you and your brother will not have an inheritance."

Thirteen

After Herr Maser left, Johanna told the Hoffmanns she wanted to rest, then broke down in tears. Karoline tucked her in and joined Wilhelm in the corridor. They descended the stairs and started walking toward the city center. Bombed-out buildings alternated with those relatively unscathed as the Hoffmanns made numerous detours around the mountains of brick and blackened timbers that blocked many of the streets. They entered the central square and sat on a bench with a good view of the Römer, the old town hall of Frankfurt.

"How do you think she's doing?" Wilhelm asked.

Karoline put her hand in his. "She's devastated. She's lost her family, she saw her friend die, she barely escaped death herself, her marriage is ruined, and she's destitute, at least until she can get new identity papers. It's hard to imagine how it could be worse."

"What can we do?"

A weary smile came to Karoline's face. "First of all and most of all, we can pray.

Surely God has brought her back so we can help her. Her most pressing need is for a personal relationship with God."

He nodded. "Which she doesn't realize."

"True. But over a period of time she may. At least God is giving her this chance. I think she will be more open now."

Wilhelm squeezed her hand. "We will pray to that effect."

He and Karoline bowed their heads as he began his simple prayer. Anxious citizens passed by them, but the Hoffmanns were alone with the Creator of the Universe.

Erich stood to the side of the apartment building's front door as the former tenants streamed by, most with yellow Stars of David pinned to their clothes. He watched in silence as the police shouted their orders, directing the people to the waiting trucks for the short trip to Berlin's Anhalter Station for transportation into occupied Poland. The men and women accused him with their eyes as they shuffled past.

Erich wanted to look away, but he couldn't. The human tide seemed to continue forever. He saw a young boy emerge from the door and stop at the top of the steps, forcing others to walk around him. The child had on a well-fitting suit complete with tie and hat. The only thing that marred his appearance was the crude Star of David pinned to his lapel pocket. Erich winced as the boy looked right into his eyes. Rather than accusation, the expression seemed bewildered and scared. Erich finally broke eye contact and looked up. Standing over the boy was a tall, thin man with a heavy black beard, obviously the father. Erich recoiled at the undisguised look of smoldering anger.

"Move at once!" came a nearby order.

Erich turned and saw a red-faced policeman come charging through the transients waving his baton. The terrified child backed into the protective arms of his father.

"Stop!" Erich shouted.

A man in a dark suit, standing next to Erich, put a cautioning hand on his shoulder. "Let it be," he said softly.

Erich shrugged off the hand and cut through the crowd, intercepting the policeman at the foot of the steps. The officer stopped, his club raised high, a startled expression on his face.

"Herr von Arendt, you must allow me to do my job."

"I'll handle it," Erich replied.

He hurried up the steps, stopping before the crying boy, who looked up at Erich as if he expected a beating. Erich felt a stinging sensation in his eyes. It took all his willpower to keep his voice steady as he tore his eyes away and looked up at the father.

"Come on, both of you," he whispered. "Resistance will only make your situation more difficult."

The man glared at him for a moment, then took his son's hand. Together they walked down the steps. The boy clung closely to his father as they passed the policeman and continued on to the nearest truck. Finally they climbed aboard.

Erich felt an overpowering sense of shame as he returned to his position near the curb. The man in the dark suit glared at him. Although Erich didn't know who he was, he suspected he was Gestapo.

"That was not wise," the man said.

"I'm not interested in your opinion," Erich answered coldly.

"Perhaps that will change," the man said, almost in a whisper.

Erich watched in silent gloom as the evacuation continued. Only when the last truck rumbled off did he go back to his car. He got in and stared out through the windshield for a long time. He knew he was supposed to return to the Main Division for Resettlement offices.

Although the car was warm and stuffy, Erich felt a chill run down his spine. He could no longer avoid the reality that had nagged him for so long. He knew personally the extraordinary magnetism of Adolf Hitler, and he had approved of the changes that helped Germany. But so much was wrong, grotesquely wrong. Erich realized he could never resolve this ugly side of National Socialism with the Christianity he had earlier embraced. He lowered his head in shame as he remembered Johanna's taunting words. No, he had to admit to himself, he didn't attend church regularly. But he still believed in Christ.

Erich slowly lowered his head to the steering wheel and closed his eyes. *Lord, I don't know what to do. This is so wrong. I ask You to come against this evil, to stop its flow. Please help me. Please show me what to do.* He waited, wondering if he would feel some heavenly response. But all he heard was the traffic on the street.

He started the car and drove slowly to the former exhibition rooms of the Berlin Academy of Arts where Albert Speer's models were housed, near the new Chancellery. He parked and walked across the grass to the building. The guard smiled, tipped his hat, and let him in. Inside, Erich paused for a moment, viewing the immense model depicting the imagined glorious future of Berlin — or Germania as Hitler intended to rename it. *What a grotesque monument to pride,* he thought.

"What are you doing here?" a familiar voice demanded.

Erich snapped his head around. Albert Speer was standing outside his office, obviously not in a good mood.

"I have to see you," he said.

"Not now! The Führer is on the way over with some visitors to see the models."

"It has to be now!" Erich insisted.

Albert glanced at his watch. "Very well. But I have only a few minutes. Come inside, but make it quick."

Erich hurried inside, and Albert closed the door.

"What is it?" Albert asked, not bothering to sit down.

"I have just come from evicting the tenants from an apartment building on Immelmannstrasse."

Albert nodded. "As I told you earlier, some resettlement is required in the rebuilding of Berlin."

"I have seen the plans, Herr Speer. This building is not scheduled for demolition."

Albert arched his eyebrows. "Then the proper authorities must be making room for other tenants. I don't know all the details. That's up to Herr Clahes. I *do* know that the number of housing units is declining, at least in the short term. Nevertheless, some people have to move out of the city — there is no other way."

"These people were all Jews."

Erich saw Albert's expression harden. "I've told you before, Erich — how Herr Clahes runs the Main Division for Resettlement is up to him. I have more important things to attend to."

"I also know that the people are boarding a train at Anhalter, and that train is taking them into Poland. I've heard rumors . . ."

"Stop right there!" Albert almost shouted. He glanced at his watch. "You must go now. But listen to me — you have a wonderful job that pays well and keeps you out of the army. I am *ordering* you to attend to your work and stop bothering me with irrelevant details. Do you understand?"

Erich choked back his anger. "Perfectly."

"Very well. If you bring this up again, it

will be the last time."

Erich hesitated. This had not ended as he wished. Nothing had been resolved, and Albert's intense gaze didn't make things any easier. Erich finally turned and hurried out.

Halfway to his car, Erich saw a tight knot of people walking toward the model building from the new Chancellery. Even at a distance Erich could see Hitler's animated expression as he talked to his guests. Germany's dictator looked in Erich's direction and waved. Erich hesitated a moment, then waved back. The procession continued toward its objective.

Erich opened the door to his car and got in. He rested his head on the steering wheel as he pondered his dilemma. Speer's orders were clear enough, and Dietrich Clahes was probably wondering where he was. Erich had to admit that he did fear losing his job, but the prospect of going into the army scared him even more. Yet, he knew that what he was doing was wrong. The memory of the young boy came back. Those sad eyes seemed to accuse him. In that moment Erich von Arendt knew what he had to do. There was no way he could continue to help the Nazis carry out their plans. If that meant being forced into the army, he would worry about that when it happened. *God, help me! Jesus, help me! I am sorry I have drifted so far, but now I want to do Your will, whatever the cost!* Erich started the car and drove off.

Erich pulled up at his house and parked behind a strange black sedan. He looked at it warily as he got out. A sense of doom settled over him as he walked slowly up the steps. He unlocked the door and stepped in. Frau Liedig was there to meet him.

"A gentleman is here to see you, Herr von Arendt," she said. "He's waiting in the sitting room."

"Thank you, Frau Liedig."

She nodded and hurried through the entryway and the kitchen. Erich heard the door to her room close as he walked slowly into the sitting room. The man in the dark suit stood, his back to the windows.

"Herr von Arendt, please sit. There are a few things we must discuss."

"Who are you?" Erich asked.

"I am from the Gestapo," the man said. "I would think that obvious. Now sit!"

Erich did as he was told.

The man consulted a small black notebook, then returned it to his coat pocket. "That was a stupid thing you did this morning. You don't seem to realize how important your work is to the Reich. Not only are you helping to rebuild Berlin, you are making new housing available for good Germans."

"And those Jews are *not* good Germans?"

The man's frown turned into a sneer. "I'm surprised at your attitude, but I'm not here to discuss racial purity with you. After the unfortunate incident this morning, I was dispatched to see you — to explain things more clearly. When you failed to return to Herr Clahes's office, I came here. You don't seem to appreciate the fact that your job keeps you out of the army."

Erich glared at him. "I don't care. I can no longer do the job I have been doing. If that means I must go into the army, I'm ready."

The man laughed. "Are you now? You might get assigned to the eastern front."

"Fine. I'm still not changing my mind."

"I seriously suggest you reconsider."

Erich felt a cold chill settle in the pit of his stomach. "Why?"

"Let me explain it to you this way." The man's expression changed to mock pity. "If you don't go back to your work, we will be forced to send your father and mother to a concentration camp."

Erich felt momentary rage but quickly quelled it. He looked at the man in utter disbelief.

"And in addition," the man added, "we will send your wife Johanna as well."

"You know about Johanna . . ." Erich began.

"We know more about her than you do," the man said. "She has been living in Frankfurt since you separated. We thought she was killed when her apartment was bombed, but she turned up again when her father's superintendent visited her."

"Is she all right?"

"Yes, yes, she's fine. And if you want her to stay that way, I suggest you do as you're told. Do I make myself clear?"

Erich choked down what he wanted to say. "Most clear."

The man stood abruptly. "Very well. Then might I suggest you return to your office?" He left without another word.

Erich thought about his earlier prayers. Where was his guidance? he wondered. The efficient Nazi machine had removed the few options he had, unless he didn't care what happened to his parents — and to Johanna. Erich slumped back in his chair and closed his eyes. He was trapped, and the Nazis knew it. Apparently even God couldn't, or wouldn't, rescue him from this terrible dilemma.

Dietrich Clahes never mentioned Erich's tardiness. This surprised the young architect at first, since he was sure his boss was well aware of all that had happened. Emboldened by this, Erich finally asked for his help in contacting Johanna. The man agreed reluctantly, arranged for Johanna to go to the Frankfurt post office on Friday, and allowed Erich to use an office phone.

Erich sat at his desk as he waited for the operator to put the call through to Frankfurt. Finally he heard the phone ringing.

"Hello," Johanna said, her voice sounding weak and faraway.

Erich's eyes grew damp, and he had to struggle to maintain his composure. "Hello, Johanna. This is Erich. How are you?"

There was a pause, and for a moment Erich thought the line had gone dead.

"It's been horrible. I almost died when the enemy bombed my apartment building — I saw my best friend die right in front of my eyes."

"Yes, I know."

"You know? How could you have heard?"

Erich glanced at Dietrich's closed door, wondering if anyone was monitoring the call. "It doesn't matter. But are you all right?"

"Yes. My feet got infected from cuts I received the night of the bombing, but they're healing nicely." She paused. "Some friends of mine, the Hoffmanns, have been helping me."

"Good. Are they friends of your family?"

The silence on the line was punctuated by a series of pops.

"Johanna, are you there?"

"Yes." He heard the break in her voice.

"What's the matter, Johanna?"

"Mama and Papa are dead. So is Sophie."

Erich closed his eyes. "No! What happened?"

"They were on the way to their house in Bavaria. Papa lost control and ran into an army truck. They were killed instantly."

"Johanna, I'm so sorry. Is there anything I can do?"

"What — you would take time off from your precious job?"

Erich sighed. Before he could reply, Johanna hurried on. "I'm sorry, Erich. I

306

shouldn't have said that. Thank you for your concern."

"I really am sorry. I liked your parents, and Sophie was so sweet. Does Bernhard know yet?"

"I sent him a letter. It depends on how quickly the post gets to Paris."

"So he's still stationed there?"

"For now."

"Do you have what you need in the bank account?"

"Yes. I couldn't use it after the bombing raid until I got new identity papers. But that's all settled now."

Dietrich came out of his office and looked pointedly at Erich.

"Good. I must go now. Please call me if you need anything."

"I will. Thank you. Good-bye."

The line clicked dead.

As Johanna's feet healed, she began to go with Karoline as she visited friends and helped groups providing aid to disaster victims. At first Johanna did it out of a sense of obligation to her elderly friend, but later because she wanted to. It gave her a sense of satisfaction to see practical results from the efforts of her own hands. Sometimes it meant cleaning and dressing wounds, sometimes providing food or listening to what a recent bombing victim was going through, something she personally understood.

Although Karoline was older and quite different from herself, Johanna began to like her more and more. There was no question that Karoline cared, and the medical treatment she'd given had been tender and thorough.

The weekend after Erich's call, Johanna reluctantly agreed to attend church with the Hoffmanns. The service defied all her expectations. The congregation didn't meet in some massive stone and stained-glass cathedral — they gathered in the basement of an office building where one of the members worked as a janitor. And the pastor didn't sound at all like the one in Berlin on the rare occasions when she and Erich had attended services. Instead of vague messages about God's love, this pastor, lacking robes or a degree, preached directly from the Bible. What surprised Johanna most was that she actually understood what he was saying.

Through the next several months, the pastor preached from a book named Romans, which he explained had been written by a Jew whose name had been

Saul but was later called Paul. Although the pastor explained each text, Johanna found her head in a whirl as she struggled to put the different concepts together. At one point Paul seemed to be telling people where they had gone wrong, but then he would tell them that Jesus had Himself paid the penalty for all their sins.

Then the pastor started preaching from a book named Ephesians. On the third sermon, he spoke urgently to his small congregation, telling them they had been saved by grace through faith, not by anything they had done. For some reason this pierced Johanna like an arrow shot by an unseen archer. She could no more set this thought aside than she could cause the war to end.

Ludwig Dorpmüller unlocked the apartment door, pushed it open, and waited for his guests to enter. Karoline and Johanna set their bags down while the men went into the small kitchen.

"Is anything the matter?" Karoline asked quietly.

"No," Johanna replied. "Why do you ask?"

"You didn't say a thing all the way home."

Johanna attempted a smile. "Are you saying I talk too much?"

Karoline smiled. "You know me better than that. And I know when something is bothering you." She became serious. "I'm not pressing, dear, but if I can help, I'd like to."

Johanna nodded. "I appreciate your concern." She paused. "It's what the pastor said — that God saves us because we believe He will."

"That's a good part of it. If we believe Jesus' offer to save us from our sins, then we *are* saved. Forgiveness is God's undeserved gift, and there isn't a thing we can do to earn it."

Johanna frowned. "I see."

"Do you? We all start out as God's enemy, but we don't have to remain that way. Would you like to become Jesus' friend?"

"How can that help? Wasn't Jesus just a man?"

Karoline nodded. "Yes, He was human. But He was also God. The Bible tells us He claimed to be equal with God the Father. And after His crucifixion, God raised Him from the dead. Paul tells us this is our ultimate proof that He was telling the truth."

"So I'm saved by believing Jesus will save me, if I depend on Him to forgive me for all I've done wrong?"

"That's right. He will save you from every evil thing you've ever done or will do. I think you know this is true. Why not receive His gift?"

Johanna saw a glimmer of hope. She knew in her heart it was true. In fact, she'd known it for some time. But she also knew that if Jesus was in charge, she wasn't, and she had struggled for some time with that. She looked into the older woman's eyes, seeing her obvious care and concern.

Johanna closed her eyes. It felt like some unseen presence was nearby, and in her heart she knew who it was. In her deepest, innermost self, she felt herself saying *yes*. It was as if some immense weight had been lifted from her, and she experienced a joy beyond any she'd ever felt before. Tears came quickly. Her heart was so full, it felt like it would burst. Suddenly she realized she'd been holding her breath. She breathed a long sigh of relief.

The weight of a short lifetime lifted from her, taken away by her new Lord and Savior. Everything was new. Everything was different. She didn't know what that would mean for the circumstances of her life, but she did know that now she belonged to God.

Fourteen

It was January 30, 1942. Erich, snug in his warm, woolen coat, peered through the tiny window of the converted Heinkel bomber at the endless white palette that spread all the way to the empty horizons as the plane droned over the desolate Russian steppes. An intermittent dark line — the railroad the pilot was following to Dnepropetrovsk in the Ukraine — provided the only relief in the blowing snow. The thin black line swelled occasionally as the plane flew over a burned-out station or roundhouse. The Russians had destroyed as much as they could as they retreated before the German blitzkrieg.

Erich turned away from the window and gazed at the other two passengers, Albert Speer and SS General Sepp Dietrich, sitting side by side. The two traded occasional whispered comments but for the most part sat in glowering silence.

A month earlier Fritz Todt, Reich Minister of Armaments and Munitions, had appointed Speer to resolve the transportation nightmare in the Ukraine, a task made almost impossible by the Russians' scorched-earth retreat and the severe winter weather. German casualties were soaring, initially from desperate Russian defense, but increasingly from the unrelenting cold and starvation. Erich didn't envy his boss's task because it looked almost impossible.

He had been surprised, but not particularly encouraged, when Speer had peremptorily pulled him out of Dietrich Clahes's organization. Erich was relieved to be out of the forced relocation business, but he no longer had any illusions about what Hitler was doing to Germany. The end of anarchy and the military victories were not worth the hideous toll on human life and dignity.

A month earlier Johanna had mailed him a letter, the first time she'd written since returning to Frankfurt. He reached inside his coat and pulled the flimsy paper out, then tenderly unfolded it and held it to the light streaming through the window.

31 December 1941
Dear Erich,
    A lot has happened since we last talked. I hope I get the chance to tell you about it, but I don't think now is the right time. But I do want to thank you for providing for

my needs. I appreciate it more than you know.

As you know, I've been worried about Bernhard being in the army, especially since losing Mama, Papa, and Sophie. He's the only family I have left, and I know you think highly of him also.

About a month ago he sent me a letter from France saying he was being reassigned to an infantry division on the eastern front somewhere in the Ukraine. Since then I haven't heard a word. I know that doesn't mean much in wartime, but I keep hearing such horrible rumors about the war in Russia.

I know I shouldn't ask, but do you think you could find out anything from someone in Herr Speer's organization? If this would cause you problems, then forget I mentioned it. Besides, I have no right to ask.

I hope this letter finds you well.

Sincerely,
Johanna

Erich folded the letter and returned it to his shirt pocket. He felt the same tightness in his throat as he had the first time he read it, only this time it was more intense. There was something about the letter's tone that did not at all seem like the

Johanna he knew. There was the natural concern for Bernhard, but also a new tenderness, a marked contrast with her earlier demanding ways.

Erich had checked with friends inside Speer's growing organization, but it hadn't done any good. A few did not wish to discuss it, and the rest had no in-depth knowledge of the growing disaster on the eastern front. He sighed and tried to relax as the German bomber droned along over the Ukraine.

Erich awoke from his nap to see the co-pilot emerge from the cockpit. The young man's eyes were very serious, and Erich half-expected him to click his heels and offer the Hitler salute. He didn't.

"Herr General," he said, "we are supposed to land soon. However, the ground crew is having trouble keeping the drifting snow off the runway, and they are not at all sure we can touch down safely."

"We have to," Dietrich replied. "We have nowhere else to go. Tell them to clear that field or else!"

"Yes, Herr General."

This time the pilot did click his heels, Erich noted in amusement. Then the humor died away as he realized he could very well be dead before the sun set. That thought spurred conflicting emotions. He had felt himself drawing nearer to God a while back, but since his inability to separate himself from the Nazis' evil doings, he wasn't sure where he was spiritually or what the Lord above thought of him.

He looked out the window beside his seat as the roar of the engines decreased slightly. He tried to catch a glimpse of the runway, but all he could see was endless white. His pulse quickened, and he felt the sharp pang of fear as the converted bomber turned sharply and started descending rapidly. The engine noise dropped away, allowing Erich to hear the slipstream whistling by the fuselage. The ground was very close now. The plane danced about in the turbulent air, and with each movement Erich was sure they were going to crash.

The plane bounced hard on its landing gear, then bounded back into the air. Erich looked out the window, his eyes wide, half-expecting the bomber to flip over. It came down again, bounced a few times, then remained on the ground. Blowing snow completely obscured the windows. Finally the plane slowed and came to a standstill. The engines sputtered once, then spun to a stop. All Erich could hear was the eerie moan of the wind. The fragile plane rocked violently with each gust.

The pilot emerged from the cockpit and walked toward the back. "My apologies for the landing, Herr General. I had to jerk us back into the air to avoid a huge snowdrift. We would have certainly crashed if we had plowed into it."

Dietrich nodded. The pilot continued aft and opened the small door. The wind wrenched it out of his hand and slammed it against the side of the plane. A frigid blast of arctic air roared into the plane, instantly dropping the temperature to below zero. Erich shivered and pulled his heavy coat closely about himself. The pilot stepped down into a snowdrift and waited to help his passengers down.

General Dietrich stepped cautiously down into the heavy snow, followed by Albert Speer. Erich came last, shivering beside his boss as they stood next to the frail-looking aircraft shuddering in the wind. The descending sun bathed the snowscape in the rich red tones of sunset.

"Where's my transportation?" Dietrich demanded as he looked around.

A young officer saluted. "My apologies, Herr General. We don't have anything that can make it through the drifts to the field. It was all we could do to get the Russian laborers to clear footpaths. If I might suggest, we must get moving — we will all get frostbit if we don't get to the rail coaches at once."

He turned and started trudging toward some oblong objects in the distance. After puzzling over them for a few moments, Erich realized they were railcars, almost buried in snow. Some distance away stood the blackened ruins of a rural station, somehow made peaceful by the drape of white.

Erich felt his face grow numb in the howling wind. He lifted his feet high as he plodded along behind the others. The snow often came above his knees as they crossed new drifts. The icy powder infiltrated his heavy boots and melted, making his feet feel like chunks of ice. For a long time the distant dark shapes seemed to come no closer. Finally, after a long half hour, they approached a railcar attached to a locomotive that puffed out jets of steam.

The guide opened the door and waited until the newcomers were inside. Then he entered and closed the door. Erich had expected the interior to be warm and cheery.

Instead he found it chilly and dismal. An odd assortment of worktables filled the converted dining car, serving as Speer's construction staff office. Haggard-looking men gazed at them as if they were unwelcome interlopers.

"Why is it so cold in here?" General Dietrich demanded.

"It cannot be helped, Herr General," said a man standing by a table heaped with papers. "We only have enough fuel to fire up the locomotive every two hours. We should have a little heat in about fifteen minutes."

"You have no supply?" Dietrich asked.

"Not for some time. And the Russians left nothing. What we're burning is what remains of the station. Also, our food is running low, and we have no report on when supply trains will be able to break through."

The general looked shocked. "Well, I'm sure it will be soon."

"I'm sure it will be, Herr General," the man replied flatly.

"Where are my quarters?"

"This dining car is our office. The next two cars provide our dormitories — our quarters. We have cleared out a space for you and Herr Speer." The man paused and looked at Erich. "Herr Speer's assistant will bunk with us."

"Very well. It has been a long day. I think I will get some rest before dinner."

"Of course, Herr General. No one will disturb you. I will show you to your quarters."

Albert was already seated next to a man, going over a thick, dog-eared report. Erich turned away in time to see General Dietrich and his guide disappear through the door at the end of the coach. Erich hesitated for a moment, then followed.

He passed through the next car, crudely converted into a dormitory with tiers of narrow bunks jammed tightly together. The closeness concerned him for a moment until he remembered the brutal winter just outside this cocoon of safety. He heard the door at the end of the car click shut. Erich hurried through the car and into the next one. Dietrich and his guide stood at the end of it. Erich couldn't hear what was being said, but the general finally nodded and moved to the other side of the blankets that partitioned the end of the car.

The other man turned, obviously surprised to see Erich there. He started back toward the front of the train.

Erich felt a chill worse than that in the

air. But after only a moment of indecision he started down the aisle between the bunks. At midpoint he came to the other man, hoping he wouldn't be challenged. The man said nothing, apparently not willing to question one of Speer's assistants. Erich squeezed past him and continued to the blankets, where he paused, afraid to continue, even more afraid to turn back.

"Herr General," he began in a shaky voice, "I need to see you for just a moment."

The rustling noises inside stopped.

"Enter," Dietrich's booming voice finally invited.

Erich pulled the blanket back and stepped inside. Dietrich sat on the bunk, his tunic draped over a chair. He had one boot off and had obviously been working on the other one. He frowned when he saw who it was.

"So, Herr . . ." He snapped his fingers.

"Von Arendt," Erich supplied. "Erich von Arendt. I am one of Herr Speer's assistants."

"Yes, yes, I know what your job is. What does Herr Speer want?"

Erich gulped. "I'm not coming for him, Herr General. This isn't business, it's personal."

Dietrich looked at him in disbelief. "Personal? Why in the world would you want to see *me?*"

Erich shifted uncomfortably on his feet. He thought about making some excuse and leaving, but he knew he had to go through with it. "It's about Bernhard Kammler. He's a private in the army, and his unit is somewhere in the Ukraine. He's the brother of — of a friend of mine. She hasn't heard from him since he was transferred, and she's worried about him. I was wondering . . . I was wondering if you could help us find out if he's all right."

Dietrich shook his head. "You dare to come to me with such a request? Everything about army operations is secret, you know that. Do you know what could happen to you for just asking this?"

"Yes. But all I want to know is if one German soldier is alive. I'm not asking what he's doing. And if anyone can find that out, it's you, Herr General."

Dietrich slowly stood. His eyes drilled into Erich's, but the younger man did not flinch. "Even if I wanted to, I wouldn't be able to find out. The military situation is changing too fast, the weather is impossible, and the supply situation is completely out of control."

"Much of this I know. My job . . ."

Dietrich snorted. "Yes, I suppose so. Well, all I can say is Herr Todt's organization better do something about this."

"Herr Speer can, if anyone can."

"We shall see."

Erich took a deep breath. Part of him said to just move on, but he also felt he must say more. "Herr General, am I to understand that you do not care what happens to the Fatherland's soldiers?"

"How dare you speak to me that way?"

"My job is to do something about this transportation mess so you can get the supplies you need. How well I do my job vitally affects your operations. All I want is information about one soldier."

Erich watched the obvious disbelief in the other's eyes. Finally the general nodded. He reached past Erich, grabbed his tunic, and put it on the bunk. "Sit," he ordered.

Erich sat down.

Dietrich remained standing. "For now I am going to forget I am an SS general, but I suggest that *you* remember it. You, no doubt, know more about this wretched supply situation than I do; all I know is that we aren't getting what we need. But I know more about how the war is going." He paused. "I must warn you. If you *ever*

323

repeat any of this to anyone, I will personally see to it that you are hanged for treason. Do you understand?"

Erich gulped and nodded.

"Very well. The war out here is not going well, contrary to what's being reported at home. I won't go into details, but Russian resistance is strong, and this winter is killing us! We were *not* ready for it. We have no idea how many men we are losing from combat, this weather, or starvation, but it's staggering." He paused and sighed. "Herr von Arendt, if your friend's brother is out here, I can't offer much hope. It is most likely she will never see him again — or even know what happened to him."

"Will you try to find out?"

"Were you listening to me? There is no way to find out. If he survives, you'll find out later."

"I see."

"Good. Now what about this blasted supply situation? What is Speer going to do about it?"

Erich sighed. "That's what we're here for. The first thing we have to do is survey the transportation system, then repair the railroads and get them going again. The Russians were very effective in destroying them."

"Can you do it?"

"Herr Speer can if anyone can."

"He'd better or we'll all be dead."

Erich stood. "Thank you for listening to me, Herr General."

Dietrich nodded. "Remember what I said."

"I will."

Erich left and returned through the two frigid cars to the dining car workroom.

Speer looked up as he entered. "Where have you been?" he snapped. "I need the production reports on railroad matériel."

"Sorry. I was talking to General Dietrich."

"What about?"

"Something personal."

Albert glared at him for a few moments, then said, "Well, where are the reports?"

"I'll get them."

Snow fell continuously during the next few days, blown into huge drifts by fierce winds. Erich marveled at his boss's stamina as Speer worked with his engineers as the true extent of the transportation nightmare began to emerge. When Speer was satisfied, Erich gathered up the reports and helped to pack for the return trip. They trekked through a howling blizzard to a train that was going to try to break through

325

the heavy drifts on a run to the west.

Erich and Albert took seats on the jammed coach and spent a restless night as the locomotive plowed through mounds of snow at less than ten miles an hour. Several times the train stopped to allow work crews to get off and shovel a path through the highest drifts. Erich awoke at each stop. Each time he noted that Albert was already awake. Erich finally drifted into a deep sleep just before dawn. He was dreaming about being trapped in the middle of a blizzard when something nudged him awake.

"We've stopped at a station. Want to get off and stretch your legs?" Albert asked.

Erich nodded as he wiped the sleep from his eyes. He followed Albert to the end of the car. They stepped down onto the platform of a burned-out station and looked around. It had finally stopped snowing. Erich shielded his eyes against the low rays of the rising sun. Something caught his eye. He looked around with growing apprehension.

"We're back in Dnepropetrovsk!" he said finally.

"We can't be."

"Well, we are. Apparently the snow's too deep to make it out."

Erich got their bags and briefcases, and they trudged through the deep snow, making large detours around drifts higher than their heads. They entered the dining car office they had left the previous day to the complete surprise of the engineering staff.

Erich found the next few days especially trying. Besides the discomfort from the frigid weather, he had to put up with an increasingly irritable boss each day as they waited for word that the westbound train was ready to try again.

At mid-morning a few days after the first attempt, Erich looked up from a report he was studying when he saw Albert enter from the dormitory car.

"Grab everything," he said. "The plane that brought General Dietrich here is leaving for Rastenburg in about an hour. The pilot has agreed to take us that far, but he has to leave immediately."

Erich got up. "Everything's packed except this." He held up the report. He quickly stuffed it into his briefcase and closed it. He pulled on his heavy coat, grabbed his bag and briefcase, and followed Albert out into the bitterly cold weather. It was clear, but the fierce wind blew the powdery snow into obscuring white curtains.

It took an hour to fight their way through the constantly changing drifts. By the time Erich saw the frail-looking aircraft, his face was numb and his fingers were in agony. The copilot stood by the open rear door and waved for them to hurry. The opposite side engine whined as the propeller began to slowly turn. The engine caught, and blue smoke billowed into the clear air.

Erich and Albert shuffled through the snow as fast as their unfeeling feet would carry them. The copilot took their bags and threw them into the cabin. The two passengers stepped up and hobbled to their seats near the cockpit. The copilot closed the door with a bang as the pilot started the other engine.

Erich fastened his seat belt securely as the converted bomber trundled over the snow. The engines went to full power, and moments later the tail came up. The plane bounced and lurched and repeatedly threatened to crash. It plowed through a huge drift, obscuring everything in a white cloud. Then with one final lurch, the plane leapt into the air. Erich breathed a sigh of relief. He glanced at Albert, who seemed unaffected. The plane droned on toward the west, away from the frozen wasteland the eastern front had become.

After landing in Rastenburg, Albert put in a call to Hitler's East Prussian headquarters. A half hour later one of Hitler's cars arrived to take them to the Wolf's Lair. The heavy sedan roared eastward paralleling a railroad line, passed the east guard post, and pulled up at a fence called "the outer wire." After a perfunctory check, the guards passed the VIPs into Hitler's fortified headquarters. Erich peered out the windows at the countless paths, huts, and machine-gun emplacements that provided the Lair's security. Finally they turned left, crossed railroad tracks, and stopped at the inner wire's guard post. The guards opened the gate and let them in. The driver dropped Erich off at his quarters, then took Albert to the Visitors' Bunker.

After dinner in the mess hall, Erich returned to his quarters. He reveled in having his own room, clean sheets, and a reprieve from the numbing cold. In minutes he fell into the first deep sleep he had experienced in several weeks.

Erich awoke with a start. For a moment

he didn't know what had awakened him. Then the phone rang again. He picked it up and heard the familiar voice of his boss.

"I need to see you at once, and bring our notes on the Russian railroad situation."

Erich was used to Albert's commands, but he sensed a strident tone he had not heard before. "Is anything the matter?"

"Herr Todt has just been killed."

Erich's mind snapped into sharp focus. "What happened?"

"His plane crashed on takeoff from Rastenburg. No one survived."

"I'm on my way."

Erich hurried to his boss's room. Albert opened the door as soon as Erich knocked.

"Let's go get some breakfast," Albert said. "We can discuss these while we eat."

The dining hall was crowded when they arrived. Erich noted the nervous chattering at the tables. He heard Herr Todt's name mentioned repeatedly as he and Albert made their way to a table near a window. They sat down and ordered. Erich plopped his heavy briefcase down on the table and opened it, pulling out the thick reports he had compiled concerning the railroad disaster in the Ukraine.

"What do you think will happen?" Erich asked as he arranged the papers.

Albert leaned closer. "I think the Führer will assign Herr Todt's construction jobs to me." He pointed to the reports. "I want to be ready in case the Führer asks me what I'm going to do about those railroads."

"I see. When do you think you will see Herr Hitler?"

"Not before noon. He never gets up early."

"Then we have plenty of time to go over these."

Albert nodded. "Give me the one about the bridges, and tell me what it's going to take to replace them."

Erich handed over a thick sheaf of papers. The waiter came out with their food and served them. Erich nibbled at his breakfast as Albert rapidly scanned each page.

Erich sat in a comfortable chair as he pored over the railroad reports. He glanced at his watch, noting it was a little after 2 in the afternoon. As expected, Albert had been summoned at around 1. Erich looked up as he heard quick footsteps. He was shocked to see his boss as pale as he had ever seen him.

"Grab your coat," Albert ordered. "We need to take a walk."

Erich thought about suggesting it was more comfortable inside but did as he was told and followed his boss outdoors. They crunched over the trampled snow as Albert led the way toward some trees.

"Did you get Herr Todt's construction jobs?" Erich asked.

Albert stopped walking when they were well under the trees. He exhaled, creating a large white cloud. "Our Führer has made me Reich Minister of Armaments."

Erich looked at him in disbelief. "What?"

"Our Führer has appointed me to the government. He's put me in charge of all military production, not merely the construction work of Organization Todt."

Erich felt something close to panic. No matter how urgently he wanted to withdraw, the horror that was the Third Reich kept drawing him ever closer. He longed for a way out, but he remembered only too well the warning the Gestapo had given him. That they would do to his family as they had threatened, he had no doubt. His conscience pricked him, but he thought of Johanna and how vulnerable she was.

"Congratulations," he told his boss weakly.

Albert nodded. "Thank you." He looked

into Erich's eyes. "I need your help now more than ever. This is going to be a huge job, and we will have definite opposition."

Erich looked at him in surprise. "How so? You're the minister, aren't you?"

Albert snorted. "Oh, yes, I'm the minister. This must go no further, Erich, but we can expect trouble from Reich Marshal Goering, and also, I suspect, from those high in the Todt organization."

"Reich Marshal Goering? Why him?"

Albert gave a short laugh. "The Reich Marshal came in right after the Führer appointed me Minister of Armaments. He asked for the position for himself and was furious when he found it had already been given to me."

"I see."

"I hope you do," Albert said after a short pause. "This isn't going to be easy. I think this will be the hardest job either one of us has ever done."

For Erich von Arendt, it would be harder than Albert Speer could possibly imagine.

Fifteen

Johanna and Karoline slogged through the filthy, hard-packed snow near the city center of Frankfurt. Each was bundled tightly against the cold, and each carried a dented metal bucket.

Johanna was more aware than usual of the war's devastation. The bombed-out buildings were obvious, but the human toll was the real tragedy, although hidden away in cemeteries or in some unknown field in the middle of a foreign country, forgotten and uncared for. Hot tears came to her eyes.

"Is something the matter?" Karoline asked.

Johanna nodded. "I got a letter from Erich yesterday."

"I see. I thought you were unusually quiet last night."

Johanna wiped her eyes on her coat sleeve. "I couldn't bring myself to talk about it then. He just got back from the Ukraine with Herr Speer. He said he couldn't go into details, but he had talked with someone who knew the war situation.

Erich said there wasn't much hope that Bernhard would survive."

"Oh, I'm so sorry, dear. This war is so horrible. Did he offer no hope?"

Johanna shook her head. "Not really. He said that based on what he knew about casualties plus what he had personally seen of winter conditions, it was extremely unlikely." She paused to wipe her eyes again. "There's something else . . . Erich was so tender and sweet in his letter. I guess that's the way he's always been, but I never noticed it before. He really cares about Bernhard and also how hard this is on me."

"Perhaps he also cares about you," Karoline said softly.

Johanna nodded, choking back her tears. "I've been thinking about that a lot. I believe he does. And I can see how I ruined everything — for him and for me."

"What do you mean?"

"I was so selfish. I only cared about what *I* wanted — the life of an artist and a romantic love that doesn't exist." She paused. "And I was mad about what my father did to me."

"Are you still mad at him?"

Johanna looked down. "No. Mama was right. Papa really was trying to give me a good marriage. It was wrong for him to decide who I would marry, but I think he wanted what he thought was best for me. And all of this blinded me to Erich's good qualities. I was so foolish."

"Don't dwell on that, dear. Pray to God, and ask Him to help you."

"I know God's there. And I'm so glad you and Wilhelm helped me find the Lord. But I've ruined my marriage."

"Trust in the Lord, Johanna. Trust Him to make restoration. We'll pray together when we get home. He'll hear you, I know He will."

Johanna nodded, but she felt no hope in her heart. No, that wasn't exactly true, she realized. There was a small glimmer of re-assurance there. She didn't understand it, but it was there. But how could anything be done about the consequences of past mistakes and the tragedies of the war?

They turned a corner and faced several whole blocks of tumbled brick and stone with pieces of timber jutting out at odd angles. Several blackened brick walls soared above the destruction, seeming so feeble Johanna wondered why they didn't fall over. Snow covered everything, as if to mask some of the horrors of war. Straight ahead the street was completely blocked by a fallen building. Women of all ages swarmed over the mountain of rubble, bringing down buckets of bricks to waiting horse-drawn carts.

Johanna and Karoline joined them. They found a mound of bricks, all that remained of a building façade. Behind it, charred blackened steps rose out of the rubble for half a flight, then ended, held up in part by a stack of pipes that extended a little higher.

Johanna dropped her bucket and started tossing sooty bricks into it. As soon as she had a load, she hauled it out to a nearby cart and dumped it in. The work was hard, and it seemed to Johanna they were making no progress. But she knew they were. This backbreaking work was all that made the inner city passable.

It was near dusk.

"Are you sure you weren't followed?" the man in the dark coat and hat asked. His breath condensed in white puffs in the freezing cold.

"No, I wasn't followed," Franz grumbled. "I know what I'm doing."

"I would feel more comfortable meeting in the country."

The two men sat on a bench.

"Tiergarten Park is safer," Franz replied. "It's close to where I work, and I often come here. It would cause more suspicion if I went out in the country for no reason. Look around. We're alone."

Franz watched as the man glanced about nervously. He almost smiled at the other's discomfort.

"I guess it will have to do. Do you have it?"

Franz slipped him a tiny roll of film. "And do you have *my* little present?"

The man handed him a slim booklet. "A Swiss numbered account as you requested."

Franz glanced at the first page, then slipped the account book into a coat pocket. "It's not much for the risk I'm taking."

"It's what we agreed on," the other snapped. "The previous information was good, I'm told, but hardly worth a raid on Fort Knox. However, if you have access to more sensitive information, the rate could go up."

"My source is impeccable, I assure you."

"I'm sure it is, but what you've given us so far is only routine intelligence."

Franz thought for a moment. "If I can get you better information as you say, what will you give me?"

"What sort of information are we talking about?"

"The man I'm getting this from has access to the highest levels of government. I can get just about anything you want."

"So you say."

"I'll get it. Just tell me how much you'll pay."

The man got up slowly. After a bit he said, "I'll have your answer soon."

Erich continued to carry out his duties because he had no choice. He watched the unfolding disaster from the intimate vantage point of one of Reich Minister Speer's most trusted assistants. He watched as the enemy relentlessly destroyed German cities and factories, only to see his boss replace the war production almost as fast as it was lost. February 1943 saw the end of Hitler's grand assault on Russia with the German surrender at Stalingrad.

Erich watched as Albert Speer became more and more wrapped up in maintaining war production, and this mania drew Erich ever closer to the dirty flame that burned at the heart of National Socialism. In August he accompanied his boss on a quick trip to Rastenburg. He was left cooling his heels while Albert met with Hitler and Himmler. Afterward Speer didn't say a word about the meeting, but Erich had never seen him so depressed.

By December 1943, Erich was spending most of his time directing engineering teams and approving plans for moving factories into various locations in the German countryside. It was depressing and monotonous work, but it was also effective. War production remained high despite devastating destruction from the bombing raids.

Erich expected December 10 to be normal, if normal meant propping up German production against an increasing rain of death. But an urgent summons from his boss's office soon had them both flying toward Weimar and the Harz Mountains on Speer's private plane. Besides the pilot, they were the only ones aboard. Erich looked down at the ground, surprised at how peaceful it looked from the air.

"There's something you need to know before we get there," Albert said.

"What's that?" Erich asked, turning away from the window.

"Herr Himmler has convinced the Führer to allow him to build underground factories to produce the V2 rocket."

"What? But that comes under your Ministry."

"Yes, I know that," Albert snapped. "But Himmler told the Führer that with the factories in caves they would be impossible for the enemy to bomb. And he promised that all the workers would come from the Buchenwald concentration camp. I was aghast. I said we shouldn't do it, but the Führer asked me for an alternative, and I didn't have one. So he approved Himmler's plan and gave it the code name Dora."

Erich felt his stomach start churning. "That's where we're going?"

"Yes. My medical director made a visit there, and he says it's like Dante's *Inferno*. I have to see it for myself, and I want you to document it." He paused. "Write down everything you see — I'm depending on your memory. I wanted to bring a camera, but we can't chance it."

"How did you get Herr Himmler's permission to visit?"

Albert gave a bitter laugh. "He doesn't know about it. I called his project director and told him I was coming as Reich Minister to evaluate the efficiency of his production methods. He didn't seem happy but apparently decided he couldn't refuse."

"What if he calls Herr Himmler?"

The plane began descending.

"Let's hope he doesn't. Oh, and one more thing."

"What's that?"

"I can't tell you how sensitive this is . . . When we get back, I want you to prepare the report yourself — don't use a secretary. Then I want you to personally see to it that it's filed properly in the Ministry archives."

Erich closed his eyes and sighed.

"Did you hear me?" Albert asked.

"Yes. I will do as you say."

"Good."

The plane made its approach and landed. A waiting Ministry car drove them deep into the Harz Mountains to the main entrance of the man-made caves and tunnels. The driver rolled down his window and presented the Ministry papers, and the guards opened the gates. After a bumpy ride over a poorly graded road, the car pulled up outside the black mouth of a large cave. A thin man in a heavy coat waited for them with a small retinue.

Erich grabbed his notepad and checked his pocket for pens. He got out and joined Albert.

"I am Hermann Olbrich," the thin man said as he shook hands. "I will be your guide today."

"Very well," Albert replied. "Shall we proceed?"

Olbrich nodded and led them toward the cave. It seemed to Erich that they were entering the mouth of some terrible beast. The cheerful outside light faded as they walked inside, replaced by the dim glow of naked bulbs stitched together by hastily installed wiring. Erich had expected to find it warmer inside, but it remained cold and damp. Dark, deep niches lined each side of the tunnel.

"What are those?" Albert asked as they walked.

"Where the workers sleep," Herr Olbrich replied. "Ordinarily the night shift would be in them right now, but they are on the factory floor for your inspection."

"You have no barracks?"

"We have no need. It's more efficient if they sleep close to where they work."

The inspection team turned a corner and entered a vast man-made cavern. The lighting was better here, and Erich could see the production line. Cylindrical V2 rockets in varying stages of completion rested on dollies. A ragged formation of men in striped prisoner's uniforms stood beside their work, waiting. Erich could smell them long before he got there, an unpleasant odor that rapidly turned into a stench. Erich felt his stomach rebelling. As he got closer he saw the filthy uniforms and the gaunt, skeletal bodies that the tattered fabric did not completely cover. They shivered in the icy dampness. A guard barked an order, and the men snatched off their caps.

Herr Olbrich pointed toward one of the V2s. "Would you care to examine the rockets, Herr Reich Minister?"

Albert continued walking until he was in the center of the prisoners' formation. Erich stopped when his boss did and stared at the grim faces. Not one of the men would look him in the eye, each one looking quickly away. Erich started scribbling furiously as he remembered his task.

"Are you here to see our production line?" Olbrich asked.

Albert looked at him. "I came to see everything," he replied slowly.

"Then may I suggest we proceed."

"Please do."

When a prisoner on the front row collapsed on the rough stone floor, Erich stopped writing and stared at the motionless man. An SS guard ran up with a raised wooden truncheon but stopped when he saw Erich. He paused for a moment as if he couldn't decide what to do. Then he dropped the truncheon and ordered two prisoners to pick up the man. Erich gasped as he saw the unconscious man's bloody nose.

"Erich!"

Erich turned to see his boss motioning impatiently.

"Come! We have more to see."

Erich dashed to catch up. The inspection party continued down the long assembly line. Soon Erich noticed another odor, different from that of filthy bodies but just as unpleasant. The inspectors passed through a small tunnel and emerged into a cavern filled with narrow tables jammed tightly together. At one end stood a row of large kettles, each one containing a dark brownish-black mixture that bubbled vigorously. Erich knew this was the source of the new stench.

"This is the prisoners' dining hall," Herr Olbrich explained.

Albert glanced at his watch. "It's almost 1. When do they eat?"

"Normally at noon. However, we had to delay serving until after your inspection."

"I will not have this!" Albert said, his voice rising. "You will begin serving immediately."

Olbrich hesitated a moment, then whispered to one of his men. The man returned to the factory floor. Soon sounds of shuffling feet drifted through the tunnel, but not a voice was heard.

"Give me some of what you're serving them," Albert ordered.

"I wouldn't advise that," Olbrich replied.

"Give it to me!"

Olbrich gave the order. A cook in a filthy white uniform dipped a ladle into a pot and deposited an amorphous glob on a dented tin plate. He had to send an assistant to find a spoon. The man returned and gave it to the cook, who inspected it, polished it with his grimy apron, and placed it on the plate. Albert walked slowly toward the cook and took the plate. Erich saw the look of disgust on his face as he dipped the spoon and slowly raised it to his lips. After a slight pause Albert put the spoon in his mouth. A moment later he spat out the food and dropped the plate.

"Where did you get this?" he shouted. "The latrine?"

"I assure you, Herr Reich Minister . . ." Olbrich began.

"This is inedible!"

The first of the prisoners began filing in, lining up before the kettles.

Erich's eyes watered as a vagrant breeze

wafted the odor over him. He looked at the nearest kettle and then at the mess at Albert's feet. The reaction was too sudden for him to control. He bent double and retched violently, splattering himself and those nearest him. He moaned as his stomach knotted up again and again, dumping its contents onto the filthy floor. He spat, trying to get the vile taste out of his mouth. Feeling a hand on his shoulder, Erich groaned and slowly stood upright.

"Are you all right?" Albert whispered, squeezing his shoulder.

Erich nodded.

"Good. Write all this down."

"What did you say?" Olbrich asked.

"We will continue with the inspection," Albert said. "I think we have finished in here. Please show us the rest of your installation."

"As you wish, Reich Minister."

Erich finished his notes. He paused a moment at the exit tunnel and looked back. The prisoners began to line the narrow tables. They scooped their meager portions from the tin plates with their bare hands. The first to sit down were finished in moments. They licked the plates clean. It was all Erich could do to keep from retching again.

★ ★ ★

Erich entered Berlin's Romanische Café and scanned the room.

Franz waved to him from a corner table. Erich made his way through the late-night crowd, wondering if there was ever a time the restaurant was not busy. He sat down and looked nervously around.

Franz exhaled loudly and peered at his friend over his nearly empty beer stein. "So, what's new besides the increase in bombing raids?" he asked.

"Will you hold it down," Erich whispered.

"But we're still winning the war." He smiled at his friend. "Don't worry. None of Himmler's goons are in here. Only us intellectual folks. If the SS or the Gestapo ever came across an intelligent idea, they'd have it shot as a traitor to the Reich."

"Will you shut up!"

Franz tilted his head to the side and drained the rest of his beer. He stared at the empty stein as if it had done something wrong, then waved frantically for a refill. Moments later two brimming steins slid across the slick table and the empty one disappeared.

"That's what I call service," he slurred.

Erich ignored his beer. "Franz, I have to

348

talk to someone."

"Well, *I'm* someone." He grinned, then held up his hand. "Say, did you hear this one? What's the difference between India and Germany? In India, one man starves for millions; in Germany millions starve for one man. Get it? Gandhi and . . ." He took a comb out of his pocket and held it under his nose. "Der Führer."

"Stop it!" Erich hissed. "You're going to get us both arrested."

Franz sat rigidly at attention and assumed a deadpan expression. "I am ready to hear your confession, my son," he said somberly.

Tears came to Erich's eyes. He wiped them with the back of his hand.

Franz exhaled slowly. "I'm sorry, Erich. The war — and my job — are driving me crazy. What did you want to tell me?"

"I saw something yesterday I don't think I can handle. I know our government has done some terrible things, but I had no idea."

"What was it?"

"Have you heard of a project called Dora?"

"No, can't say as I have."

"Well, Herr Himmler is in charge of it — that's why I asked. It's a secret factory hidden inside a mountain near Weimar. We're building V2s down there."

"Wow! That *is* something. I thought when the enemy destroyed Peenemünde, that was it for the rockets."

"Well, it wasn't. Herr Speer took me along to document everything about it, and I mean *everything*. I've never seen him so upset."

Franz took a slow sip from his stein and set it down. "Where exactly is this?"

"It's . . ." Erich began, then shook his head. "I don't think I should go into details."

Franz shrugged. "OK . . . So how did Herr Speer hear about it?"

"Someone on his medical staff told him the conditions there were horrible. Well, they are — I saw it all with my own eyes. It's the worst thing I've ever seen. The workers come from Buchenwald and . . ." Erich paused, feeling again the soul-wrenching sickness he had experienced at Dora. "What the SS is doing to those people — it's . . . it's hideous. I couldn't sleep at all last night."

"I could point out that those in Buchenwald are enemies of the Reich," Franz said.

Erich slammed his fist down on the

table. "Not all of them! And I don't care *who* it is! *No one* should be treated the way those men are being treated!"

Franz held up his hands. "Take it easy."

"It's not right," Erich said, a little more softly. "This is criminal, Franz. It's *criminal.*"

Sixteen

The man entered Tiergarten Park and walked slowly down the cleared walk between dingy piles of snow. He stopped beside the bench, looked around, and sat down.

Franz glanced at him and frowned. "I'm in awe," he said. "You must teach me how I can be a spy just like you."

"Quiet," the man hissed between his teeth. "Maybe you don't value your life, but I do mine. Now what did you want to see me about?"

"I have vital information. What will you pay for it?"

"That depends on what it is."

"I know where the V2s are being built."

"Peenemünde is rubble."

"Ah, but we've built an underground factory. My friend has seen it with his own eyes. V2s are being built at this very moment."

The man turned and clutched Franz's arm. "Are you sure?"

"Positive. So, how much is it worth?"

The man paused. "We would have to verify this."

"I understand. How much?"

"That's not for me to say. But it would be a lot — over a million dollars, I'm sure."

Franz nodded. "That's acceptable."

"So, where is this factory?"

"It's inside a mountain near Weimar — tunneled, I would guess."

"Where exactly?"

"That's all my friend told me. He wouldn't give me the precise location."

"That's not good enough. Our people will never pay for anything that vague."

Franz turned slightly and glared at the man. "You didn't even *know* about this factory. Now you do, and I've told you the general location. Can't your spies take it from there?"

The man shook his head. "We'll give you the regular payment for this. Get us the exact coordinates, and you'll get the rest."

"I don't know if I can manage that."

The man shrugged and got slowly to his feet. "That's your problem." He looked down at Franz. "If you *do* find out, contact me the usual way." He walked away.

The brutal winter of 1943 gradually released its hold on Europe. Spring came and then summer. By the first days of July,

Johanna's memories of the heavy snows were fading, helped along by the brutal reality of a city under air siege. The number of raids and the intense tension seemed to increase daily. Johanna was amazed by the resilience of those around her as they grimly refused to leave the battered city. Much of the city center now lay in ruins. With every raid, Johanna expected to find Herr Dorpmüller's apartment building leveled, but each time it still stood.

Today Johanna and Karoline sat on a bench near the Römer, Frankfurt's old town hall. It was noon, and the women were taking a break from their work of clearing rubble. Karoline opened a small cloth bag and took out their lunch, two small boiled potatoes. She handed one to Johanna, then took her hand. They bowed their heads as Karoline prayed.

"Heavenly Father, we thank You for Your many blessings. Thank You for this food You have provided. May it nourish our bodies even as Your Son nourishes our souls. Amen."

"Amen," Johanna echoed.

She took a bite of her potato. Karoline nibbled at hers.

"You got another letter from Erich yesterday," the older woman observed.

Johanna grinned. "Are you prying, Frau Hoffmann?"

Karoline's eyes twinkled. "Of course not, dear. I'm only showing normal concern for my young sister in Christ." She paused. "Of course, if you don't wish to discuss it . . ."

"I'm tempted. What if I don't?"

"Then I would probably die from curiosity, and you would have to explain *that* to Wilhelm."

"Well, I can't have that on my conscience." She paused and took a deep breath. "Yes, I got another letter from Erich. You know, I never intended to strike up a correspondence with him. I wrote him the first time because I was desperate about Bernhard . . ." The tears came unexpectedly as the painful memories returned.

"There, there, dear," Karoline said. "Bernhard is in the Lord's hands. We have to trust Him."

Johanna nodded and wiped her eyes with her handkerchief. "I know." She sighed. "I really appreciate what Erich did. His letter was so tender. I felt like I had to write him back to thank him. And then he wrote *me* back."

"And you have been wearing out the postal system ever since."

Johanna struggled with her emotions. The pain of her loss merged with her growing appreciation for a person she had never really known.

"I'm beginning to see him differently. Erich has a lot of character that I never saw. He showed me love in ways I didn't appreciate. He doesn't know much about the Bible, but I'm convinced he has a saving faith in Jesus. I sense from his letters that he's unhappy with his work, which makes me wonder why he doesn't quit."

"There has to be a reason," Karoline said. "But I agree with you — everything you've told me about him speaks of character." She paused. "I think he may still love you, Johanna. Have you thought about going back to him?"

Johanna looked at her friend in surprise. "It's too late for that. After all I did, he'd never take me back. I was a fool — a selfish fool. That fantasy about Ulrich, my dreams of being a musician . . . I nagged him constantly because I blamed him for my misery. I never tried to understand what he was going through, trying to reconcile his beliefs with his work. I think he would have confided in me if I had shown a shred of compassion.

No, I got what I deserved."

Karoline patted her hand. "I don't think things are as bad as you think. But there *is* one thing you still need to face."

"What's that?"

"Your father, and how he planned your life for you."

Johanna nodded. "Yes, I know. But Erich had nothing to do with that. All he ever showed me was love — at least until his work started consuming him. Like Mother tried to tell me, I had a good husband."

"Why don't you write Erich and ask him if you can pay him a visit, talk it out with him. Isn't that worth a try?"

Johanna thought about it for a long time. Finally she said, "Perhaps it is. I'll pray about it."

Erich answered Albert's summons immediately. He entered the office, shut the door, and sat down. He noted the familiar furrowed brow and expected trouble.

"Erich, I think Herr Himmler knows that we have documentation on the conditions at Dora. I just got a call from the supervisor of Ministry archives saying that someone in the SS — a civilian— ordered him to turn over the Dora files."

"Did they find out who?"

Albert shook his head. "No. The man flashed his identification too quickly. But the supervisor said it looked authentic, enough so that he almost turned over the files. When he said he had to call my office, the man took off."

"That sounds bad."

"Yes, it does. I'm afraid Herr Himmler might send a squad over here and take it by force."

"Would he dare?"

Albert shrugged. "I don't know. But I'm not going to take the chance. I want you to go get those files. Do you have a safe in your house?"

"No."

"Have our staff requisition the work immediately. Tell them you want it hidden. Take the papers home with you today, and when the safe is finished, keep them in there."

"What if Herr Himmler has my house searched?"

"I don't think he will. At any rate, the files will be safer there than here."

"Yes, sir."

Albert leaned back in his chair. "Ready for your trip to Rastenburg?"

"I think so, but I'm not looking forward to it."

"I know, but it can't be helped. Someone has to make sure the Wolf's Lair construction projects are completed to the Führer's satisfaction, especially the work on his bunker."

"I know."

Albert smiled. "He trusts you, Erich. Do a good job."

Erich struggled to maintain his composure. "I will."

"I know you will. You always do."

Erich hesitated. "There's something I'd like to ask you."

The black eyebrows arched. "What's that?"

"I have a lot to do, getting ready for my trip. Would it be possible for me to use a Ministry car? It would make things a lot easier."

Albert nodded. "Certainly. Requisition it in my name."

"Thank you." He started to get up, then sat back down. "There is one other thing."

"Yes?"

"You remember my wife, Johanna?"

"Yes, of course. I've always been sorry about what happened."

"Well, she's coming up to Berlin to see me. I'm not sure about what, but I'll be meeting her train tomorrow and taking her to dinner and then to the home of the friend she's staying with. Is it all right if I use the car for that as well?"

Albert nodded. "Of course. I appreciate the work you do for me, Erich." He paused. "I hope the situation works out between the two of you."

Erich looked down self-consciously. "I do too."

The doorbell rang.

"I'll get it, Frau Liedig," Erich said.

He opened the door. "Hello, Franz. I'm glad you could come on such short notice. I need the company."

Franz entered. "That's what friends are for. How are you doing?"

Erich ran a hand through his thick brown hair. "I'm not sure. A lot is going on right now, and you're the only one I can confide in." He smiled. "I hope I'm not making a pest of myself."

"Nonsense. You listen to my woes, so why shouldn't I listen to yours? Besides, we've been friends forever."

Erich clapped him on the back. "That we have. Shall we see what Frau Liedig has prepared for us?"

Franz's expression became serious. "I didn't bring my food taster with me."

"Will you stop? Frau Liedig isn't the monster you keep making her out to be."

"Let me be the judge of that."

They sat down to dinner, and Frau Liedig brought in pot roast, potatoes, and carrots. She served them and returned to the kitchen.

"Very nice, Erich. Have you heard there's a war on?"

Erich frowned. "Of course. But there are advantages to working for the Ministry of Armaments."

Franz peered at his plate. "Those potatoes *do* look like hand grenades, now that you mention it. And what caliber are those carrots?"

Erich tried to keep a straight face but couldn't. "Could we call a truce until after dinner?"

"I wasn't criticizing, believe me."

They said very little as they ate their meal. After they finished the dessert, they retired to the sitting room. They sat in the chairs by the front windows, covered with heavy blackout curtains.

"That dinner was excellent, Herr von Arendt," Franz said. "Thank you for your hospitality."

Erich nodded. "You're very welcome."

"You said there was something you

wanted to talk about?"

"Several things actually."

"Well, after a dinner like that, I'm ready to listen. Fire away."

Erich felt his stomach tighten. "You remember what I told you about Dora?"

"How could I forget?"

"Well, someone tried to steal the report I made. My boss thinks Herr Himmler knows we have it. Anyhow, Herr Speer ordered me to bring it home."

Franz sat upright. "You have the report here?"

Erich nodded. "Yes, in my office. The Ministry is building a hidden safe in there. When it's finished, that's where the report will stay."

"I hope they're making good progress on the safe. I'd feel nervous having a report like that out in the open."

"The safe will be ready in two days. But yes, I'll feel more comfortable once the report's locked up. Herr Speer isn't concerned though. I asked him about it, and he said it's surely safer here than in our file room."

Franz settled back in his chair. "I can see how this would bother you. But did you say there was more?"

Erich cleared his throat. "Yes, I did. And

I don't know exactly where to begin. I think I told you about looking for Bernhard when I was in the Ukraine with Herr Speer."

Franz nodded. "Yes. A tragic loss. From what you have told me, Bernhard was a fine young man."

"Well, after Johanna wrote me, we started corresponding, and one letter led to the next. Anyway, the last time she wrote, she asked if she could come to Berlin to see me."

Franz's eyes grew wide. "Really? Did she say why?"

"No. She said she couldn't talk about it in a letter."

"Interesting. Do your parents know?"

Erich shook his head. "No. I don't see them very often, because of my work." He paused. "Besides, I don't want to say anything to them until I see how this goes."

"I understand. When is she coming?"

"I'm meeting her train late tomorrow afternoon. We'll have dinner, and I'll find out what she wants to tell me. Then I'll drop her off at her friend's place." A wry smile came to his face. "All this on top of baby-sitting the Dora report and getting ready for my trip to Rastenburg to supervise work on the Führer's bunker."

Franz shook his head. "Sounds like you have your hands full. When is the Rastenburg trip?"

"Day after tomorrow. I'll probably be there several weeks to a month, depending on how the work goes."

"Ah, eastern Prussia in July and working for our Führer — what could be better?"

Erich frowned. "Not funny, Franz."

"No, I guess it's not. Forget I said it." He paused. "You say you don't know why Johanna's coming?"

"She didn't say."

"You have no idea?"

Erich took a deep breath. "I can't get it out of my mind. Her letters are — I don't know — they don't sound like the Johanna I remember. She even apologized for how she had hurt me. But no, I don't know why she's coming."

"Do you still love her?"

Erich's eyes brimmed suddenly. He brought a hand up and wiped them away. "Yes, I think I do — and that scares me. I'd like to believe it's possible for us to get back together, but what if I'm wrong?"

"I see. Is there anything I can do?"

Erich thought for a moment. "I hate to ask it, but can you come over tomorrow night? I should be back from taking Johanna to her friend's place by around 11." He swallowed hard. "I think I may need someone to talk to."

"Certainly. I'll be on your doorstep at 11 sharp."

Near midnight, Franz stood on Belle Vue Allee and looked into the inky darkness of Tiergarten Park. A lone car came toward him, the thin slits of its headlights providing feeble light for the unseen driver. Black monoliths rose in the distance above the park, but not a glimmer of light escaped from any of the windows. Franz heard the whirring growl of a tram before he could see the dimly lit route sign. A blinding blue flash momentarily illuminated the vehicle as it rounded a curve.

Franz felt his heartbeat quicken as he left the sidewalk and started down the path into the Tiergarten. Up ahead he saw a few tiny dots of light bobbing toward him, phosphorescent buttons on those who had to be out. He glanced down to make sure his was visible. He shuffled slowly along, trusting his shoes to warn him of unseen obstacles. An unseen pedestrian passed on his left. Franz felt an icy pang of fear as he saw someone approaching with buttons arranged in the shape of a swastika. He thought about turning back but decided that would be more suspicious than continuing on. The unseen party member passed by in eerie silence.

The pedestrian traffic grew steadily more sparse the deeper into Tiergarten he went. He left the path, inching his way across the grass toward where he thought the bench was. He stopped. Ahead, a little to the side, he saw a single, motionless button. Franz covered his button for a few seconds, then revealed it. He did this two more times and waited. For long moments he thought he had made a mistake. Then the other button winked out and reappeared three times. Franz shuffled to the bench, felt until he touched wood, then sat down.

"Why the rush?" the familiar voice whispered.

"I think I can get you the exact location," Franz replied.

" 'Dora?' "

"Yes. How much is it worth?"

"One million, in dollars."

"Very well. My chance comes tomorrow night. I will let you know when to meet me here."

Franz got up and started shuffling his way back toward the path. He couldn't see a thing as he crept along in the blackness.

Seventeen

Johanna waited until they were seated, then leaned forward over the small table. "You didn't have to bring me to Horcher's, Erich," she whispered. "But thank you."

She saw the familiar shy smile she hadn't seen for too long. He looked haggard, she noted, but was still quite handsome. She felt her pulse quicken, surprised at the feeling.

"I wanted it to be nice," he said.

"Well, it is that. I didn't think there was anything like this left in Germany."

"There is, for the Nazi elite."

The waiter came up, and Erich ordered for them. The man made a slight bow and disappeared in the direction of the kitchen.

"Johanna, I appreciate your letters. They're bright spots in my rather grim existence. And when you said you wanted to come visit — well, I didn't know what to think." He paused. "But I'm glad you did. It's good to see you."

Johanna felt a tightness in her throat. "It's good to see you too, Erich. How have you been?"

He shrugged. "Very busy. This war is a horrible trial for us all. It's like a living nightmare."

"Yes, it is, in many ways. How are your parents?"

"They're doing as well as can be expected. Herr Speer is keeping Papa busy with the Berlin models." Erich lowered his voice and leaned over the table. "Talk about 'fiddling while Rome burns.'" He straightened back up. "Anyhow, I don't see them much, and I feel bad about that, but I don't know what I can do about it."

"This war is hard on us all."

"Yes, it is." He took a sip of water. "How have *you* been, Johanna?"

She took a deep breath. "That's a difficult question. Some you know, from my letters. But the most important thing is that I've become a Christian."

Erich's eyebrows shot up. "Really?"

Johanna tried not to smile. "You needn't sound so surprised."

"Sorry." His flustered expression lasted only a moment. "But it does surprise me."

Johanna nodded. "I understand." She paused. "I'm different now. I met these wonderful people in Frankfurt — Wilhelm and Karoline Hoffmann. They took care of me during some really tough times. And they led me to the Lord. I'm even reading the Bible."

"Now that *is* serious. I'm not sure I've ever done anything but flip through the pages of one. But I do believe in Jesus."

"I know you do. And I'm sorry for how I taunted you about it . . ." She stopped suddenly. ". . . when we were still together. There's a *lot* I'm sorry for, Erich."

The tears came suddenly. She pulled out her handkerchief and wiped them away.

"Are you all right?" he asked.

She nodded.

The waiter brought their salads. Johanna waited until he was out of earshot. She knew what she had to do, but that didn't make it any easier. "I apologize for the way I treated you, Erich. Will you forgive me?"

He stared at her for a few moments. "Well, yes, I . . . of course I will." He paused. "But I need to ask your forgiveness as well. I know I was spending too much time at work, and not caring enough about your needs. That was wrong, and I'm sorry. And something else . . ."

"What's that?"

"I realized, after we were married, what your father — and mine — did without your consent. Johanna, I wanted you more than anything, but it wasn't right for them to decide your life for you."

She reached across the table and took his hand. "You didn't make that decision, Erich, they did."

"Yes, but I could have done more to find out how things really were with you." He sighed. "I made a lot of assumptions."

She smiled. "Yes, you did. But so did I."

They nibbled away at their salads. The waiter returned with the soup course, taking away nearly full plates.

Johanna tried a spoonful. "Erich, this is wonderful. This is more than I usually eat all day." She stopped in embarrassment when she saw his hurt expression. "I didn't mean that as criticism."

He shrugged. "That's all right. Believe me, in my work for Herr Speer I know how the rest of Germany lives. And I know how wrong all this is. I've seen things . . ."

She saw the pain in his eyes. "What things?"

He leaned over the table and lowered his voice. "You know bad things are going on — most Germans know. But it's far worse than you realize — I've seen it with my own eyes. But I can't say more."

She nodded. "I understand."

They lapsed into silence as they finished their soup. The waiter made his appearance and served the main course — trout, neatly filleted. Johanna tried hers and found that it brought back memories of summers spent in Bavaria.

"This is excellent."

"I'm glad you like it."

Johanna watched him as he ate. She had silently observed him ever since he picked her up at the station. She wondered about the shifts between the boyish animation she remembered and the obvious pain that occasionally came through.

She put down her fork. "I'd like to ask you something, Erich."

"Certainly. What is it?"

She took a deep breath. "I was wrong to leave you, very wrong. Do you think there's any possibility we could get back together?"

He swallowed the wrong way and had to cough. "You really want to do that?" he asked when he could.

She felt a tightness in her throat. "Yes, yes, I do."

"Why?"

Her eyes brimmed. "Because after I became a Christian, I had a long time to think about everything that had happened." She smiled through her tears. "A dear friend helped me see it. I saw that you were a fine husband, and you really *were* in love with me. I saw your strong character qualities, things I was blind to before. I realized how self-centered and shallow I was and how poorly Ulrich compared to someone like you. I wasted my emotions on a cad. Papa knew what he was doing when he got me away from Ulrich and arranged my marriage to you. I just wish he had let me come to see it for myself. I think I would have in time." She began to cry into her handkerchief. "I'm sorry for what I did," she said finally. "I don't really expect you to take me back, but I'm hoping we can try again. This time I would love you as a wife should."

He blinked his eyes and for several moments said nothing. Then she saw the wetness in his eyes. "Johanna, you have no idea how I've longed to hear you say that, but I thought it was impossible. And when you wrote saying you wanted to come see me . . . well, I wondered, but I didn't dare hope. Johanna, I love you — I've always loved you. Yes, I want you back — more than I've ever wanted anything."

Tears of joy ran down her cheeks. She wiped them away, not caring what that did to her makeup. She heaved a sigh of relief and contentment as the heavy burden lifted from her.

She looked down at her plate. "I don't think I can eat any more."

He shook his head. "I can't either. Shall we go?"

"Yes, please."

He counted out a stack of marks and left them on the table. They walked out of Horcher's and into the warm night. Erich took her arm and escorted her to the Ministry car, stopping short of the white-painted curb.

Her pulse began to hammer as he gently turned her around. She slid into his embrace as his head came down. She felt his hot breath just before their lips met. He kissed her once, barely a brush. Then again, tender but with unmistakable feeling. She returned each one with a passion that surprised her. With joy, she felt him respond. Finally they broke.

"Johanna," he gasped, "I've missed you so. I love you."

"I love you too. When I think of what I gave up . . ."

"Don't say it. That's all over now. The only thing that matters is that we're together again."

She nestled her head on his shoulder, and he stroked her hair and held her gently. A tram rumbled by in the center of the street. As it passed, the pole arced. Johanna looked up and saw Erich looking down at her, his eyes full of love.

"Does your friend have a phone?" Erich asked.

"Yes."

"Why don't we call her from the house and tell her you're not coming?"

"What?"

"We're still married, you know."

"Yes, but . . ."

"And we both want to put our marriage back together, don't we?"

"Yes, yes, we do."

"Shall we go home, Frau von Arendt?"

She looked up at his unseen face. "Yes, Herr von Arendt, I would like that very much."

He opened the door for her, and she got in. Johanna scooted across the seat as Erich walked around and entered from the driver's side. She snuggled next to him as he drove slowly through Berlin. The narrow slits in the headlights provided feeble illumination. Even so, Johanna had no trouble recognizing their route. She felt her heart quicken as they made the final turn onto their street. She smiled. It truly was "their street" again. Up ahead she saw the house. Erich parked in front. Suddenly it was quiet again and very dark.

Erich got out and came around the car. He opened Johanna's door and helped her out.

"Watch your step," he said as he guided her toward the white-painted curb.

Johanna heard a faint sound that seemed to come from near the corner. It was the unmistakable gritty sound of shoe leather on pavement. A glowing button appeared and came toward them. Johanna's heart skipped a beat as Erich stopped suddenly.

"Erich, is that you?" said a familiar voice.

"Franz, you scared me," Erich replied.

"It's the blackout. Makes it impossible to see anything."

"Let's get inside." He paused. "Franz, Johanna is with me."

"Johanna? I thought . . ."

"We'll discuss it inside," Erich said.

He helped his wife up the steps and opened the door. Johanna and Franz entered. She looked at him curiously as Erich closed the door and led them into the front room.

"Please sit down," he said to them both.

Franz took a chair by the window, while Erich and Johanna sat on the couch. He put his hand over hers and squeezed it. She turned toward him and smiled.

"Johanna and I love each other, and we've decided to get back together." He smiled. "So she won't be going to her friend's place tonight."

"I see. Well, my congratulations to you both."

Johanna wondered at Franz's strained expression. When he saw her questioning gaze, his familiar smile returned.

"Aren't you early?" Erich asked.

"Yes, I am. My evening didn't go as planned." He grinned. "No need to go into details. So I decided to come over and wait for you. Didn't have anything else to do."

"Sorry. I didn't mean to pry."

"That's all right. Listen, I know you two want to be alone. I think it's wonderful you're back together. Could I ask one favor before I leave?"

"Well, sure," Erich replied. "What is it?"

"You have a secure phone in your office, don't you?"

"Yes. It's for my Ministry work."

"I thought so. I need to contact my office tonight. It would save me a trip through this blackout if I could phone them."

"Of course." Erich started to get up. "I'll

show you where it is."

"Don't bother." He laughed. "I *know* what a phone looks like. Stay with your beautiful wife. I'll only be a moment."

Erich settled back down. Franz got up and walked toward the hall in long even strides.

Franz stopped at the top of the stairs and looked back. All he could hear was a soft murmur coming from the sitting room. He had to force himself not to tiptoe as he hurried toward Erich's office. He entered and gently closed the door. He scanned the room quickly. The desk was a mess, piled high with blueprints, stacks of reports, and books. The phone occupied one corner as if under siege by the clutter. And there in a corner chair sat Erich's briefcase, the same one Franz had given him as a wedding present.

Franz breathed a sigh of relief as he hurried over to it. He bent over, unbuckled the straps, and opened the flap. On top sat a thick sheaf of papers with one word on the cover sheet: *Dora.*

"Thank you, Erich," Franz whispered under his breath.

He stood up with the report and looked around. He needed a flat surface to photograph the pages, and that certainly was not the desk. A small table stood by the window, a table with only one thing on it — a delicately carved wooden music box. Franz picked it up and placed it on the jumbled desk.

He riffled quickly through the top pages of the report, stopping when he came to a thick document. Unfolding it, he saw a detailed Ministry of Armaments map of the Weimar area. And there, in the midst of the Harz Mountains, was a penciled X with the notation *Dora*.

Franz placed the map on the table and smoothed the creases. He pulled a floor lamp over, turned it on, and adjusted the shade to illuminate the document. He reached into a pocket and pulled out the miniature camera. He opened it, sighted through the viewfinder, and snapped several pictures. He then quickly selected several other pages and photographed them, though he knew all he really needed was the map. He pocketed the camera and put the report back together with care. He returned it to the briefcase and rebuckled the straps, making sure everything looked the same.

A sound came from the hallway, and Franz looked at the door in horror as heavy footsteps came closer. Moments later he heard the click of a light switch. Franz breathed a sigh of relief. Erich had evidently come up to the bedroom for something. A few moments later the footsteps came by again and then diminished.

Franz grabbed the floor lamp and put it back in its place. He turned it off and looked at Erich's secure phone. After a few moments' thought, he picked up the receiver. When the operator came on the line, he asked to be connected to the duty officer in his department. He waited as the phone rang. A man answered.

"This is Franz Brant," he began. "Do you have the duty schedule in front of you?"

"Yes," the man replied.

"Good. Just make a note that I will be about an hour late coming in tomorrow."

"I'll make a note of it."

"Very well. Good-bye."

Franz replaced the receiver and hurried to the door. He glanced around quickly and went out, closing the door softly. He breathed a sigh of relief as he walked down the stairs.

Johanna smiled as she held the music box up. "When did you get this?"

"When I knew you were coming. I kept thinking about how much you liked the one I got you the first time we met."

"I remember. How sweet of you to get another one for me."

She looked around when she heard footsteps in the hall. Franz came in, seeming unusually tense.

"Get everything taken care of?" Erich asked.

"Oh, yes," he said with a smile. "I'm done for the day. Thank you for saving me the trouble of going in. And now I think it is time for Franz to leave you two alone. My congratulations to you both."

Erich stood and escorted Franz out. Johanna turned the silver music box around, admiring the exquisite workmanship. She opened the lid and examined the tiny cylinder with all its minute pins. She heard the front door open, then close. Moments later Erich returned.

"Shall we go upstairs?" he asked.

Johanna held out her hand. "Yes. I would like that."

They walked hand-in-hand up the stairs and past Erich's office. Johanna saw the mess inside and something familiar on his desk.

"You kept my old music box in your

office?" she asked.

"Yes. I guess I kept it there to remind me of you."

"That's sweet, Erich."

They entered the bedroom. She watched him to see what he would do.

"Ladies first?" he asked.

"I think that would be a good idea. It takes me longer."

He bowed as she kicked off her shoes and began to prepare for her bath.

Johanna sat at her vanity toweling her wet hair. She paused and looked at the bathroom door, smiling at the muted sounds of Erich taking his bath. She started brushing her hair. She finished and looked down at her rather plain nightgown, noting that it wasn't very fancy; but it was all she had.

She got up and moved to the bed. She removed the spread and pulled back the top sheet on her side and slipped into bed. She folded her pillow and propped her head on it. She watched the bathroom door as she waited. Soon she heard the sound of water draining. Moments later the door opened, and Erich emerged wearing blue pajamas. Johanna looked at them curiously.

"Are those the same ones you wore on our honeymoon?"

He looked down. "No," he said with a grin. "I just like blue."

She smiled. "I do too."

He padded over the carpeted floor and got into bed, moving slowly until they were next to each other. She lifted her head so he could slip his arm around her. She felt her pulse race as she felt the warmth of his body through the thin cloth that separated them. He turned toward her and gently kissed her. Johanna returned it with a feeling that took her breath away. Her blood roared in her ears as they broke. She had never felt like this before.

"I love you, Erich," she gasped. "I do love you so much."

"I love you too," he replied, his voice suddenly husky.

He reached for her, and Johanna eagerly met his embrace. She closed her eyes in joy, knowing she was at last experiencing love.

Eighteen

Johanna sipped her coffee as Erich finished his toast. She sighed, realizing that for the first time in her life she was truly content. She had exactly what she wanted. "This is good," she remarked. "It's not ersatz."

"Frau Liedig's larder contains only the best," he said with a wry smile. "Courtesy of the Ministry of Armaments." He glanced at his watch. "I'm sorry, Johanna, but I have to go. I have to return the car and get ready for my trip to Rastenburg."

She nodded. "And I have to go back to Frankfurt to get my things and say good-bye to the Hoffmanns and all my friends in our church. But I'll be back in a few days, waiting for you to return."

He smiled. "And I'll be counting the days, I assure you."

"Me too, dear."

"I'll try to get done early today. Maybe we can have a little time together before your train leaves."

"I hope so. But if not, I'll understand."

He came around the table, bent down, and kissed her. He winked at her as he straightened up. "Wish I didn't have to rush off. I'd like to cart you back upstairs right now."

She blushed. "Frau Liedig might hear."

"I think she would understand, and approve."

Johanna got up and walked with him to the door, where he pulled her close and kissed her. She looked up into his eyes as they parted.

"I'll be back as soon as I can."

She nodded as he let himself out.

Johanna looked toward the kitchen. "Frau Liedig, I'm going out for a walk."

Bertha Liedig came through the door and down the entrance hall. Her beaming smile told Johanna all had been forgiven.

"Very good, Frau von Arendt. Shall I prepare you some tea when you return?"

"We'll see. Herr von Arendt is going to try to return early."

"Oh, I hope so," Bertha said.

Johanna struggled not to smile. "Why is that, Frau Liedig?"

The housekeeper looked flustered.

Johanna had to laugh. "Thank you for your kind thoughts."

"Forgive me if I seem impertinent, but I'm glad you're home, Frau von Arendt."

Johanna smiled at her. "I'm glad too."

She opened the door, then looked back. "I may be gone a while. It's been a long time since I've seen Berlin."

Bertha's smile disappeared. "It's changed a lot, Frau von Arendt."

Johanna nodded. "So has Frankfurt," she said with a sigh.

She went out and closed the door. The immediate neighborhood looked much the same; stylish houses lined the well-kept streets. But even here she noted blackened gaps here and there, although she knew the damage got much worse nearer the city center. But today even the ravages of war could not dampen the contentment and peace she felt — she was back with the husband who loved her.

Franz entered Tiergarten Park a little after 7 A.M. It seemed to him that he was stepping back in time since the bombing damage was less obvious inside the expansive greenery. He unconsciously quickened his pace as he caught sight of the lone man sitting at the appointed bench. He sighed in relief. This was one meeting that would make all the others worthwhile. The man stood as soon as he saw Franz approaching.

"Did you get it?" he asked.

"Yes. I took pictures of a map showing the exact location. When do I get my money?"

"As soon as we develop the film."

Franz handed him the miniature camera. The man pocketed it, turned, and started walking away, taking the path that would lead to one of the southern entrances. Franz watched him until he was almost out of sight. He was about to turn away when he saw two men rush up to his contact. He knew instantly they were Gestapo.

He watched in horror as the spy pulled a gun. Franz saw the puff of smoke and heard the sharp report. One of the Gestapo agents crumpled to the ground holding his stomach. His partner pulled his gun and shot the assailant. Franz saw the spy stagger backward and fall on the grass.

Icy pangs of terror gripped Franz, and he turned toward the northern entrance and started walking, keeping his pace brisk but not hurried. He scanned the deserted path before him, expecting to see dark-suited men coming toward him. He listened for rapid footsteps from behind, but so far it was quiet. The only sounds he heard were his own rapid breathing and the distant early-morning traffic. When he finally reached Belle Vue Allee, he breathed a sigh of relief. He glanced at his watch. He wasn't going to be late for work after all. He sighed as he realized the one million dollars would never be his. Then he thought about Erich. He wondered how long it would take the Gestapo to show up at his door. He cursed. He knew it wouldn't be long.

Johanna sat next to Erich on the sitting room sofa as Konrad Puttkaler faced them, his back to the window that overlooked the street. His two men stood in the hall, looking in. Bertha Liedig sat in a chair by the door.

Johanna wondered what possible interest the SS could have in Erich. She feared them but found it surprising they would interfere with someone so closely associated with Reich Minister Speer.

"I'm here to investigate the handing over of Reich secrets to the enemy," Puttkaler began. "Herr von Arendt, this morning we captured a spy who had pictures of something that belongs to you. A document recording sensitive information concerning a rather special factory."

Johanna felt her husband go rigid. She glanced at him and saw all the color drain from his face. She clutched his hand, but he seemed not to notice.

Puttkaler smiled. "I see you understand what I'm talking about. Then you also know I can't be more specific about what it is. Where is this document, Herr von Arendt?"

"I demand to speak to Herr Speer," Erich said. Johanna squeezed his hand and noted how tense it was.

"You will demand nothing! The SS reports to Reichsführer Himmler, not Herr Speer. You *will* cooperate in every respect or you will learn what happens to those who are traitors to the Reich. Do I make myself clear?"

"Perfectly," Erich grumbled.

"Shall I repeat the question?"

"It's a Ministry of Armaments document, commissioned by Reich Minister Speer himself. I can't tell you."

"I suggest you change your mind. Let me assure you that Reichsführer Himmler is in no way intimidated by Herr Speer. If you do not tell me, I will take all of you into custody. If that happens, I doubt any of you will ever see daylight again. Let me assure you, these orders come from the Reichsführer himself. Now, where is the document?"

"When Herr Speer hears of this, he will have your head."

"I think not. If you do not answer my question, we will leave for SS headquarters at once. Where is it?"

Erich closed his eyes and leaned his head against the back of the sofa. "In my office. It's in my briefcase."

"Your office at the Ministry?"

Erich glared at him. "No. My office upstairs."

Puttkaler's eyes grew wide. "You have the report here?"

"Yes."

Puttkaler snapped his fingers at the man standing behind Bertha Liedig. "Get it."

After a few minutes the man returned with Erich's briefcase. Puttkaler took it and placed it on a table by the window. He pulled out the thick sheaf of papers and scanned through the first few pages, stopping to unfold enough of the map so he could see what it was.

"Yes, this is it." He put the report back. "So someone in this house photographed parts of this document and gave those pictures to an enemy agent. I want to know who. I want to know everyone who has been in this house for the last few weeks."

Erich sighed. "This is everyone, except

for my friend Franz. He was here last night."

"This Franz has a last name?"

"Franz Brant. He works for the SS."

"*Many* people work for the SS. I'm afraid I do not know them all. But with the name, we can find him." He snapped his fingers at the man nearest the front door. "Find Herr Franz Brant, SS and bring him here immediately!"

The man rushed out. Puttkaler turned his back and gazed through the front windows. He stood motionless for almost an hour as they all waited. Then the faint sound of a car drifted up from the street.

"It seems Herr Brant is now here," Puttkaler said, turning away from the window. He looked directly at Erich. "Now, is this everyone who has been in this house recently?"

"Yes."

Johanna heard the front door open and close. A few moments later Franz came into the room and stopped.

"What's going on, Erich?" he asked.

"You'll hear soon enough," Erich snapped.

"Your papers, Herr Brant," Puttkaler ordered.

Franz gave them to him. After a few moments he got them back.

"Herr Brant, I am Herr Puttkaler. You will sit over there please." Puttkaler pointed to a chair opposite the sofa. "And I would suggest, for now, that you forget that we are in the same organization. It makes no difference in the present investigation. Do you understand?"

Franz scratched his head. "Not really, but I'll take your word for it. What exactly *are* you investigating?"

"I will get to that shortly. But *I* will ask the questions."

Franz shrugged and crossed his arms.

"Herr Brant, as I have told Herr and Frau von Arendt, we have recovered photographs of a sensitive document from a dead spy." He glanced at Erich. "This document Herr von Arendt apparently felt called upon to keep in his house."

"Under orders of Herr Speer!" Erich said.

"Do not interrupt me! The person who committed this crime is sitting in this room. Now, who is it?"

Johanna saw Franz glance at her before shifting to Erich.

"Erich," he began, "I'm sorry, but it can't be anyone but Johanna."

Johanna felt Erich jump as if he had

been hit by an electric shock.

He jumped to his feet. "No! It is not her!"

He turned and looked down at Johanna. She felt her insides turn to ice when she saw the raw pain in his eyes. She glanced over at Franz.

"Erich, what is he talking about?" she asked in bewilderment.

"Sit down, Herr von Arendt," Puttkaler ordered. "I am conducting this investigation."

Erich turned slowly toward the SS agent but remained on his feet.

"Sit down!"

Erich slumped back onto the couch.

Puttkaler turned to Franz. "Explain your remarks please."

"She's the only one who had the opportunity. Tell me, why did she come back after deserting Erich?" He turned on Johanna. "I won't keep silent about this. I know what you did to Erich, how you left him to run back to your lover in Frankfurt."

Johanna stared at him in horror. "Franz, how can you say that?"

"Because it's true. And how long have you been gone? Do you really expect anyone to believe you've suddenly come to

realize that you love him, just like that?"
He snapped his fingers.

She felt the tears coming. "But it's true.
I've changed."

"You may have blinded Erich with your
letters, but not me. People don't change
that much. And Erich and I know the details of why you left."

"But I was wrong. I explained all that
last night."

"It's obvious that you took him in. And
you got what you came for. Erich told me
there wasn't anything left of your father's
estate. I remember how much you enjoyed
the good life. Was being poor in Frankfurt
too much for you?"

"Franz, why are you saying these things?
You are terribly mistaken! I came back because I finally realized Erich truly loves
me." She reached for her handkerchief and
wiped her eyes. "And I realized I love him
too. I *did* change."

Franz shook his head. "Erich, I'm sorry I
had to say this. You know I'm your friend.
As hard as this is on you, I can't keep
silent."

Johanna turned to her husband. "Erich,
you don't believe this, do you? You
can't!"

"Enough of this," Puttkaler said. He

looked toward Bertha. "You are the house-keeper?"

"Yes. I am Frau Bertha Liedig."

"Did Frau von Arendt leave the house at any time?"

Johanna saw Bertha look at her with pleading eyes.

"You will answer my question, Frau Liedig!"

She turned back to the agent. "Yes, she did."

"When?"

"This morning, just after Herr von Arendt left for the Ministry."

"And what time was that?"

"Around 6, I think."

"I see. There is no need for further questions."

Johanna stared at Erich in disbelief. She fell on his shoulder as tears of anguish came. "Erich, I didn't do this! You must believe me!" His body seemed completely lifeless. "Erich, say something!"

"What is there to say?" he said in a low monotone. "You betrayed me once, and now you've done it again. I was a fool to believe you."

"Erich!" She felt like her heart would stop when he refused to look at her. "Erich, you can't desert me like this! I'm your wife. I love you."

"Enough of this," Puttkaler said. He looked toward the door. "Take Herr and Frau von Arendt into custody."

"Why me?" Erich demanded.

"Until we know more about this document you will remain with us. If you resist it will be hard on you."

The two SS men came forward and escorted their prisoners out into the hall.

Puttkaler waited until he heard the front door open, then close. "Herr Brant, I see no reason to detain you. But I must warn you not to leave Berlin. I may have further questions later. Do you understand?"

"Yes, Herr Puttkaler."

"Very well. You may go." He turned to Bertha. "Frau Liedig, you may go about your duties. However, you must not leave this house until this matter is settled. Is that understood?"

"Yes, Herr Puttkaler."

The SS agent departed.

Nineteen

Johanna gazed out the window of the speeding car as it roared out of Berlin toward the west. She was still numb from everything that had happened that morning. Her only hope for happiness had been ripped away from her. The SS agents had driven her and Erich to their Berlin offices. She still remembered Erich's haunted expression as they led her away. Fresh tears came as she struggled with Erich's rejection. It was bad enough that the SS had accused her, but that Erich believed it was more than she could stand. He hadn't said another word, even though she had pleaded with him.

Now as she was being taken someplace else, she closed her eyes. *Lord, why are You allowing this?* she prayed silently. But her prayer seemed to fall back on her, unheard. *This is wrong. Don't You care?* Again all she felt was a numbing silence. *Dear God, why?*

The car finally turned onto a narrow road. A mile further they passed through a heavily guarded gate. Inside the high fence enclosing the heavily wooded compound were a series of one-story buildings spread out among the trees. "Where am I?" Johanna asked.

"Be thankful," the heavyset matron sitting beside her snapped. "This is a VIP camp. You could have gone to a regular concentration camp. You can thank your husband's job for our mercy."

Johanna looked out at the drab huts. She did not feel thankful.

An SS agent opened the door. Albert and Erich swept past without even slowing down. They hurried down the steps and out to Speer's waiting car. Erich got in the passenger side; Albert took the wheel.

"Heinrich Himmler is an insufferable idiot!" he fumed as he cranked the car. Erich sat staring silently. His boss glanced at him out of the corner of his eye. "I am truly sorry for what happened."

Erich sighed. "I am too. I believed her. I thought she had changed. I was such a fool. And on top of that, I lost the Dora report."

Albert shrugged. "I regret that too, but I understand. I'll try to get it back, though I doubt Herr Himmler will turn it loose. Still, we both remember what we saw." He paused. "Which means we will have to be careful. He has a long memory when it comes to his enemies."

Erich nodded.

"Are you ready for your trip?"

"No, but I will be. All I have to do is gather the blueprints in my office and pack my bag. A Ministry car is taking me to the train station."

"I could arrange a plane."

"No, thank you. The train will give me time to rest and review the plans."

"As you think best." He glanced at Erich. "Are you sure you're up to this?"

"I don't have any choice," he snapped. He noted his boss's shocked look. "I'm sorry. This has been very hard on me. Yes, I'm up to it. I know how important it is. I'll make sure the Führer is pleased."

Albert smiled. "I knew you would be ready. He trusts you, Erich."

Erich made sure his boss did not see his frown. "Yes, I know he does."

They passed the rest of the trip in silence. Albert pulled up to the curb and let his passenger out. Erich watched as his boss drove off.

He trudged slowly up the front steps to his house, longing for some escape from his misery. He opened the door and walked in. He heard faint noises from beyond the kitchen, and presently Bertha rushed into the hallway.

"Oh, Herr von Arendt, I'm so glad you're back. I was worried sick."

He nodded. "I appreciate your concern, Frau Liedig."

She twisted her hands. "Where is Frau von Arendt?"

Erich struggled to maintain his composure. "I don't know, and I don't really care."

"Oh, how can you say that?"

"Because she betrayed me again!" he replied, raising his voice.

She drew back, shocked. "Forgive me, sir. I did not mean to offend." She paused. "Please, may I say something?"

Erich sighed. "Yes, of course. And I'm sorry — I didn't mean to take it out on you."

"That's all right. I know you're under a lot of pressure. I heard what Herr Brant said, but it's not true — it can't be. Frau von Arendt could not have done this. If you ask me, it was Herr Brant."

"Stop. I will not hear another word. Obviously enemy agents sent Johanna up here to seduce me in order to steal state secrets. As much as I hate to admit it, nothing else fits."

Bertha shook her head. "No, sir. She

couldn't have. I saw both of you together. Frau von Arendt *loves* you. She did *not* do it."

"We will discuss this no further. I have to get ready for my trip to Rastenburg."

"Yes, sir."

Bertha returned to the kitchen.

Erich trudged upstairs and entered his office. He longed for a way to avoid the trip to Hitler's Wolf's Lair but knew there was no way. He picked out the blueprints he needed, rolled them into a single bundle, and slipped them into a cardboard tube. His eyes swept over the cluttered desk and came to rest on Johanna's music box. It seemed to mock him, and not for the first time. He was near tears as he picked it up and put it back on the table he had reserved for it. Did he really want it there? he wondered. It was, after all, a constant reminder of this great failure in his life. He finally left the office and entered the bedroom to pack.

He pulled out his suitcase and placed it on the bed, then looked at the bedside table on the left. There he saw Johanna's crumpled handkerchief. He gritted his teeth as he thought about how gullible he had been to be taken in by her tears. Some inner voice seemed to urge him to pray.

This startled him, but he decided he was imagining things. But the thought came again. For a moment he wavered, then he turned and walked to the dresser. *Why should I pray to God?* he thought in irritation. *Johanna almost had me convinced God was bringing us back together. But if He exists, He either doesn't care or He can't do anything about what I'm going through. Either way, I do not wish to pray.*

Erich yawned as he scanned the concrete Führer's bunker, the bombproof refuge inside the Wolf's Lair near Rastenburg, East Prussia. His plan to sleep on the train had come to nothing. Twin nightmares had pursued him all night — Johanna's betrayal and his dread of working close to Hitler. After the short car ride from the Rastenburg station, he had dumped everything in Speer's office. Picking out the blueprints he needed, he left immediately for the bunker to inspect the progress.

Erich glanced at the construction supervisor hovering at his shoulder. "The structural work is basically correct, except for a few details I marked on the print. One section of wall is rougher than it should be, but the wood paneling will cover that. However, the detail work will never do."

Erich shook his head. "The paneling that's already up will have to be redone. The seams don't line up, you didn't patch the nail holes, and I saw a lot of dings and gouges. Take it all down and do it right."

The man sighed. "But, Herr von Arendt, it is impossible to do good work and also meet this difficult deadline. Also, the paneling and some of the other supplies are substandard, and I haven't been able to get anything better."

Erich turned and handed him the marked blueprint. "I will take care of the supplies," he said. "You will take care of the sloppy workmanship, *and* you will stay on schedule or find yourself in a new line of work. Do I make myself clear?"

The man blanched. "Yes, Herr von Arendt. I will see to it personally."

Erich nodded. "Good. That is why I'm here. If you have any problems, let me know at once. Do you have any questions?"

"No, Herr von Arendt."

"Very well. Carry on then."

The man shouted an order and called for all the workers to gather around. Erich watched for a moment, then left the large room to inspect the entrance hall, which led to the stairway and the blast-proof compartment. This work, he was relieved to note, was better, though not perfect.

He was checking panel seams when he heard footsteps coming down the stairs. He looked up in time to see Hitler come through the door, dressed in complete uniform. Erich felt his chest tighten with dread.

"Herr von Arendt," Hitler said with a smile of recognition. "I thought Herr Speer told me you were coming today. Inspecting the work?"

"Yes, my Führer."

Hitler came close and turned to examine the paneling section. "Hmm, what do you think?" he asked after a moment.

"It's good, for the most part. A few seams are a little off, and the color doesn't match on one section."

Hitler walked slowly along the wall, then returned to Erich. "Yes, I see what you mean. Good eye. I'm glad Herr Speer sent you."

Erich looked into the familiar blue-gray eyes, aware as always of the man's mysterious charm. "Thank you, my Führer."

Hitler nodded. "I imagine you're glad to be back in architecture and construction, even if it's only for a little while."

Erich nodded. "Yes, I am. But Herr Speer made it clear I was coming back to Ministry work after I see this work completed."

"Well, it is *all* important." He paused. "However, I think you share my passion for building things."

Erich felt the old ambivalence toward Hitler. He knew him to be a monster, but at the same time he could not deny the man's charm. "Yes, I do."

Hitler glanced toward the door leading into the bunker proper. "How goes the rest of the work? Will it be done on time?"

"I'm having some things redone. But the work will be completed on time, my Führer."

"Good, good. I'm tired of holding meetings in the briefing hut. It's primitive and . . ." He paused. ". . . and it's unprotected."

For the first time Erich saw the stress in Hitler's eyes. "Once we're done here, you won't have to worry about that anymore."

"Yes." He clapped Erich on the shoulder. "Keep up the good work." He turned and left the bunker.

Erich stood there, a willing captive of his own confusion and regret.

Although there were difficulties, Erich was generally pleased with the construction work at the Wolf's Lair over the next few weeks. He glanced down at his neatly typed work schedule as he ate a hurried breakfast in the Mess one morning. The date, 20 July 1944, was stamped boldly on the title page as if to remind him that time was growing short, and he had to keep pushing the work crews. The thick sheaf of papers covered many projects, but he could see the major one through the Mess windows. The entrance to Hitler's bunker was less than a hundred feet away.

Erich shook his head as he pondered his work at Rastenburg. Everyone told him how important it was — Albert Speer, his associates at the Ministry of Armaments, and of course Herr Hitler. Were the inmates in charge of the asylum? he wondered. The western front was crumbling faster every day as the Russians drove relentlessly from the east. And this very day the Führer was scheduled to meet Mussolini, whom SS Colonel Otto Skorzeny had sprung from an Italian prison in a daring raid the previous year. To what purpose? Erich mused. Though the war would obviously be lost, the Führer still commanded the army personally, apparently convinced of ultimate victory. But Erich did not share the confidence.

Erich turned a page and noted that because of the construction going on in the Führer's bunker, Hitler had reserved Organization Todt's briefing hut for the meeting. Since it was scheduled for that afternoon, Erich decided to spend the morning supervising work in the bunker, then check the hut around noon to make sure it was ready.

The morning's work went smoothly. The supervisors obviously knew Erich meant what he said about attention to detail. They also knew he checked *everything.* He lost track of time until his growling stomach sounded an alarm. He glanced down at his watch. It was just after 12:30. He thought about having lunch before checking the briefing hut but decided to swing by there first, in case anything needed his touch.

He left the bunker and stood blinking under the bright sunlight. He set out across the grass toward the enclosure that surrounded the hut and the Visitors' Bunker. As he started across the road to the enclosure's main entrance, he saw a staff car rush out and turn toward the road leading to Rastenburg. Two officers sat in the back, both looking rather grim, Erich thought. One he didn't recognize, but the other was Count Claus von Stauffenberg, General Fromm's chief of staff and an acquaintance of Albert Speer.

The guards immediately cleared Erich into the enclosure. As he approached the hut, he knew something had changed. The hut should have been empty, but guards were posted outside. He approached an SS colonel he knew by sight but whose name he could not remember.

"Is someone using the briefing room?" he asked.

The colonel nodded. "Yes, Herr von Arendt. The Führer rescheduled his briefing because of his meeting with Il Duce."

"It would have been nice if someone had told me," Erich grumbled.

"It was a last-minute decision."

"Yes, I'm sure it was. This is Organization Todt's hut, and I wanted to make sure it was ready. Now it's too late."

"Don't worry. I saw the room before they started. Everything was in order."

"Good." Erich looked down the side of the building toward the briefing room windows. A single sheet of paper fluttered in the grass, in plain view of those inside.

"Who left that litter on the ground?"

"I'll send a man to fetch it," the SS colonel said.

"Don't bother. I'll get it."

Erich hurried to the spot and snatched up the paper, acutely aware he could be seen by those inside the briefing room. He stood up and turned back toward the entrance. In that brief instant he heard and felt the blast. The shock wave slammed him down like a giant hand as shards of glass and wooden splinters whizzed past. Something struck him in the leg, throwing him to the ground like a discarded rag.

He stared up into the sky, uncomprehending as debris rained down all around him. After a few moments he felt an excruciating pain in his left thigh. He vaguely heard nearby screams and moans as he looked down at his side. A large jagged wooden splinter stuck through his pants leg, the ripped cloth already red and sopping wet.

"Help me!" he screamed as he rolled around in agony.

No one came. He turned his head toward the hut. Gaping holes marked where the windows had been. Soldiers picked their way cautiously through the debris. Erich heard one say, "He is dead." Then he realized, through the haze of shock, that someone had set a bomb for the Führer, successfully it appeared. Then he saw the familiar thin figure in his distinctive uniform being helped out by a soldier. Hitler was still alive, though Erich found it hard to believe that anyone had survived. Some had died apparently, but not Hitler.

Erich turned his head toward the building's entrance. Officers and soldiers milled about like drones around an endangered queen bee. He saw an officer look directly at him but just as quickly turn away. Erich gritted his teeth as he gripped the gaping wound to try and stanch the blood flow. He felt dizzy and hoped he would not lose consciousness.

How long he waited for aid, he did not know, but finally a soldier came toward him. Without saying a word he stooped down and examined the wound, then called for a stretcher. Then he gripped the wooden splinter and tried to pull it out. Erich screamed in agony and passed out.

The week after the failed assassination attempt on Adolf Hitler at Rastenburg, East Prussia, was a week that would remain etched forever in Erich's mind — a week of pain, delirium, and depression.

After initial treatment at Rastenburg, Albert Speer had intervened, arranging for Erich's evacuation by train to Berlin and subsequent medical treatment in a hospital reserved for the Nazi elite.

Erich rested on his back, staring at the door to his private room, his vision swimming in a morphine haze that gave him a respite from pain. The door opened, and a tall blur entered. Erich squinted, and his boss came slowly into focus.

"How are you, Erich?" Albert asked.

"They won't tell me anything!" Erich paused, tears coming suddenly. "Did they cut off my leg?"

Albert shook his head. "No, but for a while they weren't sure they could save it. The injury was very bad."

"Am I crippled? Tell me the truth!"

Albert sighed. "I have always told you the truth, Erich. The doctors tell me you will have some disability. How much, they don't know. But I can assure you of this — you *will* have the very best medical care."

"Thank you."

"It's the least I can do."

Albert brought over a chair and sat down.

"What happened at Rastenburg?" Erich asked.

"It was an assassination attempt on the Führer. At first they thought one of the workers in the Organization Todt had done it. Later they found out that Count von Stauffenberg planted the bomb. It was a conspiracy, Erich, an operation they called Valkyrie — an attempted *putsch* to take over the Third Reich."

"How did they do it?"

"A group of senior officers decided to kill the Führer and seize control, and they almost succeeded. All over Germany, army officers were waiting to take over. An army battalion in Berlin had the government buildings cordoned off. The only thing that stopped the coup was when Herr Goebbels told that unit's commander that the Führer was still alive. He put a call through to Rastenburg, and the man talked to Herr Hitler himself. And that ended the *putsch,* except . . ."

"Except what?"

"Except a lot of men were executed last week. And I'm sure many more are to come."

Erich slumped back on his pillow. He looked at Albert with a weariness that seemed next to death. "What is the point? The war is lost."

Albert came closer. "Quiet," he hissed

under his breath. "Don't you realize how dangerous any disloyalty is? You must keep such thoughts to yourself."

"But it's true," Erich whispered through his tears. Albert hesitated for a moment. "Yes, I know. But there's nothing we can do but continue our work — and try to stay alive."

By mid-September 1944 Johanna was sure. It had been over two months since her fateful trip to Berlin — two months since her last hope for happiness had been snatched away. Grief overwhelmed her whenever she remembered that one night of bliss followed immediately by the disaster she still could not comprehend.

But something else had happened on that July evening. When Johanna did not experience her menstrual period in August, she began to suspect . . . and when the same thing happened in September, she was sure. What should have been her highest joy only added to the despair that threatened to destroy her. She was carrying Erich's child.

Twenty

From late July until mid-December 1944, Erich had endured three operations intended to repair the damage done by the jagged piece of wood. Each time the doctors assured him the recommended procedure would repair the damage and speed his recovery, and each time the doctors were wrong. Erich appreciated his rehabilitation nurses' perpetual good cheer and enthusiasm, but he also saw their looks of concern when they thought he wasn't looking.

The constant enemy air raids added to Erich's troubles; the Americans by day and the British by night bombed Berlin, apparently determined to drive Hitler from his lair. Even though the hospital was located outside the city center, there had been several near hits. Erich didn't know which frightened him the most — the possibility of being permanently disabled or of dying in an air raid. What he would do when the ground war came to Berlin, he had no idea. But by February 1945 he knew the end was near.

Erich turned his head toward the door

when he heard the quick click of heels in the corridor. A man in a white coat strode through the door and grabbed Erich's chart, reading it before addressing his patient.

The doctor shook his head. "This is not good. The wound is not healing properly. I'm afraid we will have to operate again."

"No," Erich said.

The doctor lowered the chart and for the first time looked at his patient. "What did you say?"

"I said no. You will *not* operate on me again."

"You don't understand, Herr von Arendt. If we don't operate, you will be lame for the rest of your life."

"You've operated on me three times, and I'm not getting any better. At least I can hobble around on crutches."

"But we are responsible for you. You *must* have the operation — that is our decision!"

"The war is lost, doctor. The Russians are probably only weeks away from capturing Berlin, and I don't intend to be here when they do."

"That's not what I hear."

"I work for Reich Minister Speer. I know

what I'm talking about! Don't you understand?"

The doctor pursed his lips as he made a few quick notes on the chart and threw it back into the metal basket attached to the end of the bed. "I have scheduled your operation for 6 A.M. tomorrow." He turned without waiting for an answer and stalked out.

Erich listened as the rapid heel clicks gradually dissolved into the background noise of the busy hospital ward. He felt sweat under his arms despite the coolness of the room. He slumped back on his pillow as his despair verged on panic. He could see no way out. If they operated, he felt sure he would be no better. And if he was recovering from surgery, how would he evade the approaching enemy armies? The western juggernaut frightened him, but what really brought him terror was the approaching Russian bear. Erich's shiver had nothing to do with the chill in the room.

Erich's analytical mind churned, searching for an answer. An impulse to pray occurred to him several times, but other thoughts quickly crowded it aside. He closed his eyes in an effort to ward off his hopelessness. Again a single word, *pray,* seemed to come from nowhere. It sat for a moment in the center of his consciousness as Erich pondered where it had come from. A strange peace seemed to overshadow him but quickly fled as he focused again on his dilemma. Finally, reluctantly admitting there was nothing he could do, he gave up on his own resources.

Lord, please help me. He paused as doubts assailed him. *I know I'm not the Christian I should be, but I ask You to get me out of here. If they operate on me . . .*

He stopped, convinced he was wasting his time. He collapsed back on his pillow. Would they hold him against his will? he wondered. He was not sure.

Night approached with agonizing slowness. After what seemed forever, a nurse came in at ten o'clock with his sleeping pill. He smiled at her as he put the pill under his tongue and took a sip of water from the glass she gave him. He waited for her to leave, then spat out the sedative. Then came the long wait for her midnight check.

He began to suspect she had forgotten when he finally heard her soft steps squeaking along the polished corridor. He closed his eyes and feigned sleep. He heard her enter the room. The squeaking stopped, and he imagined her looking at him. Why was she taking so long? he wondered. He had almost decided to peek when the squeaking resumed, trailing off as she continued her rounds. He cracked one eyelid and saw to his relief that she was gone.

He threw back the covers, barely noticing the chill. He swung his legs over the side and almost cried out at the sudden pain that shot through his wounded leg. He waited for a few moments while he got used to the dull throbbing. He looked toward the closet, wondering if he could make it there without collapsing. He put his feet on the floor and stood up. At first he thought he might pass out from the agony, but the pain gradually eased. He started shuffling toward the closet, favoring his injury as much as he could.

He opened the door, pulled on his shirt without even thinking about buttoning it, grabbed his trousers, and hobbled to a chair. Gritting his teeth, he sat down and began the laborious task of pulling his pants on. At first he thought he would never get them over his injured leg, but finally he managed.

He stood up again and shuffled back to the closet. He wished he had a coat, but the only things left inside were his robe and cane. He pulled the robe on and grabbed the cane. He hobbled to the corridor and peered out, pulling back just as quickly. The ward matron was sitting at her desk, as he should have expected. He couldn't afford to be so careless. What now? he wondered.

A clattering crash suddenly came from the next wing. Erich looked out again. The heavyset matron was already on her feet and rushing toward the disturbance.

Erich hurried into the corridor and toward the abandoned station as quickly as he could. He grimaced at the noise he was making and his agonizing slowness. As he turned toward the stairs he hazarded a glance down the other wing. There was no sign of the matron or nurse, but he had no idea how long that would last.

Finally he reached the stairwell and stared down it anxiously. As he carefully began to negotiate the steps, he saw the matron come back into the corridor. His head dropped below floor level, but he wondered if she had seen him. He heard no sign of pursuit.

Though the heavy cane took most of the impact, he winced with each jarring step. He reached the second landing and saw that floor's matron busily engaged in paperwork. Erich hurried down the stairs, hoping she wouldn't look his way.

His shirt was soaked with sweat by the time he reached the bottom. He paused for a few moments to catch his breath. The first floor was momentarily deserted. His cane made heavy thumping noises as he crept along the dimly lit corridor. Finally he reached the front door. He twisted the handle and pushed it open, the wind almost tearing it out of his grasp. He stepped out quickly, gasping as the winter chill cut through his thin clothing.

He hobbled down the steps and onto the sidewalk, then almost panicked when he remembered that the nearest tram was over a mile away, if it was still running. He shivered violently as he shuffled along as quickly as he could.

Hearing a muted rumbling noise somewhere behind him, he turned and saw the headlights of an approaching vehicle. Not daring to risk suspicion by just standing where he was, Erich stepped into the street and started across, hoping whoever it was would see him in time. As the growling sound came closer, Erich faced the headlights and waved his cane. Just when he thought he would surely be run down, he heard the squeal of brakes as the vehicle slid to a stop a few feet away.

Erich crept up to the darkened cab and saw it was an army truck. The driver's window rolled down.

"Are you trying to get killed?" the man yelled.

"Please help me. I need a ride."

"I can't take you. It's against regulations."

Erich closed his eyes against his pain and the numbing cold. "It's all right. I'm with the Reich Ministry of Armaments."

"Yeah, I bet you are. I don't have time for this. It's late, and I'm tired. Now get out of my way."

"Wait, please . . . If you leave me out here, I'll freeze to death. Please help me."

The truck's engine idled unevenly as Erich waited. Finally the man said, "Get in."

Erich walked around the front and opened the passenger's side door. He cried out in pain as he climbed up into the cab's bench seat.

"Are you hurt?" the driver asked.

"Yes, a leg wound."

The driver put the truck in gear and stared out. "How did it happen?"

Erich looked out through the grimy

windshield. "You wouldn't believe me if I told you."

"Really? . . . Well, where can I take you?"

Erich gave him the directions, then tried to get comfortable in the jouncing truck. Erich reflected on his earlier prayer as blacked-out Berlin swept past his window. Although he hadn't felt particularly sincere in that prayer, he had to admit that he was now out of the hospital, just as he'd asked. However, what he would do now, he wasn't sure.

The trip lasted less than an hour. Erich thanked the driver and stepped down into the winter chill. As the truck drove away, he looked up at the dark structure of his home, still standing despite the devastating air raids. He doubted it would remain un-scathed much longer. He hobbled up the steps and rang the doorbell. He waited as patiently as he could as the raw wind stole away his meager body heat. He rang the bell again. Long minutes later he heard soft sounds approaching.

"Who is it?" came the familiar voice from inside.

"It's me, Frau Liedig — Erich von Arendt."

The lock clicked, and the door opened a

crack. Then it swung wide.

"Herr von Arendt!" Bertha gasped. "Come in, come in! What are you doing out on such a night?"

"It's a long story," he said as he entered, the heavy cane keeping time with each step.

"You're hurt. Didn't they take care of you in the hospital?"

"Not very well," he grumbled. "I must sit down before I collapse."

"Oh, yes, of course. Let me help you."

The only thing Erich wanted was a clear path to the sitting room couch without interference, but he allowed his housekeeper to take his arm. She'd always been so compassionate. Arriving at the couch, he turned and sat heavily, wincing at the sudden pain.

"I can't tell you how good it is to be home," he said.

Bertha's look of concern lightened a little. "I'm glad you're home, sir. Would you like something to eat?"

Erich thought about that. "It's late, but I think I would like a sandwich."

"I'll make anything you want. Would you like some soup?"

He shook his head. "No, thank you. Just the sandwich and a glass of water."

"I'll be right back."

Erich turned to the blackout curtains as Bertha left the room. He stared at them as he listened to the distant, energetic sounds in the kitchen. The heavy black material seemed to suggest mourning cloth, appropriate attire to commemorate the death of Germany. His fears began to circle again as Erich wondered what he should do. The Russians would be in the city in a matter of weeks — a few months at most. They must not capture him. The English and Americans were approaching from the west. To whom should he surrender, and how?

Bertha returned with two large sausage sandwiches and a glass of milk. Erich started to protest but stopped when he saw her eyes.

"Thank you, Frau Liedig. I don't know if I can eat two, but I'll do my best."

"Yes, sir. And if you want anything else . . ."

"No, this will be quite enough. Then I'm turning in. I'm exhausted."

"I'm sure you are."

He picked up one of the sandwiches and took a bite. "This is excellent. You have no idea how bad that hospital food was."

She smiled. "I can imagine."

She turned to leave but hesitated.

"Is anything wrong?" he asked.

"Sir, have you heard anything about Frau von Arendt?"

He frowned and put the sandwich down. "No, and I don't want to. I'll never forgive her for the way she betrayed me. I was such a fool."

"Oh no, sir. Please forgive me for again speaking my mind, but she couldn't have done it. I saw her with you. She's changed. She loves you, I know she does."

"That's enough, Frau Liedig."

"But, sir . . ."

"I mean it. She fooled you just like she fooled me. I don't want to hear any more about it."

"Yes, sir." She turned and left.

Erich ate a few more bites before struggling to his feet. He grabbed the cane and headed toward the hall. Reaching the stairs, he began the painful ascent.

He paused at the top and looked into his office. The desk was still a mess, since Frau Liedig was forbidden to do anything except sweep and dust there. Blueprints littered the desktop. He remembered the last time he and Johanna had passed that door. He frowned as he recalled what she had said. How often would that wooden music box haunt him? he wondered.

He stopped suddenly as her words drifted through his mind. He looked through the doorway at the desk. "You kept my music box in your office?" he recalled her asking. His brows furrowed. He knew something was wrong without knowing what.

He crept slowly into the office. He remembered finding the music box on his desk when he was preparing to go to Rastenburg. But it had been on its table earlier, he was sure of that. And Johanna had not been in the office.

With cold horror, he finally realized what had happened that awful night. Franz must have moved the music box so he could use the table. Erich closed his eyes. *Franz photographed the Dora report, not Johanna.* The sudden realization of the truth nearly overwhelmed him.

He stood there before his desk as tears of despair came, mixed with anger at Franz's betrayal. *Johanna really does love me, and I abandoned her to the SS!* He felt an overpowering desire to track Franz down and make him pay, but that dissolved into an inner agony so sharp he felt he would die. Johanna was likely dead by now, and if not dead, surely doomed. But then, they were all doomed! So much had gone wrong, so many dreams had become sawdust blown aside by a windstorm — for Germany, and for him and Johanna.

Erich hobbled around to his chair and collapsed into it. Wild thoughts raced through his mind — thoughts of suicide or simply giving up and waiting for the Russians to capture Berlin. *I've ruined everything. I destroyed my marriage, and when I had a chance to make things right, I believed Johanna betrayed me. And how can I ever justify what I've done to help the Nazis with their depraved madness! They threatened me, but I didn't have to give in. I took the easy way out.* He had been a fool, but not in the way he had thought.

He laid his head on the desk and wept.

Twenty-One

Erich spent a sleepless night, longing for a way out of the escalating horror. At the first hint of dawn, he dressed and went downstairs. To his surprise he heard Bertha Liedig moving about in the kitchen.

"Frau Liedig," he called from the hallway.

She opened the kitchen door. "Yes, Herr von Arendt?"

"Please join me in the sitting room."

He hobbled along the hall and into the front room, went to the window, and peered out. It was still quite dark. He turned back to see her standing at the door. He motioned toward an easy chair by the window.

"Please sit down."

She looked uneasy but did as he said.

He sat in the opposite chair. He struggled with his emotions, not sure he could trust his voice. "I found out last night you were right." He paused to wipe away a sudden tear. "Johanna didn't betray me — Franz did. He did it when he went up to phone his office. And I didn't believe

Johanna — or you."

"I'm sorry, sir. But I'm glad you know the truth. Herr von Arendt, can't you do something?"

He shook his head. "I haven't slept all night thinking about it. I'll try, but I don't think there's any chance. Once the SS or Gestapo takes someone, no one can do anything to help. Besides, I don't even know if she's still alive."

"Oh, don't say that, sir. You must not give up hope."

He waved toward the window. "What hope do any of us have? Soon the war will be over. The Russians will take Berlin as the American and British armies attack from the west. Everything's lost."

"There's always hope."

He wished that were true. "I'll check with some people at the Ministry. Meanwhile, I think it would be wise for you to leave Berlin." He paused. "Do you have any friends or relatives west of here?"

She shook her head. "No, sir. I have a few friends in Berlin, but no one close. I have no family."

"I see. Would you like to come with me when I leave? I don't think you would like being under Russian occupation."

"That is most kind of you, Herr von

429

Arendt. Yes, I would appreciate going with you. But, sir . . ."

"Yes?"

"You will try to find out about Frau von Arendt?"

He nodded. It took him a few moments to get his voice under control. "Yes, of course I will." He didn't believe he would find her, but the kind housekeeper's words made him at least want to try.

The trip through the devastated city center did nothing to improve Erich's outlook. Bombed-out buildings and mounds of rubble seemed to press in on every side. Several times the Ministry driver had to detour to avoid a blocked street. Many buildings were devoid of window glass and appeared deserted. Berlin seemed on the verge of total collapse. And for the first time there were no work crews.

Erich got out with difficulty and made his way over the unswept sidewalk and into the building. He paused outside his boss's office and knocked.

"Come in," came the reply.

Erich was shocked by the haggard face that greeted him.

"Sit down," Albert said.

Erich eased into the chair. "Thank you

for seeing me — and for sending a car. When I phoned this morning, I didn't expect you to be here."

A look of irritation came to the man's face. "I'm not here very often. I'm trying to save what's left of Germany." His expression softened. "But enough of that. I appreciate your service to me — I think you know that. How is your leg?"

Erich hesitated, not knowing how much he should say. "They wanted to operate again — for the fourth time. I said no, and when they insisted, I left."

A wry smile came to Albert's face. "I don't blame you a bit. I almost died when I trusted a doctor who happened to be an intimate friend of Himmler's. Your leg, I take it, isn't healing properly."

"No, it's not."

Albert drummed his fingers on his desktop. "I could get you into another hospital, but I don't recommend it."

Erich nodded. "The end is near, isn't it?"

"Of course it is. You know that as well as I." He lowered his voice and leaned forward. "The only one who doesn't accept the truth is our Führer."

"He's here in Berlin?"

"Yes, in his bunker under the Chancellery. His advisers are trying to get him to go to Berchtesgaden, but I don't think he'll go."

Erich took a deep breath. "Herr Speer, I would like to ask your help."

"I will if I can. What is it?"

"You know what happened to Johanna. After I came back, I found out it was not she who betrayed me — us." His voice turned hard. "It was Franz Brant — my best friend, Franz."

"I am truly sorry to hear that."

"Herr Speer, is there anything you can do to get Johanna away from the SS?"

Erich knew the answer before Albert spoke. He felt his only hope slipping away as he saw his boss shake his head.

"I have no authority over Herr Himmler's organizations. And as you know, I have no influence over Herr Himmler." He paused. "I didn't tell you, but I tried to find out where they took her. All I discovered was that Herr Himmler himself is interested in her case — probably because of your association with me. I'm sorry."

Erich closed his eyes and struggled against his tears. "I understand. Thank you for trying."

"Of course." Albert paused. "What will

you do now? You can't work with that leg, not that I would ask you to."

Erich struggled to maintain an outward calm. "I want to leave Berlin. I certainly don't want to be here when the Russians take over."

Albert nodded. "To be with the British or Americans would be better."

"But travel is impossible. And I can't walk with this leg."

"Yes." His eyes took on an unfocused look. "The trains are reserved for the military. It is the same for cars and trucks." He grabbed his phone. "Come into my office please," he said into the mouthpiece.

A secretary hurried in moments later, pad in hand.

"Take this order," he said. "This authorizes Herr Erich von Arendt to use any Reich transportation for his execution of Ministry of Armaments and Munitions business." He waited until she finished writing. "Make that up in the proper form and bring it back for my signature."

"How soon do you need it?" she asked.

"Immediately. I am dispatching Herr von Arendt today."

She hurried out. They sat in silence. Erich's mind whirled as he tried to bring order to his involvement with Adolf Hitler's thousand-year Reich. What had seemed so good in the beginning had always had its dark side, although he hadn't seen it until later. He tried to comfort himself with the knowledge that he had only participated in constructive jobs. Then he remembered the nightmare of working for Dietrich Clahes in what they euphemistically called resettlement. He had helped Herr Clahes send Jews to their death. The fact that the Gestapo had threatened him and his family seemed a weak excuse now.

Erich looked around as the secretary returned. She placed the single piece of paper on Speer's desk and left. Speer glanced at the document on his Ministry's letterhead, then quickly signed it.

"Here," he said, extending it to Erich. "This may help. I think you're wise to leave Berlin. I'd suggest taking a train to Hannover, then waiting until it's over."

Erich took the paper and stood. The two men looked at each other for several moments. At first Erich thought Albert would say something more, but he didn't. They shook hands, and Erich left.

Outside, he opened the rear door of the Ministry car and got in. He folded the paper and put it in a pocket as the driver took the first detour on their tortuous exit from the inner city. After a moment's thought, Erich leaned forward and gave the man a new destination.

Erich heard the Ministry car drive off as he rang the bell. His parents' home appeared unscathed, although the neighborhood had its share of bombed-out houses and blocked streets. The smell of charred wood lay heavily on the morning air. He heard plodding steps approaching. The lock clicked, and the door opened.

After momentary confusion, Julia von Arendt beamed at her son. "Erich, what a pleasant surprise." She rushed forward and embraced him. "What are you doing here?"

He smiled. "To see you, Mama," he said as he limped in.

"What are you doing out of the hospital?"

He felt a sharp spasm of pain. "Could we discuss it in the sitting room? My leg is acting up."

"Of course, dear. Let me help you."

He submitted gracefully as his mother took his elbow and guided him into the dark room. She waited as he sat in an easy chair, then pulled back the blackout curtains. She looked tired, he noted, and older.

"Can I get you something to eat or drink?" she asked.

"No, Mama. Please sit down. I just came to see you."

She hesitated, then sat in the chair opposite his. "How is your leg, son?"

"It's not good. They operated on it three times, and each time it did little good. I couldn't let them do it again, not with everything that's going on. But that's not why I'm here. Where's Papa?"

"Herr Speer sent him out on a trip to visit cities along the Rhine, something about helping them prepare for the enemy."

Erich nodded. "I remember Herr Speer talking about that. Hitler ordered everything to be destroyed when the enemy is approaching — the cities, the bridges, the railroads — everything. But that is just more of his foolishness. Whatever's destroyed now will just make things harder on the ones who survive."

"Your papa doesn't tell me details."

"He probably doesn't want to worry you. Do you know when he'll be back?"

"I don't know."

"You know the end is near," Erich said softly.

She sighed. "Yes, your father told me that much."

Erich patted his pocket. "Herr Speer has authorized me to use Reich transportation, and I'm leaving for Hannover as soon as possible. Come with me. We can leave Papa a note."

She shook her head. "No, dear. My place is here."

"Do you know what Papa's going to do? Are you and he leaving Berlin?"

"No, we're staying here. Berlin's our home."

"But the Russians are going to take it."

"I know, but that doesn't change things. Your father won't leave, and my place is with him."

Erich slumped in his chair. "I wish you wouldn't, but I understand." He hesitated. "There's something else you need to know before I leave."

"What's that?"

"Johanna didn't betray me like I thought. It was Franz. *He* photographed the report." He broke down and wept.

"Oh, Erich." She hurried over. He heard her sob as she took his hand. "Erich, I'm so sorry."

He brought up a hand and wiped his eyes. "She really does love me, and I let her go without saying a word."

"But you didn't know, dear."

"No, but I should have. I should have trusted her. Now she's gone."

"Can't you tell the Gestapo what really happened?"

He shook his head. "I don't have any proof they would accept. Besides, the Gestapo runs by Herr Himmler's rules. They take whoever they want, regardless of the facts."

"I'm sorry."

He sighed. "I am too." He grabbed his cane and struggled to his feet. "I must be going."

"I wish you'd stay awhile. It's been so long since I've seen you."

"I wish I could, but I must get ready to leave the city. Please give Papa my love."

She walked with him to the door. "I will, dear."

He hugged her and bent down and kissed her on the forehead. He looked down into her caring eyes, knowing he would probably never see her again. He struggled to control his voice. "Good-bye, Mama."

"Good-bye, Erich. May God go with you, son."

He opened the door and went out. The

two-block walk to the tram stop almost exhausted him. All the way home he thought about the powerful armies that were closing in on what remained of the Third Reich. He choked back bitter rage as he considered Adolf Hitler. The man who had terrorized the world for years was now hiding in his hole underneath the Chancellery.

Erich and Frau Liedig stood on the platform waiting for the boarding announcement. He ignored the curious stares from the surrounding crowd of soldiers, officers, and government officials. Speer's authorization plus Erich's papers had worked exactly as he had expected. He and his supposed secretary were booked on a night train bound for Hannover.

Finally the announcement came. Erich and Bertha joined the crush and pushed their way aboard. In the third car he finally found two seats. Bertha took the one by the window, while Erich collapsed next to her. After a few minutes the train lurched and started forward. Soon they were out of the terminal and rumbling through the inky blackness of Berlin. Once Erich thought the train would stop when searchlights came on and antiaircraft guns began firing. But the train continued on its way out of the city. After a while Erich heard muffled explosions behind them as bombers unloaded on the Third Reich's capital.

Despite his anxiety and fear, Erich felt his bone-weariness, never far away, return with full force. In moments he was asleep, where dreams of destruction waited in ambush.

Erich awoke with a start. Frau Liedig was already awake and staring out the window. The gray of dawn revealed falling snow and a nearby forest. Brakes squealed as the train shuddered and slowed. The conductor entered from the front of the car and strode rapidly down the aisle.

"Why are we stopping?" Erich demanded.

The man hesitated, then stopped. "The track's out. Trucks are being sent out from Hannover to pick up passengers."

"Where are we?"

"About halfway between Wolfsburg and Hannover. Now, if you will excuse me, I have things to do." He left without waiting for an answer.

Erich turned to Bertha. "Are you ready?"

"Yes."

Pain shot up his leg as he levered himself up with his cane. He gritted his teeth as he waited for a gap in the suddenly full aisle. He stepped in front of an SS colonel, blocking the way until Bertha got out. They shuffled to the end of the car and stepped down into the snow. Erich gasped as the frigid wind tugged at his heavy coat, dumping icy flakes down his collar. He caught up to Bertha and hobbled along beside her. The other passengers hurried past, anxious to reach the waiting trucks. Erich soon lost sight of them as they disappeared into the trees.

"Can you make it, Herr von Arendt?" Bertha asked.

"Yes, Frau Liedig," he gasped, short of breath. "But I'm holding us back."

"Don't say that. We'll get there."

They entered the trees without another soul in sight. Erich plodded along as the pain in his leg grew steadily worse, sapping what little energy he had left.

"I have to stop," he said finally. He stood gasping for breath. Bertha watched him with obvious concern.

"You must keep going, Herr von Arendt," she said. "Let me help you."

She came around and held out her hand for the cane.

"I'll be all right," he said.

"Give it to me. I'm stronger than you think."

He saw her determination. He gave her the cane and put his arm around her shoulders. She put her arm around his waist with a grip that surprised him. Together they continued toward the unseen road.

By the time they stepped out of the trees, only one small truck was left.

"Hurry up!" shouted the driver, standing by his open door. Three other passengers waited in the uncovered back, sitting on wooden benches. Erich and Bertha hobbled up to the truck's high bed.

"My boss is injured," Bertha called up. "I need your help."

A portly man in a suit frowned at her but stepped down. He and Bertha managed to help Erich up until he could grab the bench and pull himself the rest of the way. He sat heavily and slid along the bench until he was next to the SS colonel he had seen earlier. The businessman took a seat across from them, next to an SS captain who was obviously traveling with the colonel. Bertha sat next to Erich.

"Now maybe we can continue our trip," the colonel said.

The driver slammed his door. The rear wheels spun briefly as they started out. As the truck jounced along the narrow country road, the snow gradually decreased and finally stopped. The early morning light revealed snow-covered trees and fields. Erich looked up into the high overcast with increasing apprehension.

"What's wrong?" Bertha asked.

"These are perfect conditions for an air attack," he replied.

The colonel turned on him. "I will not sit here and listen to such defeatist talk."

Erich faced him. "Colonel, I work for the Ministry of Armaments and Munitions. Perhaps the SS is not aware of what's happening in Germany, but I am. Now, since I am not under Herr Himmler's authority, I suggest we call a truce."

The officer glared at him for a moment, then turned to face forward.

Erich saw a long bridge approaching. Automatically he scanned the skies as they approached. The truck lurched and skidded up the long entrance and onto the narrow two-lane structure. Erich felt his pulse quicken as he saw four dots off to the south. For a while they continued toward the east, but then two split off and dropped lower, growing rapidly larger. In a few moments Erich identified the large oval shapes of the approaching planes.

"P-47s!" he screamed as he turned toward Bertha. "Jump!"

He grabbed her by the arm as he staggered to his feet and shuffled toward the back of the truck. Out of the corner of his eye he saw the lead fighter's tracers lancing out toward the truck. When Bertha hesitated, Erich pushed her, then tumbled down after her. He cried out in agony as he landed on his right side, rolling and sliding until he bounced against the bridge's narrow curb.

"Keep down!" he shouted to Bertha, who had come to rest a little behind him.

The truck raced along, swerving violently on the slick surface. Erich watched as the tracers finally found their mark. The heavy .50 caliber slugs tore into the truck and forced it into the bridge's guardrail. Pieces flew off as the vehicle disappeared inside a cloud of smoke. The heavy American plane thundered over the bridge, clearing it by less than ten feet. A split second later the wingman roared past in the first fighter's wake. Erich watched as the two planes pulled up, swept around in a big arc, and returned just fifty feet over the bridge.

"Don't move," he told Bertha.

"I don't think I can," came the reply.

The planes continued on to the south. Erich waited for a minute, then cautiously got up. He saw two dots near the horizon join with two others as the fighters continued their sweep into Germany.

"You can get up now," Erich said. He held out his hand while he braced himself using his good leg. He helped Bertha to her feet.

"What will we do now?" Bertha gasped.

"I don't know," Erich said as she helped him along.

The two SS officers and the businessman lay sprawled on the truck bed like bloody dolls. Hundreds of holes pierced the left side of the truck. Erich shook his head as he examined the mangled metal. Somehow the tires had escaped, he noted. As he got closer he heard a hissing sound. The radiator had not been so fortunate. Erich grabbed his cane as he limped past. He reached the cab and pulled the door open. The dead driver tumbled out onto the bridge, leaving a bloody trail on the seat.

Erich pulled him to the side, then stood up. "Get in on the other side. We'll go as far as this thing will take us."

Bertha hurried around the front and got in as Erich pulled himself up into the driver's seat and slammed the door. To his relief, the truck started immediately. He put it in gear and let out the clutch. They continued across the bridge as he fought to keep the truck from skidding. Two miles down the road as they topped a hill Erich heard a loud noise under the hood just before the engine quit. He glanced down at the temperature gauge.

"The truck will go no further," he said as he pushed in the clutch and slipped the transmission into neutral.

"What do we do now?" Bertha asked.

"Wait for someone to come along who is going to Hannover."

They coasted down the hill, the truck finally rolling to a stop near a creek. Erich opened his door, took his cane, and stepped down into the snow. He walked around the front of the truck.

"What's that over there?" Bertha asked, pointing to a thin curl of smoke above the trees to the right of the road.

"I don't know. Let's go see."

As they clumped along toward the trees, they saw that the snow was heavily trampled. Soon they came to a large clearing where they saw a large barn-like structure beside many crudely constructed huts.

"Oh," Erich said when he saw them.

"What is it?"

"A refugee camp. These are springing up all over Germany. After people are bombed out of their cities, they come to places like this."

"Do you suppose they'll help us until we can get to Hannover?"

Erich looked toward the east. "I think we would be better off here than in Hannover."

Twenty-Two

Johanna finished her prayers and pushed herself up off her knees. She sat heavily on the bed with a sigh of relief. Considering her condition, she wondered if the Lord would hear her prayers just as well sitting or lying on her cot. She decided He would, but she knew she could continue using her knees for a little while longer. She looked down at her swelling belly, wondering anew at the baby's growth as she neared the eight-month mark. She placed her hand on her taut skin as she felt the tiny kicks start. *He always seems to know when prayer time is over,* she thought. *Time for his calisthenics.* Somehow she always assumed she would have a son.

She knew very little about her prison, except that it was somewhere north and west of Berlin. Trips outside were strictly supervised, but these revealed roughly a dozen one-story buildings nestled inside a dense forest, surrounded by a high fence and guard stations.

She'd asked God repeatedly why He had allowed her imprisonment. Her prayers had been full of anger, so much so that it scared her sometimes. Then she remembered Karoline Hoffmann's words, that God was always God, even through the hard times, and that He would be with her no matter what. And Johanna had finally come to accept that and find comfort in it. But she still longed for her husband. She sighed as she wondered where he was and what he was doing.

She looked up and saw Margarete watching her. The young woman, also pregnant, had become her roommate a few days ago. Until that time Johanna had had the small room to herself.

"Why do you pray?" Margarete asked. "What good does it do?"

"I pray to thank God for what He's done for me and to ask for His help."

"You thank Him for being here? You thank Him for these SS butchers?"

Johanna felt a twinge of doubt and sent up a silent prayer before answering. "No, I don't thank Him for the SS or this place. However, the Bible says that everything works together for good to those who belong to Him and live according to His will."

"You can't really believe that."

Johanna felt a confidence she didn't understand. "Yes, I do. Jesus is with me no matter where I am. You have no idea what a comfort that is, *especially* in a place like this. Don't you long for real peace and security, a home where you are always welcome?"

Margarete swept her arm about the tiny room, her face a contorted mask of hate. "If your god allows monsters like these to do as they please, I don't want Him."

Johanna saw the hurt in her eyes. "I'm sorry for whatever you've been through. I'll pray for you."

"Don't bother."

"I hope you change your mind."

"Change my mind? What difference would that make? Don't you understand? None of us will ever get out of here. I will die. You will die. Even that baby you care so much about will die. And there's not a thing in the world you can do about it."

With that, Margarete turned her back on Johanna and faced the wall.

Margarete's words echoed in Johanna's ears later that morning when the nurse escorted her to the clinic for her regular prenatal exam. Johanna had always wondered about the large medical staff at the prison and the well-equipped clinic, but she had assumed it was because the inmates were related to government officials.

The nurse helped her off with her shoes and into her gown. Johanna struggled up onto the table. Moments later the doctor came in, wearing his usual immaculate white jacket. A round mirror on a head strap and a dangling stethoscope completed his professional appearance.

He was aloof but appeared to know what he was doing. Although he occasionally made comments in her presence, he never talked directly to her. Johanna always reserved her questions for the nurse who, though always reassuring, never offered any specific information.

The doctor performed the examination with even more care than usual, Johanna thought. When it was over, he removed his gloves with loud snaps, staring at her with intense blue eyes behind heavy glasses. For a moment Johanna thought he was going to say something to her, but instead he turned to the nurse.

"I think it's time," he said. "Stay with her while I consult with my colleague."

"But, doctor, I have to go get another patient."

The man fiddled with his stethoscope for a moment. "Then go *get* your patient." He glanced toward Johanna. "This one will remain here until you return."

"Yes, doctor."

The nurse left the room, closing the door quietly. The doctor gazed at Johanna for a few more moments, then left by a different door.

Johanna thought over what the physician had said about it being time. Time for what? She knew the baby would not be born for about another month, and she could see no signs that the baby might come early. After a few moments she got up and moved softly over the shiny floor in her bare feet. She hesitated at the door the doctor had gone through, then twisted the handle. She pushed the door open slowly and saw a deserted corridor with a series of other doors. The one at the end was ajar, and although she could hear two people talking, she couldn't make out what they were saying. She stepped into the corridor and started tiptoeing toward the door, stopping when she was several feet away.

She heard her doctor speaking. ". . . would be beneficial. But so far only one fetus has survived, and it was essentially a vegetable after the operation."

"Yes. That is most unfortunate, but

that's the price we must pay for advances in medical science. To be able to do extensive surgical procedures on pregnant females without adversely affecting or killing the fetus is a worthy goal."

"Do you think you have the right anesthetic mix this time?"

Johanna heard the other doctor pause.

"I can't be sure, of course, but I'm much closer. At least the last fetus didn't die when you removed the mother's breast."

"Very well. We'll perform the operation tomorrow at 10."

Johanna's heart raced in near panic. She turned quickly and hurried back to the examination room, hoping she would not be discovered. She passed through the door and closed it. She was tiptoeing back to the table when the other door opened and the nurse returned.

"What are you doing up?" she demanded.

"I didn't know when you'd be back, so I thought I'd walk around a little."

"Well, we don't do anything around here without the doctor's orders. Now come with me."

Johanna fought down her feeling of terror as she accompanied the nurse back to her room.

★ ★ ★

Johanna spent the rest of the day and much of the night in prayer. In the early hours of the morning she finally released her fate to her Lord as best she could. She felt an inner peace, although she realized that she, and her baby, were still in grave danger. But the Lord knew that, and she believed He would see her through. Finally she gave in to her exhaustion and slipped into an uneasy sleep.

What seemed like moments later, the overhead light clicked on. Johanna struggled to comprehend what was happening as the last cobwebs of sleep gave way to reality.

"Time to get up," the nurse said as she approached. "It's almost 9:30."

Johanna's stomach growled. "I missed breakfast."

"No breakfast for you this morning. You're scheduled for surgery."

Johanna glanced at Margarete. Her roommate's eyes were very wide. She had her blanket pulled up to her chin.

"There must be some mistake. I'm not ill."

"Now calm yourself . . . This is doctor's orders. I'm sure he didn't want to worry you with what he found yesterday."

"What did he find?"

"I can't tell you that."

"I want to see the director."

"I'm afraid that's not possible. Now, either come with me or I'll have to get some orderlies."

Johanna struggled to her feet and slipped into her robe and shoes. The nurse escorted her to a wing of the building she had never been in before. She considered running but realized how utterly futile that would be. She plodded along with her captor down the long corridor toward the operating rooms.

Johanna felt her heart race as they pushed through the door and saw the operating table and the two men in white. One was the doctor who had examined her yesterday and the other, she was sure, was the doctor he had been talking to. The nurse helped Johanna remove her shoes and get into the hospital gown.

"Strap her down on the table," her doctor ordered. He looked around at his colleague. "Do you have your anesthetics ready?"

"I'm prepared. Is your scalpel ready?" he responded condescendingly.

The nurse tightened her grip on Johanna's arm and shoved her toward the table.

"No," Johanna whimpered.

"Move," the nurse hissed. "If you force me to get help, you won't like it."

Johanna turned to her. "How can you do this to me?"

The older woman paused. She lowered her voice and leaned close. "I don't have any choice, any more than you do. Cooperate. It's all you can do."

"What are you saying?" the surgeon demanded.

"I am just telling her to do as I say."

"Well, get on with it! I don't want this taking all day."

Johanna almost bolted, despite knowing it was futile. But something seemed to urge her to cooperate. The nurse helped her onto the high table and started attaching the arm and leg straps.

"Why are you doing that?" Johanna demanded.

"So you won't move during the operation," the nurse explained. "You could roll off and injure yourself."

Johanna winced as the nurse drew each strap tight.

The surgeon approached the table, looked down at Johanna, and turned away. "Take her under. Let me know when she's ready."

The other doctor approached with a large syringe. He tapped the glass cylinder to get the bubbles out and squirted a little of the solution into the air. "No ether for you. Let's see what this does."

"But what about my baby?" Johanna wailed.

"Quiet!" the doctor replied. "Soon you won't feel anything. Now be a good girl. Don't struggle or this will hurt."

Johanna felt the quick chill of the alcohol on the inside of her right elbow. Then came the sharp pain as the needle slid in.

Dear God, no. Johanna's silent prayer shot heavenward even as the needle slid deeper.

"What's that?" the nurse asked suddenly.

The doctor stopped and looked around. "What are you talking about?"

Then Johanna heard it too. A low rumbling sound that gradually grew louder. All questions disappeared when the air raid sirens started going off.

"Surely they won't hit us?" the surgeon said. "We're out in the country."

"Don't count on it," the nurse replied. "There's a solid overcast. The bombers can't see their targets."

"You hold your tongue!" the doctor said.

The rumbling noise grew louder, and the sharp cracks of antiaircraft artillery rattled the windows. Moments later they all felt as well as heard the heavy concussions of high-explosive bombs, distant at first but marching ever closer. Glassware on the shelves started jumping with each impact.

"They're coming right at us!" the surgeon screamed.

The whole building shook from a near hit, then the door blew open. Debris flew through the air as acrid smoke filled the operating room. Johanna's ears rang from the explosion. The lights blinked off with the next blast.

"Let's get out of here!" someone nearby shouted.

Two more blasts came in quick succession. Something large whizzed by and tore a jagged hole in the outside wall from the roof to the floor. Light streamed in, illuminating the destruction and bringing with it a biting winter wind. Both doctors lay crumpled on the floor, one impaled by a section of pipe, the other also obviously dead. Johanna looked away quickly. A mound of debris near the operating table shifted, and the nurse struggled to her feet and looked around.

"Help me!" Johanna shouted. Her voice sounded tiny and faraway in her ears.

The other woman turned toward

Johanna, a confused expression on her face as if she didn't know where she was. She looked down at the doctors, and for a moment Johanna thought she was going to walk away. Then she returned and started releasing the straps, fumbling with them as she struggled to keep her hands from shaking. Finally she finished and staggered off without a backward glance.

Johanna eased her bulk off the table and put her bare feet on the rubble-strewn floor. She winced as the sharp debris bit into her soles. She shuffled her way across the floor as quickly as she could as the sounds of explosions drew farther away. Her heart raced as she searched frantically for something to wear. She started to enter the corridor when she heard distant voices. She retreated to the back of the operating room and pulled open a door. Inside she saw two coats and two pairs of heavy boots. She pulled on one of the coats, grateful it was quite large. She sat in a chair and struggled desperately to pull on a pair of wool socks and boots, panting from the exertion by the time she was through.

She got up and hurried back to the center of the operating room. Again she heard voices toward the front of the building complex. She stepped over the debris, made her way to the gaping hole in the outside wall, and looked outside. It was snowing now, and judging by the gloom, it would soon be heavy. She stepped over what remained of the wall and started walking away from the building. She reached the trees and looked back. The entire building had been leveled except for the operating room and the rooms nearest it. Bomb craters covered most of the surrounding grounds.

Johanna kept walking, desperate to not lose her new freedom. The snow swirled about her, obscuring everything except the nearest objects. After a few minutes she saw a dim shape ahead. She realized too late that it was one of the guard stations on the perimeter fence. She had almost decided to turn back when a gust of wind blew aside the curtains of snow. The tower had received a direct hit, leveling it and the fence for a hundred feet on either side. Johanna looked right and left. The other towers were hidden in the snow. She plodded past, thanking God for her release but wondering where she should go.

Johanna trudged through the snowdrifts, trying to ignore her hunger and the bitter cold. She kept her hands in the coat pockets as much as she dared, pulling them out only to push her way through the bushes. Eventually she came to a narrow road and turned to follow it toward the west. Once she had to hide in a grove of trees as an army truck rumbled past, heading toward Berlin.

A little later she topped a small hill and immediately smelled wood smoke. It was still snowing steadily. She turned into the wind and followed the gently rising ground, leaving the road at her back. She reached the gentle summit but still couldn't see anything. She started downhill, continuing through the thick woods as she followed the smoke scent. Finally she saw a small farmhouse, with a barn and several outbuildings. Desperate, she hurried down to the narrow front door and knocked. After a few moments a thin middle-aged woman peered out.

"Please help me," Johanna pleaded.

The woman opened the door wide. "What's wrong?" she asked, as she stood back to let Johanna enter.

"I'm freezing," Johanna replied.

"Here, come to the fire. Who are you, and why are you out in such weather?"

A cheerful fire roared in the stone fireplace of the large room. Johanna shuffled over to the fire and held her hands out. "It's a long story," she said, shivering violently. She sighed in relief as she felt the warmth on her hands and face.

The woman threw two more logs on the fire and arranged them with the poker. She pulled a chair up beside Johanna. "Here, sit down and let me have that coat. I'll hang it by the fire where it can dry."

Johanna hesitated, then let her remove the heavy garment, revealing Johanna's hospital gown and a very swollen belly.

"Oh my! Where *did* you come from?" she asked as she draped a welcome quilt around her guest.

Johanna felt fear rise up within her. She knew the danger of saying too much but could see no way out. "I've escaped from an SS camp," she said.

A look of horror came to the woman's face. "Oh, no."

Johanna looked up at her, her eyes pleading. "You won't turn me in, will you?"

The woman's eyes turned hard. "Turn someone over to the SS? No, of course not." Her scowl softened to a look of concern. "You're safe with me and my husband. Surely the Lord sent you to us."

"You're Christians?"

"Why, yes, dear, we are."

"Thank God."

"Thank Him indeed. We'll take care of you."

Johanna's tears came freely, as if a dam had suddenly broken. "Oh, thank you. I don't know what I would have done if I hadn't found your house."

Her hostess brought a handkerchief. "There, there. You're all right for now." She poked at the fire again, then sat in the chair beside her guest. "Oh, forgive me, I haven't told you my name. I'm . . ."

"Please don't," Johanna interrupted. "Under the circumstances, I think it best if we don't know each other's names. That way, you can truthfully say you don't know."

The woman held her hand to her mouth. "Oh, yes, I see what you mean. I guess that would be best." She looked down at Johanna with sorrow in her eyes. "But I'm sorry it must be that way . . . I would very much like to know you."

Johanna smiled. "You do, in the ways that count. And maybe after the war . . ."

The woman sighed. "Yes, I suppose that's something we need to be thinking about. Will it go on much longer, do you think?"

Johanna shook her head. "No. I think it will be over very soon now."

"But not soon enough for some people, I suppose."

Johanna sighed. "No, not for some."

The woman stood. "Let me get you something to eat. You must be starved after what you've been through today."

"Thank you. Yes, I'm very hungry."

"I'll bring you some soup and cheese."

She got up and left for the kitchen.

Late that afternoon the sky began to clear, revealing patches of blue among the white clouds, tinged a reddish hue by the approaching sunset.

Johanna was standing at one of the front windows when she heard the distant sounds of a car approaching. She felt a sense of dread that quickly changed to icy fear. "Does your husband have a car?" she asked.

The other woman hurried to the window. The car was not yet in sight. "No. All we have is the horse and wagon he uses to deliver our milk cans and cheese."

"It has to be the SS — or the Gestapo. They're looking for me."

"We must hide you. Sit down." The woman dashed to the fireplace. Johanna sat heavily as her friend helped her on with the now-dry socks and boots. Johanna stood and struggled into the coat as she followed her new friend to the back door.

"Step where I step," the woman said when they were outside.

They hurried through the farmyard to the large dairy barn. The woman opened one of the doors and held it to allow Johanna to enter. Inside it was musty, smelling of hay and cows.

"Up in the loft?" Johanna asked.

"No. We've been searched before. They always look up there."

"Searched for what?"

"You'll see."

The woman led Johanna back to a stall, then opened the gate and led the cow out.

Johanna looked at the beast in apprehension. "You want me to hold her?" she asked, eyeing the rope.

"No need. She won't go anywhere," she said as she returned inside the stall.

Johanna looked into the cow's large brown eyes, wondering what she would do if the large animal *did* decide she wanted to escape. Fortunately, a trip outside didn't seem uppermost in the cow's mind.

The farmwife hurriedly swept aside the straw and a layer of dirt, revealing sturdy planks about five feet long. She pulled one up and leaned it against the side of the stall. Then she removed five more, revealing a large root cellar.

"Come, let me help you down. You'll be safe down there. The Nazi goons haven't discovered this yet."

Johanna found little comfort in those words. Surely searches for prison escapees would be more rigorous. She approached the pit with a sense of dread. A steep, sloped ladder led down into a larder stocked with sacks of potatoes, blocks of cheese, and an assortment of boxes and glass jars. She turned around and backed down the steps, feeling for the bottom with her feet. Finally she touched hard-packed earth. Her head was almost level with the floor of the stall.

"I have to cover you up now. Spread those empty burlap sacks over the potatoes for a place to lie down. I'll come back as soon as they leave. Don't make any noise."

"Don't worry, I won't."

Johanna spread out the sacks and sat down. She watched as her friend quickly lowered the planks one by one, gradually cutting off the light. Finally the last one thumped down, and Johanna heard scraping sounds as dirt and straw covered her hiding-place. A short while later the boards groaned as the cow returned to the stall. Then everything was silent.

Johanna placed her hand on her belly as her baby started kicking. She wondered how much longer they would remain alive.

Twenty-Three

The blackness was total. For a long time Johanna heard nothing except occasional noises from the overhead planks when the cow moved. Then came a sound she had a hard time identifying. It was a heavy plopping, and it continued for some time. Finally Johanna figured out what it was and hoped that the dirt over the boards would provide a good seal.

A little later she heard muffled voices approaching, then the sound of the barn door banging open.

"Please," a woman said, "if you disturb the cows, they won't give milk."

"Keep silent!" a man said.

"Want me to search the loft?" another man asked.

"Yes, and do a thorough job. She could be anywhere. We know these farmers are quite clever in hiding *other* things from us."

"What do you mean?" Johanna heard the farmwife ask.

"Don't pretend you don't know," the man said. "The food. The food that should go to the good Germans of the Reich."

Johanna held her breath as she heard heavy thumps directly overhead. The planks groaned and shifted. A narrow gap opened up suddenly, and a beam of light lanced down as dirt and something wet fell down from above. Johanna almost cried out as she caught sight of a man. All she could see was his head.

"What is the matter with that beast?" the man asked.

"You've scared her."

"Hmm. Perhaps, but maybe it's something else. I think I'll have a look in there."

Lord, help me, Johanna prayed silently.

"I would advise some boots," the farmwife replied.

"What?"

Johanna could see the man's eyes as he looked into the shadows at the back of the stall.

"What is that stuff?"

She laughed. "Cows do not give only milk, I'm afraid. Do you want the boots?"

Johanna saw the look of disgust on his face.

"No, that will not be necessary." He looked up suddenly. "Find anything in the loft?"

"Nothing."

"Very well. Come down immediately. We

have other farms to search."

The man disappeared out of Johanna's view. The last thing she saw was the farmwife's quick glance. Then she left as well.

The sun sat on the horizon, red and weak. Erich hobbled back to where Bertha Liedig was waiting. He held his cane in his left hand while gripping two rusty tin cans precariously in his right. Bertha sat on a log beside a small fire that gave scant heat to the dozen or so gathered around it.

Erich handed her the cans, then sat down. The log rocked a little as he tried to find a position that would minimize his pain. He stopped when the man on the other side of Bertha scowled at him.

"They didn't give us much," Erich said. "Some thin broth and two small chunks of rotten potato."

"But we should be thankful, Herr von Arendt."

He felt his face grow warm despite the chill. "You're right, Frau Liedig. I guess I should give thanks to the Lord for our food."

"I think that would be nice."

He bowed his head. "Lord, we thank You for meeting all our needs. We give You thanks for this food. Please continue to watch over us . . ." He paused. "And please take care of Johanna, wherever she is. Amen."

"Amen," Bertha said.

Erich looked up and saw most of those around them looking at him curiously. Some nodded silent agreement, some looked puzzled, while others were clearly irritated. Erich shrugged and sipped the broth. It tasted bitter and was nearly cold now. He fished the potato out of the can and ate it, trying not to think about what the black specks were.

"What are your plans, Herr von Arendt?" Bertha asked.

"I don't really have any. All we can do is try to survive until the war ends. And this camp is as good a place to wait as any, certainly better than if we were in a city." He gave a bitter laugh. "We have two choices, as I see it. We can either be captured by Montgomery's forces or Eisenhower's. Herr Speer seemed to favor the British, so I guess we're in the right place since Montgomery has been allotted the north. His armies should come along in due course, provided General Eisenhower manages to get him to move."

"How do you know all this?" a man on

471

the other side of the fire asked.

Erich looked him in the eye. "It doesn't matter. It really doesn't matter."

The farmer opened the door and looked past his wife. Johanna saw his look of surprise mixed with apprehension. He attempted a smile as he removed his coat and gloves.

"I see we have a guest," he said to his wife.

"Yes, we do. She has escaped from an SS camp."

His eyes grew very round. "She has?"

"Yes. And under the circumstances, she suggested it might be best if we don't know each other's names."

"That would probably be best." He turned to Johanna. "You are welcome in our house. Please sit down." He walked past and hung his coat beside the fire.

"There's something else," his wife added.

"What's that?"

"The Gestapo were here this afternoon."

"They didn't find anything, did they?"

"No, but they nearly did. I hid our guest in the root cellar, and the cow kicked one of the boards loose. The stall was quite messy at the time, which was all that saved us. I think they'll be back."

He shook his head. "This is bad."

"I'm sorry," Johanna said. "I didn't mean to bring this on you."

As he looked at her, his frown turned to a weak smile. "Now, don't you worry. This isn't your doing. It's those Nazis. We'll take care of you."

"But how? If they keep coming back, they'll eventually catch me. I don't want you to suffer because of me."

He scratched his beard and glanced at his wife. "Let us worry about that. But you're right, they are persistent."

"What can we do?" his wife asked.

He shook his head. "That's hard to say." He looked at Johanna. "You need to get far away from here. Do you have any friends or relatives?"

Tears came to her eyes. "I'm from Frankfurt, but my family's dead."

"Oh, I'm sorry, dear." The farmwife handed her a handkerchief.

"Do you have friends there?" he asked gently.

She nodded. "Some very dear Christian friends. They'd take me in if I could get there."

"Frankfurt would certainly be better than here, especially with the SS looking for you. But the problem is, how can we get you there? Travel is almost impossible, though I think I can help you get as far as Magdeburg. I have to deliver a load of milk and cheese to Havelberg tomorrow. From there the food goes up the Elbe by boat. I know the owner, and I'm sure he'll take you."

"Will she be safe?" his wife asked.

"Safer than she will be here." He paused. "I'll be glad when this war is over."

Johanna felt her baby kick. "So will I."

Even though the day dawned crystal-clear, the weak winter sun did little to warm the narrow wooden dock. The wind whipped around the freight soon to be loaded into the narrow riverboats that waited with their cargo hatches gaping open. Most of the boats were operated by families that lived on the river, the boats being their homes as well as their livelihoods. But an old bachelor owned and operated the *Oder* with the help of a single crewman. The captain appeared past middle age. He was short and stout with a full white beard. He wore rough work clothes that were as neat and clean as his vessel. His assistant stood at the forward hatch, waiting to load the boat. He was tall and thin, and his clothes looked like they had been slept in.

The green water of the Elbe surged smoothly past the dock on its journey to the North Sea. The scene was deceptively peaceful, a sharp contrast to all the horrors Johanna had been through. She watched while the farmer explained her situation to the captain. The man glanced at her with keen blue eyes, nodding as the other filled him in.

The farmer returned to where Johanna waited. "He'll take you."

"Thank you for all you and your wife have done for me."

"No thanks are necessary. We're glad we could help." He handed her a sack of food. "Here . . . My wife fixed this for you. She says you must eat well for the baby."

She smiled. "I will."

The farmer looked past her. "I think the captain is ready for you to board. I explained your situation, so they won't ask your name."

"May God bless you."

"Thank you. And may our Lord be with you — and your child."

She turned and walked up to the captain.

"So, you are my passenger, yes?"

"Yes. I'm grateful for your help."

"You're welcome. We'll take good care of you. My crewman will take you to a special hiding-place in the forward hold — we've done this before. After we're on the open river, you can have my cabin."

"Oh, no, I can't do that."

"Oh, yes, you can." His blue eyes twinkled. "I'm the captain, and you have to do what I say. Don't worry about me. I'll be just fine in one of the other cabins."

He led her up the narrow gangplank and over the deck to the forward hold. "We have a special passenger. Please show her to the hiding-place."

The man nodded and turned without a word. He walked to the forward hatch and stepped quickly down the steeply sloped ladder without turning around or holding on. Johanna marveled at how he could do it without falling. She heard a laugh behind her and turned to see the captain smiling.

"It's something sailors learn how to do. I suggest you turn around and hold onto the rails."

"Yes, I think I will."

Johanna started down backwards, finding it difficult in her present condition. She paused with her eyes at deck level and looked around, taking in the beautiful morning. Then she descended into the hold.

The crewman was waiting patiently. Once she turned around, he led her forward on the starboard side. He suddenly stopped and began working on what appeared to be the boat's hull. After a few moments, he lifted away a section the size of a large door, revealing a space about three feet deep next to the real hull.

"This is where we carry our special cargoes — including the human kind." He pointed to the cot. "Lie down there. I'm afraid it's a little close in here, but you'll be all right. I'll come down for you when it's safe."

"Thank you."

She sat on the cot, swung her legs around, and lay on her back. The crewman quickly closed up the false hull. Johanna sighed as the gap of light narrowed, then winked out.

She tried to rest as the strange sounds of water commerce invaded her hiding-place. She wondered what was happening as she listened to the mysterious thumps and grunts of physical exertion. On the other side she could hear the gentle lap of water against the hull. This went on for what seemed like an hour until she heard one final, heavy thump. A few moments later the engine started, sending a light vibration through the boat as if it had become alive. Soon Johanna heard the soft whisper of moving water against the hull. They were underway.

A few minutes later she heard the footsteps she had been waiting for. Something scraped above her head, and the secret panel moved away. The crewman helped her up and led her aft to a small hatch over a narrow vertical ladder. She started up, keeping her eyes fixed on the narrow square of morning sky. She reached the deck and clambered through, standing a little uneasily even though the boat was absolutely steady.

The captain opened the door to the wheelhouse and stepped out. "Welcome on deck."

Johanna shivered as a frigid wind whipped across the open bow. She pulled her coat tighter.

"Come join me in the wheelhouse. I think you'll find it a little more comfortable in here." He went back inside and closed the door.

The crewman led her aft and up some steps. He held the door for her while she entered, then closed the door and continued walking aft.

Johanna stood beside the captain as he looked ahead through the large wheelhouse windows, occasionally moving the wheel slightly. The wide Elbe moved swiftly past them as the *Oder* fought its way upstream near the bank.

"It looks so peaceful," Johanna said as she scanned the river and the nearby shore.

"Right now it does," he agreed. "But looks can be deceiving."

Johanna noticed that the green water was carrying its own freight down toward the sea. She saw logs and bushes float past and later a large number of wooden boxes, all clumped together. Several grayish oblong objects trailed along behind. It took Johanna several seconds to realize they were dead German soldiers.

"Don't look," the captain said.

Johanna couldn't tear her eyes away. The bloated objects drifted past and were soon lost astern. The *Oder* rounded a sharp bend, revealing a narrow highway bridge over the river. The right-hand span lay in the water, a crumpled mass of iron and shattered concrete. The captain spun the wheel, pointing his boat toward the left-hand section that still stood. The burned-out remains of a military convoy littered the bridge deck. The front end of a truck hung over the end.

"When did this happen?" Johanna asked.

"Recently — perhaps yesterday or the day before. It was still standing last week on our trip downstream."

Johanna looked up apprehensively as they passed underneath the bridge. After a brief moment of shade, they came out into the morning sun again.

"So the war has come to our rivers as well," she said.

"Yes, it has. Things are much worse for us now that enemy fighters can reach this far into Germany."

"Is it safe for us to travel during daylight?"

She saw the tension in his eyes as he answered. "No, it's not. But I'm in a hurry to get home. Our home port is just outside Magdeburg. Once we get there, we're tying up until this is all over."

"How likely is an attack?"

He shrugged. "Hard to say. The trains and military convoys are the main targets. But if a fighter catches us out in the open, you can be sure he'll attack."

Johanna ate a quiet lunch with the captain as the *Oder* continued to plod its way upstream against the current. At first she scanned the horizons continuously, looking for the tiny glints of light that would spell doom for them. But hour after hour they continued their lonely journey toward Magdeburg as if they were the only ones left alive in northern Germany.

By late afternoon she began to believe they would reach safe harbor without incident. The *Oder* rounded a bend, and in the distance Johanna saw a narrow railway bridge, its steel structure seeming to be no more substantial than a spiderweb. But it grew more real as they approached, towering above the river.

"Look over there," the captain said, pointing.

Johanna saw a smudge of black smoke off to the left, signaling an approaching train. She felt a sense of growing dread. She looked past the bridge toward their destination and at first saw only the trail of smoke rapidly approaching the river. She held her breath when she spotted two silver glints winking in the distance. Then she lost sight of them.

"I think there's something to the south."

"Yes, enemy fighters."

"What are you going to do?"

He kept his eyes on the approaching bridge. "Hope they leave us alone. They're after the train."

The silver specks reappeared and grew rapidly. The train reached the bridge and started across. The locomotive's drive wheels blurred, and black smoke trailed back from its stack.

"That engineer is giving it everything he's got," the captain said.

"Will they make it?"

"We'll see, but I doubt it."

The lead fighter dropped down until it was nearly level with the tracks. White puffs of smoke spouted from the wings as tracers lanced out toward the target. The lethal hail sloped upward as the pilot corrected his aim, and the deadly bullets raked across the locomotive. Pieces flew off it without seeming to slow the train down at all. The fighter pulled up at the last moment and roared over the bridge. Johanna looked up at the blunt wings as the pilot turned sharply to the right. The second plane lined up on the locomotive, and again machine gun fire converged on the target. Moments later the steam engine disappeared in a white cloud. Metal flew in all directions, making large splashes in the river below.

"The boiler blew up," the captain said.

The second fighter swept past. It also turned away to the east. The train slid along the tracks, metal screaming against metal. Finally it ground to a stop, almost in the middle of the bridge. The *Oder* continued toward the span.

"Shouldn't we turn around?" Johanna asked.

"Wouldn't do any good. They know where we are. But for now they're more interested in that train."

"They've already blown up the engine."

"Yes, but what's in those boxcars?" He pointed up the river. "See?"

The lead fighter screamed in from the right on a path diagonal to the bridge. His tracers led the way to the front of the train and raked their way along its entire length in one long burst. A boxcar near the end erupted in an orange and black ball of flame. The concussion hit the *Oder* a moment later, cracking one of the wheelhouse windows. The captain spun the wheel hard to the left. The boat hesitated for a moment, then started coming around. Heavy debris rained down all around them, raising hundreds of geysers. Some of the metal and wood slammed into the decks, creating large holes and gouges.

Another blast enveloped the bridge, and the span underneath buckled and collapsed, dropping what remained of the railcars into the river. Twisted girders followed them down. The wreckage disappeared momentarily inside a white wall of water.

The *Oder* continued turning until it was headed downstream.

"What was that?" Johanna asked when she could speak.

"Munitions. At least two boxcars, I'd say."

"What do we do now?"

The man looked her in the eye. "The best we can."

He opened the wheelhouse door and stepped quickly outside. He looked astern, then toward the bridge. He dashed to the wheel and spun it to the right.

"Come on," he said as he held the wheel against its stop.

The boat turned sluggishly as it fought the swift current nearer the center of the river. Slowly the *Oder* came around, seemed to hang broadside for a moment, then continued turning until they were once again pointed at the bridge. Dead ahead lay the pier closest to the fallen section. Flames and smoke engulfed the cars still on the tracks.

"Where are the planes?" Johanna asked.

"One is orbiting to the south, but the other one is making a run toward the bridge."

Johanna caught a glint of silver just off the water and headed right at them. The captain adjusted the wheel slightly. The bridge pier slid slowly between the hunter and his prey. When the fighter banked, re-appearing on the right, the captain adjusted course to the left. The bridge pier loomed larger as they approached the dingy shaft of concrete hiding them momentarily from the attacker. Twin fountains of water marched toward them as the machine gun fire sought them out. A few slugs slammed into the hull, but most of the fire went by on either side. The plane pulled up and flew over the bridge. Johanna looked up at the plane's belly as it roared past.

The *Oder* was almost to the pier now. The captain made a course correction, and they passed close on the right-hand side. Once clear, they turned to the left toward the collapsed section of the bridge.

"Get down on the deck!"

Johanna knelt down, then sprawled awkwardly in the right front corner of the wheelhouse. She looked up at the captain as he made a minor correction to the wheel. She saw him glance to the left. He hesitated for a moment, then dove for the deck. She heard the staccato rattle of machine guns over the roar of the approaching fighter. She wished she had something better to hide behind as bullets slammed into the boat. Large holes pierced the top of the wheelhouse, blowing out all the windows. Johanna covered her head with her hands as wood splinters and glass shards showered down on them. As the slugs continued to explode into the small compartment, Johanna's heart raced as each moment she expected the deadly barrage to rip her body apart. The next moment the only thing she could hear was the roar of a racing engine as the fighter pulled up and over the bridge. She took her hands away and looked up cautiously.

The captain got up and crunched over the glass to the wheel. He peered to the south, then spun the wheel to the right. "You can get up now. They're gone."

Johanna struggled to her feet and looked toward the south. The two silver glints shrank quickly as they turned toward the west.

"I thought we were dead," she gasped.

He pointed his thumb astern. "If it hadn't been for the bridge wreckage, we would be. Most of that horrible racket was ricochets off the girders."

"Do you think they'll be back?"

"Not those two. They're out of ammunition."

Johanna looked up the Elbe, once again peaceful. She closed her eyes and leaned against the back bulkhead of the wheelhouse. She tried to still her heart as she prayed silently. *Lord, thank You for protecting us. Please continue to watch over us — and help me get home.*

Twenty-Four

Johanna stood outside the warehouse while the *Oder*'s captain explained the situation to the wagon driver. She had spent a restless night in the master's cabin on the boat, worrying over how she would get back to Frankfurt. Magdeburg was roughly seventy-five miles from Berlin, and her destination was still over 200 miles away — and all of it over war-torn roads.

She shivered despite her coat. It was cold again today as the weather continued clear, but she knew that could change quickly. She shaded her eyes against the low rays of the sun as she watched the ongoing transaction. Several times the driver looked her way. Finally both men came outside.

"He will take you as far as Sangerhausen," the captain said. "There he thinks he can get you on another wagon going to Weimar. It's slow, but it's about the only transportation available."

"I appreciate your help," she said. "I wouldn't have made it this far without you."

He seemed flustered. "Oh, I don't know

about that. Glad to do what I could."

"What will you and your crewman do now?"

He sighed. "Wait for this blasted war to end." He paused. "I hope you make it home. Good-bye to you."

He touched his cap and was gone.

The driver nodded toward the loaded wagon. "We'd best be going. It's a long trip."

"I'm ready."

She entered the warehouse with him. He helped her up, and she sat heavily on the hard seat. He went around, removed the horse's feed bag, and placed it in with the cargo. He pulled himself up and sat down beside Johanna. He released the brake, took the reins, and shook them gently, clicking his tongue as he did so. The horse leaned into the harness and started pulling the heavily laden wagon forward. Johanna sighed. Two hundred miles, in the middle of a war, was a long way to go.

A biting wind swept across the field at Toul, France. First Lieutenant Andy Redpath shivered as he approached his olivedrab P-47 Thunderbolt. He shielded his brown eyes against the early rays of the winter sun as a vagrant gust messed up his straight black hair. He was tall and thin, the usual physique for fighter pilots.

He viewed his plane with a sense of awe, undiminished by his forty missions with the 365th Fighter Squadron. Most pilots called the P-47 a "Jug" because it looked like one if viewed from the side. Others called it the Republic Streamlined Crowbar, a tribute to its brute strength. Andy glanced at the two 1,000-pound instantaneously fused bombs that would explode on contact. The day's mission called for train killing. For some reason he thought of his latest letter from his wife, Helen. It had been the usual — the events in Tuscumbia, what little Sam had been up to, and so on; but at the end she told him she was praying that God would protect him. Andy looked up at the massive fighter. *This is what I depend on to protect me,* he thought as he prepared to climb aboard, *not some distant deity.*

"Mornin', Lieutenant," came a gravelly voice on the other side of the aircraft.

"Morning, Pops," Andy replied, using his crew chief's nickname. "Is Helen ready to go?" He glanced at his wife's name painted on the plane's nose.

"You bet she is. You just point her where

you want her to go, and she'll get you there — and back."

"That's what I want to hear."

Andy climbed up on the wing, walked forward, and stepped into the cockpit. He settled into the seat as his crew chief, standing on the other wing, helped him strap in. The man then hurried off the plane as Andy slid the canopy shut. Moments later the huge, four-bladed propeller started turning. The 2,000-horsepower engine caught and settled into a smooth idle.

Andy taxied out with the rest of his flight, making wide S turns to avoid running into the aircraft in front of him. Minutes later they were in the air, climbing for altitude and thundering toward Germany.

After passing Pirmasens, Andy began looking for trains by scanning the tracks below, leading to Landau. The line twisted and turned as it followed the valleys, disappearing at frequent intervals as it passed through tunnels. Today it looked like a black shoelace against a backdrop of cotton. Andy heard his earphones pop.

"I see smoke up ahead," his wingman said over the radio.

Andy looked past the P-47's long cowl and turned slightly for a better view. "I see it. Follow me in."

"Roger."

Andy dropped lower and pushed the throttle all the way forward. He roared just a few feet above the fir trees as he rounded the intervening foothill. He hoped to pop up on the far side and gain enough altitude for a dive-bombing attack. Too late, he saw the train was too close to the tunnel it was approaching.

"He's gonna make the tunnel, Andy," his wingman said. "You'll have to catch him on the other side."

"Roger."

The locomotive swept into the tunnel trailing nine or ten boxcars. Andy pulled straight up and over on his back, rolling out and traveling in the opposite direction. His wingman, he noted, was right with him. Andy gained altitude rapidly to get into position for the attack. He pulled back on his throttle and started a wide turn to the left, keeping the western tunnel mouth in view at all times. The locomotive did not appear.

"Ah, Andy. I think the guy's stopped inside the tunnel. He won't come out as long as we're up here. Let's go on down the line and see if we can find another train."

"He's not going to get away with this!"

"There's nothing we can do. Let's go."

"Not on your life. I'm going to get him! Stay up here, junior. I'm going in by myself."

Andy glanced down at the track below. Then he flew to the next tunnel to the west and racked the heavy fighter around in a tight turn to the left, rolling out almost in line with the track.

"Andy, you can't skip bomb him. Those fuses are instantaneous. If you hit the tunnel face you'll blow yourself up."

"I won't hit the face."

He dropped even lower. Now he was right over the rails, roaring toward the black circle of the tunnel that was hiding his target. Closer and closer it came. Andy flicked off the safety, made a minor correction, then held steady. He knew this had to be just right. He jabbed the firing release button and pulled the stick back and to the left a fraction of a second later. Each moment he expected to be blown from the air as he continued his climbing turn.

"You did it!" his wingman shouted. "Both bombs skipped down those ties like they were on wires — went right inside the tunnel! I bet that was one surprised German!"

Andy heard the explosion but couldn't see it until he pulled back around. The spouting white cloud amid the boiling smoke told him all he needed to know.

"That'll teach him to try and hide from me."

"I'm glad you're alive to tell me about it."

Andy pulled back up to where the rest of the flight was orbiting. "Come on, junior. Let's go see if we can find you a train."

"Roger."

Helen Redpath sat on the bed in the front bedroom of her parents' house in Tuscumbia, Alabama. She brushed her long auburn hair away from her face as she smoothed the flimsy letter out so she could read it. She felt the familiar pain in her heart as she thought of the one who'd written it.

The clatter of little feet sounded on the side steps to the porch, and a blurred figure raced past the window. Moments later she heard the front door slam. Four-year-old Sam dashed by the bedroom door, apparently not expecting his mother to be in there. He slid to a stop, turned around, and came through the door, dropping the sadly deflated leather football as he ran to the bed.

"Up," he demanded.

She set the letter aside, reached down, and lifted him into her lap. She looked at him with her lively brown eyes. He so reminded her of his father.

"I'm hot," he announced.

"Well, no wonder. You haven't been still since you've been up." She removed the heavy sailor's coat and draped it on the bed. "Is that better?"

"Yes."

"Thank you?" she prompted.

"Thank you, Mommy."

"You're welcome."

"What's that?" he asked, pointing to the letter.

"A letter from Daddy." She watched the puzzled expression on his face. Other kids in town had fathers, and he couldn't understand where his was. She felt her eyes grow moist. Little Sam had been less than two when Andy had shipped overseas to join his fighter squadron. "Do you want to hear it?"

He scrunched up his face. "I guess so. Where's Daddy, Mommy?"

She sighed. She had given up trying to explain about the war and fighter planes and Germany and Hitler and France and

. . . everything. "He's gone on a long trip, honey."

"Why can't he come home?" He looked up when he heard her sniff. "Why are you crying, Mommy?"

"I miss your daddy." She brought out a handkerchief to wipe away her tears.

"Don't cry, Mommy."

"I'll be all right, dear. Why don't you go see what grandmother is doing." She forced a smile.

He smiled back. "OK."

He jumped down and ran for the back of the house.

She picked up Andy's letter.

January 12, 1945
Dear Helen,

I miss you and Sam more than I can say. Please don't worry about me, I'm being careful. Besides, I'm very good at what I do.

There's not a lot I can tell you. I'm in Toul, France — can't be more specific than that. Things are going well, and I don't really see how the war can last much longer.

The P-47 is a real brute. I named mine for you — hope you don't mind. Anyhow, the Thunderbolt takes good care of me, thanks to Pops, my crew chief. I have nothing but admiration for the Republic Aviation Corporation.

I've decided I want to stay in the Army Air Corps after the war. My CO told me I should consider volunteering for the occupation army in Germany. He said it would help me in my career. I'm thinking about it.

Well, got to go. Got a briefing in five minutes.

Love,
Andy

Tears fell gently on the letter, causing the ink to run. Helen closed her eyes as she longed for the war to be over. She thought about the letter. What would it be like to go overseas with Sam? What would it be like to live in Germany? She shivered and bowed her head.

Dear Lord, Andy is so far away. He tells me not to worry, but I know he's in danger. Please watch after him and protect him. I pray You will reunite us as soon as possible. Amen.

Johanna couldn't believe the damage to Frankfurt's city center. The old Römer still stood, but not much else. She had already gone to Herr Dorpmüller's building. A huge pile of rubble was all that remained of the entire block. She tried to find other members of the church but to no avail.

It was now early March 1945. It had taken Johanna two long weeks to travel from Magdeburg to Frankfurt. Now she wondered if it had been worth it. The biting wind whipped about her, tugging at her very round coat. She looked down at the prominent bulge. That morning she had felt several minor twinges and wondered if it was time. Now she felt the pain again, but stronger this time. She started walking north.

A half hour later as she plodded along Reuterweg, a powerful contraction hit her. After it eased, she looked in the direction of Grüneburgpark, a large greenbelt north and west of the city center. All she could see was destruction. There wasn't a soul around.

She looked up into the winter sky. *Lord, help me! Show me where to go! Send someone to help me! Don't let me have the baby here, alone, amidst all these ruins of war!*

She thought about turning around to try and find someone in the city but decided against it. Another contraction seized her. She knew she would need help soon, but all she could see were bombed-out buildings and houses. She continued down the road, wondering how long she could keep going. Soon the contractions were just minutes apart.

She leaned against the rusting hulk of a burned-out car while she caught her breath, then looked up. Off to the left stood a forest and open country. A moment later she saw a thin wisp of smoke somewhere inside the park. Having nowhere else to turn, she started toward it.

Oh, Lord! Help me make it there! And please have someone there who can help me!

Every few moments she had to stop because of the pain. But after each contraction and urgent prayer she started walking again.

"I'm not going to make it," she groaned. But something seemed to urge her not to give up.

She plodded on, seeing only what was immediately in front of her. She could no longer see the smoke but hoped she was still going in the right direction. Finally she rounded a grove of trees and saw a refugee camp. Dozens of crude huts dotted the hillside in front of her. A man chopping firewood looked up and saw her.

"Help!" she screamed as another contraction hit her. "I'm having a baby!"

The man dropped his ax and ran into the camp. Moments later a woman and two men hurried to her side.

"Carry her," the woman ordered one of the men.

He picked her up and followed the woman to the nearest hut. She went first. After he took Johanna in, he returned outside.

"Get me some hot water and rags," the woman said from inside.

Two hours later it was over, and Johanna rested under a pile of blankets. In her arms she held a tightly wrapped bundle, with only the baby's very red face showing. She looked toward the woman who had helped her.

"I can't thank you enough," Johanna said.

"I'm glad I was here to assist. What will you call him?"

Johanna's smile was mixed with grief. "His name is Erich."

The woman nodded. "A fine German name."

Franz Brant slouched as he reached the door. The windows on either side were gone, hastily patched with scraps of lumber. He twisted the handle and pulled, but the door was jammed. He cursed and pulled harder. Finally it broke free from the warped frame and sagged on loose hinges. The chill wind snatched at his coat as Franz stepped onto the neglected sidewalk and turned toward Tiergarten Park. His nervous eyes darted about as he trudged along. Berlin was a hollow, crumbling shell now, apparently about to collapse completely, a huge pile of rubble marking the open grave the enemy was digging for Hitler and his National Socialist party. It was a grave that had plenty of room for Heinrich Himmler and all the other high Nazis as well. It had room for him too, he thought, as he crossed the street and entered Tiergarten.

The park seemed dead and deserted. Trash blew everywhere, and the grounds were shaggy and unkempt, so unlike Tiergarten's proud past. And it was deathly silent. He kicked a rotten branch out of the way. *The birds are smarter than we are. Who but fools would stay in Berlin waiting for the inevitable bombing raids, the raids that Reich Marshal Goering assured us would never happen.* He stepped off the path and approached the bench where he had met the American spy. He sat dejectedly and looked toward the east as if he could see the Russian army approaching to seal their doom.

His thoughts turned to Erich. Poor, gullible Erich. Franz had finally admitted to himself that he really had no friends. His grief was compounded by the fact that Erich had been a friend to him, with a loyalty Franz knew he didn't deserve. He didn't regret his decisions as much as their failure. And yet, what he had done to Erich — and to Johanna — weighed heavily on him, a debt he somehow couldn't put out of his thoughts. *Well, there's nothing I can do about it now. It's over. I'll be dead and forgotten in a few days, along with all our idiot leaders.*

The faint sound of muffled artillery fire came from the east. *Pretty soon their tanks will be in front of the Chancellery, if it's still standing.*

Erich's image bubbled up in Franz's mind again, like a specter that would not go away. There was something Erich needed to know, however much Franz tried to resist the thought. He tried to tell himself it wasn't worth the effort, not with everything he was going through. But finally he gave in, deciding he would never have peace unless he tried to find Erich. But where was he? The only one who might know was still in Berlin. But would he tell Franz?

Erich looked up from the fire at the sound of an approaching car. Military traffic up and down the road was not that unusual, but none of those vehicles stopped at the camp. This car did. Erich watched the driver's door open. His mouth fell open when he saw who it was.

He grabbed his cane and stood, all caution lost in his rage. "Franz! How dare you come here!"

Erich started toward him as fast as his injury would allow. As he neared the car, he raised the cane over his head. Franz ducked back behind the car. Erich, too angry to watch where he was going, stepped into a hole and tumbled to the ground. The cane flew out of his hand and clattered against the car. Franz hurried around to grab it.

"Hold on!" he said as he cautiously approached Erich. "I came here to see you. I . . ."

"I don't want to see you! I want to kill you!" He struggled to rise.

"Let me help you up."

"Stay away from me!"

Franz stepped back. "Have it your way. But I *still* have to see you. I have come here to help you."

Erich winced in pain. "What could I *possibly* want from you after all you've done?"

"I have news about Johanna."

This caught Erich by surprise. He clenched his teeth. "What about Johanna?" Then the rage returned. "Franz, if I could, I'd strangle you for what you've done to both of us!"

"I know, and I deserve it. But I didn't come all this way to let you do that. I came to tell you something." He paused. "It took me a long time to get Herr Speer to tell me where you were. Now, do you want to hear what I have to say or not?"

Erich glared at him as he tried to get control of his emotions. He knew his blind rage would accomplish no good, and yet . . . "OK, OK . . . What is it you wish to tell me? But I warn you . . ."

Franz sighed and handed him the cane. Erich snatched it and relieved the pressure on his bad leg.

"The enemy bombed the camp Johanna was in."

Erich's anger quickly turned to concern. "What? When did . . ."

"Hold on . . . I have better news . . . She

escaped." He stopped, and Erich thought he saw a look of remorse. "I did what I did for money. I know that was wrong, and I'm sorry for what it did to Johanna — and to you. You were such a good friend, and I betrayed your trust. I know what I am doing now doesn't fix anything, but I wanted you to know what happened."

A faint glimmer of hope rose in Erich's heart. "Where is she?"

"The SS traced her as far as a nearby dairy farm — they think . . . They're not sure. They know the farmer made a trip to Havelberg with a load of milk and cheese. The boat that took his cargo went to Magdeburg. That's all they know. The SS goons snooped around a little more but couldn't turn up anything else."

"Do you think Johanna made it to Magdeburg?"

"I think so. We know for a fact she didn't die at the camp. Think about it, Erich . . . If you wanted to go to Frankfurt in the middle of a war, how would you do it? She can't travel by normal means, even if she could get the proper authorization. But food shipments have to continue or we all starve."

"We may yet. You should see what we get by on here."

Franz nodded. "Yes, yes, I know. Anyway, if she had contacts with people who deliver food shipments, she might very well be in Frankfurt by now."

Tears came to Erich's eyes as he wondered if he dared hope. "Do you really think she's alive?"

Franz took a deep breath. "There's no way of telling for sure, you know that. But I think there's a good possibility she is. And *if* she is, I'd be willing to bet she's in Frankfurt."

"I hope so. I hope she is all right."

"Believe me, Erich, so do I. And there's one more thing . . ."

Though anger still smoldered deep within him, Erich felt emotionally drained. Quietly he asked, "What is that?"

"She's pregnant."

Erich stared at him for a moment, unable to reply.

"Did you hear me? Johanna's pregnant. She's expecting your child."

A deep yearning grew in Erich's heart until he thought he would pass out. "I must get to Frankfurt."

Franz glanced toward the west. "I advise you to stay here for a while if you want to live."

Erich nodded. "So Montgomery has finally crossed the Rhine?"

"Yes — last night. That's why all the military traffic is coming through here. It won't be long before the front is right here. I'd find a place to hide and wait until this is over."

Erich nodded slowly. "That would probably be wise."

"I have to go." Franz paused as he reached the door of the car. "I'm sorry for what happened, Erich. I am truly sorry."

Erich looked at him, not knowing what to say.

Franz got in the car and drove off.

Twenty-Five

The British sweep through Hannover did not come as quickly as Erich expected, even though he was well aware of Montgomery's legendary caution. But when the battle line neared, there was no mistaking it. Retreating German vehicles were the first through, a disorganized assortment of trucks, personnel carriers, and tanks. Following these came the army troops. This continued for many hours until the lead British elements approached. Erich and Bertha pulled back into the trees, away from the camp to see what would happen.

"Is that the last of our men?" Bertha asked, pointing toward the road.

"I think so. Fairly soon we should see the British scouts followed by some tank units."

"So it's almost over."

"Yes. But it's *been* almost over for a long time. If it weren't for Herr Speer, the war would be over now."

"What will happen next?"

"That depends on the Americans and the British, and to a lesser extent the Russians and French. They'll probably take over our government for a while — they'll adjust our borders for sure . . ." He paused. "And they'll probably do something about the crimes the Nazis committed."

"What will they do about those?"

Erich shook his head. "I don't know. But they ought to hang them all."

He heard a whistling scream approaching. "Get down!"

Erich buried his head against the ground and waited for the impact. The first artillery shell exploded about a hundred feet away. Dirt clods and dust rained down for some time, and then the barrage began in earnest. The ground shook with the impact as the shells walked ever closer to where Erich and Bertha hid, like a rampant giant searching for new victims. Each blast lifted them off the ground, and with each round Erich thought they were doomed. He tasted dirt and felt something wet running down his face. He touched it with his hand, and it came away bloody.

It seemed to Erich the barrage would last forever, but gradually it tapered off and finally quit. He waited a few minutes to be sure, then turned over. He looked over at Bertha Liedig. Other than being covered with chunks of dirt, she appeared to be in one piece.

"I think we can get up now," Erich said.

She didn't move. He touched her arm. "Frau Liedig, I think it's over."

Icy fear gripped him as he saw the dark red tide just beyond her head. He crawled over, still on his hands and knees. He almost vomited when he saw that a piece of shrapnel had torn away the entire right side of her head while leaving the left unscratched. He was sure death had been immediate.

He rolled over on his back as the tears came. He thought of all the years Bertha had faithfully served him. Even when she had disagreed with him, she had been on his side. She had survived this horrible war right up to the end, and finally, when it was almost over, she had died like this.

He grabbed his cane and struggled to his feet. There was one more thing he had to do. He hobbled over to the camp and found a shovel. Then he buried Frau Liedig.

For hours Erich waited for the approaching British army as he thought about the German soldiers retreating eastward. He had mixed emotions about this. He knew personally the evil of Hitler's Third Reich and that it deserved to lose. But he was still German, and Germany had been here before Adolf Hitler. Hopefully a decent Germany would rise from these ashes, free of the cancer of National Socialism. But that depended in large measure on what the victors did.

Eventually Erich saw the lead tank units and approaching infantry. The tanks clattered past in a long column while the soldiers fanned out around them, their rifles held at the ready. Many of the men stared at those in the refugee camp as they continued pursuing the retreating German army.

Late that afternoon Erich saw an American jeep coming from the direction of Hannover. He approached the road cautiously, shading his eyes against the setting sun. As the jeep drew abreast, the officer in back gave an order Erich didn't understand. The jeep slid to a stop, and the officer jumped out. Now Erich could see he was an American army major. He felt deep apprehension as the officer looked him over.

"Who are you?" the American asked in quite good German.

"I am Erich von Arendt."

"Von Arendt, hmm? Are you an army officer?"

"No."

Erich saw the suspicion in the man's eyes. "You're quite young to be a civilian. I see the cane. How did you get injured?"

Erich took a deep breath. "It doesn't matter now. The war's over, or will be very soon."

"Let me be the judge of that. Tell me how it happened."

"My leg was hit by a large wooden splinter. I've had several operations, but it's not healing well."

"Were you in a battle?"

"No. I was standing outside a briefing hut at Rastenburg when a bomb went off."

The officer's mouth fell open. "You were at Hitler's Wolf's Lair on July 20, 1944?"

"Yes, I was."

"So, you're not an army officer, but you had access to Rastenburg. Who do you work for?"

"No one now."

The American pointed a finger at him. "Enough of this! Who *did* you work for?"

Erich sighed. "I worked for Albert Speer, Reich Minister of Armaments and Munitions. I was one of his executive assistants."

"So you're a Nazi."

Erich felt a quick chill of fear along with deep indignation. "No, I am *not* a Nazi!"

"Right. Funny thing — I've talked to quite a few Germans, and I haven't run into a Nazi yet." Erich saw an eager look come to the man's eyes. "Do you know where Speer is?"

"The last time I saw him was in the Ministry offices in Berlin."

"What are his plans?"

"I'm not sure. He's been trying to keep the generals and mayors from destroying the cities and transportation. He told me he was thinking about giving himself up to the British in northern Germany once the end came near."

"Well, the end's near now."

"Yes, I know."

The major pulled his Colt .45 service automatic and trained it on Erich. "Herr von Arendt, you are my prisoner. You will accompany me back to my headquarters."

Erich felt his hope slipping away. "Why? What have I done?"

"I don't have to tell you anything. But for your information, I think we'll want to talk to you about Nazi war crimes."

"But I told you, I'm not a Nazi."

The American waved his pistol. "Get in the jeep now!"

Johanna stood on the edge of Grüneburgpark, gazing toward Frankfurt's city center, marveling at all that had happened since she had arrived back home, if you could call a devastated city under foreign occupation home. She looked down at her son's peaceful face as he slept in her arms. *Well,* she thought, *at least little Erich is happy enough.* She kissed his forehead.

With June had come warmer weather. May 7 marked Germany's official surrender to the Allied Forces — and the final end of Hitler's mad plans for a world empire ruled by the Fatherland. The American army continued to pour into Frankfurt as the occupiers tried to come to grips with the almost complete destruction of German commerce. Johanna found herself wondering what they would do to feed the citizens.

Little Erich squirmed in her arms. She looked down at him, but he didn't awaken. She sighed. *Had Erich survived the war?* she wondered, not for the first time. *If he had, where was he?* She felt a deadness in her heart that even her beautiful baby could not completely dispel. She had prayed for

Erich often, but there seemed to be no answer.

Erich again sat in the starkly furnished room as he waited for the interrogator. In the long months since he had been held in the small hotel in Dusseldorf, an endless stream of Americans and Englishmen had questioned him, first about the Reich Ministry of Armaments and Munitions, and later about whether he had participated in Nazi war crimes. These questions paralleled those he had asked himself ever since he had found himself inside the Reich government.

Although he had known about the slave labor, he had not been involved with it, except for the short time he had worked for Dietrich Clahes. Other than the rumors he couldn't bring himself to believe, he had not known about the death camps until after the war was over. He felt guilty before God, but at the same time after he began working for Speer, and especially after the Gestapo had threatened him and his family, there was nothing else he could have done.

His conscience pricked him. *No, that is not so — I could have done something. But it would have been dangerous, very dangerous.*

He had taken the easy way out, as had so many Germans. And now quite possibly he would have to reap the consequences of his choice.

The nameless interrogator came in and sat down. He opened his notebook and took out a pen. He peered at Erich through wire-rimmed glasses. "Tell me what you know about Dietrich Clahes and the Main Division for Resettlement."

"You already have that."

"Tell me again."

Erich sighed. "As you wish."

"Well, what do you think?" Andy Redpath asked.

Helen released little Sam's hand and watched him go racing around the house. She was still weary after the long bus ride from Bremerhaven to Frankfurt.

She turned around in the large entryway. "It's huge. We're going to be living here?"

"Yes. The military government requisitioned it. It's the nicest house in the compound."

"What compound? This is the only house standing for blocks around."

"I know. We're technically part of a compound two blocks to the north. That's where we get our lights and water. It's also

516

our neighborhood, I guess you'd say. I already know several of the families, and we'll soon get to know them all."

She smiled at him. "Well, it certainly is nice." Sam swept past and raced up the stairs, taking them two at a time. "And your son apparently loves it."

Andy took her in his arms. "Helen, I'm so glad you're finally here. I've missed you so much." He kissed her. She returned it, feeling the full awakening of all the longing she'd felt for him since he'd been gone.

"Well," she said when they broke, "I don't think there's any doubt about that."

They heard something clatter to the floor upstairs. They both looked up the stairs, but it was quiet now.

"What do you suppose that was?" Andy asked.

"I have no idea. But Sam definitely takes after his father."

"Handsome and dashing?"

"Yes, and full of mischief."

Johanna cradled her baby in her arms as she waited for the American army sergeant to examine her application for employment. She knew selection was not likely, but with winter approaching, she was desperate. Early September had already seen a few cool days.

"I see you didn't put anything down for marital status," he said as he fingered the application.

Johanna struggled to maintain her composure. "I don't know what happened to my husband. I've inquired with your army and the civilian authorities, but no one can tell me anything."

"I'm sorry. This is a very difficult problem."

"Yes. But meanwhile I and my son must live. Can you find any work for me?"

"Your English is acceptable, and that's a plus," he said. "But we don't normally hire young mothers."

"*Please* accept me. My son will not cause a problem. I will work hard. I promise complete satisfaction."

"Well, that will be up to Lieutenant and Mrs. Redpath. Would you like to go meet them and see what they have to say?"

"Yes, please."

The sergeant drove Johanna and her son through Frankfurt and over the bridge to Sachsenhausen. She watched as the heaps of rubble swept past, wondering if the once-elegant neighborhoods would ever be rebuilt. Her growing suspicion finally proved correct when the American turned onto what had, a long time ago, been her street. He pulled up in front of the house she had last seen — how long ago? She couldn't remember exactly.

"This is it," the sergeant said as he parked the jeep and got out.

They walked up to the front door and knocked. After a few minutes a young woman opened the door. Johanna looked down and saw a little boy hiding behind his mother's skirt. She smiled at him, and he grinned back.

"Yes?" the young woman said.

"Mrs. Redpath. I'm Sergeant Allen. Lieutenant Redpath requested we provide a housekeeper for you." He glanced back at Johanna's baby. "We don't normally consider young mothers, but we're having a hard time finding qualified applicants. She speaks English. I told her it would be up to you and the lieutenant."

Helen turned to Johanna. "Well, we do need someone. This is such a large house." She smiled at the young German woman.

Johanna smiled in return, surprised at how open and friendly the woman appeared. *Was this the enemy of Germany?* she wondered.

"I'm Helen Redpath." She held out her

hand. This also surprised Johanna. She took her hand gingerly and shook it. "And behind me is Sam."

"I am Frau — *Mrs.* Johanna von Arendt." She glanced down. "And my son Erich."

"Your English is very good."

Johanna smiled. "You are kind. I know it enough to get by." She paused. "I hope you and your husband will hire me. I will do anything you want."

Helen turned to Sergeant Allen. "We'll take her. What do we have to do?"

He handed her a slip of paper. "The lieutenant will have to sign this and drop it by our office." He hurried back to his jeep.

Johanna looked at the American, finding, to her surprise, that she really liked her. Those brown eyes were so full of life and joy.

"How do we begin?" Helen asked with a laugh.

Johanna grinned as she remembered how awkward she had been with Frau Liedig. "I can start by cleaning. If you want, I can help you with the shopping. I can translate for you, of course. And do you want me to do the cooking?"

"Yes, I think so. The first time I ever cooked — a meal, that is — was after Andy and I got married. I'm not very good at it, but I'm getting better. Perhaps we could do it together."

"I have a confession. I'm not a very good cook either. My husband . . ." Her voice faltered, and her eyes brimmed with tears.

"What's the matter?" Helen asked.

"My husband is missing." A tight knot appeared in her throat. "I think . . . I think he is dead."

"Oh, I'm so sorry."

Johanna looked into the woman's eyes and knew she was sincere. "Thank you. Anyway, before the war we had a house-keeper in our Berlin house. I'm afraid Frau Liedig was a much better cook than I was. But I watched what she did. What I don't know, I can learn."

Helen laughed nervously. "Well, maybe we both can."

"I'll do my very best for you and your husband. Would you like me to start by cleaning the upstairs?"

"If you like. Do you need me to watch Erich?"

"Oh, no. I can watch him while I work."

"OK. But if you need help with him, let me know. I love children."

"Thank you."

"Would you like me to show you around the house before you begin?"

A shy grin came to Johanna's face. "That won't be necessary."

"Why is that?"

"I used to live here. I grew up in this house."

Helen's eyes grew very round. "Really?"

Johanna nodded, a swirl of emotions nearly overcoming her.

Johanna finished up in Bernhard's old room in the late afternoon. She sat on the bed and looked out the window as she tried to resolve how she felt about her new circumstances. Her family was gone, and their house was now occupied by Americans. Still, she found it hard not to think of it as *her* house. It looked much as it had, although the rest of the neighborhood was gone. Except for what her parents had taken, all the furniture remained, though the clothing had been packed away. Even her mother's silverware and china graced the large hutch downstairs. The strangeness of the situation made her feel sad and a bit confused. This was what Hitler's war had brought to her and to millions of other Germans.

Although Helen had offered Johanna her old room upstairs, Johanna had assured her this was not appropriate and suggested the downstairs room that had been Herr Exner's.

Johanna sighed. She got up and returned downstairs, finding her employer in the kitchen.

"Shall I start dinner?" she asked.

"Let's do it together." Helen rummaged around in the pantry.

"I'm afraid all I've got right now is Spam, canned vegetables, and some potatoes. We can make a trip to the commissary tomorrow."

She pulled out the canned meat. "It'll be just us. Andy's on TDY to Munich. He'll be back this weekend."

"TDY?"

"I think it means 'temporary duty.' Anyhow, we can cook to suit ourselves. I personally don't like Spam, but it's better than nothing."

Johanna's mouth watered as she eyed the two rectangular cans. "I'm sure it will be wonderful."

After Johanna had the string beans on the stove, she pulled out the silverware and napkins to set the table. "I presume you and Sam want to eat in the dining room."

"Why don't we *all* eat in there?"

Johanna put down the napkins. "That would never do. The help does not eat with the family. It isn't done."

"Where will you eat?"

"In the kitchen, over there."

Helen glanced at the table. "Well, can Sam and I join you?"

"Really, Mrs. Redpath, this is your house, and I am your servant."

"Please, I'm a long way from home and don't know anyone. I like someone to talk to."

Johanna looked down. "I also would like someone to talk to."

Twenty-Six

"This is daddy's airplane," Sam announced, storming in with a small metal toy. He dashed around the kitchen, twisting and turning as he imagined himself flying a military airplane.

"Honey, go play in your room," Helen ordered.

He stopped and looked up at her, his eyes pleading. "Right now."

He resumed his flight and ran for the stairs. Moments later Johanna heard the clatter of tiny feet on the steps. She checked the chair where Erich lay sleeping peacefully. "He's a dear," Helen said.

Johanna smiled. "Your Sam is a sweet boy."

Helen nodded. "Yes, he is. He's a handful at times, but I like that. I think the Lord knew what I needed when He sent me Sam."

Johanna smiled. "Then you are a Christian?"

"Yes, ever since I was a little girl."

"I'm glad to hear that. I did not believe until after I was married. Erich — my husband — was a Christian. He didn't know much about what the Bible says about Jesus, but I know he believed. And I gave him such a hard time about it." She sighed. "I know I'll see him in the life to come, but somehow I had hoped he would survive and find me. I wish it had been the Lord's will to give us back to each other in this life, but apparently it wasn't."

"I'm sorry."

"Thank you. One thing I have learned — there will always be hard things in life. But I do believe the Lord will see us through it all. He said so."

"Where does it say that?"

Johanna looked at her in surprise. "Why, in the Bible. 'I will never leave you nor forsake you,' for example."

"Oh . . . I've never read the Bible much."

"But you are trusting Jesus to save you?"

"Oh, yes. He's my Savior, I'm sure about that."

"Would you like to study the Bible together — learn more about what your faith is based on?"

Helen nodded. "Yes, I think I would." She looked down. "And there's something else."

"What's that?"

"I'm embarrassed to say it, but Andy's

not a believer. We never really discussed it when we were courting. I just assumed he was. I found out he wasn't after we were married." She paused. "He's never made fun of me, and he wants me to take Sam to church with me. But he says religion isn't for him."

"Oh, you have to do something about that."

"What?"

"To start with, love him and pray for him."

Helen smiled. "That's what my mother said. She said she would pray for him and in time the Lord would save him."

"That's a good start. It should certainly help him to choose when the time comes."

"I hope so. I appreciate your concern, Johanna, especially after everything you've been through."

Johanna found herself liking this American woman more and more. It was a great comfort to learn she too was a Christian. "May I make a suggestion?"

"Yes, please."

"Let's pray for your husband right now."

"Thank you. I'd like that. And let's also pray that your husband will be found. Let's ask the Lord to bring him back if he's still alive."

Johanna swallowed the lump in her throat. The hope Helen suggested was what she wanted more than anything. Dare she hope?

By early November Erich had heard about the Nuremberg trials. Albert Speer had been indicted in September, and Erich feared he would be called there also, or to one of the other courts being set up to try war criminals. So when he received an early-morning summons, he was not surprised.

But instead of going to the interrogation room, his guard led him to the lobby of the hotel-turned-prison. An American army colonel met him near the front desk.

"Von Arendt, consider yourself lucky. The prosecutors have decided there's not enough evidence to indict you. Personally, I think you're guilty as sin, but my opinion doesn't matter much."

Erich sighed. "I *do* share in the guilt. I know I participated in things that were wrong. My conscience will never let me forget that."

"I don't think any of you Germans *has* a conscience."

Erich found he really couldn't get angry with the man. "I understand why you feel that way. But I don't think it's fair to blame all Germans for what the ones in power did." He hurried on when he saw the man open his mouth. "Please let me finish. Yes, I was one of the ones in power. I'm guilty."

The officer glared at him. "No argument from me on that. But the legal beagles said to turn you loose, so that's what I'm going to do."

"Loose?"

"Yes. Loose. Free to go. Is my German clear enough for you?"

Erich nodded. "Yes, certainly."

"Then get out of here. There's your coat and personal belongings."

A few moments later Erich put on his coat. Then he picked up the tiny bag of toiletries and grabbed his cane. With a nod, he passed under the colonel's glare and out the door.

The biting wind cut into him at once. He pulled the coat tighter and looked into the cold, gray sky. He could think of only one thing — traveling to Frankfurt.

On his first day of freedom Erich had been hopeful of some kind of transportation. But the only persons who had cars and trucks were the Allied Forces, and they didn't give Germans rides. Erich finally gave up as he trudged slowly along the highway from Dusseldorf to Cologne. He tried not to think about how far it was to Frankfurt.

Erich stopped at a refugee camp just after midday, but all they offered him was a tiny chunk of raw potato, which he gratefully accepted. He hoped to find another camp by nightfall, but the only thing dusk brought was a light snow and a bitterly cold wind. He shivered inside his coat as he longed for some kind of shelter. The snow turned quickly into a winter storm, covering everything with a heavy white cloak. Soon it was too dark to travel. Erich kept pushing through the enveloping blackness until he stepped into an unseen hollow. He tumbled forward, his cane flying into the air. He landed painfully on his side and rolled down the slope until he reached the bottom. He cried out as his lame leg struck something hard.

He thought about trying to find his cane but knew that would be futile. He heard flowing water nearby and crawled toward it. He found the small stream by touch, then crept further forward on his belly so he could taste it. It was cold but good. He drank his fill. Not knowing what else to do, miserable in the blowing snow, he crawled alongside the stream until he heard the wind die down. After a few more feet the snow let up sharply, and he felt a little warmer. Unable to go any further, he rolled himself into a shivering ball. The last thing he thought of was Johanna and her radiant smile, all he had left from that one wonderful night in Berlin — how long ago? Tears pushed their way through his closed eyelids, and he fell into the uneasy sleep of sheer exhaustion.

Erich cried out, awaking what seemed like moments later, jarred loose from sleep by a sharp pain shooting through his lame leg. Still on his stomach, he reached down and massaged it until the agony receded into a dull throb. He looked about in the feeble gray light of dawn. A heavy overcast shrouded the sky, but at least the snow had stopped. The stream splashed along at his side, and a concrete culvert sheltered him.

Erich rolled over and struggled to rise, only to fall back in exhaustion. He tried to ignore the gnawing hunger in his stomach as he crawled into the fresh snow on his hands and knees. He looked around for his cane, but all he could see was the smooth blanket of white. He crawled toward a nearby tree so he could use it to help him stand up, trying to ignore the growing numbness in his bare hands. His right hand banged into something, sending needles of pain through his fingers. A long, straight crack appeared in the snow. Joyfully, Erich reached out, grasped his cane, and knocked the clinging snow off it. Using the cane, he struggled to his feet, every joint in agony. He hobbled to the tree and leaned against it. He thrust his hands into his coat pockets and waited for them to warm up.

A few minutes later, with a weariness that scared him, he made his way back to the road and resumed his shuffling walk toward the south, paralleling the Rhine River. By mid-morning he saw a thin tendril of smoke coming from the forest off to the right. He left the road and made his way slowly through the trees until he saw a crude camp up ahead. Gaunt faces regarded him as he approached the fire. An elderly woman tended a blackened pot that had once been a German army helmet. Without a word, she scooped a tin can into the helmet and offered it to him.

"Thank you," Erich said as he took it. He burned his tongue on the thin soup as he sipped it. As meager as the meal was, he felt welcome strength extending outward from his cramped stomach. He finished the meal and handed the can back. The woman didn't offer more, nor did Erich ask. He simply turned and retraced his path to the road.

Although he looked for refugee camps for the rest of the day, he found none. When he could travel no further, he spent the night in a burned-out German armored personnel carrier. The next morning he forced himself to get up, although part of him wanted to give up. Several hours later he caught his first glimpse of Cologne. Slowly the jagged ruins approached. It took him over an hour to pass through the skeletal walls and the mountains of crumbled bricks, stones, and blackened timbers. The Allied traffic was heavier here, hurrying through the streets of a city that for the most part no longer existed. Erich felt a sad relief when the destruction was behind him. Ahead were Bonn and Koblenz. He tried not to think of how far he yet had to go. He had his goal, and he was determined he would reach it or fall by the side of the road in the effort.

Erich finally lost track of the days, but he guessed it had been about two weeks since his release. He knew he was near the end of his endurance. For over a day he had been traveling along the Main River, the nearness of Frankfurt bringing him a slim hope. Soon the tumbled ruins of the city came into view from a low hill. He entered Frankfurt in the late afternoon, long dark shadows stretching out before him. His heart beat faster as he approached the city center with agonizing slowness.

He paused at an intersection. Although he couldn't remember the exact address, he remembered Johanna telling him the name of the street Herr Dorpmüller lived on. Wonderful visions of Johanna waiting for him drifted through his fevered mind. Erich hobbled toward the street with new, though frail, energy. But when he turned the final corner, he found the whole block a massive pile of rubble.

What do I do now? he wondered. He thought about checking with the Americans or the civilian authorities, but that would have to wait until the next day. He made his way slowly out of the city center. After hobbling a few blocks, he looked down the street leading to Sachsenhausen. He felt an urge to turn down it but knew it was pointless. Yet the feeling would not go away.

Erich turned south and plodded along without any thought except going just a little while longer. When night fell, he would try to find some shelter. He crossed the bridge and started trudging up the gentle hill.

After a while he saw a lone house off to the right. So Johanna's house still stood. But of course it wasn't Johanna's house anymore, and she wouldn't be there.

Erich turned onto the street. His goal, if he could call it that, was near. But so was the end of his endurance. The two-story house swam in his vision as he staggered up the front walk. *Someone is living there. I see lights, and smoke is coming from the chimney.* This just confirmed the futility of finding Johanna there. Only Americans had power and heat. He knew he could go no further, and consciousness left him, along with what little had remained of his hope. He collapsed and fell heavily on the walk.

"Can I go outside and play?" Sam asked, tugging at his mother's dress.

Helen glanced over at Johanna. Johanna smiled. "It's nearly sundown, dear. Why don't you play inside."

"Outdoors, please — just for a little while?"

Helen put her hands on her hips. "Five minutes," she said sternly.

Sam beamed. He dashed for the front door, opened it, and raced out.

"Sometimes I don't know what to do with that boy," Helen said.

"Enjoy him," Johanna said.

Helen smiled. "You're right, and I do. But sometimes he tries my patience."

They heard the front door open again.

"My, that was quick," Helen remarked.

Sam dashed in. "Mommy, there's a man sleeping on our walk."

"What?"

"Come and see."

The two women walked to the open front door and looked out. Sure enough, someone was sprawled on the sidewalk. Johanna knew this wasn't unusual. Many Germans were malnourished and starving. She and Helen stepped out cautiously and walked down to where the man lay on his face.

"What should we do?" Helen asked.

"I don't know. Call the army authorities, I guess."

"Yes, I suppose you're right." She reached down and turned the man over.

Johanna gasped. The man's face was thin and covered with a scraggly beard, but she knew instantly who it was. "Oh, dear God, dear God — it's Erich! It's my Erich!" She fell down on her knees and pulled his head into her lap. "Erich, speak to me! Oh, Erich!" Tears poured down her cheeks as if her heart would break.

She saw his eyelids flutter. Then he opened his eyes and looked at her for a few moments. "Johanna?" he asked, his voice low and feeble. "Johanna," he said in a hoarse whisper. "Thank God, I've found you!"

She cradled his head as he lay there. "Erich, oh Erich, God led you here. He's brought us back together, dear." She closed her eyes. "God, thank You — my Erich is alive!"

Epilogue

Erich limped into their room and closed the door. Johanna sat on the narrow bed, her back to the window. She looked up from feeding little Erich. A warm, gentle breeze blew through the open window, carrying the scent of budding roses from the Redpaths' garden.

"I've finished weeding the garden and mowing the lawn," Erich announced as he pulled off his gloves. "Butlers' chores have certainly changed since before the war." He paused as his son came up for air. Johanna placed the infant on her shoulder and patted vigorously, rewarded moments later by a surprisingly loud report.

Erich sat in a chair by their small table. "Not that I'm complaining," he continued. "I'm extremely grateful Frau Redpath was able to convince her husband to keep me on as a butler." His eyes twinkled. "Even though I'm not qualified."

Johanna smiled. "God has indeed been so good to us."

Erich smiled, then looked out the window. "Yes, He has," he replied after a bit.

Johanna could tell that his thoughts were far away. "Is anything the matter, dear?"

"I was just thinking about Papa. I don't suppose we'll ever know what happened to him."

Johanna felt a stinging sensation in her eyes. "No, Erich, we might not. I've often wondered about the Hoffmanns and Herr Dorpmüller as well. So many people disappeared without a trace. No one knows what happened . . . But at least your mother survived — and her house."

He came and sat by her on the bed. "Yes, I'm grateful for that."

Johanna slipped her hand into Erich's as their son drifted off to sleep. Tears of joy sprang forth as she felt his gentle touch, her heart full of grateful love. "Oh, Erich, I thank God for bringing us back together despite my foolishness — despite this horrible war." She looked down. "And for giving us our son. In spite of all our grievous errors, our waywardness and stubbornness, God has shown us the mercy of salvation and has given us a new life."

He squeezed her hand and touched his head to hers.